*Nicholas Shakespeare*

## THE DANCER UPSTAIRS

Nicholas Shakespeare grew up in the Far East and South America. His novel *The Vision of Elena Silves* won England's most prestigious Somerset Maugham Award, and he was chosen by *Granta* magazine as one of the Best of the Young British Novelists in 1993. He lives in London.

Also by Nicholas Shakespeare

*The Vision of Elena Silves*

*Bruce Chatwin*

"A fascinating and wholly compelling novel, lucidly and expertly told and ringing with unmistakable authenticity. Nicholas Shakespeare has found his voice as a writer and it is marvelously assured."                                      —William Boyd

"Shakespeare is a good writer and a clever and ingenious storyteller. . . . This is as good a book as we are likely to get about the atmosphere of the Sendero years."      —*The Times Literary Supplement*

"Nicholas Shakespeare enlightens us in his intelligent, beautifully written and terrifying novel. . . . Issues and actions and the murderous degradations imposed by ideology come to terrifying life in Shakespeare's prose."      —*The Commercial Appeal* (Memphis)

"Shakespeare again explores an explosive situation in Latin America, deftly mingling love and suspense in a powerful, persuasive narrative. . . . Precisely written, beautifully detailed, with a remarkable grasp of tension in a society not the writer's own: a tale both faithful to its time and utterly timeless."      —*Kirkus Reviews*

"*The Dancer Upstairs* is a twist on an old formula—a *Heart of Darkness* journey up the Amazon that ends with a confession to a journalist—but here it works. Shakespeare has given us a richly layered character in Rejas, as contradictory and infused with fatalism as Peru."      —*Newsday*

"A tautly written thriller—full of dialogue as brisk and knowing as the imagery is vivid. . . . It is Shakespeare's fully realized depiction of Rejas as Everyman that makes *The Dancer Upstairs* so memorable."      —*The Oregonian*

"There is an old-fashioned nobility about Nicholas Shakespeare's gripping new novel. Layering love and politics over a landscape of intense tropical gloom, it tackles the kind of large moral questions that most of us have never had to confront."
—*San Francisco Chronicle*

# THE
# DANCER
# UPSTAIRS

# NICHOLAS SHAKESPEARE

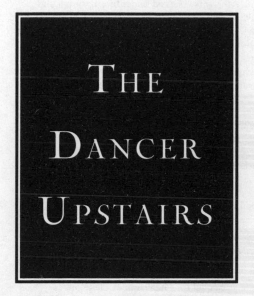

THE
DANCER
UPSTAIRS

Anchor Books

A DIVISION OF RANDOM HOUSE, INC.

NEW YORK

First Anchor Books Edition, February 2002

*Copyright © 1995 by Nicholas Shakespeare*

All rights reserved under International and
Pan-American Copyright Conventions. Published
in the United States by Anchor Books, a division of
Random House, Inc., New York. Originally published in
Great Britain by The Harvill Press, London, in 1995.
Subsequently published in hardcover in the United States
by Nan A. Talese, an imprint of Doubleday, a division of
Random House, Inc., New York, in 1997.

The words of "I'll Remember April" are reproduced by
kind permission of MCA Music Ltd.

Anchor books and colophon are registered trademarks
of Random House, Inc.

The Library of Congress has cataloged the Doubleday
edition as follows:
Shakespeare, Nicholas, 1957–
The dancer upstairs / Nicholas Shakespeare.
— 1st ed. in the U.S.A.
p. cm
Sequel to: The vision of Elena Silves.
1. Revolutionaries—South America—Fiction.
2. Guerrillas—South America—Fiction. I. Title.
PR6069.H286D36 1997
823'.914—dc20 96-15219
ISBN 0-385-48513-1

Anchor ISBN: 0-385-72107-2

*Author photograph © Renate von Mangoldt*

www.anchorbooks.com

Printed in the United States of America
10 9 8 7 6 5 4 3 2

*For Ruth Shakespeare and Donna Tartt*

This novel may be read on its own or as a sequel to *The Vision of Elena Silves*. Like that book, it is a work of fiction. Although it is inspired by the capture of Abimael Guzmán in September 1992, none of the characters are based on anyone involved in that operation, or drawn from anyone in life.

I am indebted to many people for their help and generosity, including Patricia Awapara, Sally Bowen, Toby Buchan, Richard Clutterbuck, Frederick Cooper, David and Jane Cornwall, Iva Fereira, Celso Garrido-Lecca, Nigel Horne, Adam Low, Christopher McLehose, Juan Ossio, Christina Parker, Roger Scruton, Angela Serota, Mary Siepmann, Vera Stastny, Cecilia Valenzuela, Antonio Ketín Vidal and Alice Welsh.

*"I have always thought that if we began for one minute to say what we thought, society would collapse."*

—ALBERT CAMUS, quoting Sainte-Beuve

# THE
# DANCER
# UPSTAIRS

# 1

Night was swallowing the square. The cobbles glistened with river mist and it was impossible to see more than a few steps ahead. Strange screams—he couldn't tell if they were human—penetrated the fog, and from the old fortress at the end of the quay came the thump of a samba rhythm.

Dyer remembered the restaurant being on the waterfront, at the corner of the square. He knew that he was close, for he could hear the river slapping against the steps. Then the wind picked up and through the parting mist he recognized the sign swaying beneath a wrought-iron balcony above him: CANTINA DA LUA. Light streamed down from the dining room on the first floor and one of the shutters crashed against the tiles.

Later, when he thought of those evenings and his walks across the square, there would come back to him nights which smelled of mango rinds and woodsmoke and charred fish. But mostly he remembered that wind, leaping in warm gusts over the waterfront, rattling branches on the rooftops, banging the shutter.

A waiter squeezed onto the balcony, secured the shutter with a loop of wire and stepped back inside. That was when Dyer saw the man for the first time, an outline defined by the overhead bulb. Dyer was struck by the stillness with which he held himself. How could he not have been distracted by the shutter's banging? But the man stared at the river pouring into the night as if nothing else existed.

Dyer passed beneath the balcony, through a doorway and up a stone staircase. At the head of the stairs a bead curtain stood guard over the entrance to a whitewashed room; burgundy-colored table-cloths, bentwood chairs, an old-fashioned till on a bar. Each table had a tiny vase and a flower. The restaurant was empty save for the waiter and the man at the window.

Straight-backed and attentive, wearing a navy blue polo shirt, he was talking to the waiter in Spanish. A book lay open on the table.

Dyer heard the waiter say, "How is the señora today?"

"She's better. Thank you." In that moment he looked up, took in Dyer, and then his eyes dropped back to the book.

Dyer saw a man a year or two older than himself: early forties, middle height, short black hair, clean-shaven. And, in that brief glance, eyes whose intelligence had been tempered by extremes of suffering seen and suffering borne.

Dyer could not have said from where, but he recognized him.

When the ultimatum came, Dyer was on the point of leaving for Ecuador to cover the flare-up on the border.

> I do wish we had the chance to talk this through. It's much easier across a desk than across the Atlantic. Long story short, the cutbacks we've got to make are so draconian that I can't see us maintaining the Rio bureau. I gave it my best shot with the proprietor. He said he didn't know why I bothered. The accountants want him to shut down three offices—and yours is first on his list, John. If there's another Falklands, we can always fly you out.

Everyone agreed, Dyer was the doyen of Latin American correspondents. No one more richly deserved another big challenge, etc., which was why the editor could make the following proposal:

> You can have either Moscow or the Middle East.

The only other question he needed to address was the date of his return.

The receipt of this rapid, handwritten note from his editor did not keep Dyer from flying north, but in the jungle it pressed on him. He spent four days and nights with units of the Ecuadorian army. Once, wading across a stream, he was fired on by a man leaning out of a helicopter. Throughout these days he felt a weight on his heart and behind his eyes, like mountain sickness. He could muster not one iota of enthusiasm for Moscow or the Middle East. This was the region which had formed and blooded him. Anywhere else he would be out of his depth.

He returned to Rio and the office on Joaquim Nabuco, from where he sent nine hundred words describing the dispute. Twenty minutes later the telephone rang. The foreign desk, no doubt, to suggest cuts. Anxious about his fate—the imminent parting from friends, from his wife's family, from his whole geography—he had overwritten.

The voice belonged to his editor, booming into a car phone. "If you won't get in touch, John, I'll have to give it to you straight. The accountants have decreed: Shut Latin America. Full stop. So which is it to be: Moscow or Jerusalem?"

Dyer walked to the window. He held the receiver an inch from his ear to distinguish the voice from the catarrhal crackle. "That's it?"

He stared down the street toward Ipanema beach. A paper kite had caught in telegraph wires and a white-skinned boy looked up at it.

"Believe me, this is the last thing I want," said the editor, overly sympathetic now. "But I speak after another bruising meeting with the proprietor. It's down to this price war. We haven't any money. If you were in my seat, what would you do?"

Dyer kept his eyes on the kite. "We're talking about fifteen years."

"Look, I know how good you are," said the voice across the sea, probably on its way to its club. "But our C2 readers aren't switched on to your neck of the woods."

"Twenty-one countries?"

"I can't hear what you're saying. Are you there? John? John?"

Dyer last heard a long, bracing obscenity and the line went dead.

He put down the receiver and leaned against the desk, waiting.

On the wall hung a watercolor he had painted of Astrud. His eyes fastened on her face while he toyed with the alternatives. The BBC had last month replaced their bureau chief in Buenos Aires. *Le Monde* needed him, God knows, but would probably not appoint an Englishman. The *New York Times*? A long shot, and the present incumbent was a friend.

The telephone rang.

Astrud smiled at him from beneath a green beach umbrella.

"There you are. These things are hopeless for abroad. I was about to say, can we look for you at the end of April?"

"I really can't. There's a book I'm supposed to be writing. I do have to finish it before I leave."

"How long do you need?"

"To assemble the bits—four, five weeks."

"Fine. Then next month is holiday. In June I want to see you here."

"All right," Dyer said rapturelessly.

"I give you this time-off on one condition. You write me a major piece. We can run it Saturday and Sunday. Allow yourself twelve thousand words, but give Nigel plenty of warning about pics. You have the background taped. There must be a story you really want to do? Something we can syndicate?"

Always Dyer had cherished the idea that if ever the time came to leave this continent, he would go out on one wonderful note. His book was to be an introduction to the cultural and social history of the Amazon Basin. But he thought of it as a task he had to complete. It was not a grace note on which to end his South American career.

On the other hand, the editor's valedictory commission did at least give Dyer the freedom to pull off an interview which every journalist down here would be envious to see in print, and which would be the logical climax of the story he had been tracking for a decade.

"There is something I'd like to write," he said. "Do you remember the terrorist Ezequiel?"

"The chappie in the cage?"

Ezequiel was a revolutionary leader who had been caught after a twelve-year hunt. His guerrilla war against the institutions of his Andean country had resulted in thirty thousand deaths and countless tortures and mutilations. Ezequiel's public humiliation—he was indeed shown to the international press from inside a cage—had captured headlines across the world a year before.

"You can get him?" It showed the editor's lack of awareness that he could ask such a question.

"It's not Ezequiel. No one's allowed to see him." After being paraded through the streets under military escort, Ezequiel had been kept underground in a lightless cell. He had not spoken a word to the press.

"It's the person who put Ezequiel in the cage."

"What's he called?"

"Tristan Calderón."

"And who is he?"

"On the face of it, a humble Intelligence captain. In fact, he's the President's right-hand man. He runs the country."

"Has he been interviewed ever?"

"Never."

"What makes you sure you can crack it?"

"I have a good contact."

The contact was truly a good one. Calderón was infatuated with Vivien Vallejo, an Englishwoman who had given up her career as a prima ballerina with the Royal Ballet to marry a South American diplomat. Calderón called her the whole time and sent presents, much to the annoyance of her husband. Vivien was Dyer's aunt.

"Why haven't you suggested it before?"

"I have. Twice." The foreign desk, under pressure to reduce expenses, had judged it too obscure.

While it was nowhere in his nature to shelve a story which excited him, he was aware of his aunt's hostility to the press: gossip-column pieces, photographs of Vivien on the arm of someone not Hugo, had jeopardized her marriage more than once. For this reason Dyer had not wished to enlist her support until he could be one hundred percent sure of an appropriate space in the paper.

"That's it, then," said the editor, sounding pleased. "You get me the Calderón interview and you have a month off. Nothing would make me happier than for you to come out with all guns blazing."

Dyer looked down the beach to where he had painted Astrud. The kite was still there, but the boy had gone.

When, two days later, he saw the gray-tiled turret above the jacaranda, he felt he was coming home.

The garden walls of Vivien's house on the seafront had grown since the summers he had lived here as a child. Topped with broken brown glass and electrified wire, they surrounded a building conceived in imitation of a Gascon manoir. The effect was wide of the mark it aimed at. The house resembled nothing so much as a subtropical folly, crammed, because of Hugo's profession, with objects of little beauty but plenty of nostalgia.

It was to this address on the Malecón that Dyer had sent his fax. He was coming to stay, he informed Vivien. He hoped this wouldn't be an inconvenience, but he found himself in desperate straits. He begged for her help in fixing an interview with Calderón—on or off the record. He had signed the faxed letter, perfectly honestly, with his love. Vivien, his top card, happened also to be the person he most wanted to say goodbye to before he was made to depart South America.

Until the last, when the taxi turned into her street, he had forgotten how much he missed his aunt. He had first driven up this road as a six-year-old, after his mother died. In that doorway had stood a small, vivacious woman. By the way she held herself, he had thought she waited to greet him, but she was saying goodbye to a neat bald man who soon excused himself. Catching sight of the boy, she had run out, flung open the car door, plucked him into the sunlight. Her understanding hands caressed his face, looking for her sister. Then she hugged him to her neck and laughed.

The sound of Vivien's throaty laugh was among his earliest memories. Her bold blue eyes would bewitch anyone they looked on. Unlike most charmers, she had known suffering of her own, so that those same eyes also shone with the pale brightness of someone who has peeked over the rim. As a young girl, she had been wasted by a rheumatic fever which no doctor, and certainly no one in her family, expected her to survive. Recovering, she had taken up ballet in order to develop her weakened muscles. "No miracle, my dear, I just decided one day that every hour was a gift and I liked being alive." It was not long before she had become famous as a classical dancer—and for renouncing everything the moment it came within her grasp.

She had been in her tenth season with London's Royal Ballet when she met Hugo Vallejo after a performance of *Giselle* in Lisbon. Hugo, at that time an attaché at his country's embassy, told her: Did she know? It was incredible, but in shape and color the birthmark on her right cheek matched exactly the drop of tea he had splashed that afternoon onto a tablecloth at his ambassador's residence.

"It was the corniest shit, and I told him so." That night they dined at Tavares. A month later she exchanged Covent Garden for South America.

Her body had thickened since Dyer had lived with them. In those days she attracted to the house a corps of dedicated admirers. Gossip accused her of reserving her most accomplished steps for the dance she led her husband. "I married Hugo," she told Dyer in one of those phrases of hers he never forgot, "because he didn't put his hand on my knee after dinner and say, 'What do you want to do now?' He put it here, on my hip, where it mattered." And if she had disengaged those fingers once or twice to indulge a passionate life behind Hugo's back, their marriage had still endured. Now approaching seventy, she remained devoted, balanced and worldly; and, despite her accent, modulated like that of a 1950s radio announcer, very un-English.

Neither the excitement he felt in Vivien's presence nor the fact she was his aunt did anything to conceal from Dyer her essential toughness. She was an effective figure in her adopted country and skilled at getting things done, something she ascribed to her Covent Garden training. "All ballet dancers are made of iron, my dear. If you work nine hours a day, your life is regimented, orderly and extremely strict. You can't have an ounce of woolliness." And it was true. When Vivien said, albeit with perfect grace, "This is what I want," people by God jumped.

Greatly loved, she was also well aware, not least through friends like Calderón, of the political processes of the country. Too wise to take sides, although her opinion and her company were deliberately courted, she acted as a sort of "ambassador without portfolio"—and at one stage was invited to be special envoy to UNESCO. She declined, offering as an excuse her worry that she might lose her British passport. Besides, diplomacy was Hugo's bag.

For Hugo she might have given up dancing, but she did not sever links with the world of ballet. As Principal of the Metropolitan, she had kept her name prominent—if not sanctified—in that milieu. Of late, though, she was more associated in the public mind with the Vallejo Orphanage.

The story was famous, how Vivien, driving through the outskirts of the capital, spotted some children playing beneath a water tower. She assumed the creature they were teasing as it thrashed on the ground was an animal. Then, through the circle of legs, she saw a boy. Telling Hugo to stop the car, she had pummeled her way past the children. Their victim was no older than five or six. His mouth was locked open in a spasm and his moans bubbled through saliva trails flecked with sand. One of the boy's tormentors lifted a foot and wiggled his toes between the caked lips.

Vivien had pushed him aside, gathered the boy in her arms and made Hugo drive to the hospital in Miraflores, where she had agreed to meet the medical expenses.

The boy spoke almost no Spanish, but phrase by incomplete phrase she had pieced together his history. He came from near Sierra de Pruna. His father had been executed by Ezequiel. His mother had fled. He had contracted meningitis. Such handicaps are a stigma in the highlands. His mother set out for the capital, and when she got there, she abandoned her son by the roadside.

"It changed my life. It would have changed anybody's life. What else could I have done? Left him there? Just be thankful you didn't find him, my dear."

In the weeks ahead Vivien learned of other cases. Two sisters from Lepe, alone in the city, their parents victims of the military. A girl, her family destroyed by a car bomb. A two-year-old, his mother seized by three men disguised as policemen.

"For every child I found, another two popped up—dazed, hungry, sick. My heart wrinkled to see them, but we simply didn't have room."

She began to call in favors.

Vivien's international status as a dancer had always endowed her with a snobbish appeal for a certain kind of powerful person. Now she sought their patronage. She cajoled and bullied friends for donations, rented a house in San Isidro and, before quite realizing it, had set up an institution for the orphans of the violence. Within eight weeks she found herself responsible for sixty children. Dyer would hear them during rehearsals at the Metropolitan, hiding under the seats, hitting each other, bawling. Once the music started, they shut up.

Among the influential people whom Vivien had badgered was the sometime lawyer Tristan Calderón. He was now a director of the orphanage.

On a silver tray in the hallway, under an authentic, moss-colored ballet slipper, an envelope waited for Dyer. The letter was on stiff cream paper. Vivien had flown the coop.

J—Paths have crossed/Must fly to Brazil, organizing charity gala at the Pará opera house/Can't wriggle out since it was *my* idea in first place/Meanwhile you're here/*Too* maddening.

Got your message/But Darling, I *can't*/For one thing, T's not doing *any* interviews/As you are *perfectly* well aware/For another, how can you possibly expect me to help after what happened last time with the President/What you wrote was most unkind/It was unworthy of you.

I feel badly about your job/But I'm an Old Lady and suddenly I cannot face one more of my friends saying to me: "Your Bloody Nephew, I only agreed to see him for *your* sake—and now he's revealed this Appalling Secret/ Did he think we lived so far away we'd never find out?/etc. etc."

You know I love you, Johnny/It's your profession I

can't stand/Do remember: Hugo and I have to live here/So while part of me is on your side and hopes you get your story, this time you are going to have to do it all on your own/Sorry.

Your birthday card was sweet/Tell your father Thank You for the lovely umbrella/By the way, could you take this ballet slipper back when you leave/The shop's somewhere behind Copacabana/I've taped the address inside/Ask Hugo—he knows/It's so bloody frustrating/I keep writing to them to say it's *this* kind of leather I like and they send me some other kind/I want them actually to see the shoe/ And, Darling, do make sure it's the Emerald—not the Forest.

Make yourself at home etc./Hugo is looking forward to your visit/You'll find him much better.

Love—V.

PS  It is your home, whenever you need it/Do come back soon/Don't wait until there's another war.

PPS  There is no such thing as off the record/As you jolly well know.


Dyer reacted with panic. When you sit in an office a thousand miles away, it is easy to make rash promises. Vivien's advocacy had been crucial to his getting the interview. Without her, he couldn't hope to track down Calderón.

He tried the obvious sources. There was a Deputy to whom Vivien had introduced him two years ago. He left three messages on an answering machine. Either the man was away—or had no desire to renew acquaintance.

Nor did the local press, commonly a rich seam of unexplored leads, prove useful. His buddies on Caretas and La República were happy to see him, but as soon as he mentioned Calderón's name, they became guarded in a way they had never been about Ezequiel. Not even in the days when his organization was killing them.

Dyer resorted to the official channels, but the people he had known at the Palace had been replaced. Captain Calderón was a functionary of average rank, nothing more; and it was not government policy to grant interviews to the media.

On the second evening, he took Hugo out to dinner at the Costa Verde.

"How's that pretty girlfriend of yours?" This was the first time he had seen his nephew on his own.

"She's been gone for ages," said Dyer.

Hugo, humbled, shook his head. "I shouldn't ask so many questions."

His uncle had been with him in the Rio clinic when Astrud died. Vivien was touring Argentina with her dance company. Hugo flew over after things took a turn for the worse. Astrud had gone into labor prematurely. Dyer and Hugo sat outside the operating theater. Winter sunlight spreading lozenge shapes on the lino; down the corridor a man selling magazines; the doctor taking off his glasses to wipe the bridge of his nose.

The amniotic fluid had entered her bloodstream. She died giving birth to a stillborn girl.

Hugo took control. He dealt with the hospital, the burial, the foreign desk in London. He spoke with Astrud's parents in São Paulo and her grandmother in Petrópolis. Then he brought Dyer home to Miraflores.

That was eleven years ago. Since when, Hugo and Vivien always welcomed him with an unwavering warmth. "This is your home, Johnny." He must invite anyone he wanted to. So the house on the Malecón became the place where Dyer brought his new girlfriends.

"I'll get Mona over tomorrow night." Hugo mentioned the name of a dull cousin, recently divorced.

"I'm here to work," said Dyer.

Hugo nodded. He didn't ask about the nature of this work, nor did Dyer tell him. He had no wish to involve his uncle in his quest for Calderón. Hugo had not been well of late, and in any case had always preferred to turn a blind eye to Vivien's adventures.

While they ate, Hugo discoursed about Vivien's orphanage, to which Dyer supposed she would be donating the proceeds of the Pará gala. He ran through the membership of the Jockey Club, where he was now Secretary; and when conversation petered out over coffee, he turned to the subject of genetically modified vegetables, in which, since his stroke, he had developed an interest. About the civil war which had disemboweled his country, he said not a word.

"What are things like here now?" Dyer inquired at last.

"There's an uneasy peace," said Hugo cagily. "It's real because it's happening, but maybe something more is going to happen."

"You were brave to go on living here. Why in heaven's name didn't you leave?"

"It's not me. It's Vivien," said Hugo, and not for the first time Dyer was conscious that few conversations he conducted with Vivien's husband ever hit the nub of the matter.

"When is she coming back?"

Hugo had been adroit so far in steering away from this subject, and he remained vague. "I was expecting her home by the weekend. Or maybe she'll stay in Pará some more."

"I forgot Pará had an opera house."

Hugo raised what had once been an eyebrow. The stroke had removed both brows and given to his features, already bald, an unprotected air. "Pavlova danced there."

By Sunday there was still no sign of Vivien. "She's bound to be back tonight," said Hugo, who had spent all day at the racetrack. But she did not reappear.

Nor did she turn up on Monday.

On Wednesday morning Dyer joined Hugo for breakfast in the conservatory. Before going to bed, he had been rereading Vivien's letter.

"Hugo, what is it with this slipper?"

"Is that the shoemaker in Rio? She swears by his shoes. I discovered him by chance when I was staying with you that time."

Hugo accepted the letter from Dyer and studied it. His face was normally difficult to read, but not on this occasion. "If you ask me—and this is just a hunch—it's Vivien's way of saying she's not going to come back until she is sure you're gone."

"Why would she behave like that?"

Dyer sensed his uncle's reluctance to hurt him. "I didn't want to tell you," said Hugo. "But perhaps it's not such a bad thing, you know." The truth was, his last article had made Dyer persona non grata in one or two circles. "It frightened Vivien quite a lot. I've also had my share of barbed remarks at the club."

"About what?"

"Something you wrote upset Calderón. From what I understand, he intimated to Vivien that there might come a time when she is going to have to stop talking to you. He finds it disconcerting to have people around who are so well informed."

"I was hoping to get an interview with him."

"Well, exactly, but you can put that out of your mind. You're a good journalist, Johnny, and that's what makes you dangerous. For some people in our society, the whole practice of journalism menaces their peace of mind. Half the dinner parties Vivien goes to, she's terribly proud to be your aunt. The other half, she keeps very, very quiet about it."

There followed two fraught days. Dyer, his options running out, spent his time in the library of the Catholic University, using the opportunity to read early explorers' accounts of the Amazon. By Thursday it was obvious that Vivien was going to stay on in Brazil. Hugo spent conspicuously more time at the Jockey Club, but continued to behave with unflagging hospitality on the few occasions they met.

Unwilling to be more of a headache to him, Dyer announced his intention to go upriver. There was research on the Ashaninkas he needed for his book. Not to alert Vivien, he told Hugo he would be spending a few days among an Indian tribe near Satipo. But he had decided to smoke out his aunt in Pará.


The Pará opera house is a coral-pink building across the Praça da República from the Hotel Madrid. On the morning of his arrival Dyer walked down an avenue bright with mango trees to an entrance swathed in scaffolding.

The young woman in the administration office confessed herself perplexed. She had, of course, heard of Senhora Vallejo, but did not believe the Metropolitan was dancing in Pará. Besides, no performance would be possible until the municipality had completed the work of restoration. She suggested Dyer try the Teatro Amazonas in Manaus.

He telephoned Manaus and drew another blank. Six hundred miles upriver and no Vivien, no ballet. He contacted theaters in Santarém and Macapá. By midafternoon he knew he was wasting his time. The ballet story was a ruse. His aunt had left home because she knew he was coming.

He walked down to the river, then back through the bird market to his hotel. The air was humid, sweetened overripely with mangoes; beads of sweat tickled his neck and he wanted a shower. Afterward he lay down on a hard bed under the window, unable to sleep. He squeezed a hand over his eyes, but with each mango-laden breath the sensation increased. It was four in the afternoon in a place where he didn't want to be, and he was furious.

He was stuck. He saw that now. He had bought a fixed-date ticket; the return flight another week away. He was loath to give up the chase on Calderón. He thought it yet possible to snare his aunt with a last-ditch appeal. But what could he do in the meantime? It was pointless to fly back to keep Hugo company. The most sensible course would be to take a leaf from Vivien's book. Lie low for a few days, then surprise her.

Next morning he moved into a hotel close to the British-built port; a plaster-fronted building with white shutters and a veranda perched over the immense river. This was the old quarter, built during the rubber boom. Once prosperous, it had grown decrepit. Many of the houses were boarded up, with trees bursting out of the roofs. Others, like the building opposite, stood no deeper than their façade. To Dyer, the emptiness behind the preserved frontage mimicked one of Vivien's stage sets. Standing on his veranda, he could see the cloudless sky beyond the windows, the slanting drift of vultures between the architraves and, every now and then, the agitated flight of a black and yellow bird, the bem-te-vi.

*Bem-te-vi, bem-te-vi*—"I've seen you, I've seen you."

Frustrated, lethargic, crushed by the heat, Dyer could not hear that call without thinking of the slave hunters who trained the bird to hunt down fugitives. Catching sight of those yellow wings hovering in the sickly sweet air, he wanted to shout out, "Go and find her, you stupid bird."

*Bem-te-vi, bem-te-vi.*

He tried to be calm about his fate. He had been given free run of the world he cared about, the fount of his stories, and he had failed to deliver. If he telephoned Hugo, that would blow the whistle on Vivien. If he telephoned his editor, he ran the risk of having to return to London immediately. What could he find to do in Pará—except what he ought to be doing anyway?

The proposal of a book on the Amazon Basin had interested him when originally he was approached by a London publishing house. He had long been fascinated by the area and had no doubt that he was qualified to write an introduction—although, in the absence of any reminders, it did cross his mind that his publishers might have gone the way of his newspaper. Vivien's vanishing act gave him an excuse. He had the notes he had made in the Catholic University library, and had had the foresight to bring with him several learned works. And hadn't this wild-goose chase landed him by sheer chance in a seaport which he needed to write about? Rather than cooling his heels for a week, he would spend the time sketching out captions for as yet imaginary photos, studying texts, gathering information.

No sooner had he switched hotels than he began to enjoy Pará more. Due to its position on the equator, it was a place which lived obstinately in its own time. Pará time never altered. And then there were the hours kept by the rest of the world.

He liked the fact that the sun rose and set at the same time each day. He liked the unforgettable smells of the port, and the torpor of the riverside, which met a commensurate emotion in him. Something having snapped in his bond to the newspaper, he suddenly looked forward to this time on his hands, time to reflect on the future, time to lay to rest one or two hungry ghosts, time to plot his book. There was nothing and no one to distract him, he remembered thinking, as he walked toward a restaurant he had marked out earlier in the day.

Only Euclides da Cunha, whose *Rebellion in the Backlands* he was thankful he had brought with him.

2

Dyer sat down at a table and at once began reading. He had read a chapter by the time the man at the window called for the bill. Dyer smiled, trying to remember where they could have met. The man responded with the unfavoring half-smile people reserve for helpful shopkeepers. Dyer looked away.

The pattern repeated itself the following night. The two diners sat together in that room for no longer than twenty minutes before, punctual as the last ferry, the man called for his bill. They read and ate their meals in silence. It must have confounded the waiter to watch his only clients sitting like that, not exchanging a word.

Dyer would have taken the man for a fellow stranger to Pará had not the waiter treated him so respectfully. Emilio hurried for no one, yet when signaled by the man at table 17, he stopped whatever he was doing and directed himself between the straw-seated chairs, clasping his black folder as though it contained not a bill for a grilled fish but the freedom of the city. A moment later, walking like someone out of uniform, his other customer brushed past Dyer's table.

But Emilio could not satisfy Dyer's curiosity. The courtesy with which he brought and removed plates concealed a splendid disdain. Emilio, if Dyer was reading, was not above lifting both book and plate and dusting away the crumbs, all the while smiling apologetically, as though he were somehow to blame for their presence on the table. His manner seemed determined by the assumption that Dyer would leave no tip. Emilio would call at his back as he left, "Good evening, senhor," as if he didn't mean it. These words, spoken in correct Portuguese but with the trace of a Spanish accent, were the only three he addressed to Dyer. When asked about the person at the window, he shrugged.

Not until the third night did the man pause at Dyer's table.


Dyer was so engrossed in *Rebellion in the Backlands* that several seconds passed before he became aware of someone looking over his shoulder.

The man held out his own cloth-bound volume. They were reading the same book.

"I don't believe it. Extraordinary!" Dyer got to his feet. The coincidence was not so extraordinary, at least not in Brazil. But in that scarcely patronized restaurant it was strange indeed.

Dyer gestured at the chair opposite. The man checked his watch.

"I cannot stay long," he said, in Spanish. He drew the chair to him and sat on the edge of the seat, facing away. "I am expected at home."

Dyer sought Emilio, but observant as ever, he was already advancing.

"Beer?"

"A coffee, I'd prefer."

The man placed his book, the Spanish edition, on the table. "If only the author could see!"

Dyer said, "You know how people go on about a book, then you are disappointed. But it's as good as I hoped."

"I've come to reading late." His face had a preoccupied look. "My father had a library, but I never made use of it. At last I have time."

"Then we're in the same boat."

The eyes which inspected Dyer were brown and steady. He was neither good-looking nor ugly, and while he would not have turned a young girl's head, someone older might have been struck by his face and the evidence of a passion which had left its traces.

"Don't you think that each time a good book is written it's a triumph for everyone?" said the man. "The same each time someone is cured of a disease or a criminal is caught. It's one more tiny victory against the darkness." It was touching, this faith in books. He'd only just discovered them and now he had discovered them terribly.

"But da Cunha and his kind," said Dyer, "aren't they practitioners of a dying art? The public want to watch videos. They don't want to read *Rebellion in the Backlands*."

He chose not to answer. "You're not Brazilian?"

"I'm English."

"You are here on business?"

Dyer found it sensible all over South America to avoid telling people he was a journalist. "I'm finishing a book."

"About Pará?" He gazed steadily at Dyer.

"I mean to concentrate more on the Indians."

The man sighed. "When we go to Europe, we're looking for civilization. Yet when you come here, you are seeking for the primitive."

Dyer said awkwardly, "And you, what do you do?"

Nothing in the eyes hinted at what the man was thinking. His gaze rested on the books which had brought them together.

"I used to be a policeman."

"Used to be? At your age? You mean you've retired?"

"Not exactly. But I am required to do less and less."

Family matters had brought him to Pará. He was spending some time with his sister, who was ill, taking turns with her Brazilian husband to sit by her bed.

"You don't come from Brazil either?"

"No," and he picked up Dyer's book, keeping the place with a finger. "Tell me, where have you got to?"

Dyer had been reading an ode celebrating the death of a soldier who, kneeling beside his commander's dead body, fought on until the ammunition ran out. On the day after the battle, the leading Rio newspaper had devoted the lion's share of their front page to this poem. Dyer had been musing over the likelihood of the foreign subs in Canary Wharf being able to coax iambic pentameters to bed.

"I'm a little further on than you." He looked at Dyer over the book. "May I see—to test my English?"

"Please do."

He peered at the type. "You write in the margin." Then, twisting the book, "But I can't read your hand."

"It's a habit," said Dyer.

"I share it. I went through my law books the other day. All those illegible scribbles. Like a different person."

In that second the man's face relaxed and Dyer remembered who he was.

He was aware of palpitations in his chest. His breaths came fast. He watched the bubbles rising in his beer, calculating his next move.

"The most wanted man in the world." Headlines had debased the phrase, but for twelve years it might have applied to the philosophy professor, Edgardo Vilas—or, as he became known, President Ezequiel. Sitting less than three feet away, so near that Dyer could, if he wanted, touch his sleeve, was the man who had captured the Chairman of the World Revolution.

No one knew the story. The policeman had been forbidden to speak. He had defied his orders; had not immediately handed Ezequiel over to Calderón, who would certainly have executed him. Everyone had expected the revolutionary to be shot, to fight his way out, to take his own life. Only this man could say how Ezequiel had been arrested without a struggle.

His name was Agustín Rejas. For years he had worked undercover to capture the Public Enemy Number One. For years he had been an unknown police colonel. Then, suddenly, his name was on the lips of a whole population. Within a few days he was being touted as a presidential candidate. The following week he had vanished. Which is how things were in his country.

All Dyer knew of Colonel Rejas was that he was forty-four, that he came from a village north of Cajamarca. For twenty years he had served as a policeman and for twelve of those years he had been responsible for one case. It was about this case that Dyer had been trying, a week earlier, to contact him, though not with any expectation of success. His pretext had been to gather background material for the Calderón profile. Had he had the spectacular good fortune to meet Rejas, he would have wanted to discuss a great many other things as well. But this was a man nobody met. People said he was out of the country. He was unfindable.

"Apparently he's in a witness protection program," Dyer had been told by the BBC stringer. She was the most reliable of the local foreign correspondents. "Although I have also heard that he's abroad, talking to the Americans."

They were drinking chocolate in the Café Haiti. Dyer told her of the call from the editor.

"Maybe the fellow up there's telling you something." She blew her nose. "Maybe it is time to get out."

Lonely, in need of a companion, he would have asked her out to dinner, but she was taking her younger lover to a Brahms concert in the Teatro Americano. A year ago, with Ezequiel still at large, such an event would have been unthinkable.

"Has Calderón come to terms with Rejas?" Dyer had asked.

"I doubt it. I'm sure Calderón wanted to snuff out Ezequiel there and then. My contact in the Palace says that when he saw Rejas presenting Ezequiel to journalists, Calderón was so enraged that he put a whisky decanter through the television screen."

One year before, from a friend at Canal 7, Dyer had borrowed a videotape of Rejas reading aloud his prepared statement. On the tape, the policeman stood outside the Anti-Terrorist Headquarters in Vía Expreso. He held himself erect, hardly moving. The speech was impressive for its modesty. Thanks to the hard work, patience and discipline of his men during twelve years, the man styling himself President Ezequiel had been taken into custody at eight-forty the night before. Rejas said that he had not completed the process of interrogation. He concluded by speaking of his hope for the country; his belief in the institutions of justice and democracy. He would donate any reward to charities for children orphaned by the violence.

The camera had been jostled frequently. For a second it had focused on Rejas as he read, his chin caught in the same position as Dyer would see it in the restaurant. And here was the extraordinary thing: he betrayed not a trace of exultation.

Two days later a curt bulletin from the Palace announced that Ezequiel had been removed from Colonel Rejas's charge.

"There's a widespread feeling that Rejas has been treated extremely shabbily," said Dyer's BBC contact.

"So he's not given his version of events?"

"Apparently not. After they robbed him of his spoil, there was a quiet promotion. He serves as Quartermaster of the National Police, a post having no executive responsibility whatever. And it means that Calderón can keep tabs on Rejas. I can't tell you how much this sudden popularity unnerved the Palace." She took Dyer's *Spectator* and slipped it into her basket. "But Calderón must have some hold over him—or else why hasn't Rejas spoken out? Everyone would have listened. The people here worship him."

"Are the rumors true?"

"That he will run for President? All I know, there's a group of Deputies, quite influential. They've been to see him."

She gave the names. An impressive list.

"What chance he'll accept the nomination?"

"The people badly want someone of his caliber, a truly heroic person who is also a modest man. But who knows? Since the blaze of publicity, he's disappeared off the scene."


When Dyer's plan to interview Calderón was scuppered by Vivien's defection, he did not want to think about such characters again. Now, in a seaport on the Amazon, fate had thrown him a bigger prize, a man who could help incidentally over Calderón, but who knew more about Ezequiel's organization than anyone alive.

Dyer knew he had to suppress his excitement. He had this astonishing and wonderful catch. He must not scare him off. If he tried for too much, he might wreck everything—but there was no time for an elegant, oblique approach.

Rejas was still reading when Dyer said, "So, a policeman. Did you have anything to do with that terrorist who was captured?"

Rejas raised his eyes from the book. "Which terrorist?"

"The President Ezequiel."

Rejas threw back his head and laughed. The laugh was not unpleasant or cruel. An outsider might have taken it for an amused laugh, one that said, How could you imagine such a thing? But to

Dyer, the laughter contained the sound of hatches being closed, of shutters going up, of a man protecting himself. It declared that Rejas wouldn't tell Dyer a thing, that if he made an attempt to pry, he would be steered from the subject and the policeman would leave the restaurant, and once the beads had settled behind him, he would not be returning to that table by the window and Dyer would never see him again.

"It's another interesting coincidence," said Dyer, "but I believe my aunt is a good friend of an associate of yours."

Rejas lowered the book. "An associate?"

"Tristan Calderón."

Too late he saw that he had alerted Rejas, had shown him that he knew who he was.

Rejas replaced the book behind the paper tulip.

"Who is your aunt?"

"Actually, I believe she's quite well known in your country. Vivien Vallejo."

"The dancer?"

"That's right."

"The ballerina"—as if he wanted to be certain—"who runs the Metropolitan?"

"Yes."

Dyer watched him roll the thought in his head, approving it. "Do you have an interest in the ballet?"

"My daughter has a picture of your aunt on her wall. A great admirer. And there are others I know . . ." When he spoke again, he was looking not at Dyer but at the river. "Her philanthropy is very much appreciated."

"I would be honored to give your daughter an introduction."

"That's very kind, but . . ." Rejas didn't finish his sentence. A light moved across the black backcloth beyond the window, one of the palm-thatched boats puttering upriver.

"Naturally, if she knew it was your daughter . . ." Dyer said, seizing on the slenderest excuse to keep Rejas at his table. At the same time, why would such a rigorously secret man speak to him? This was not an Ancient Mariner. He was here to get away from his country, not to talk about it.

Rejas did not answer. And there was not a thing more Dyer

could think of to say. Here he sat, helpless, tired, a bit drunk, watching his thoughts flow out through that window with Rejas's gaze, unable to stop them.

At last, turning back into the room, Rejas said, "Did you know that we caught Ezequiel above a ballet studio?"

3

"Did you know that we caught Ezequiel above a ballet studio?"
"No."

Rejas considered this lie.

"Have you seen a man with his head cut off?"

"No."

"Once I saw a man with his head cut off," said Rejas. "The body remembers what it used to do, what it was told to do seconds before, and it just keeps on going, shrugging blood, shuffling forward. It's a little while before it gets the message the boss man isn't there."

"Where was this?"

"A tiny hamlet. Jaci. Way up in the—hills. You wouldn't have heard of it. I was trapped there on the morning Ezequiel's people invaded. I watched the execution through an earth wall, on my stomach. The man was ordered to kneel and come forward on his knees. After the machete struck, he continued several paces as if at the end of a long day's pilgrimage to Fátima. My nights are still haunted by that rippling body. He jerked about on the ground, spraying up dirt, quivering, not dead at all. Then his executioner, a girl about seventeen, picked up his head and swung it like a lantern across his chest, yelling, 'Look, pig! Look!'

"That was the most extraordinary thing. The reaction of the face, I mean. Try to imagine the expression of a man's face staring at his own body. You see, the head goes on working too. For a few seconds he is still capable of registering sight and sound and thought. The eyes blink open, the lips pucker. He can even mouth a sentence or two. Well, almost. The words bubble to the lips, but you can't hear them because the vocal cords have been sliced. When I told our pathologist, he dismissed it. Muscle contraction, he said. But that's not what I saw.

"The man they'd executed was the sacristan: they'd discovered he was my informer. I think of the sacristan's face when I remember the situation in my country after May 1980. Ezequiel, when he declared his revolution, intended to slice off the state's head. He intended to swing us by the hair, force down our eyes, shout in our ears. He wanted us to recognize our past vileness.

"But perhaps you have no idea what I'm talking about."

Rejas leaned back, dug a hand into his jeans and produced a wallet from which he drew a small wrinkled photograph.

"Why I keep this, I don't know." His eyes flickered over the image, his expression neutral. With a forefinger he slid it across the table.

Dyer picked up the photograph, taken head-on in black and white, and held it to the light of the overhead bulb. It showed, patterned by finger marks, a handsome, clean-shaven man in his early thirties with mixed-race features similar to Rejas's own: dark eyebrows, a nose broadening at the base, narrow eyes. The eyes stared at the photographer, but telling nothing. It was a face from which all emotion had been extinguished.

"You know who that is?"

Dyer nodded. How many posters of it had he not seen, with details of a million-dollar reward across the top. It was for ten years the only known photograph of Ezequiel.

"It was taken at twelve-fifteen in the morning, the seventeenth of May, 1980. That is," Rejas said, "on the day he vanished."

Dyer looked at the well-remembered features. The chin raised defiantly. The thick black hair, swept back in iron waves from a high forehead. The unreflecting eyes. The dark scarf around his neck. No one visiting Rejas's country in the past decade could have failed to see this face.

"He's sitting on an empty beer crate."

Dyer looked closer. "Really? How can you be sure?"

"I took the photograph."

I met Ezequiel only twice. The first time I was thirty-one. I was coming to the end of my stint in Sierra de Pruna, a small town north of Villoria. Sylvina hated it, called it the Styx. "I didn't marry you for this," she said. But after the election we would be moving to the capital. I'd been promoted to a unit protecting foreign diplomats. Soon Sylvina would be among friends. Laura would be able to play with their daughters.

This was the first democratic election since the coup. Twelve years ago now. We'd forgotten what to do, although we anticipated trouble. My job was to set up roadblocks outside the villages and check documents. Very tedious work, like sentry duty at the Tomb of the Unknown Soldier: six months of vigilance in case someone blew out the flame! It did fail once, during a gas workers' strike; I had to use our Primus stove. Roadblock duty was like that. After three years in Sierra de Pruna I'd reached a point where I wasn't doing my job well. The routine was wearing me out. Just as much as Sylvina, I looked forward to a new start under a government elected by the people.

Hardly any traffic passed the police post on that morning. Then at eleven-thirty I stopped a red Ford pickup heading toward town. In the front, staring intently at the hot hood where I'd rested my hand, was the man in that photograph; next to him, bolt upright, both hands gripping the wheel, sat a long-nosed mestiza of about twenty. Three Indians were standing in the back, their hair snagged with bark and grass. Probably they had slept outside.

"Documents," I said.

They produced identity cards, all except the man in the passenger seat, who patted his pockets as if his card was there somewhere.

I was about to raise the barrier when my eyes ranged over the pickup and I see, lying in an odd sort of heap, a large jute sack. An animal's tail, the black and white fur clotted with blood, poked from the sack's mouth.

The girl, slender, wearing a loose-fitting skirt, got out of the car. "We ran it over."

She leaned over the back. "It came from nowhere onto the road."

I peeled back the sack to the tail's puckered pink base.

"A dalmation, it looks like," she said.

Who is the owner? Why did you pick it up? What are you going to do with a dead dog? But I didn't ask these questions. I didn't even bother to check the bumper for dents.

"We're going to a funeral." She pushed back her hair and the sun lit up a pulse on her temple. "My uncle—he's being buried this afternoon."

"Where?"

"Pelas." Twenty miles east. "He was a machine operator. All his life he sits on the same chair, then he drops dead." She clicked her long fingers, the sound cracking in the dry air.

I walked around to the passenger window. "Found it?"

The man inside shook his head. It was a scalding day, but he had tucked in at his throat a brown alpaca scarf. He was wearing a red shirt, collar up.

"Got to be somewhere." The girl had followed me. Her face in the side mirror looked anxious. "Come on, you must have it."

"Guess I left it at home," he muttered. He picked a packet of cigarettes off the dashboard, tapped one out, lit it. Behind his ears on his neck he had a skin rash.

"Where do you fit in?" I asked.

"He's family," said the girl.

I asked Sergeant Pisac to cover me and opened the door. "I'll need to take your details."

I typed out the notes in the small office, the man sitting opposite; a basic description to pin to a photograph:

*Name:* Melquiades Artemio Durán
*Sex:* male
*Age:* 34
*Race:* mestizo
*Profession:* laborer
*Height:* 5 feet 8 inches
*Build:* thin
*Eyes:* brown
*Dental state:* 5 fillings in lower jaw
*Distinguishing marks:* skin rash—possibly eczema

"Where were you born?"

"Galiteo."

"On the Marañón?"

"Yes."

"Then you know La Posta?"

He nodded.

"That's where I come from," I said.

"Really?" He lit another cigarette, a Winston, and blew out two smooth trails of smoke.

That's it. That's all there is. You cannot imagine the number of times I raked over that scene. The whole conversation, according to my notes, lasted seventeen minutes. From what he said it would have been impossible to believe this man was a philosopher who, twelve and half hours later, would initiate a world revolution.

Hindsight is like using powerful binoculars. I should have detained him. I should have waited, sent the woman back for his documents. I should have asked a lot more questions. But next day I was leaving Sierra de Pruna. I was not going to pay over-much attention to mislaid identity papers. And I was sentimental. We came from neighboring valleys, the man in the alpaca scarf and I, and he was going to a funeral.

At five minutes to twelve I escorted Melquiades Durán into the backyard, sat him on a crate and took his photograph using a police-issue Nikon on a tripod.

Probably he moved, because the contours of his chin are blurred. See? He's not well lit either. At the lab they thought the camera might have had a light leak. But that shaft of light is there because the sun was coming up over the roof. I didn't have much experience with a camera. He looks like a figure from a medieval painting, don't you think?

At twelve twenty-four we came back inside the police post, where the woman driver and the three Indian men waited under guard. I handed her the keys.

"Go to your funeral."

They went out. The engine didn't start immediately. The three Indians looked at me with accusing faces. Beneath them the pickup rocked back and forth.

"Wait. Give it a rest," I called. She had flooded the ignition.

She waited, then brushed back a strand of hair and turned the key, eager to be on her way. This time it fired.

I leaned against the barrier, watching the truck pull away. I expected the woman to wave, but she didn't. The man I had photographed stared at me from his side mirror. The pickup turned the corner, the sun flashed on the roof and they faded into a trumpet of dust.

The next time I met Ezequiel I found him alive, on a sofa, in an upstairs room in the capital. He had altered beyond recognition, only his scarf the same. But that was thirty thousand deaths, two thousand car bombs and twelve years later.


I now know that when I stopped him at the roadblock, Ezequiel was driving with his wife and his three bodyguards to a safe house in Sierra de Pruna. If I had dismantled the truck, I would have found explosives stolen from a tungsten mine concealed beneath the seats. I should have realized that there was something odd about a dog being in a sack, about the dog being in the truck at all.

That night Ezequiel would address a group of comrades packed into a storeroom behind Calle Junín. The meeting was tense. To fortify their spirits, he read aloud passages from Mao, Kant, Marx and *The Tempest,* including the line "No tongue! all eyes! be silent." At one minute after midnight, speaking in a low, precise voice, occasionally sipping from a glass of mineral water, he called for the armed struggle to begin. One by one he embraced his audience, kissing each person on both cheeks. He would not see them again until the revolution succeeded. After he walked through that door, he would be going underground, with another identity.

At twenty minutes past midnight, having been told that the road was clear, he left.

For me, though, the story of Ezequiel really begins seven months later, with another dead dog.

I am standing on a bridge in the capital, staring up at a street-light. It is two o'clock in the morning of the twenty-seventh of December. Suspended in the dark, the orange capsule of the lamp is surrounded by a yellow haze. But there's something wrong. A black weight dangles beneath the bright artificial light. It has torn ears and a wedge-shaped mess across its neck.

I will never find a better allegory of the horror prepared for us.

"Why have they cut his throat?" whispers Sucre.

"So the soul can't escape through the mouth."

In my village, when you died, your dog was hanged from a tree. Dogs, my mother instructed us, were good at crossing rivers in the underworld. But we didn't slit their throats.

"Christ," says Sucre, who is going to be a policeman only until he inherits his father's fruit orchards.

Above me the body twists in the breeze. The animal has been hanged by the tail. His front legs, bound with telegraph wire, stretch down to below his head. As he revolves, he resembles one of the brass reindeers I assembled above our Christmas candles, except he isn't tinkling. A drop splashes my face.

"He's got something in his mouth," says Sucre.

I step back. The jaws have been forced open, something holding them apart in a frozen pant. A placard hangs down from the legs.

Twice I jump up, but the dog is too high. My attempts to pull him down disturb the flies at his eyes. I drive the car onto the curb and stand on the roof to cut the wire. The body drops to the ground, expelling a gasp of air. In the orange light I read the words "Deng Xiaoping."

I untie the placard and hand it to Sucre. Puzzled, he reads

aloud the message written below: "Your fascist leadership has betrayed our world revolution."

He frowns. "Who's President Ezequiel?"

But I am concentrating on the dog. From the mouth pokes a narrow truncheon of dynamite. My first thought is for the traffic below.

The sun would rise on dogs hanging from streetlamps in Belgrano, Las Flores and Lurigancho. Four more mutilated animals were found along the highway to the airport and another outside the Catholic University. People gathering beneath them experienced the same bafflement. No one had any idea who or what Ezequiel was. Nor his world revolution.

In the morning I spoke to the Chinese Embassy. Despite the references to Deng Xiaoping, no threats had been received. After a fortnight without more such incidents, I put the events of that evening from my mind.

Sylvina was relieved to be back in the capital. I had not seen her so happy since the early months of our marriage.

For about a year we rented the flat of her cousin Marco, who had moved with his wife to Miami. Eventually we found a modest basement apartment in Miraflores, three blocks north of Parque Colón. It wasn't as nice as Marco's flat, or the flat we had lived in six years previously, when I worked as a lawyer; and I couldn't easily afford the lease. But her mother's death had left Sylvina with a modest inheritance. How we would cope when this source exhausted itself, neither of us found the courage to contemplate. Meanwhile the inheritance paid for a cleaning lady and the subscription to the tennis club in San Isidro where Sylvina played four afternoons a week.

Our daughter Laura was growing up to look like my sister: large brown eyes, a strong body and masses of black hair which Sylvina insisted on braiding into a plait. Already Sylvina was talking about ballet lessons.

We had lived a year in the new apartment when I was promoted to assistant head of the Diplomatic Protection Unit. Despite that, Sylvina remained convinced that I was crazy to stay in the force. Who could imagine becoming a policeman? They were all either psychologically disturbed or they'd had run-ins with the law. "And all of them are poor." But I worked regular hours, and it was a quiet time in our marriage and in the capital.

One morning in November I am summoned to an office on the third floor of a building in Vía Expreso.

I reported here for duty on my return to the capital, but have had little occasion to come here since. It is a cheerless place, and when the wind blows off the sea, as it does this morning, the corridors smell of car fumes and maize cobs and urine. Because the place was always known as one of the ugliest office buildings in the city, money has been spent to brighten up the exterior with an unnatural-looking green wash which makes it even more charmless. The color does not sit well with the barbed-wire emplacements at the entrance or the concrete blocks which prevent people from parking.

General Merino is a large-shouldered man with the trace of a mustache and small shining eyes pouched into a gray face. He wears a black turtleneck shirt, a half-sheepskin jacket with belt-flaps, and looks at me from one side of his face, then the other, like a chicken. There is no tic at the corner of his eyes, as there is to be later. It is a benevolent look.

Merino is our most distinguished policeman. As a cadet in the sixties, he helped crush Fuente's revolt, and he protects his service with a similar ferocity. He has a reputation for hating the army and is known to be honest, brave and overworked. His joy in life is fishing. A rod is propped against the map on the wall behind his desk.

"You speak Quechua, right?"

"Yes, sir."

"You know the north well?"

"Yes, sir."

There is a glass bowl with oranges on his desk.

"Want one?"

"No thank you, sir."

He takes an orange and peels it. "To corner a tomcat, Colonel Rejas—I call you Colonel, you understand, because I am promoting you—what do you do? You don't send two Alsatians up an alley. They'll play havoc with the garbage cans and the cat just leaps up the tree. No. You send in someone who knows the area, the other's way of thinking, what he smells like. You send in another tomcat."

The General, I will learn, is someone who reaches a decision quickly, is reasonably intelligent, and once he has delegated a problem, he has no intention of being bothered with it again. He gestures to a thick blue folder on his desk. "I want you to be our tomcat, Rejas."

He gives me until next morning to acquaint myself with the contents.

At home I slip open the adjustable metal fastener. The files catalogue incidents in the countryside since 17 May 1980, the day of the last general election. On that night, seven months before their appearance in the capital, dogs were hung from lampposts in four villages of Nerpio province. The symbol was, apparently, a Maoist one. "In China a dead dog is symbolic of a tyrant condemned to death by his people." Nor was it limited to the Andes. In the weeks ahead, dead dogs would hang under the streetlights of Cajamarca, Villoria and Lepe, culminating in the incident I have described on the bridge over the Rímac. The capital had no more such incidents after that first spate.

The animals that came next were alive.

In February, in Cabezas Rubias, a black dog ran through the market, frothing at the mouth. A fruit seller was chasing him away with a broom when the dog exploded. Three people suffered appalling wounds and a meat stall was blown all over the marketplace.

In Judío a donkey, galloping wildly, exploded into a thousand bloody pieces outside the police station. No one was hurt, but the blood seemed to have been etched into the stucco of the building.

In Salobral, during a meeting of the council, a hen was introduced into the Mayor's office and spattered the walls with feathered blood.

In none of these cases did anyone claim responsibility, but the dog and the donkey had evidently a placard around their necks proclaiming EZEQUIEL.

"A delinquent!!!" declared the Mayor of Salobral. "An Argentine," hinted the local bishop in a sermon recorded from the pulpit. "An American," avowed someone in a bus queue, this quoted by the correspondent of *El Comercio*.

There were also reports from the deep country areas.

From the police post in Tonda: eyewitness accounts of a public assassination, the victim accused of stealing bulls.

From Anghay: two prostitutes assassinated on a crowded street.

From Tieno: the assassination of the Mayor in a barber's shop.

Again, the name Ezequiel associated with these atrocities, sometimes scrawled onto the walls in the victim's blood, sometimes spelled out in rocks on a hillside: VIVA EL PRESIDENTE EZEQUIEL. VIVA LA REVOLUCIÓN.

This name repeated itself in valley after valley. Whoever this Ezequiel was, he was everywhere. At the same time, he was nowhere. He had published no manifesto. He never sought to explain the actions taken in his name. He scorned the press. He would apparently speak only to the poor.

This was why the government had ignored him.

You've spent time in my country. You must understand why Ezequiel could describe the capital as "the head of the monster." His "revolution" passed unnoticed there. His actions, if ever they reached the newspapers, were dismissed as an aberration, the work of "delinquents" and "thieves."

But you know what the capital is like. It believes itself to be the whole country. Everything beyond its limits is the great unknown. It only starts caring when the air conditioner is cut off or there's no electricity for the freezer. So long as he operated in the highlands, Ezequiel was no threat to our metropolis. And all this while his movement was stealthily encroaching underground. A gigantic scarab growing pincers and teeth. Ignored. Until the moment, one week before General Merino summoned me, when a boy nearly the same age as Laura walked into the foyer of a hotel in Coripe and blew apart.

That frightened people.

The photograph from the *Diario de Coripe* is dated 10 June. It must have been taken in a photo booth, because doubt is wandering onto the good-looking face. He holds his smile, uncertain, waiting for the flash.

In the article his profile is placed alongside a shot of the hotel's gutted lobby. Six bodies are arranged on stretchers. Paco, according to the manager, who survived the blast, was dressed in smart Sunday clothes with a brown leather satchel slung over his right shoulder. The manager remembered seeing his face, shielded by his arm, appear at the door. Local parliamentarians had convened in the foyer to discuss the building of a milk-powder factory. Catching sight of Paco's eyes bulging against the glass, the manager opened the door. The child had an urgent message for his father, the chairman. He must deliver it personally. "Over there," said the manager, indicating the chairman already rising to his feet, puzzled by the boy running toward him, holding up a satchel, and calling out "Daddy, Daddy!" The fact was, he had no son.

*"Viva El Presidente Ezequiel!"*

"This Ezequiel, sir, do we know anything about him?" I asked General Merino next day.

"Motherfuck all. Nothing beyond what you will find in that file." The General had trouble grasping anything in the abstract.

"We were a small unit, never more than six in the early days. Our brief was 'to investigate and combat the crimes perpetrated in the name of the delinquent Ezequiel.' But it is hard to establish an effective intelligence system from scratch. You need money—and we had little of that. One year we couldn't afford new boots. It takes also time."

"You had twelve years," Dyer pointed out.

"You sound like the General. And I tell you what I told him. Intelligence is no different from any other art. It's about not trying to push things. It's about waiting. Do you know how long it takes a sequoia seed to germinate? A decade. Of course, there's a time for impatience, when you must act quicker than you've ever acted before. Until then it's about collating and analyzing information.

Ezequiel, remember, had prepared his disappearing act since 1968. Once he disappeared, we would spend another twelve years tracking him down. But that's how long the Emergency lasted in Malaya.

"Success might have come sooner had we reacted earlier, with a clear policy and an image of the state as just, generous and firm. Unfortunately, the state wasn't that. It was directionless and its mongrel policies fueled Ezequiel's appeal to the country people and, of course, eventually also to people in the cities. By the time we decided to take note of him, it was too late. He had gathered momentum to such a degree that he could not be contained.

"I was glad to be entrusted with the case. My vocation, for which I had abandoned a prosperous position, had fallen short of my hopes for it. So I dedicated myself to the pursuit of Ezequiel.

"From the start, I was amazed by the fanaticism of his followers, by the degree of their subjection to his discipline. His cells proved impossible to penetrate. They relied on no outside group. They stole dynamite from the mines, their weapons from the police. We rarely made arrests, because their intelligence was better than ours. The few we captured refused to speak. When someone talks, it's to get off the hook, but not in the case of Ezequiel's people. It was evident they had been training since they were children. A good many of them *were* children. And when Ezequiel tapped a child on the shoulder, that child became a killer. To a ten-year-old boy or girl, it was a game. They competed. Put a satchel of dynamite or an AK-47 in the hands of a ten-year-old and annoy him—you don't want to be around.

"The finding of Ezequiel and his top echelon was my aim. My orders to my men didn't change. To defeat our enemy, we must be aware of his attractions. If we wanted to capture Ezequiel, whoever he was, we had to win over the same people. In no circumstances would we kill or torture a suspect. Frustrating though it was, we stood for the rule of law. Oppression must be seen to come from the other side. Intimidation wouldn't give us the answer. We might learn about the past, what had happened. But we forfeited a suspect's cooperation in the future.

"We were far more likely to achieve success by 'turning' a suspect. We should concentrate on scrutinizing those in the community who betrayed any sympathy for Ezequiel. Through details, however tiny, that's how we'd find him. The color of a wallpaper, the pattern of a dress, the contents of a garbage can.

"So we stacked up the evidence.

"We rifled garbage cans. We watched houses. We noted what suspects wore. Slowly, patiently we would build up a picture until we could present our suspect with a stark alternative: Prosecution or Reward. Any human being when faced with two doors, one saying LIFE, the other DEATH . . . well, you can predict which one they will choose.

"Which is what happened when I confronted the sacristan in Jaci."

He was awkwardly thin, his crinkled skin hanging on his face like something borrowed. I found him in the church, removing the candle stubs from a row of spikes. It was vital that he should not view me as yet another official from the coast conversing in a language he didn't understand. This was why the General had asked if I spoke Quechua.

We sat on the front bench.

"This is you?"

"Yes."

In the photograph, taken from the roof of the village school, he was receiving money from a masked figure. His benefactor's other hand clutched a captured police rifle.

"And this?"

The sacristan sat in a boat, two armed men in the prow.

"I can explain." The hospital would do nothing without money. He had taken it to pay for an operation. His mother was dying. Cancer of the lymph glands.

"A judge would give you twenty years. Maybe more."

"You don't understand."

"I do."

There were four more photographs, but he had seen from the start that I had the evidence to convict him. His face collapsed.

After he had agreed to help, I spoke to him with sympathy. I promised to have a word with the hospital. I tried to win him over.

I don't know if I succeeded. But he said he would have the information ready—names, dropping-off points, dates and places of future actions—when I returned.

I came back in plain clothes. The village lay in a bowl surrounded by steep, treeless hills, by a river with little water. It took three days to reach by bus and another morning in the back of a lorry. The driver was buying cheap potatoes. Passing as his mate, I helped load them into sacks.

I had arranged to meet the sacristan at midday. As I walked toward the church, I heard hooves galloping over loose timbers. In the street, there was a stirring. People gathered up their produce, speaking in quick, hushed voices. Doors slammed. The horses must have crossed the bridge because the clatter faded. Then they rounded the high wall of the school.

I could tell who the riders were. They were masked, about ten of them. Teenagers, led by a woman, her hair tucked beneath a baseball cap. Her short legs, bulging in their faded jeans, kicked the horse in the direction of the church where I was headed. The ground vibrated as she galloped past. She rode up to the church door, urging the horse up onto the stone step until its head and bristling shoulders filled the doorway. Then she got down. One of the masked riders took her reins. She hoisted up her belt, from which hung a machete in a leather scabbard, and walked into the vestry, where the sacristan awaited me with his information.

I fled uphill, up a narrow twisting street, to find a hiding place. The villagers had vanished behind their shutters, but I could feel their eyes. Eventually I took refuge behind an adobe wall—nothing but empty fields behind me—from where I looked down on the church. Minutes later, to the ringing of bells, five men were pushed into the square. The riders had known who to take, where to find them. The Mayor, two adulterers, the driver of the lorry which had brought me. And the sacristan. They were forced to their knees while the villagers watched. The bells fell silent and a young woman's voice burst from the loudspeaker tethered to the ankle of a stone figure above the church door. She spoke in fluent Quechua

on behalf of Ezequiel. He had come to free them from their past.
For Ezequiel the past was dead, as—shortly—these criminals
would be. The five men symbolized a world in total disorder. The
only way to change it drastically was not through reliance on natural political means but through the agency of someone divine. Ezequiel was this divinity. He was the Eternal Fire, the Red Sun, the
Puka Inti, beyond human control. In his presence it was impossible
to remain neutral. He was not just a law of nature but the fulfillment of our oldest prophecies.

"Weren't you promised clinics?"

Several heads nodded.

"Weren't you promised roads?"

"Yes."

"Weren't you promised telephones?"

"That's right!"

"Ezequiel will bring you telephones, clinics, roads. He will
strip the flesh of the reactionaries who denigrate your customs, and
throw the scraps of their offal into the flames." She held up a fist.
Her voice rose to a strident pitch. "Under his banner the unbrib
able soul of the people will triumph over the genocidal forces of
the law."

From the wall, after adjusting her shawl, an old woman hurled
a stone at the men kneeling in the dust. I had stopped at her stall
earlier to drink coca tea.

"This Ezequiel, you support him?"

"Yes."

"Why?"

"I am no longer a cabbage," she had said, not looking at me.

"Have you seen him ever?"

"Yes."

"What does he look like?"

She had pointed to a configuration of stones on the hillside.

Below, the campesinos were being as easily won over as a child
with a sweet. Terrifying. He was using our myths for his purposes.
But even had the villagers understood, they wouldn't have cared.
Today in this square he offered what for five centuries the government had denied them.

A murmur fluttered through the crowd. In the sun, something metal flashed. There was a shout and one of the masked riders jabbed a rifle into the sacristan's back.

"Forward!"

The man's head rested, bowed and shaking, on his clasped hands. The force of the blow had knocked his cap to the ground.

"Go forward!"

Another blow on his shoulders. I heard him whimpering. He babbled about his sick mother, how she needed medicine. My fingers scratched the earth. He was about to be punished because of me. If I had been there, I would have been seized too. Who had betrayed him? Where was the information he had prepared for me?

He threw back his head. In a hoarse summons to the surrounding bowl he shouted, "Rejas!"

My name ricocheted from hill to hill.

"Forward, traitor!"

One knee tested the ground an inch ahead. Then the other. In minuscule shuffles he advanced toward the masked figure with the machete.

She tested the blade with her thumb.

"Rejas!" And madly his eyes followed the echoes, as if they would delve me into the open.

"*Viva El Presidente Ezequiel!*"

I tell you, I still wake up and it's his call I'm hearing. Rejas, Rejas, REJAS.


In this fashion Ezequiel persuaded the people to consider him divine. As a man of flesh and blood, he had ceased to exist. He had dismembered and scattered his body, and now thrived like a monstrous Host in the heart of anyone invoking his name. One day he was in Jaci, his name daubed in dripping letters on the church wall. On the same day he was six hundred miles east, robbing the Banco Wiese. If ever we approached him, the old coca lady had warned, he would transform himself into a canopy of feathers and lift into the sky. "He can never be caught."

But Ezequiel was no condor or circle of stones. He existed, all right. Who he was and what he looked like—small, large, one-legged, wall-eyed—we had not the least idea. But someone who condoned public beheading; well, we didn't think to look for a man of culture. We had marked him as a jungle-tested leader in the mold of Guevara or Castro, or those revolutionaries whom the General had fought in the sixties. Which is why it was such an extraordinary shock when we discovered Ezequiel's true background.

Six months after the execution at Jaci, Sucre led into the office a senior lecturer in philosophy from the Catholic University.

"He says he knows who Ezequiel is."

The philosopher—stooped, bloodshot eyes, white mustache—was frightened. A colleague had overheard his boast and mentioned it to another colleague, who at some point had told Sucre's cousin, a second-year student in the same faculty.

Contemptuously, Sucre piloted him to a chair. "He now denies it."

"Who were you talking about?"

"It doesn't matter. It was a quarrel, a long time ago."

He wore a maroon corduroy jacket buttoned up, which he undid to reveal a brown cardigan, also unbuttoned, covered with biscuit crumbs. His skin was drink-ruined, and he had the deflated cheeks of a boaster.

"Tell me about this quarrel."

It was nothing serious. Just an academic squabble.

"About Ezequiel?"

"No, with Ezequiel."

"You're telling me Ezequiel was an academic at your university?"

In the corner Sucre chewed air.

"He was a philosopher of no small distinction." Tetchily, he drew the wings of his cardigan over his shirt. "Only he didn't answer to Ezequiel. His name was Edgardo Rodríguez Vilas."

And slowly it came out.

It had happened in Villoria, in the mid-sixties. Our informant—let us call him Pascual—had been recruited to the newly opened University of Santa Eufemia. He had been happy in his position, until the appointment of this man Vilas to the same faculty.

Vilas was a Maoist, Pascual a Marxist. It was the time of the Sino-Soviet split. They'd argued.

"I was pro-Castro. Vilas thought Castro was a chorus girl."

One day Pascual complained to the Dean. Said he didn't approve of what Vilas was doing. A sinister, antihumanist influence. So fixed in his political ideal that all things became instrumental to it.

Somehow his complaint reached the ears of Vilas. In charge of personnel, he removed Pascual from the faculty board.

There was an added complication. One student over whom Vilas had exerted his influence was Pascual's girl. Vilas had gone off with her.

"You mean an affair?"

"To my knowledge, he did not actually have a physical relationship with her," he said coldly.

"Then why did she leave you?"

"I understand she found his absolutism attractive. Such people are always hungry for imperatives when those imperatives coincide with their own."

"Which were?"

"Like a lot of types unable to relate to others, he could excite in them a romantic possibility of violent revolution."

"Which you couldn't?"

He buttoned up his cardigan. "I tend to see the other side of the coin."

"And your colleague Vilas, he was capable of violence?"

"Possibly. He was always talking world revolution. But it was the sixties. Weren't you?"

"Where is he now?"

"Look, he's probably still in Villoria."

"Describe him."

"This was twenty years ago."

"Concentrate."

"Average height, glasses, black hair, thin."

"Do you have photos?" My attention had waned. At that time

a lot of radical professors, because of the expansion of the univer-
sities, woke up in positions they didn't have the intelligence to
maintain. Suddenly they had power. They possessed the truth. So
they used revolutionary ideology to shatter the system. Until it
threatened their pension plans.

"He would never be photographed," Pascual was saying.

"Really? Why not?"

"Hated it. Which we found odd because he wasn't shy. If you
ask me, it was vanity. He had this skin complaint."

My interest quickened. "Get the albums, Sucre."

There were six of them. "Take a look."

The philosopher turned the laminated pages. On one side we
had stuck pictures of Ezequiel's victims; opposite, the faces of
those so far interrogated.

"I didn't realize . . ."

"No one here does."

He leafed through the album. Page after page of mutilation.

"He was responsible for this?" He stared at the sacristan's
corpse. He was frightened. He remembered something. Something
was coming back to him.

He reached the end. "No, not there."

"Try an earlier one."

With relief he closed the second book. "Nothing."

"Another."

We were nearly done. His cardigan buttoned up, he wanted to
go.

"Tell me. You're a man who understands history," I said. "If
you want to start a revolution, why not issue a manifesto? Why
not show the people who you are, what you're doing?"

He leaned back, grateful to explain. "That's perfectly understandable. Socrates wrote nothing down. Neither did Jesus. The
problem with text is that it assumes its own reality. It cannot answer and it cannot explain."

"So if you wanted to be effective, you'd leave no trace?"

"That's right."

I opened another album, the earliest. "Last one."

Impatiently he turned the pages. Halfway into the album he
dislodged a photograph. I retrieved the print from the floor and

inserted it back under the plastic sheet. Pascual lifted the next page, and even though he had not been concentrating, I saw the hairline hesitation. His hand came up, scratched the side of his nose. Something forced him to hurry on, cover up the image which had made his eyes contract.

"Stop!" I pressed my hand down on the album, turned the page back.

"Is that him?"

The philosopher's cheeks sagged. His eyes flicked wildly over the face. I could only see it upside down. I wrenched the album from him. He had been trapped by a photograph of a man wearing a brown alpaca scarf, taken on a scalding morning near Sierra de Pruna. Taken by me.


A curious and not very comfortable feeling comes over me when I look at prints of my wedding or of Laura's christening: as soon as I see them, my memory of the occasion is subverted. In a vital way, what they celebrate has ceased to exist for me.

So it was with that photograph of Ezequiel. Each time I looked at it, I remembered less. The image, already distant, became encrusted with a further memory of my failure to remember anything more. The live face was, if you like, lost, bullied out by subsequent events.

At the office there was jubilation. At last we knew who he was and what he looked like. Professor Edgardo Vilas was the laborer Melquiades Artemio Durán, who was the Maoist revolutionary leader Ezequiel. The General hoped the sight of him might prompt additional memories, as if, by remembering one tiny detail extra, all would be solved.

"Think hard, tomcat. Think back. There must be something other than his Yankee cigarettes and the rash on his neck."

But there wasn't. Lifeless, unreal, boiled in time, he had become a nonface. He wasn't a man anymore. Not someone you could see in a café drinking tea and say, "Yes!" He had become an icon. When I looked into those narrow black eyes, all I saw was a stiff tail sticking out of a sack.

Pascual couldn't help. Two days later, when he was required to come back in and verify the photograph before General Merino, the faculty informed me that he had taken unexpected leave. He never did come back.

It does seem incredible in the age of the camera that someone can avoid having their picture taken for thirty-four years. From outer space it is possible to frame the scowl of a man perching on a beer crate in a country yard, yet for all this time what printed image did we have of Ezequiel? Apart from that black-and-white print, not one. Think of it: no high school portrait, no family picnic, no face gazing from among a group of friends. That this distinction should have been achieved by the holder of a prominent chair at Santa Eufemia University is remarkable.

With the same reverence for detail that characterized his dissertation on the Kantian theory of space, he had excised from the record all trace of his physical presence. When I inspected his dissertation, his appointment to the professorship, his library card, I found in each case the same rough, near transparent patch, lighter in color than the surrounding page, where a photograph had been torn out or removed with a knife.

It is not the first time an intense search has yielded nothing. At the Police Academy we were lectured on the American D. B. Cooper, who was the first person to hijack an aircraft. Our tutor credited Cooper with being the forerunner of modern terrorism. Decades later he may be still at large, walking cheerfully down some main street in Mississippi, popping his pink gum at the sky. For three hours, the length of the flight, he existed as D. B. Cooper, after which no one saw him again. He parachuted out of history, and the last image anyone had of him was the light on his silk chute drifting toward the pines.

Once he had climbed back into his pickup, that's how it was with Ezequiel.

———

I won't go into detail about the months and years which followed. The people who had met him, the rooms he had lived in, the shop where he had bought his mineral water—all these I traced until the moment of his disappearance. But I was trying to carve a statue out of shadows. I might have been excavating one of those burial mounds at Paracas. To the General, my exhibits appeared indistinguishable from the sand.

It proved impossible to conjure Ezequiel from such remnants. He was not a man to whom stories attached themselves. His character, assembled from hundreds of interviews, was a hollow, papier-mâché construction. The sentences canceled each other out. You heard only the echoes.

"He wouldn't hurt a fly." Classmate, San Agustín College, Galiteo.

"He said that violent revolution was the only way to seize power and transform the world." Classmate.

"He had no girlfriends." Classmate.

"Women pushed and shoved to be near him." Pupil, Santa Eufemia.

"His lectures were repetitive. He was not a particularly interesting phenomenon." Fellow teacher.

"He was handing down the Commandments." Pupil.

"He only bought mineral water." Shopkeeper, Lepe.

"I saw him smile once. It was in the street and he was drunk." Fellow university student, Lepe.

"He said that flowers made him sneeze." Secretary at Faculty of Philosophy, Santa Eufemia.

"Every day for lunch he ordered the same dish: a flavored yogurt." Cashier at university canteen, Lepe.

"He asked me to turn down my music." Neighbor, Santa Eufemia.

"In the middle of a conversation he would tell you Albanian olive oil was the best in the world." Visiting Peace Corps lecturer.

"He never took off his jacket. He always wore a scarf." Pupils, various.

Read cold on the page, these statements were inert or comical. One element united them. In each case, I heard the hush in the speaker's voice, the kind of hush people use when they should not be speaking.


Where was he?

Possibly he was not in the country at all. He could easily, without risk to himself, have directed his operations from some hotel in, say, Paris. But I didn't think so. My instinct told me he remained locked into this soil, driven into it with the force of an axe, identified with his revolution so as to be indivisible from it.

He really was a charismatic leader, you see. This was a man in command, who was not commanded. An unquivering spirit seemed to lie at the center of him, stilled into place by a terrible ambition. He didn't have to participate himself. I doubt he ever fired a gun. But by the act of being there, of showing his face, he could infuse a terrible energy into his followers.

And the throat slittings and the killings and the bombings and the robberies and the kangaroo trials and the dogs hung from lampposts—these ceased when he left an area. They followed him wherever he went, and when he was no longer there, they stopped. He was, if you like, one of those washerwomen in times of plague who contaminate everything they touch even as they wash it. Our own Typhoid Mary, except he believed he was making clean the lives of our people. He was scrubbing out the dirt and the corruption and the abuses which had oppressed us since the Spanish Conquest. He was leading us toward his fresh new dawn.

That's how he earned his nickname at university. Behind his back they called him Shampoo. Because he brainwashed people.


He wasn't abroad, but where was he? Believe me, it is difficult to disappear. Your ability to hide is restricted if you stand out in any sort of way. If you are bigger or more intelligent or if you come from somewhere else. Ezequiel would have stood out.

When people are after you and want to kill you, you have three choices:

You go to a place where there are no people.

You never leave your room. But it's not easy to hide an extra person; you knock over a chair and always there's someone downstairs who had thought, until then, that there was no one else up there.

You remain in the open, but you change yourself in every way possible. If you are an obsessive coffee drinker, you drink tea. If you wear glasses, you change to contact lenses. If you like to wear your hair one length, you wear it another. You put tacks in your shoes so your mother would not recognize your walk. You change your instincts. The Gestapo caught one of your agents in Paris because she looked to the right as she crossed the road. If you have to go into the street, you guard against anyone catching sight of your profile. Even on a rainy evening it's easy to recognize a person you know. You might not have seen them for twenty years, but no downpour will disguise the contours of a familiar cheek spotted through a car window.

In short, you change your habits, your instincts, your face.

But one thing you can't change is your illness.


You remember how I typed "eczema" on the basic description of Melquiades Artemio Durán? Well, Ezequiel suffered from psoriasis.

It's not a pretty disease. The new cells push up before the old cells are ready to leave and you erupt in nasty weeping yellow scabs. But what's odd about psoriasis when you consider Ezequiel is that you don't find it among the Indians. It's a Caucasian disease. A white man's disease.

It's also incurable. It might fluctuate and there may be periods when it's not present, but always it comes back. What you've got to watch out for is the stage when it becomes rampant, because that's when the sores become infected and the smallest movement is agony.

For a long time Ezequiel's bad skin was my most concrete lead. After any attack by his people on a village, I would interrogate the chemist. Sometimes they'd lie, sometimes there would be no records, but where records existed, these often revealed a sale of Kenacort E.

It suggested Ezequiel's illness might be worsening. If this was the case, I was confident he would be forced soon to abandon the high altitudes. You see, at a certain altitude his blood would coagulate. He wouldn't be able to go on breathing, and that's why he would want to make his way down to the coast.

I have no proof to back this up, but I suspect Ezequiel's ailment was connected with his decision to go underground. His behavior did suggest a certain vanity. All those spots—would you want to be seen in that condition? How else does one explain the quantum leap from Professor Edgardo Vilas, the mild-mannered philosopher, into President Ezequiel, the revolutionary?

I am not a Kantian philosopher. I find his work hardly intelligible. But I understand it enough to know that Ezequiel took an à la carte attitude to Kant's works, and made such a meal of his philosophy that its originator would not have recognized it.

Kant does have one image which holds some meaning for me: the bird which thought it could fly faster in a vacuum, without air to beat against. For me, that is where Ezequiel's reading and his texts and his philosophy had led him, to airless haunts where all gusts of life were extinguished. He'd started out with his ideology, but he was dealing with people for whom ideology meant nothing. Blood and bone and death were all that mattered to the people in my valley. It was idiotic to think they would care about Kant or Mao or Marx, and so he taught them in blood and bone and death, and he had become intoxicated.


My pursuit went on.

I got used to the overlarded soup of the canteen, the wary nods in corridors, the unanswering shelves of documents and photographs, the despair of an unfinished case.

I drove home.

I crouched before Laura as she sat in her playpen and shielded with both hands the flicker of my love for Sylvina. But my vocation had generated a deepening hostility. The unsolicited touch of our first meeting, that look across the table in the faculty library, such intimacies had fled into a darkness from which I could not retrieve them.

Day after day passed like this. Year by year. Twelve of them.

It came as a shock, therefore, when Ezequiel's death was announced. On 3 March 1992, Alberto Quesada, Minister of the Interior, gave a television interview in the course of which, questioned about the insurrection in the highlands, he adopted this line: Ezequiel, a criminal, a one-off, was certainly dead. If he wasn't dead, why didn't he show his face? He was the Eternal Flame. How could you conceal his splendid blaze?

Because, Quesada jeered, he had perished. He was like one of those tyrannical sultans whose death is not admitted, and whose pavilion is raised each night. He was like El Cid, and they had strapped his carcass to his horse. He had, in short, been blown out.

It was tempting to believe Quesada. But his bellicose message was as crude as the posters distributed by his ministry, showing my photograph of Ezequiel prancing on cartoon cloven feet and embellished with the tail of a devil. If such a pivotal figure were dead, there would be some sign that he was no longer on the scene. If the army had killed him in a shoot-out, they would have flaunted the body. They would have treated him like Che Guevara.

My own belief, which I had submitted in my latest report to General Merino, was that, on the contrary, Ezequiel had never posed a greater threat.

I expected to hear back from the General, but three weeks after Quesada's broadcast the police went on strike. None of us had been paid for two months. Outside the Ministry of the Interior a thousand policemen held up our symbol, a worn-out boot. The strike ended with Quesada giving his personal assurance that all salaries would be paid by the end of the week. Two days later the General summoned me. It was, the summons said, important.

I never could predict what the General regarded as important. I hoped he wanted to discuss my report. But he might want to talk about Quesada's pay settlement; or possibly he wished to know more about Hilda Cortado, a woman we had arrested the previous afternoon for distributing subversive leaflets. It was rare to catch someone red-handed like this.

In fact, it was about none of these things.

Preparing his tackle, he fiddled with a lure dangling with

hooks. "Forget it, tomcat. It's over." He rolled down his turtleneck and, with the lure, slit the air an inch from his neck. "Your pal Ezequiel, he's dead."

He sketched the details for me brusquely. Skirmish on a dirt road above Sierra de Pruna. Lorry refuses to stop. Army opens fire. Lorry, packed with dynamite from copper mine, explodes. Body found. Ezequiel.

Merino was annoyed. "We work on this for twelve years, then the army waltzes in. General Lache is going to be unspeakable."

"When did this happen, sir?"

"A month ago."

"A month ago! Why weren't we told before?"

"Lache wanted to be certain. He tells me Quesada's very happy."

It was true I had observed a lull in Ezequiel's activities. Normally during this period we might have expected forty, fifty incidents in the provinces. Since Quesada's broadcast my unit had reported seven.

Could Ezequiel be dead?

I expected the story to lead the news on Canal 7, but it was transmitted near the end, after an item on the national women's volleyball team. In the capital Ezequiel remained virtually unknown. The announcement of his bandit's end on a dust road a thousand miles away merited twenty seconds. There was film of a truck on its side and a plump corpse covered with an army blanket. An anonymous hand drew back the blanket, and the camera closed in on a man's head, lingering over charred features and a body which resembled a burned sofa.

Sucre looked to me for confirmation. "That's him. Isn't it, sir?"

"It could be."

You know how you look forward to something which you never believe will happen, and when it does, you are overcome with exhaustion? That was my feeling on seeing the blackened mess which was Ezequiel's face. With this fulfillment of my task, desire had faded. There was none of the anticipated elation. I felt stripped of my shadow.

Quesada, a small dapper figure in a white suit, was filmed clapping the shoulder of General Lache, who looked massively pleased with himself. Delighted, the Minister knocked on the camera lens. "As of this moment, Ezequiel no longer exists."

General Merino would have attributed it to professional resentment, but I had no wish to see the body.

# 5

"When did you next see Ezequiel?"

It was the second night and Emilio had removed their plates. Dyer, arriving early, had found Rejas already sitting at the corner table.

"See him? Five days after he was pronounced dead. But I didn't know it was Ezequiel."

"Who did you think it was?"

"How well do you know my capital?"

"Reasonably well."

"Then you know Surcos?"

Dyer did. A prosperous new suburb in the northern outskirts. Rejas leaned forward, raising his chin.

Picture this. It's about eight-thirty at night. I've parked my car and I'm looking up at the first-floor window of the building opposite. A yellow curtain—it is obviously a child's room—is drawn. There are cartoons of some sort decorating the fabric, but since the room is in darkness, I can't tell what they are. The sliding window is open at one corner, where a breeze sucks at the curtain, distorting the characters. I am trying to decide who they are—whether it's Mickey Mouse or maybe Dumbo the Elephant—when a light cuts on and a strange blue glow, full of underwatery movements, flickers over the ceiling. A figure moves across the light. I see someone pause behind the curtain and very slightly part it.

Although bracing myself for an uncomfortable interview, I do remember wondering who is in that upstairs room and whether the person framed by those eerie fluorescent shadows is Laura's teacher—or whether the apartment is even part of the dance studio.

It's Laura's teacher I'm waiting to see. There's been an embarrassing incident. Due to Quesada's delay in paying our salaries, my check for Laura's lessons has bounced. I hope the embarrassment is temporary. Deprived of Ezequiel's terror, I have tired of my profession overnight. It's as if Ezequiel's death has set me free.

But Ezequiel is not dead.


Surcos, if you have to live in the capital, is a pleasant enough suburb. It's about thirty minutes' drive from Miraflores and twenty from Laura's school in Belgrano. It smells of cooking oil, geraniums and, before it rains, fish.

Calle Diderot is a wide street, well tended, and you can imagine children running along the pavement or playing on the tidy beds of grass between each house. Populated by lawyers, doctors and teachers who have migrated from the coast, the street has a café, its own video store and an estate agency operating from a garage.

Jacaranda trees on each side of the street give speckled shade to eighty houses, painted brightly to remind owners of their fishing villages. The houses are modern, two-storyed, with barbed wire between the roof terraces. Their little front gardens are enclosed by walls or by iron fences, sometimes with a dog's muzzle poking through.

That's how it is now, and that's how it was then, on the night I'm talking about.

The ballet school was unremarkable, and was entered through a wall painted the same peppermint-green as the building it concealed. One by one the mothers pulled up outside to wait for their daughters. They parked bumper to bumper and sat in their cars, varnishing their nails. Now and then one of them would turn to shout "Get down!" at an uncontrollable poodle.

Many of these women had been Sylvina's friends since childhood, but they didn't marry policemen. They drove new cars, lived in properties facing the sea and could afford cooks. Sylvina saw them often. Iced coffee at the Café Haiti; tennis at San Isidro's Country Club; aerobics in the Hotel María Angola; and—the latest excitement—a literary dinner which required the wife whose turn it was to host the event to deliver a short talk on a modern novel, explaining why it interested her.

"Agustín!" Marina, sitting in her cherry-red BMW and tilting her face to the side mirror, had been applying her lipstick. She had returned from Miami with a slightly different profile, a little less nose, a little more chin. She left the car and crossed the road.

"I haven't seen enough of you!" Divorced from Marco, she had been two months back in the city.

We kissed. Miami had given her a taste for tight pants, long fingernails and streaked hair.

"I've been busy."

"How pleased you must be. I saw the news on television. I didn't realize until Sylvina told me he was the one." She touched my arm, partly secretive; partly not. We had asked Marina to keep quiet about my profession. When the girls at Laura's previous dance school found out I was a policeman, they had teased her. So had the ballet mistress.

Marina, squeezing my arm, said, "What will you do now?"

"I don't know. Maybe it's time to go back to the law."

"Sylvina will be thrilled!"

"I suppose so." That's what I'd promised my wife. Once Ezequiel was caught, I would look for a better-paid job.

"Is Sylvina all right?"

"She's at the vet."

"We're looking forward to her talk on Wednesday. You know we're meeting at your place?"

"She's very excited about it."

"I can't fault Marco. He's been extremely generous, sending us copies of the novel. Which I still have to read." The divorce, Marina wanted us to gather, had not been acrimonious.

"And Laura," she said. "Is she happy with her new teacher?"

"Oh yes. A great success."

"When I heard how miserable she was with Madame Offenbach . . ."

There was a commotion behind Marina. The ballet class filed out of the door in the green wall. Beautifully turned out, erect, with splay-footed steps they scattered toward the cars.

Marina, recognizing a pampered girl in pink tights and a smart blue leotard, said, "There's Samantha! Bye for now."

It was easy to tell my daughter apart. The other girls left talking to each other. She was by herself. Slightly heavier than the rest of them, and smaller, she was made taller by a head of hair which she pulled back in a way that gave a crushed look to her features. It was hair she could sit on, long and thick, the color of freshly made coffee. The other girls in her class had the blonder hair of their mothers; and the lighter skin.

Laura, seeing the gray Peugeot, walked toward me at a tilt. Conscious of her short neck, she held down her shoulders. Despite the warm night, she hid her body with leggings over her leotard. Sylvina was always after her to lose weight—"If you're not careful, you'll see your dinner in your behind"—and she would prepare a special fat-free chop which Laura devoured in a second.

Continually struck by the girl's resemblance to my sister, I asked on one occasion, "What's wrong with her? She looks all right to me."

Sylvina flicked the white hands which had once fascinated me. "Certainly she looks all right. Now."

My wife was the force behind the decision that Laura should take up ballet. This was what her friends did with their children. Through Laura, Sylvina could live out the dreams she had harbored for her younger self. She wanted Laura to be pretty, to walk nicely with ribbons in her hair, to be up there onstage as a Cinderella fairy. In other words, she wanted Laura to put on a tutu and forget where she came from.

The matter was never brought up; it lay unexploded between us. I had once overheard Sylvina speaking to Marina on the telephone. I wouldn't have listened had she not been talking in such an apologetic tone. "Samantha's so lucky with her looks. Laura's very dark, you see."

Quite why this should have cropped up then, I don't know. It had never been an issue before. When I met my wife—at university in the late sixties—it was a time of "indigenism," the country en-

joying one of its spasmodic celebrations of self-discovery. For
Sylvina it was an assertion of identity to be seen in fashionable
company, white hand in brown, and I was not immune either.
Now, twelve years on, she believed learning classical ballet might
go some way to removing the jungle from Laura's face.

But you only had to look at Laura to understand she wasn't
built for classical ballet. It agonized me to watch her struggling,
bewildered, before the mirror we had installed in the hall. I could
see the pain she inflicted on herself, trying to make her joints go in
a way they were not meant to; doing things which did not come
naturally to her body.

When I mentioned this to Sylvina, she said, "To be a good
ballerina, you have to deform yourself."

I said nothing, but it made me angry. Laura had her own poise,
her own beauty. She required nothing more.

However, this was not the matter I needed to discuss with her
teacher.


I asked Laura to sit in the car.

My knock resounded in the street. Over the wall I heard a
sliding door being opened, footsteps, the drawing of a bolt.

She was dressed in black: black round-necked leotard with
long sleeves, a gauzy black ankle-length skirt over it, black ballet
slippers.

"Yolanda? I'm Laura's father."

She pointed to her smiling mouth, which was full. She put a
hand to her throat, as if this would make her swallow quicker.

"There. Sorry." She held up a slice of banana cake on a paper
plate. "I've just made it. Want some?"

"No thanks."

"But Laura's left. Haven't you seen her?"

"She's in the car."

"Do you want to bring her in?"

"I'd rather not. It's about your letter."

"Oh. Yes," she said, as if she had forgotten. It's an embarrassing thing, to tell someone their check has bounced.

She unfastened the door chain. Beneath the streetlight her face gleamed pale, still wet from where she had toweled off her makeup. Wide brown eyes set on high cheekbones, a clear skin, fine dark hair. She looked frank, honest, conscientious—the kind of person you might tell everything to on first meeting.

"Please. Come through."

I followed her across the patio. We entered the studio through a glass door and she slid it shut after me.

The room smelled of cigarettes, sweat and the musky scent of rosin. A wooden barre, slung with pink tights and tracksuit tops, ran around two mirrored walls. Laid out on the shiny parquet floor were inflatable gray mats for breathing exercises and, against the near wall, a cassette player, a tin box scattered about with white powder, and a leather trunk. One door, half-open, covered in photographs of dancers, led into a kitchen; another, also ajar, into a shower room. The mirrors were steamed over.

She put on a tape, Tchaikovsky—quite loud, as if that were what I would expect—and raised her arms in an apologetic spread at the tatty state of her studio. "So. This is it."

Beneath the strip lighting, there was something original and unfeigned about her. Also a graveness, as if she had been marked by a bad love affair.

"Laura warned you? Once inside, you have to do everything I say."

Before I could answer, she raised one hand above her head and slid her fingers down an invisible rope to her neck. Speaking in a strict Germanic accent, she said, "The best position for a dancer is the one when you're hanged, because it's very well placed. The hips are over the feet. The shoulders are over the hips. The head is midway. *Ja,* it's a wonderful position." The imitation was good. She made me want to laugh.

"Madame Offenbach?"

"Not a success, I gather?"

"No."

I could see Yolanda wanted to say, "I hope Laura's happier here," but she held the words back, her lips skewed sideways, her front teeth showing at the corner of her mouth.

She scooped something from the floor. "They never pick up their plasters!"

She threw it into the rosin box "Coffee? Or would you like lemonade, if they've left any?" She watched me, biting a nail.

"Laura's waiting. I'd better not."

To Laura, not Sylvina, she had entrusted her simple note:

Dear Señor Rejas,

I regret to tell you the bank has refused to honor the money you owe me for Laura's ballet lessons during December and January.

Yolanda Celendín

I was nervous, which made her nervous. "Here's the money I owe. I'm sorry about the check."

With a smile all neat and laced, she said, "We hadn't met, but I thought it was better to tell you than Señora Rejas."

"My employers are two months in arrears with their salaries."

She accepted the money and, without counting it, folded it onto the plate beside the remains of her cake. "That's terrible. Already I've had to let three girls go because they couldn't afford it. I've regretted it ever since. They came every day from Las Flores. They were so excited, the parents. They watched their daughters in their beautiful dresses and they dreamed. I should never have let them go. They were three lovely dancers, I could tell as soon as I saw them."

"Can you tell, that quickly?"

She nodded. "Some girls, you only have to see them standing still to know they're dancers. Others might be good at barre work, but when you bring them into the center, they're terrible."

"And Laura?" I risked.

"Your girl, she's a spot of sunshine. That's a real child you have. Not a little adult in lipstick." And she imitated with exaggerated eyes someone I knew at once to be Marina.

At my laughter, she raised her hand. "No, I mustn't be so disparaging. They're probably your friends. It's just that in six months I have attracted the worst sort of ballet mother."

I was still smiling. Her mocking of Marina's values struck a chord. She was not the dupe of anyone's wealth. But she hadn't answered me.

"It's hard for a parent to ask this. Should we encourage Laura?"

Her face remained serious. "How much do you know about ballet?"

"Not much." Through Sylvina I had met a few dancers. They seemed to me dim, uneducated and self-absorbed.

"Laura has nice ideas," she said, "but she should take risks. I love people to take risks. Very often it works."

"She wants to join the Metropolitan."

"You've put her down for classical classes, which is fine," she said carefully. "You can't be an engineer without studying mathematics. If you've been classically trained, you can do things in modern dance no modern dancer can do. But she might find her natural aptitude is for the kind of contemporary dance I'm involved with. It can't hurt to try."

Politely, conscious of the time and of Laura waiting in the car, I said, "Do you still dance?" I knew nothing about her. We had found the school through Marina. Keen for Samantha to maintain the standards of Miami, she had recommended the teacher in Calle Diderot as a first-rate communicator. But I had no idea whether the teacher performed.

"I did and then I didn't and now I do again. As of this moment I'm meant to be preparing a ballet with a small group at the Teatro Americano, but it's getting desperate. I can't find a subject." She tucked her hands behind her back. "But you're not here to discuss my problems. Is there anything else about Laura?"

In fact, there was. I was worried my daughter was the one the pretty girls laughed at. I knew they called her Cucumber Body after a livid green all-over which Sylvina had bought in a sale. Once through the kitchen door I had heard Laura, in tears, telling Sylvina, "Samantha says my feet are claws around a branch and I look like a parrot in a storm."

But if Laura had been teased, she wouldn't want me to know. And no parent cares to inquire too closely into the particulars of their children's suffering. So I said, "I'm worried about her feet."

"Her feet?"

"Is it right for Laura's feet to bleed?"

"Can I ask you something? Laura wants to join the Metropolitan, but how serious is she—I mean, about wanting to be a dancer?"

I pictured my daughter night after night before the hallway mirror, beating her new shoes with Sylvina's toffee hammer to make them quieter, soaking her feet in salt water, spreading mustard on her blisters, inserting foam between the toes, raising one leg and then the other, her legs taut as triggers, her breasts shuddering as if she were going to be sick, her body crying out with fatigue.

"She is serious."

"Then she'll have to go through this hell. If you want to be a dancer, you can't have a normal life. You don't have boyfriends. You're not really a woman in most people's eyes. There's a sense in which you have to dance yourself to death. You're aiming for a perfection which your body isn't meant to give you. The pain is intense. Intense. You dance with pain. But the feet, you don't have to worry about them."

She hiked up her skirt, easing off her ballet shoes. In a graceful movement she lifted her leg until her bare foot rested in the air, perfectly still, not far from my face.

"See those corns? When they're well set in, she'll be able to dance on them. They'll be deformed, but her feet won't bleed anymore."

Yolanda's foot, it was more a sea creature's flipper. Ugly, discolored, with red calluses, the nails ridged into shapeless chips, the skin on the toes sharpened into a permanent crease. It reminded me of the turtle with a bitten shell I'd seen on the beach at Paracas.

I averted my eyes. "Does she have to starve too?"

"I don't understand." She lowered her leg.

I told her about the diet Sylvina insisted upon.

"Laura's not on a diet? You must take her off it. You'll never get a classical figure by dieting. She's growing. She needs energy. Oh, these Western ideas of beauty make me sick. Little girls' looks are just different. She's beautiful as she is."

I thought so.

"Of course she is! She should treasure what she has, make the most of it. That's what'll make her a dancer. Your daughter's much richer, much lovelier than all those Miami babes with chocolate-chip noses and frosted hair. Look at her. She has all of our country in her face."

I had never heard anyone talk like this. Those elements which Sylvina found distasteful in our daughter were mine as well. By supporting Laura, her teacher had given me, my origins, validity.

"At the Metropolitan I got into the most awful fights with the teachers. Be honest, look at us, I'd say. Most of us, we're brown-skinned and stocky. Classical ballet was invented by the Europeans, and is danced with different bodies in mind, different sensibilities. We have Andean bodies, Andean minds. How can we respond to what is going on around us if we're dressed like this and all the steps are spoken in French. We can't!"

"What did they say?"

"They'd laugh, except the Principal, who was English. Señora Vallejo was sympathetic, but she wasn't allowed to sack anyone. For the other teachers, the world didn't exist outside that European stage." She looked at me, amused. "In my last term I put on this dance. A scandal it caused with the parents. Much too dark, they found it. We don't understand your work, that dance you did with spiders. Spiders, I asked? Or was it homosexuals? Do you know what it was? The Condor Festival, one of our oldest ceremonies. And they thought this was sodomy!"

Until this moment I had thought of Yolanda as someone a little bit nervous who was talking a lot. I had said to myself, She's bound to be edgy, it's after-hours, maybe she's worried she's about to lose another pupil. I will give her the money I owe and after a polite interval I will leave. Now I wanted to stay.

"Haven't you forgotten about Laura?" she said.


Laura sat in the car, one foot over her knee, peeling off skin. When she saw me, she leaned across the seat and opened the door.

"Isn't she nice! I knew you'd like her. Was it about that letter?"

"A little bit."

"Was it a love letter?"

"About you."

"What have you been saying?"

"You should try modern dance, she thinks."

"I'd like that." She uncrossed her leg. "Today I danced a painting."

"How did you do that?"

"It's easy. She said, 'This is a painting. These are the dark colors. These are the light. Now express the colors for me.' I was the light. Then she divided us into two groups. 'Over here you're angry. Over here you're not interested. Dance it.' "

"Which were you?"

"I was angry, which was fun."

It was a world away from cloche-hatted Madame Offenbach.

"You haven't told her what I do?"

"No, Daddy."

"If she asks, say I'm a lawyer."

"I need new shoes."

"Mummy will get you some."

She slipped on her ballet slippers. Their color was disfigured by a watermark and the toes were rusty with spots of dried blood.

"And unlike Madame Offenbach she can dance," Laura went on.

"Is she a good dancer?"

"When she left the Metropolitan, she was the best ballerina in the country. That's what Samantha told me. She danced a wonderful story for us today which she'd picked up in the mountains. She called it 'The Dance of the Weeping Terrace,' after a terrace people go to when they say goodbye. They hug and cry because they don't know their destination. That's why it's called a weeping terrace."

"Darling, I told you there was a terrace like that in our valley."

"Did you? No, you didn't. I wish you had."

Her teacher had made it more memorable.

"You promised to take me to La Posta," she said cunningly. Until now Ezequiel had been the reason we couldn't make the journey. According to intelligence reports, his men had been observed in the lower valley.

"You've no excuse now."

"I'll have a word with Mummy."

"Do you mean that?"

"Of course I do."

"And we can see the coffee bushes and Grandma's parrots and

Grandpa's library?" She had never met my parents. Like my sister, she would have run rings around them.

"That's right."

"You are coming home tonight, aren't you, Daddy?"

Often I didn't come back at night. I might be in the sierra, chasing some shadow connected with Ezequiel, or, if in town, I might be watching a suspect house. The extra money I earned from surveillance had—so far—covered Laura's tuition fees.

"Yes."

Beside me Laura loosened her damp hair. She gathered it up, fastening it with an agate hairclip I had given her. In contented silence we drove toward the supermarket in Miraflores.

"We must remember the cat food for your mother," I said.

The night was sticky and at the traffic lights on Parque Colón I shrugged off my jacket and laid it on the backseat.

"Aren't you hot in those leggings?" I asked Laura.

"Daddy, do you have a girlfriend?"

I was unable to reply for a second or two. "Darling! What makes you ask such a thing?"

"You never come home."

"I've been working, Laura."

"Samantha says her mother likes you."

Feeling angry, I was about to say "Well, I don't like Samantha's mother" when, without even a warning flicker, the lights in the street went out.

Laura looked outside. "What's happened?"

"Just a power cut."


The supermarket was a block away. An assistant shone his flashlight over the pet food shelves. He hoped it wouldn't last long. At nine there was a volleyball match.

There hadn't been a power cut since the military coup, but I was not concerned. At the plant in Las Flores they had been rumbling on for months about low pay. I was more put out by Laura's question.

We were about ten blocks from home when my jacket started to bleep. Sucre. I pulled over outside the Café Haiti. Lanterns had been placed on the tables. In the subdued light I saw men speaking into their mobile phones, checking to see all was well at home, in the office.

I listened to the confused details. The darkness sheeting the city had nothing to do with industrial action.

"Have you told the General?"

"He's on his boat."

"I'll meet you at the theater."

I gave Laura the handset. "Take this."

"What is it? What's wrong?"

She realized something terrible had happened. She fiddled joylessly with the machine. She was trying to imagine this terrible thing.

"It's Ezequiel." I said the words quickly, not hearing what I was saying.

"But Daddy, he's dead."

I accelerated along Vía Angola. Our street was not far now. I braked noisily outside the house, leaving a track of rubber.

"Listen, honey, I'm sorry. I'm not making sense. Explain to Mummy I can't stay."

I pulled the door shut behind her and drove flat out along Calle Junín. Sucre's message had resurrected the dread which Quesada only five days before had put to rest. It meant one thing: Ezequiel had not lain blackened and featureless beneath a coarse army blanket; instead, he had taken a tighter grip still on our destinies. It meant he was alive after all and had decided to rise from the earth. It meant he had descended finally to the capital. And the capital, "the head of the monster," was the perfect place in which to hide.

By the time I reached the theater, the audience had bundled out into the street and were assembled on the sidewalk in a state of shock. My men had arrived and were attempting to detain them, but many had slipped away already. The crowd spread out under the plane trees and waited for taxis. Some, nervous as birds, stumbled between the tramrails. They followed the rails to the sea, not caring where they walked.

From a French playwright who had been sitting five rows from the stage I pieced together what had happened.

Lionel Grimaud, unaware of the power cut outside, had taken the blackout to be a part of the experimental drama he was watching, in full keeping with the poster which had beguiled him here.

The poster showed a young woman with white-chalked cheeks and eyes made up to look like a cat. She peered at her right hand, in which she held a minute version of herself fashioned into a glove puppet. From the tight ceramic mouth poured the words:

> Literature! Dance! Theater! Film! All this in a drama that is absolutely contemporary. Are you sick of injustice? Are you sick of feeling helpless? Are you sick of believing there's nothing you can do? Our actors will startle you out of your indifference. In *Blackout* you will see human existence taken to its extremes. You will see fanaticism. You will see darkness. You will see intolerance. You will see hope. AND YOU WILL SEE *Blackout* TONIGHT!

Twenty minutes into the play the theater lights went out. Already a negroid face, filmed behind an empty desk, had appeared on a large screen talking about alms. Then an angel had skipped onstage. Dressed in red rubber gloves, a gray suit and cardboard wings, he had hurled the contents of a bucket of water into the front row.

As an irritated section of audience mopped themselves dry, the voice of Frank Sinatra could be heard singing "This lovely day will lengthen into evening, / We'll say goodbye to all we ever knew . . ." The angel floated off, wiggling his red fingers, to be replaced onstage by four dancers, their backs to the audience.

Grimaud—who was emphatic on this point—said the dancers were girls. Each wore a black stocking over her head, with a thin black garter strap binding her face. They bent into a provocative stance, waggling their buttocks and slowly turning until they faced the audience on all fours, their tongues out. The only sound was of a fast breathing—"the sound of dogs panting"—and this, mixed with Sinatra's voice and, at the edge of the stage, the silhouette of the angel lip-synching his words, provoked a horrifying impression.

Sinatra was singing "I loved you once, in April . . ." when the moan of a recorded siren interrupted the words, followed by the rattle of gunfire.

It was then that the blackout occurred.

"We couldn't very well understand what was going on," admitted Grimaud. Onstage a disembodied light swung up and down. All eyes fixed on this erratic firefly, which plunged swiftly into the auditorium. There was the clatter of several people being tugged against their will onto the stage.

The audience shifted uneasily. Behind Grimaud an elderly woman hissed, "Claudio, you did not warn me that it was one of those audience participation plays. We should have sat farther back."

Then three shots, in quick succession.

The same woman said, for all to hear, "You promised it would be a musical."

Things were by now so confused that people didn't know if

this exchange was part of the play. The smell of cordite wasn't agreeable either, nor a warm sticky substance like scrambled eggs which had landed in several laps. After five more minutes of waiting in the dark, those in the front row who had earlier been sprayed began to hiss angry asides.

But even so, they sat there. And this was the strange thing: at least ten minutes passed before anyone had the nerve to stand up, and only because they saw, shining behind them down the aisle, another flashlight.

It swept along the rows, giving substance to the people sitting there. Soon it reached the stage, jerking upward to reveal a drawn curtain and three figures sitting on deck chairs about six feet from the back wall.

When you light something from below, you know how exaggerated it becomes? Imagine the sight of those bodies. The beam wavered across their legs and chests, magnifying huge shadows on the back wall.

They sat at an angle. Something had happened to their faces.

Quesada, his body bent backward, had a red caste mark on his forehead. The back of his head was no longer there, but you could see the eyes, nose and cheeks. His mouth had been gagged with theater programs screwed up into little balls.

Beside the Interior Minister sat his wife. You could tell it was a woman from the shadow cast on the ceiling by her curly, well-cropped hair. Her neck was twisted, with one shoulder thrust back to show her lapis necklace. They had shot her in the left eyeball, through her glasses, and her hair was sparkling with broken glass and what looked like phlegm, except it was her eye.

The bodyguard slumped forward next to her. The hollow-point bullet had entered the back of his head and his face was somewhere in the audience.

The silhouettes slipped back into the darkness as the manager rested his flashlight on the stage and climbed up. You saw its beam pointing at the woman's feet, where there was an awful lot of blood. The manager picked the flashlight up and staggered through the puddle toward the chairs, shining the beam directly into their faces, so now everyone could make out those terrible looks, the splatters on the stage set, like ink blots from a fountain pen which has been shaken violently, each splatter larger than the head, each self-contained, except for a thick vertical mark behind Quesada's chair where a chunk of his skull had struck the wall and slid down.

The light scanned the wife's sparkling hair, the pulpy red mask of the bodyguard and Quesada sitting there, a cardboard notice on his paunch, the lettering, sketched in his blood, reading DEATH TO ALL TRAITORS. VIVA EL PRESIDENTE EZEQUIEL!

The manager gave a choking sound. People in the audience gasped.

"Believe me," came a man's voice, "this is part of the play."

As soon as I read the sign around Quesada's neck, I knew that Ezequiel had come down from the mountains. He was among us in the city. Anywhere in the city.

But he was not just "anywhere."

I now realize that, earlier in the evening, he would have turned on the television. Careful to cut out the sound, he wouldn't have wished to attract the attention of the ballet students below. Laura's class had ended. The girls having taken their showers, he would have walked to the window to watch them leave. He would have pushed back the curtain with the back of his hand—and that's when, through the narrowest of gaps, he would have seen me.

Admittedly, in the dark neither of us could make out more than the outline of the other. But for a second or two we looked at each other. All that separated us was a yellow nursery curtain.

That curtain was permanently drawn. Ezequiel would stand behind it for minutes on end, absorbing the street. He liked to stand in the same position, his face against the glass of the window, which he would slide open a few inches. At the end, when I was observing him through my binoculars, I could see him inhaling the air, feeling it on his raised face like a dog pressing its nose to a car window. That's probably what gave him his cough, because a few days after Quesada's death Laura came home with a fever, and by the end of the week Sylvina had caught it too.

I can describe what he would have seen through that chink. By the time I ordered in my men, I knew everyone in that street, what they did, when they left home, what time they returned, their love affairs and peccadilloes. Afterward I wandered a lot around that room, standing where he used to stand, imagining him. Once, a movement drew my eyes to the house opposite. A young girl pushed a man, laughing, onto a bed. A leg was raised at right angles into the space where they had stood, then it disappeared. When the girl next passed the window, she was naked. Seconds later I heard the sound of a toilet flushing.

The toilet was fed from a water tank on the roof. It's a funny thing, but for six months almost the only word Ezequiel would have seen in the world outside the room was the manufacturer's name: Eternity.

If I close my eyes, I can follow the street to the hill at the end. Sometimes the outlines of the slope are clear and I can make out paths and the colors of a garbage dump. On other days it remains a blurred shape, the same color as the fluffy gray sky which our poets liken to a donkey's belly.

I hear the sounds of a middle-class street. A gate closing, a car door opening, a bird singing. The tree where the bird sits is a jacaranda. It's been growing purpler by the day, as if someone had dipped the branches in the afternoon sky. I don't know about you, but I hate the sound of birdsong in the evenings.

Opposite, below the lovers' room, Milagro, the maid, starts to beat an imitation Persian carpet against the fence. The noise causes an Alsatian to leap up, paws spread against the railings, barking. A while ago, while reversing into the street, Milagro's employer ran over one of this dog's puppies. That's why she paces up and down, thrusting her snout between the bars, her black eyes roving over anyone who passes.

Milagro shouts for the Alsatian to be quiet, but is ignored. She is habitually ignored. Every day she bustles after the boy who collects bottles. Too late she hears his shout. She scuffles in the wake of his bicycle cart, but never attracts his attention.

"Bottles!" shouts the boy. Casually he lifts both hands above his head, so that for a few dangerous yards no one is steering the cart. Then he grips the bars, leans into the corner and disappears.

Milagro lurches one or two paces and stands in the middle of the street, panting helplessly, holding to her breast a bag which clinks with empty Cristal beer bottles. "Señor . . . Señor . . ."

The barking frightens a face to a window of the house on the corner. Did Ezequiel know what went on in that room every afternoon? The face at the window belongs to Señora Zampini. At three o'clock, when Dr. Zampini is lecturing on geriatric oncology at the Catholic University, an orange Volkswagen Beetle draws up and out steps a tall man in a brownish suit with shiny dark patches on the elbows of the jacket. He stands up stiffly, pulling his shirt cuffs back down his sleeves. He's not as excited as he used to be. He comes without the verve or the flowers that attended his earlier visits. Has Señora Zampini noticed his listlessness? When the door opens, hers is the face in the shadow, grim with anticipation. He enters, kisses her hand. The door is bolted behind him.

What else do I hear? The conversation from the corner café over cups of scalding, cardboard-tasting coffee. Cars leaving for the beach, their drivers hooting as they pass the video store, the air sweet with the lotions they've rubbed on their arms and faces. The panting of two middle-aged joggers, women in turquoise tracksuits, their hairdos ravaged by sweat.

It is easy for me to picture myself as Ezequiel. How hungrily I watch the street. I yearn to be outside, moving. There are occasions when I want to yield to the violence I have unleashed, taste it for myself, experience the fear I have become immune to. I touch the window and cough. I feel the air against my hand. Despite my cough, I press my cheek to the draft. I belong downstairs, not in this locked room. I touch the door handle and dream of the world downstairs. At half past three every afternoon, Kant walked under his lime trees. For six months I haven't abandoned this space.

So there Ezequiel stands, waiting for Laura's class to leave, waiting to count the girls out so he may watch television or listen to his music.

There is a box crammed with loose cassettes—Beethoven, Schumann, Wagner and a Donizetti opera, *Lucia di Lammermoor*. There are also recordings of Frank Sinatra, but they haven't been played in a while. Ezequiel's taste in music has changed since he left the mountains. As the psoriasis devours him, eating its way between his buttocks, he no longer wants to hear a human voice. Not that he spelled any of this out during our interrogation. I had to retrieve these bits and pieces from a tide of belligerent nonsense about fascist continuismo and the Inevitable New Dawn. The utopian garbage he spouted contained few clues about what actually went on in that room. Only the room told me anything.

It was not much bigger than my office. There was a double bed and at the center, with its back to the window, a high-backed armchair covered in red velvet, in which he spent much of his time reading.

His books were arranged in alphabetical order on a shelf above the cassette recorder. This was Ezequiel's third safe house in eighteen months and he had with him only essential texts, each one annotated in his close, backward-sloping handwriting. Had they let me study them, I might be able to tell you more about the way his mind worked. But they didn't.

On the arm of the chair, a tin Cinzano ashtray overflowed with Winston stubs. He loved American cigarettes. That, and his psoriasis, and his passion for Kant, and the fact that he liked drinking mineral water constituted pretty much the whole of the picture I had of the man until I met him face to face in that room. By that time there would be no yellow curtain between us, no merry cartoon elephants floating down on striped parachutes. Down to what, I don't know.

What else was up there? In such a space everything becomes an icon. Two pairs of shoes on the floor, making steps without him. On the white walls a small picture of Mao and a framed photograph of the Arc de Triomphe at night. He'd never been to Paris, but he admired Napoleon. These types do. A hotel trolley which he used as a desk, and also to eat from. The food, prepared in a back kitchen, was brought to him by Comrade Edith. She was the only person allowed to enter his sanctuary, kept locked at all times. Edith was the reason, I am sure, he had abandoned the mountains. His wife Augusta was the girl who had driven the red pickup (and was formerly the girlfriend of Pascual). She would have wanted him to remain in the countryside. Like him, she had envisaged the revolution achieving its triumph after his death, in much the way that cathedral architects were content not to see their work completed in their lifetimes.

But that was a young man's dream, the fantasy of a provincial idealist. Augusta's death and his disease had pinched him back into this life. He no longer had the patience of a snake. He had grown restive, and Edith found it easy to exploit this impatience. She urged him to enjoy the fruits of his revolution now, in his lifetime. All they required was one final, decisive action. But for this he must come down to the capital. His physical presence was needed to plan the operation. To monitor and inspire it. To be there when his people removed, once and for all time, the rotten, crumbling keystone of the state.

I don't know whether he and Edith slept together in that unmade bed. Rumors said he slept with all his female followers, who regarded him as holy. But I don't believe that.

A small bathroom led off the bedroom. Here he swallowed his capsules and applied his creams. Have you smelled petroleum jelly? Well, that's how the bathroom smelled. There were medicines everywhere, on the floor beside the perished rubber mat, on the shelf below the shower, ranged along the top of the cabinet above the basin.

What struck me was the lack of a mirror. I can only suppose that Ezequiel had become revolted by his image and no longer wished to be reminded of his obese, diseased, almost immobile self.

So here he stood, this sick body—the psoriasis worsening by the day—restless, in pain, and of course he was going to be aware of the beautiful girls below. Since he couldn't see them, they must have been the more beautiful in his imagination. You see, the dancers' bathroom was directly below his. He would have heard snatches of conversation as they soaped their exhausted bodies under the shower. Think of it. Here was a man in a locked room preaching liberty while downstairs, only a matter of feet away, they were free.

They were being trained to fly and he was caged. Doesn't that make you laugh?

He must have seen me get out of my car. I'm not sure what can have passed through his mind when he saw me crossing the street.

I guess while I talked with Yolanda downstairs he would have sat in his armchair and watched a silent television screen. Then, when the power cut came, he would have waited for news from the theater.

I left the Teatro de Paz at three in the morning and drove cautiously home. The only lights came from cars and a few candles twitching behind windows. The city was quiet too. All I could hear were the waves stampeding on a dirty gray beach. Not until I reached Vía Barranco did I learn why the silence was sinister.

My headlights picked out packs of children tearing along the sidewalks. They were sticking paper sheets onto doors and windows. I swerved at them and they ran off. Getting out of the car, I walked toward the face which stared at me from this door and the next, and from the doors of every house in Vía Barranco.

My photograph of Ezequiel, blown up by Quesada's ministry and used in the countryside, had been translated into thousands of head-sized posters. They were signed PRESIDENTE EZEQUIEL, while across the top of each, in the same handwriting, were the words BLOOD DOESN'T DROWN THE REVOLUTION BUT IRRIGATES IT! EZEQUIEL'S THOUSAND EYES AND THOUSAND EARS ARE ON YOU!

I had the sensation that the eyes in the poster mocked me personally. As a clue to what I look like now, this morning, they said, this face is worthless.

The dawn confirmed his prevalence. In San Isidro a general's widow woke in the half-dark and thought she had died because Ezequiel's face, which she mistook for that of her husband coming to greet her, had been pasted over both bedroom windows. His uninhabited eyes stared from the garbage cans, from movie posters, from beneath the glass tops of the tables left overnight outside the Café Haiti. He floated in the fountains of the Plaza San Martín. He was caught in the treetops of the Jardíne Botánico, as though dropped from the sky. He looked up from doormats in Belgrano, having been slipped, like a locksmith's circular or a Chinese restaurant menu, beneath the front doors.

Like the Passover Angel, he had spread his wings over the capital.

So long as it stirred the dust of unseen terraces far from the capital, no one believed much in Ezequiel's revolution. Now everybody was fervently interested. When there is a victim at once familiar and powerful, the anxiety of a nation is easily engaged. The identity of the murdered Minister underlined our gross incompetence. The man onstage, his mouth grotesquely stuffed with theater programs, had, among his other responsibilities, been head of the national police force. He was, politically speaking, our boss.

At eight-fifteen in the morning on the day after the Teatro de Paz killing, General Merino called me to his office. When he had learned the news of Ezequiel's death, already he had taken a holiday. He should have been on his boat. Instead, he stood by his desk and looked at me with misgiving, his lower lip pushed forward a little. He was slightly tipsy and smelled of the cigarette he had cadged off his secretary. Because of the power cut, the air-conditioning wasn't working and he had removed his jacket.

"I've been asked to stand by. Calderón wants to speak to me."

"Fuck," I said.

" 'Fuck' is right."

He grabbed an orange from the glass fruit bowl and started to dismantle it. A sticky hand indicated a poster on his desk, black letters screaming SICK OF INJUSTICE? SICK OF FEELING HELPLESS? SICK OF BELIEVING THERE'S NOTHING YOU CAN DO?

"Once," he said through a mouthful of pulp and juice, "I made the mistake of buying a ticket for one of these so-called plays. Believe me, there was nothing I longed to do more than climb onstage and grab the actor by the throat and say to him, 'This is no damn good.' "

He shook his head and sucked at a segment of orange.

"You know what Calderón is going to say, tomcat. How did we so completely underestimate Ezequiel?"

"We didn't, sir."

"What's that? Speak up, can't you?"

"A copy of my report was sent to the President's Office."

The warning had been there on the first page. In the third

paragraph, I referred to the mimeographed pamphlet discovered on the woman we had arrested in Las Flores. This pamphlet, entitled "Washing the Soul," constituted Ezequiel's sole declaration to date. "Our process of the people's war has led us to the apogee; consequently, we must prepare for the insurrection, which becomes, in synthesis, the seizure of the cities."

My message, underlined in yellow marker, was clear. On the presumption that the pamphlet was not a forgery, and regardless of the welcome lull in Ezequiel's activities, we ought to brace ourselves for an escalation of violence. "We cannot rule out that he will try a political assassination."

I doubt whether General Merino had read the report. He was unable to take Ezequiel seriously, regarding him, with mannered disdain, as a college professor who had dropped out. Revolutionaries who showed their faces—that's what he was used to. But Ezequiel was sneaky. He wasn't a manly Castroite like Fuente, who boldly and openly entered a bar and, in full view of his victims, shot dead fifty of them. The General, faced with my attempts to describe Ezequiel's revolutionary philosophy, would dismiss them with an air that suggested he had seen it all before, in far more virulent form.

"You think Ezequiel's people know about Mao and Kant and Marx, but they're just going back to the same buzzwords. They sit around the fire and pretend to warm their hands with European nostalgia. Really, they're itching to get out their knives. Especially the women. They adore to kill. It's an event. Then they make love for three days after. No, tomcat. This isn't a world revolution. It's a fuckathon."

His attitude exasperated me, but his hands were full elsewhere, his mind preoccupied with staff morale, pay, an epidemic of internal corruption. There was pressure on him from the government, the military, the drug enforcement agencies. The "world revolution" came low on his list. The capital was the General's priority, and to date Ezequiel had restricted his actions here to one or two attacks on the Central Highway, some tires burned and a demonstration on Labor Day. And dogs hanging from the streetlights, of course. He was irritating in the way a cigarette butt in the lavatory is irritating, still bobbing up after every flush. So the General had left me to deal with him. I wasn't on the take, so he could trust me. Because of my Indian blood I could be expected to shed light on the phenomenon. Better than some of his officers anyway. And most important to his way of thinking, I'd met Ezequiel, hadn't I?

Now the lavatory had blown up in his face.

He'd had a presentiment of this. Or so he would confess in one of the watchful nights ahead. One evening after work he'd be sitting in his favorite bar by the port, dreaming fish, and—snap!—the lights would go out. He would order another drink while they hunted for candles, and half an hour later a tapping at the window would divert him from his cinnamon-flavored brandy and Sucre would be making goldfish lips against the glass.

"What's that, Lieutenant? Stop that nonsense. Come inside."

"It's Quesada."

"What about him?"

"He's been shot."

And he'd feel this pain—actual pain—in his clouded head and all the bright days when he shouldn't have taken the boat out would slyly wink at him from his brandy glass.

The prospect of a meeting with Calderón filled him with apprehension. He began adjusting the position of his mobile telephone.

"It's in your report, I know. You've done a good job, tomcat. But remind me. How did this begin?"

"In Villoria. At the university."

"Villoria, eh?" He looked at the map on the wall behind his desk. An orange slice moved uncertainly over the Andes. "Now Villoria," he said, as if considering the matter for the first time. "Isn't that a strange place to start a world revolution?"

He turned to me. And the questions fell out of him until they lay between us in a pathetic heap. Why weren't we catching him? Where did he get his funds from? What did China have to do with our country? How many men did he have? Why communism? Wasn't communism dead? On and on, with me doing my utmost to answer, until he finally said, "What does he want, for Christ's sake?"

"Absolute power."

"Why?"

"He says the state doesn't care for the people."

"Amen to that," said the General.

He sucked at another orange quarter, then looked at me over the rind. "You know what worries me—"

The telephone on his desk began ringing, long pauses between each ring. He rolled his eyes despairingly and threw the peel into the bowl.

"Time to swallow the hemlock," he said.

He extended the mobile's aerial and climbed inelegantly to his feet, walking to the window. "Yes, Captain," said the General. "Speaking." Perhaps he decided he was being rude, or maybe he wanted me to share the burden, because he walked back to where I was sitting, drew up a chair and sat down next to me, facing his own empty chair across the desk, and held the mouthpiece between us so that I could hear too.

The voice was clipped and quick, too low for me to catch.

"I do understand," said the General reasonably. His cheek all but touched mine. I smelled the brandy.

"Do you think we haven't—"

The other voice broke in. The General listened, breathing heavily until it subsided.

"It is a sorrowful state of affairs. Twelve years . . ." He was echoing the words he'd just heard. "It's difficult to say, Captain. Perhaps you have no idea how diff—"

Another angry outburst. Again he listened, nodding. He reached for the fruit bowl, edged back. "Do you think that is necessary? I mean—" He looked at the space above the chair where he had been sitting.

"Of course. I understand, Captain. I will do what I can."

He slapped down the telephone and shook his head from side to side, testing the bridle of Calderón's order.

"I tell you. Tomcat, I feel just like . . . like . . ." The simile escaped him.

He walked around his desk and collapsed in his chair. "He's canceled all leave."

"I'll tell the men."

"If we don't find the assassins, he'll bring in the army."

"I have no names for you," I said.

"Then who do I tell him was responsible for putting a bullet through our boss's head?"

"They were dancers, sir. A man and four women."

"And why can't we catch them?"

"They're known as 'annihilation detachments.' Twenty years old, often younger. They probably came in from the countryside and disappeared there afterward."

"Who helps them?" No pause for breath.

"No one who helped them would have known who they were."

"Women? Jesus. What's happened to the women in this country? Have they gone nuts or something?"

"I don't know, sir."

"There must be thousands of poor bastards who don't know what's going on in their women's minds. The point is not that these women are terrorists, but that there are all these stupid husbands who don't know what the hell's going on."

I said nothing.

"These women, have we ever convicted any?"

"The evidence is never enough."

"We let them go?"

"Yes." He knew all this.

"Don't we have any suspects at the moment?"

"There's the woman we arrested with those pamphlets—"

He leaned forward, alert. "Who is where?"

"Downstairs. We have her in detention."

"Then we have nothing to worry about," said the General, springing from his chair.


The lift was not working. We walked downstairs, the General stumbling behind me in the dark. As we reached the basement, the lights flickered on.

Hilda Cortado sat on the corner of her bed, rubbing her eyes. We studied her sad face through the grille. She was muttering to herself, readjusting to the light. According to my notes, she was nineteen.

"She's a sexy drop," said the General, polishing another orange on his shirt. "Where's she from?"

"Lepe."

"Indian, is she?"

"Yes, sir."

"At police college we used to make the Indians eat dog shit," he said wistfully.

Hearing him, she turned to face us.

The arrest of Hilda Cortado a week before had, for me, first raised the possibility that Ezequiel might be preparing the fifth and penultimate stage of his New Democracy: the assault on the capital. Deceived by Quesada's broadcast, by a cindered corpse beneath a blanket, we had overnight lost interest in her. Now she incarnated all the General's earlier failures to take notice of Ezequiel.

"Okay, tomcat, I'll be the good cop," said the General genially, unlocking the door.

Once inside the cell, he took up position in the corner farthest from the bed, beaming.

I approached Cortado. "I have some questions."

The spit landed on my forehead. I left it there, not reacting, then stepped toward her. Her eyes flared and she braced her head, expecting to be hit. Holding her stare, I wiped the spit from my forehead and touched the wet fingertips to her lips. She pulled back, tightening her mouth.

I crouched before the bed, looking down at the floor. It hadn't been swept. She had scratched some words in the dirt: VIVA EL PRESIDENTE EZEQUIEL.

I took a breath and became the bad cop.

"Hilda Cortado," I began. My voice rose. "Listen up, bitch."

"Hey, calm down, buddy, calm down." From the corner the General made mournful eyes and shook his head. "She's young. She's got a right to her silence."

I turned from him to glare at her. "You had something to do with planning that business last night, didn't you? Didn't you?"

She sat very still, unblinking, her expression not altering. If I accused her of too much, she might confess to something. That was the idea, at least. But I'd interviewed her already. I knew she wouldn't confess to anything, even if I had found her with a dripping knife in each hand. Yet I wanted the General to see this for himself. I wanted him to understand that Ezequiel wasn't an invention, a rumor, an abstraction. I wanted him to know the frustration of dealing with people who never speak.

"Three murders," I said. "That's a life sentence. Three times over. The rest of your life in a cell like this. And you know who we're going to pin those murders on, Cortado? You." I held up a pamphlet, one of two hundred we'd found in her bread basket. I opened it. "Incitement to rebellion. Ten years for that. But after last night I think most judges would link you with Minister Quesada's death. Don't you?"

Her expression didn't change. Even if she didn't know anything about the Quesada operation, she wouldn't say. She had been trained for this.

"But that's not an option, is it?" I said. "Oh, no, Cortado. Because you know what we do with assassins like you, don't you?"

She'd know about the cattle prods, the buckets of water, the magnetos wired to genitals. Fuente had been sat on a box of dynamite and blown into the sky.

I produced a pamphlet and stroked it back and forth against her nose.

"Where did you get this, Hilda? Who gave them to you?"

"The wind blew it into my hand." She hissed the words. Her lips had no sooner opened than they clamped shut.

I rubbed out the letters on the floor. My fingers were still damp with her spit, and the dirt stuck to them. I began again, quieter. We had been preparing for this interview when General Lache's men blew up "Ezequiel" in his truck.

"Lepe, eh? I used to race around that square when I was your age. Jorge, the grocer, remember Jorge? I could beat him."

She wasn't looking at me, but listening. No one beat Jorge, the grocer.

I wiped my hand on my trousers and glanced up, catching her eye. She turned her face away.

"Benavides? Remember how he used to let down our tires?"

She closed her eyes. I no longer saw her large pupils. I knew too much. The thought of that possibility beat at her defenses.

Kindly, I said, "And Domingo. You know my godson?"

On the bed the body tensed. Another hiss. "He never mentioned you." This time the lips remained open, glistening with spittle.

"Remember that ship in a beer bottle? On the shelf where he kept his music? Remember his guitar eyes, Hilda? Remember him going on about Mao and Marx, reading aloud from those books? Well, I gave him those books." I straightened. "We're fighting the same people, Hilda."

She stared at me, her body slumped, miserable, the slope of her shoulders like Sylvina's after an argument.

From the corner I heard the moist slap of the General's tongue. I was being too gentle. This, after all, was the role he had elected for himself.

I brushed the pamphlet against one cheek, then the other. "Ezequiel, where can I find him?"

But the General had heard enough. He stepped from the shadows. "Get out, tomcat," he ordered. "Let me stay with her a few minutes." He looked toward the bed, his eyes filled with consideration. "Hilda, can I have a word?" Even someone who knew the trick usually ended up telling the good cop something. But the General had never dealt with anyone like Hilda Cortado.

Full of concern, he went on smiling at her. "I'm sorry about my colleague here. He's a hothead," and he jerked a thumb in my direction. "He gets out of line sometimes." He put a hand on her cheek and tilted her head, like a man studying the label on an unfamiliar brandy. "Want a piece of orange, kid?"

The spit hurtled into his left eye.

If she was surprised by the ferocity of the General's assault, she didn't show it. Without blinking, she allowed herself to be slammed against the wall.

"Tell me where Ezequiel is, you bitch."

For the first time she smiled.

## 7

The blackout had sent the clocks haywire. I found Sylvina stacking plastic bags of thawing food on the kitchen table. The freezer door was open and ice dripped into a bucket.

"Thank heavens you're home. I've no idea how to reset anything."

I lifted the clock from the wall and turned back the numerals to 19:20. Then I advanced the date from 24 to 25 February. I could sense her eyes scanning the side of my face.

No one had told her about Quesada's death. She had been asleep when I returned in the early hours, and I had driven away before she awoke. But she had guessed. We had enjoyed our burst of hope and we had been deceived.

The weekend before, to celebrate, Sylvina had borrowed a beach house in Paracas belonging to one of her tennis partners. A hired boat chugged us to the island, where Laura threw potato chips at the sea lions. On the shiny brown sand she danced between the jellyfish. After dinner Sylvina and I made love.

"What will you do?" she asked.

"I'm not sure." In the dark I heard the dislocated bark of the seals. For as long as I could remember, my thoughts had condensed on the harassing figure of Ezequiel.

"There were times when I suspected he might not be a he."

She deserved to be happier than my circumstances had allowed. I would make it up.

"Maybe it's the moment to leave," she whispered in my ear.

We had met in my second term at the Catholic University. I

was standing in the canteen after a lecture and she stood one place ahead. Round, elegant spectacles, a brooch at her neck, and white hands seamed with blue veins. I couldn't take my eyes off those hands, so different in color from my own. She waved them, exasperated, then noticed that I was looking at her. "Help me. What shall I have to eat?"

Sylvina took another bag from the freezer and put it on the table. "I hope there won't be a blackout for my party. What was going on last night anyway?"

"They've killed the Interior Minister."

"Quesada?" She stopped, still holding the plastic bag, its contents obscured by droplets of condensation.

"Yes."

"So he's not dead? After all that?"

I put the clock back on the wall. "Does that look right?"

"Christ, I was at school with Quesada's wife."

"She's dead too."

"What happened, Agustín? Tell me. You might as well tell me."

I described the events at the Teatro de Paz. It was the kind of play Sylvina might have enjoyed. Patricia, who had lent us the beach house, was on the theater's board and occasionally gave Sylvina tickets.

"Lucky she didn't this time." Her eyes had watered, but she tried to sound bright.

We talked about her literary evening. She worried the blackout might have ruined the casserole. "How long do you think it can keep?"

"Did you cook it with milk?"

"It's the one I make with smoked trout."

"If it has milk, are you supposed to freeze it in the first place?"

"I guess that means I shouldn't refreeze it."

"I'm sure it's all right."

"Or is it pushing things?"

"If it was me, I'd put everything back in the freezer."

"But I thought you said it couldn't be refrozen."

"Maybe I'm wrong."

"I also broke the pepper grinder. I can't get a new one anywhere . . ." She ran to snatch the bag from the cat, and immediately relented.

"She's eating!"

She seized a spoon, urging onto a saucer more of the half-frozen casserole.

"Look, Agustín. She's eating!"

She turned and looked at me. There was a spark of pleasure in her eyes and I wondered if she was seeing again what she had seen when I was a stranger?

I stroked the cat, as though I would benefit from the affection. I took Sylvina's hand, but she drew back. She pointed to the telephone on the trolley. "You haven't reset the answering machine."

I rewound the message tape and heard myself apologizing for not coming home: "I'm sorry. I'll explain later. You'll understand when I tell you . . ." The voice, high-pitched, aloof, uttering the decayed phrases of conciliation, didn't sound like my idea of myself. Though I stood only an arm's length from Sylvina, I seemed to be eavesdropping on some private grief.

She slithered the rest of the bag's contents into a blue container. "Laura said you had plans to take us to La Posta."

"She's keen to go."

"You can't. Not now."

"What shall I do? I did promise."

"You'll have to tell her it's out of the question."

"Where is Laura?"

She looked at the clock. "I'm collecting her in half an hour."

"She seems nice, her new ballet teacher."

"I'm not sure about this sudden interest of Laura's in modern dance."

"Can it hurt?"

"I haven't decided. I don't want anything to interfere with her chances at the Metropolitan."

"Isn't it her birthday soon?" I had been reminded as I fiddled with the clock.

"Next Thursday."

"How old is she?"

"Twelve, Agustín."

"What are we getting her?"

"Some ballet shoes, I thought. I'll also need some money from you to pay back Marco."

"Sylvina, why do we owe Marco anything?"

"He sent me the book I've got to talk about tomorrow."

Marco was her second cousin, a lawyer I disliked even more than I did Marina, his former wife. I felt bad when I complained about them to Sylvina, but the pair of them appealed to her worst instincts. They had gone to live in Miami soon after we married, and at their farewell dinner Marco had made me intensely angry. Standing by the fireplace in his creamy Nehru suit, he had told me that I ought to get my money out of the country: there was no future in a place where half the population were Indians who couldn't speak Spanish. I realized that he thought I was like him, and it enraged me. I had drunk rather a lot, and had begun to feel Sylvina was also looking down on me. I lost my temper. We were the ones who should be setting an example, I said. Instead, he was fleeing to Miami. I can't remember what else I said. Too much, probably. It makes me embarrassed to think how self-righteous I must have sounded. I remember the contemptuous look on his face. "So what are you going to do?" he said to me. "Become a fucking policeman, or what?"

I'd never thought about it before that minute, but that's exactly what I did. Laura was born in July. In August I was accepted by the Police Academy of San Luis, and things were never the same.

The knowledge that I owed money to Marco spurred me to tackle Sylvina about our financial circumstances. I was about to say something, but her mind was exercised by her literary evening, now only twenty-four hours away.

"You will be here to help, Agustín? You won't wriggle out of it."

I counted out the notes for Marco. "No, darling."

The prospect of having to talk for fifteen minutes about the novel Marco had sent had unnerved Sylvina for several days. At Paracas, lying on the beach, she had explained the plot aloud to clarify her thoughts. "It's about a cowboy who's also a photographer and he's always bringing light into these women's lives. Marco saw the guy who wrote it on a television show. Apparently he's really interesting, and he sings as well. Marco's sure the women down here would love him. I just hope Marina doesn't find out where I got the idea."

Over the weekend she had shown me passages from the book. I didn't care for it.

"I think this is trashy."

"Well, Marco doesn't. He thinks it's good."

She lodged the blue container in the fridge. "I don't care a damn what Ezequiel does, you've got to be here."

Poor Sylvina. Nothing went right for her, no matter how hard she tried. When he chose his next victim, Ezequiel couldn't have known that among the casualties would be my wife's literary dinner.

On that day I would complete my investigation at the Teatro de Paz.

None of the theater staff had seen the performance. *Blackout* had been a low-budget production and the players—students, it was thought—had insisted on operating the lights and curtains. They had left behind no trace save for a cassette, discovered under a chair, of Frank Sinatra's album *Point of No Return*.

"I . . . I was grateful for the business." Sixtyish, mustached, polite, the manager was the sort who likes to greet his audience as they leave. He sat on his hands wearing a formal satin jacket, which he refused to take off, apprehensive about his future. Nobody would want to be part of an audience where you risked being dragged onstage to have your head blown off.

He knew nothing of the cast. The one person he did remember was the director. He had been in his late thirties, of average height and build, with his hair concealed under a soft black cap somewhat like a beret—"but not a beret." He had spoken courteously in the accent of the capital, with a discernible whistle when pronouncing certain words—although which words exactly the manager couldn't remember. At first he described him as clean-shaven; later, he would not be confident even of that. The man had rented the theater for a fortnight, paying cash, with the option of extending the period should *Blackout* prove the success he sincerely believed it would be. Madame Offenbach's production of *The Nutcracker* was two months away. Rather than have his theater lie empty, the manager had accepted payment in the name of a student theatrical group from the Catholic University.

I don't need to tell you, no such group existed.

I never found out why Quesada let himself be lured that night to the Teatro de Paz. True, he had a liking for theater, but even so—*Blackout?* You see, Ezequiel couldn't have orchestrated his death without feeling confident he would be in the audience. Free tickets had been sent to five other government ministers and eight ambassadors; later, another of the envelopes was found unopened in a pile of correspondence addressed to the President. The publicity material, fortunately, attracted nobody but the Minister of the Interior. One can imagine the devastation had Ezequiel decided to stage, say, *My Fair Lady*.

I had the envelopes analyzed for fingerprints, but the technicians failed to come up with a match. I also submitted the handwriting on Ezequiel's poster to a graphologist. Her findings reached me late in the afternoon and told me nothing I didn't suspect. The low slope of the letters combined with thick, clublike finals indicated a cold character ruled by the head. It was the hand of a male; clannish, methodical, authoritarian and determined to succeed in spite of every obstacle. The lasso loops suggested a lover of music. From the short downstrokes she judged that the author suffered from an illness or physical weakness.

The analysis concluded: "This is a person who is successful in what he does, but who derives little pleasure from life."


Sylvina had a sweltering day for her dinner. At five-thirty I telephoned to say I was on my way.

"What happens if there's a blackout?" she said.

"There won't be."

"It's so hot."

"Borrow a fan, then."

"Who from?"

"The people upstairs, they'll lend you one."

"I can't. I complained to them this morning about blocking the garage."

"How's the casserole?"

Twice at breakfast she had opened the fridge, run her nose over the lid and sniffed.

"It should be all right. Although I did ring Marina to check. She says the amount of time is much longer than you're meant to keep something cooked with milk. I didn't tell her it was what we were having tonight."

"Have you worked out what you're going to say?"

"I've written two pages. That's enough, isn't it?"

I had suggested she practice her speech in front of the mirror, without looking at what she had written.

"You will be home, Agustín?"

"I'm leaving now."

Knowing the center would be congested, I headed through Rímac. There was more traffic than I expected, but that was all right. She didn't expect her guests until seven. I would arrive in time to insert the leaves into the dining room table, remove the two armchairs to the bedroom and act as a supporting presence. I would devote myself to making Sylvina happy, and afterward . . .

The mobile rang inside my jacket pocket. I pulled the car over onto the shoulder. The transmission was half drowned in static.

"What is it?"

"Sir, can you hear me?" Sucre.

"I'm here. Go ahead."

"It's Prado."

"Oh God." Admiral Prado, the Defense Minister, had been one of the other officials who had received free tickets for *Blackout*.

"Two girls. They've shot him."

I stopped the car. "Where?"

"La Molina, outside his house."

This morning I had been on the telephone to Prado's office. "No restaurants. No beaches. Not even a church."

"I don't believe Almirante Prado is a churchgoing man," said the secretary.

Yet even with the Defense Minister on his guard, Ezequiel had been able to strike.

A girl no older than Laura had killed the Admiral on this hot afternoon. There had been little to distinguish her from the thousands of schoolgirls who spilled into the streets after class. The Admiral and his driver, about to leave home for the Assembly, would have sat in the car, watching the bulletproof security gate slowly rising and the young legs juddering into view. The attention of both men would have been tantalized by the blue canvas shoes growing into the white ankle socks, the sunburned calves into bare knees, the thighs spreading into the neat hems of a brown and yellow summer dress just like my daughter's. Perhaps the driver kept his whistle to himself. Perhaps the Admiral whistled. His corpse would have the exhausted face of a womanizer.

She stood in view. They would have noticed her white headband. Two other girls joined her on the drive, blocking the path.

The driver hooted. Indifferently, they stood aside. The girl in the white headband rummaged in her satchel, tilting it toward the rear window, as if searching for a crayon.

The driver spotted the aimed satchels and delved inside his jacket.

The Admiral, his smiling face flattened to the glass, was shot twice in the neck. According to the Admiral's maid, who had run to the window at the first two shots, there was then a single explosion. In fact, three more bullets were fired.

Two rounds struck the driver. The car jerked forward and stalled in the road. The third hit the Admiral's assassin, who fell to the pavement, her jaw blown away.

Somehow the two unwounded schoolgirls managed to tug Prado and his driver from the car and lift their injured companion inside. The maid saw the dark blue Mercedes driving southward.

I turned my car around and headed for the house in La Molina. Five minutes later Sucre rang back. A teacher had contacted police headquarters.

"There's a car abandoned near her school in Lurigancho. It sounds like the Mercedes."

It was. I found it sideways in a ditch on the edge of the road to the airport, two wheels in the air. A tracery of blood covered the windshield, and more dampened the back and front seats. Flies buzzed between the sticky surfaces. In the heat the blood had begun to smell.

A hundred yards from the car a group of children volleyed an orange ball over a rope strung between lampposts. It was growing dark, but the ball remained bright, as if drawing to itself the fading light. I left my car beside the Mercedes and walked over.

The children—five girls, five boys—continued thumping their ball, not looking at me. I waited until the ball came near, then caught it.

"That car," I said to the girl who ran up. "Who drove it?"

She squinted at the Mercedes.

"Never seen it before, chief."

A boy with a peaked Coca-Cola cap sauntered over with the other boys. They looked from the car to me, hands on hips, panting.

I ignored them, and I asked the girl, "How long have you been playing here?" She drew an arm across her nose, sniffing.

I walked between the boys to a little girl at the back.

"You? How long have you been here?"

Her black hair was matted with sand where she had fallen.

"Ten minutes," she whispered. They had started late. It was too hot to play earlier.

"You saw nothing?"

She shook her head, concentrating on her toe as it scraped a meaningless doodle in the dust.

Kneeling before her, I'm thinking I ought not to be here. Sylvina expects me at home. Six-thirty. Her friends will be arriving soon.

"What's the score?"

At this, the girl smiled. "Three–one. To us."

"They would have come this way—the people from the car." I bounced the ball. The boy with the peaked cap made a grab for it, but I was too quick.

In houses around us the lights snapped on. A shadow moved, drawing my attention to a girl I hadn't noticed. She bent over, transfixed by a patch of ground at her feet. I walked along the shadow toward her.

"What have you seen, little one?" I squatted on my haunches beside her, but she didn't answer. She didn't have to, because as soon as I touched a fingertip to the dark spot on the sand, I realized it was blood.

I ran back to the car to radio Sucre for help.

"Here's another!"

I replaced the mike and saw in the distance the boys gathering in a huddle. They strode back across the pitch in a group, led by Coca-Cola Cap.

"Chief, what will you pay us for every drop of blood we find?"

"If we find what I'm looking for, I'll give you something."

"No."

My men wouldn't arrive for another ten minutes. There wasn't time to barter. "One peso."

Two boys nudged each other.

"Five," Coca-Cola Cap insisted.

"Two." I wouldn't be able to claim it on expenses.

He looked at me, weighing up my offer, old eyes in a young face.

"Three."

"Okay, three."

His lips came together in an awful smile. He half turned and, inserting into that smile a dirty forefinger and thumb, he whistled.

I watched his acolytes haring up the bank. The girls didn't follow. They remained on the pitch, picking up their jackets, reluctant to take part.

I heard a shout: "Here's one!" As before, the boys gathered around it. The drop of blood held them in, then released them.

"Here's one!"

"Here's one!"

They receded in the deepening dusk, drawing together, then separating again, a monstrous anemone expanding and contracting in the dark.

I tossed the ball to the girl with sand in her hair and set off after them, unfastening the holster on my belt.

The drops of blood led into a labyrinth of pale brick houses. Rusted angle-iron entrails poked from the roofs, and corrugated sheets leaned in bundles against the unpainted walls. I pictured the wretched group struggling this way. Had they known where to go? Was there a safe house in an emergency? Were they expected?

The boys had assembled outside a single-story house with low railings around it. They pointed to the steps, the concrete specked with blood. I drew my pistol. The boys stepped back a pace, all but for Coca-Cola Cap, who stood with his hands in his pockets, head at an angle, eyes missing nothing. I spoke again on the mobile. The nearest car was six kilometers away. I would have to act now, this minute.

I opened the gate and walked up the path. I felt no terror. That would come later, in the car driving home, in bed with Sylvina.

The door opened to my touch. I stepped into a narrow corridor. Ahead was a kitchen, to the right a glass door. Somebody flitted behind the glass. I pushed down the handle and kicked the door open, keeping back.

A body faced me on the floor, half propped against a black vinyl sofa and covered to the neck with a blanket. The head had been clumsily wrapped in a pink bath towel. All that could be seen of the face was a mouth, open at an angle, as if the skull underneath had twisted around and no longer fitted the skin. From the mouth came a wheezing sound.

Out of sight, a window rattled. I rushed into the room in time to see a flash of yellow hem disappearing over the sill. There was a loud report and the body at my feet jerked. I threw myself to the floor, in the same motion firing twice at the window. I counted to five. When I ran to look, there was no one there, and no one in the alley outside, and no noise.

I hurried back to the sofa. Under the bullet's impact the head had dropped to the floor and the blanket had slipped, revealing the brown and yellow uniform beneath. I peeled off the sodden towel. Still recognizable above the shattered jaw were the nose and eyes and hair of a young girl. Dead.

My mobile bleeped. Sucre, by the Mercedes, needing directions.

Outside, the volleyball team waited for me. When they heard the door open, they jumped off the railings. Their leader advanced up the path. He held out his arm, opening his fist. He was even younger than the dead girl inside, younger than Laura.

"Two hundred and forty-nine pesos."

That night, after the ambulance had removed the body to the police mortuary, we continued our search of the house. Sucre and I went through the front room while the forensic people completed work on the sofa. They had marked and tagged the towel and blanket and were tweezering the last fabric samples into a zippered plastic bag.

Around us, the havoc of a dismantled room.

"Hello." Sucre had unscrewed the back of a stereo loudspeaker. Wedged inside, a black leather Filofax.

I flicked through the pages. There were some words written in blue Biro, making no sense.

"I'll look at this tomorrow."

I drove home.

The kitchen clock said ten to midnight. Sylvina was washing up. Her guests had left half an hour earlier.

"They killed Prado," I said.

She didn't look up from the sink. "I know." Consuelo, the last guest to arrive, had heard the announcement on her car radio.

"How was your evening?"

"It went well, thank you."

Her shoulders betrayed her. Last night she had looked beautiful when trying on the dress.

"Sucre did call you?"

"Yes. Thanks." She was angry, but pretending she wasn't.

"I'm sorry I couldn't be here."

"I know. I understand." She might have lost her temper, but she understood.

She stacked another bowl.

"I've kept some food for you." She fetched the plate from the oven. Looking up, about to say something, she saw my shirt. "Agustín! You're covered in blood."

Fourteen years ago she had rushed toward me like this. It was my third week at the Police Academy. Then it hadn't been blood, but dog shit.

She made me take off the shirt, emptied the sink, filled it with hot water, dropped the shirt in it.

I sat down and began to eat.

"Probably it's disgusting," she said.

"She was only eleven or twelve."

"Who was?"

"The girl from the group who killed Prado."

"A street child?" She didn't mean to sound bitter.

"No."

You can tell a lot about a corpse. She'd come from a family like ours. Mixed blood; good dental care in the few teeth spared by the bullet; tidily dressed—the headband we later traced to a sports shop used by Sylvina; and little opal earrings concealed by the hair she must have washed only yesterday. This wasn't a deprived child or an orphaned child or an illegitimate child abandoned to the streets. This was a well-tended child from a good home, and with parents who loved her.

"This is the extent to which Ezequiel indoctrinates people."

I looked up. By the way Sylvina was pounding my shirt in the sink, I realized that I was behaving with no consideration for what my wife had been through. If you worry about something, you worry about it. She'd listened to me, but she had suffered her own miserable evening.

"Tell me about your dinner. Were you terrific?"

"Not here, Agustín. I'm tired."

In bed, naked together, she said, "Please don't. I can't. I don't want to."

I rolled back, lying beside her in the dark.

"Do you want to hear or don't you?"

"You know I do."

She spoke for half an hour, conducting her own postmortem. She talked at random, remembering what someone had said, providing another person's reaction. Until she drifted into sleep, one arm across her forehead, I was able to lose myself in another person's wretchedness.

I'd attended one of my wife's dinners a year before. The vogue then was charity, not books. Within six months they'd stopped raising money.

I conjured up her friends, braying women with their teeth in braces, tugging dogs into the hallway, plucking their blouses from their shoulders because of the heat. The images volleyed back and forth, and sometimes they were mine.

"But Sylvina, what a wonderful pied-à-terre."

She was too ashamed to invite these women home. I pictured them clinging to her in the gloom cast by the fluted Portuguese lamps, devouring with their degrading glances the tiny front room, the chairs in which they would sit before and after the meal, the lacquered dresser behind which Sylvina had tenderly arranged an incomplete set of green French coffee cups. From such inherited belongings she wove the mantles of her nostalgia.

I see Sylvina, elegant in her mother's dress and bracelets, hastening to close the kitchen door, calling over her shoulder, "I'll just do this as an anti-cat measure," before urging Patricia and Leonora to leave their dogs in Laura's room, where I hear Patricia whisper, "She looks like she's robbed the burial mound at Ur!" and I watch Leonora nod, indicating with a cruel uplift of her brow the tutu which Sylvina bought secondhand, and after they have shooed from the door their pets, a red setter and a dachshund, I follow them down the corridor, follow them past the mirror, observing their little flounce, follow them into the stifling room, where, bounding up to their hostess, they say in unison, "What a dear little flat you have," and Sylvina, blushing a little, starts to thank them when Marina interrupts, "Where's Agustín?" and Sylvina replies, "He's sorry, he has to work late," and Marina says, "Consuelo's just told us, isn't it terrible? I mean, tonight Prado, Quesada on Monday, and weren't we at school with his wife?"—this stimulating Leonora to admit through the braces on her teeth, "It's awful, I always found her so difficult," prompting from Patricia, "They tell me at the theater it was a woman who shot them," and Sylvina to react, "Oh, I think I can relate to that.

We have a repressed internal violence. Don't you think so?" which shocks Marina into saying, "But could you kill, Sylvina?" and Sylvina to answer, with her mind on me, on her smoked trout casserole, on the carnal adventures of a photographer cowboy, "I feel I could kill. I say that, but I don't know why," before leaping up, having spotted a tail under a chair, "Pussy! I thought I'd locked you away!"—this provoking Bettina to apologize, it must have been her, she'd mistaken the kitchen for the bathroom, but gosh it looks good, whatever it is, which reminds Marina to ask Bettina from the side of her mouth, "The bathroom, tell me, I've forgotten?" and Marina walks from the room trailing in her wake a silence which is filled by the sound of Consuelo's electric fan— she's brought it with her—and by Patricia, who says, "Remind me, did Marina leave Marco or did he leave her?" to which Sylvina, getting up, replies diplomatically, "Oh, I think it was mutual," as she prepares to offer each guest a monogrammed napkin and a plate arranged with slabs of veal pâté and thick sausages of cheese, which she encourages them to spread on squares of bread—"I'm sorry it's so soft, but I can't bear cheese that's been in a fridge"— and so on around the room, all accepting save Amalia, who declines with the words, "This man everyone's talking about, Ezequiel, doesn't he sound fascinating?" to which Sylvina says, "Amalia, how do you keep your skin looking like that?" causing the other women in the room to concentrate, first on the portrait above the electric fire of Sylvina's great-uncle, for six months a Vice President during the Bermudez dictatorship, and then, more respectfully, on themselves caught in the hallway mirror, which, noting the direction of their glances, Sylvina explains she has erected for Laura, who now has a marvelous teacher, "All thanks to Marina," so releasing everyone to talk at once, even the taciturn Consuelo, the hostess of their last literary evening—a splendid affair on a lawn—who bursts out, "Don't tell me! That's wonderful," this encouraging Sylvina, on her way to collect the casserole, to add in a raised voice, "She's hoping for a scholarship at the Metropolitan," leaving her guests to nod to one another as if to say, "That dumpy little girl!" while they wait for her to wheel out the trolley—"No, it's quite all right, I can do this"—and out of politeness accept a small amount, "No, far too much, although it does look good. Really, I don't know how you do this on your own," as Sylvina resumes, "She'll be able to dance in New York, London, Paris," to which Leonora says, "Where our dogs come from," and Amalia jokes, "And some of our second husbands too!" and everyone laughs, before they coax the evening to its climax, the unavoidable moment when eight faces look up from their abandoned plates and forget the casserole and the heat and the absence of her antisocial husband and reassure Sylvina in a chorus warbling with anticipation, "Isn't this delicious? Isn't this fun?" and merge into a single creature, an oriental goddess with sixteen arms who pats her cat, her chair, her arm, and says, "Now, Sylvina, this book you've made us read . . ."

In less than a week Ezequiel had scrambled from the unmarked grave prepared for him by Quesada. From now on he would seek to burn his name on hillsides which could be seen from China to Peru. Every Cabinet Minister daily expected death.

We had no leads for Quesada's murder. At least the assassination of the Defense Minister provided two solid clues. They survived the night and were there when I awoke. There was the small body in the mortuary, which might be traceable. And there was the Filofax Sucre had discovered in the loudspeaker.

The diary pages were blank save for two entries, which read like assignations: "C.C. 9:30" (23 April) and "C.D. 6:00" (15 July). Maps of the capital and of Miami were inserted into the front, and a guide to phrases in English: "Please give me Thousand Island dressing"—that sort of thing.

The importance of Sucre's find was limited to two unlined pages clipped into the Filofax immediately after the diary. These had been filled in arbitrarily, with the randomness of notes jotted down at different times. One page consisted of a crude diagram in the shape of a church door, four mathematical calculations and a reference to page numbers 27 to 31 of the medical journal *The Lancet*. We would trace this eventually to an article, two years old, on a breakthrough in the treatment of erythremia. The sums might have been straightforward adding and subtracting—somebody balancing their checkbook or checking a grocery bill. Or they might have meant something else.

Ten phrases were listed on the facing page. Some, obviously, were book titles, but it wasn't clear if these were works someone had read or books to be bought from a shop.

Life of Mohammed, W.I.
Rhetoric and dialectic in the speeches of Pausanias
Revolution among the children
Revolution No. 9
To know nothing of oneself is to live
There is always a philosophy for the lack of courage
Arquebus
Situationist Manifesto
One invariably comes to resemble one's enemies
Kant and samba

Most I couldn't decipher. For all I knew, "Arquebus" was a racehorse—or was it some cold-blooded code word? The few words or phrases I understood meant nothing. "Revolution No. 9" is a song by the Beatles. "Pausanias" was a Greek traveler and a tedious character in Plato's *Symposium*. I guessed "W.I." to be Washington Irving—and this in fact I verified when Ezequiel, during my interrogation, began quoting a passage about how certain desert tribes, if their dedication were great enough, could gallop out of nowhere to conquer an empire.

As for the other phrases, well, only last week I was sitting here, reading a book—Pessoa, it was—when that line about knowing nothing of oneself leapt out at me. It made me think that if I live long enough, perhaps I'll come to understand the rest of them.

Nothing on that list was as important as the three handwritten addresses on the reverse of the page. All were in the capital. One might be the house of the girl with the white headband.

They didn't let you smoke in the mortuary. The pathologist finished his cigarette in the corridor, then pushed open the door. He slid her from the refrigerator and with both hands drew back the sheet. He repeated the process with the Admiral and the Admiral's driver until the three bodies lay side by side, as if members of the same family. The ammoniac smell reminded me of Sylvina's sink.

Two reddish mosquito bites pimpled the Admiral's chin. Otherwise his face, frozen into its tired expression, had the bluish white blush of ice. The skin wrinkles had stiffened and there were scabs of mucous about his nose. More disturbing than the fatal mess to his neck was the bloated angle of his penis. Resting against his stomach, it seemed cocked in the semiarousal which sudden death, pathologists tell us, can bequeath.

The eyelids had sprung open. The pathologist closed them.

When you get down to it, a dead body isn't something most of us can bear to talk about. We treat death by conventions. People are neatly removed by a single bullet. They drop to the ground in midstride. They die immediately.

Except that they don't die immediately. They keep moving. Breathing. Thinking. The Admiral died as instantaneously as it is possible for a man of sixty-five to die. Shot twice in the throat, he had suffocated to death. He had to have blood and he had to have oxygen, and both had been cut off by the girl's bullets. He was three minutes from the end when the first round caught him, but three minutes is three minutes. Struck by the bullets, he had passed into shock, yet his brain had continued working. For three minutes he would still have had his thoughts; confused and delirious, but thoughts nevertheless. He would have felt some pain, although not to the degree you might have imagined, since that part of his brain which enabled him to feel pain was dying.

Certainly he wouldn't have experienced the kind of torment his assassin suffered over the next two hours. She had had a much harder time. Until the moment she was fired at from the window, she could still breathe.

It is not usual even for policemen to come across dead children. I forced my eyes from the calm forehead to the ruined face. The jaw was a frayed tangle of blackened flesh. Part of her tongue fell free, tasting the air where her chin should have been. The face was the same color as mine, except at the back of the neck, where the blood shone purplish through the skin. The upper teeth, intact and healthily white, formed the top half of an expression. Whether of pain or something else I couldn't tell.

What had she been trying to do, this girl? Had this been a game? When the bullet removed her jaw, did she see everything in a different light? Or, even then, was it worth it?

For a few seconds she had been alive with me in that room in Lurigancho. Four feet away, that's how far apart we'd been, the same distance as now divided her from the Admiral—and I had heard her breathing. After I kicked open the door, her eyes blinked up at me, but because of the towel around her face it was impossible to read her expression. Did she know what was going on around her? What had that look meant? It had to mean something, from such a small creature in such extremity. Because the horrible thing about pain is that you're alone. No one can help you. I might have been able to help her, a little. But then the people she had thought her friends had fired a bullet into her chest.

The pathologist was speaking. "She had a nice little lunch beforehand. Lettuce, rice, meatballs, swallowed down with Inca-Kola, topped off with a Mars bar." He pulled back the sheet. "Before I tuck you away, little one, I'm going to put these up your nose." He talked to her as though she lived: to cope, I suppose. When I arrived, he had just sawed apart her chest.

It may sound silly, but in the days ahead I hoped someone would recognize her. To track down her parents, her grandparents, anyone who had known her, we circulated an artist's impression to schools. For any person in the world, there are hundreds of people who recognize their face. Think of those who would have come across this girl. She must have ridden on a bus wearing her brown and yellow uniform. From someone she must have bought her Mars bars and her Inca-Kola. To someone she must have shown off her little opal earrings.

We heard nothing. No one came forward. That, to me, was Ezequiel's most terrible legacy. The idea that someone could not only send this child to her death, but not claim her.

Later that morning General Merino returned from the Palace.

He had driven off at nine o'clock, flanked by two police motorcyclists. He sat upright in the middle of the backseat, clutching my report, rehearsing, not seeing the houses he once cherished, dreading the interview ahead.

The room was almost pitch-dark, he told me, just a light in a corner by a leather armchair. Calderón, in a black suit, finished writing something on a pad. He did not offer the General a seat. He stood up and sat, one leg dangling, on the edge of the desk. He wore black lace-up shoes, a tie of red and white horizontal stripes, round tortoiseshell glasses. His receding hairline was lavished neatly back, emphasizing the shape of its M.

"One of those faces you see in the business pages, tomcat, with a smile thinner than his shoelace."

Calderón had folded his arms. "Let us imagine that I am your superior."

"Yes, Captain."

"I would wish to know why this man, this delinquent . . . No. Let me put this another way. I want what you have on him. Everything. All records. Is that understood? Nothing kept back."

"No, Captain."

Merino had seen the goblin shark, and it was kinder.

Without energy the General walked to the window and looked out toward the sea. He spoke rapidly, his hands behind his back, getting rid of the words as fast as he could. "Calderón's ordered a curfew. From ten o'clock tonight. He's letting in the military. From now on it's a joint operation. We furnish the army with copies of our files, help any way we can. He has no choice. Prado was their man. Lache feels he's been made a fool of, especially after receiving Quesada's televised congratulations. His blood is up. It's bad, Agustín, bad, bad, bad."

Already he'd had General Lache on the line. "A heap of underperforming blubber, that's how he described us."

Behind his back, one hand twisted inside the other.

"Let us imagine Calderón's orders to Lache. 'If you catch anybody who looks mean or looks like they once had a mean thought about the way things are here, slap him in jail. Use any means. Screw due legal process. Plant drugs, torture them, keep them by force. If necessary, shoot them. You can't treat these people like rose petals.' "

He turned, looking at me. "You can see their point, tomcat. We've been in charge of this for twelve years and what do we have to show for it? A girl from Lepe whom we haven't yet charged because she won't speak." He brought one hand out from behind him, grimaced at his watch and made a calculation. "Well, forty-five minutes ago, four of General Lache's men went careering into the basement to sort out that particular problem. God knows where they've taken her, what they'll do." He turned his head from one epaulette to the other. "I'm sorry, Colonel."

I was leaving when he called me back. Something he had overlooked. Calderón, to finance the army's assistance in this joint operation, had trimmed our budget.

"It means no more overtime."


The cancellation of my overtime was a blow, I admit. The bank agreed to extend my overdraft for a short period. Regrettably, they could not increase the limit. Too many customers shared my predicament—those who hadn't had the sense to transfer their money abroad.

The need to discuss money with Sylvina had become more pressing than ever. But I dreaded the thought of her protestations. I knew what I meant to say, and quailed. She, not I, was in the right. She had been good about money. She had spent her mother's inheritance on us. She took care to buy everything as cheaply as possible. Yet for twenty years she had been forced to endure the torture of her friends' sympathy.

It shames me to acknowledge this, but I found in Sylvina's demoralization a further excuse to prevaricate. Her nerves had grown frailer in the phoenix days following Ezequiel's reappearance. Two days after her literary dinner she had a noisy row with the couple in the flat above, newcomers from the coast, who parked outside our garage. About to leave for work, I had asked the husband to move his car. He obliged, but then his wife started shouting from the window. This was everyone's street. Just because we'd been here longer, it didn't mean I had a right to tell people where to park. "We're proud in Judío, too!" She withdrew her head, then, as an afterthought, yelled, "Poof!" I drove off, but unfortunately Sylvina, coming outside to see what the matter was, heard the insult. She stood in the middle of the street and raised her fist. "My husband is not a poof! Park your bloody car somewhere else!"

Once more the woman stuck out her head. "Poof!"

This was too much for Sylvina. She marched back inside and reemerged clasping a long screwdriver. In full view of the street and ignoring the woman's anguished cries, she scraped and scratched at the offending hood. She stood back to reveal the words: THIS STREET SHOULD NOT BE LIVED IN BY PEOPLE LIKE US.

I agreed to meet the repair costs, but that, together with the blood money I had paid Coca-Cola Cap, meant I was almost at the limit of my overdraft.

The curfew lasted from ten o'clock at night until six in the morning. Any person stopped on the street between those hours without a permit risked arrest.

Hungry for information, people started to pay attention to earlier reports from the provinces. As the press caught up with nine-year-old atrocities, mothers throughout the city could be heard telling their children not to accept parcels from strangers, no matter what they offered.

Nothing retained its innocence. A group of schoolgirls on a sidewalk shimmered with menace. In the suburbs, schools broke up early.

The curfew, introduced to defuse tension, exacerbated the panic. Ezequiel's shadow had darkened us. Not a day would pass when we didn't feel the draft from his wings.

In the cathedral, minutes before a service due to be led by the Arch-Cardinal, a bomb constructed from mining gelignite was discovered under the altarcloth.

The president of a television channel sympathetic to the government was shot in the chest outside a flower shop.

Four civil servants died at a restaurant in Monterrico when a beer can, hurled through the window from a llama sling, landed hissing on their table.

Car bombs exploded outside the Carnation Milk Factory, at a

Miss Universe Pageant and outside the American Ambassador's residence.

Criminals fed on the chaos. In the richer districts, families prolonged their holidays, leaving their houses inadequately guarded. Sylvina's friend Patricia returned from Paracas to discover the contents of her living room missing, down to the brass light switches.

Soldiers patrolled the streets to meet the unseen threat. Tanks rolled into the square outside the Palace and took up positions from which they rarely moved. At night you saw the gun barrels aiming at the stars, the drivers watching the buildings through night glasses. Somewhere, inextinguishable in that darkness, murkier than any vapor, lay Ezequiel. But the army hadn't been trained to swat shadows. The soldiers couldn't grasp what they were fighting. Desperate for a severed head to brandish to the crowd, they could produce no one except Hilda Cortado, the nineteen-year-old pamphleteer. She was executed—God knows how—keeping her silence to the last.

Three weeks after the blackout at the Teatro de Paz, General Lache lost patience. In a crude parroting of Quesada's assassination, he exacted his reprisal on a group of drama students.

I have no doubt the Arguedas Players were innocent. I know that the man in the beret who booked the theater for *Blackout* had mentioned the Catholic University. A student theatrical group, remembered the manager. But, crucially, no name. My men had three times interrogated members of the Arguedas Players, the university's sole drama group, and absolved them of suspicion. Humiliated, dishonored, furious, General Lache reopened their case.

On the first Tuesday night in March, due to the director's car running out of petrol, the Arguedas Players started their audition for *Mother Courage* thirty-five minutes late.

The group which assembled in a lecture room of the agronomy faculty comprised ten men and six women aged between eighteen and thirty, the number increasing to seventeen with the arrival of the director, an untidy, square-faced man. Apologizing energetically, he unpacked from his wife's shopping basket five large bottles of Cristal beer and a pillar of paper cups.

At seven forty-five the caretaker looked in to tell them he was locking up at nine. He had the drama group marked down until eleven o'clock, in fact, but the booking had been made before the curfew order. With little to do, he asked if he might watch from the back. The director saw no objection. The caretaker would be the only survivor.

At seven fifty-five Vera, a nervous, striking-looking girl who hoped to play the lead, began reading from the text in a singsong voice. She spoke a few lines and stopped. She stubbed out her cigarette and, after a cough, began from the top, less mechanically this time.

She had read for perhaps a minute when there came a crash from the corridor. The door burst open and twenty men in black masks kicked their way through the chairs toward her.

Vera, unsure whether to continue, sought the director's cue. The script was slapped from her hand. An arm was clamped over her mouth, ripping her blouse at the collar. Someone forced a sweater over her head and, with her arms twisted behind her back, she was bundled outside.

On his hands and knees under the table, the director screamed for help until one of the masked men jerked him out backward by the ankles, smashing his nose on the floor.

Two minutes later a postgraduate student ran down from the library into an empty room. Scattered about the floor he found women's shoes, spectacles, pens, cigarettes and a script foamy with beer. At the back sat the caretaker, unhurt.

Not one of the Arguedas Players had been seen since.

General Lache laid the kidnapping at Ezequiel's door. Few believed him. The press interviewed distraught relatives and lovers— in one article mentioning by name the officer believed to have led the squad. It made no difference. That was the terrible thing. Among Sylvina's friends it was felt that the army wouldn't have acted without a reason. Therefore, those drama students must have been guilty.

"But, Sylvina, if we kidnap people without proof, we're no better than Ezequiel. Why choose us rather than him?"

She had come to equate me with the problem, not as part of the solution. "I don't care. It shows something's being done."

---

While the army retaliated—searching schools, arresting the in-nocents, filling prisons—I sat in a parked car and watched one or other of the three houses listed in the Filofax. About the addresses there could be no dispute. They were bricks and mortar. They existed.

Title checks couldn't tell me whether the houses belonged to friends or enemies. They were innocuous, well-kept buildings in the south and east of the city. They were lived in by a chiropodist, a professor of ethnology from the Catholic University and an American in the fish business, recently married to a pretty girl from Cajamarca.

Maybe these people were potential targets, people Ezequiel wanted to kill. Maybe they were his assassins. I had no idea. I just knew some violence was in store, some catastrophe, and I didn't want to risk questioning anyone in case we scared off Ezequiel. For this reason I had not relinquished the Filofax to the army. I felt I couldn't do anything for the time being except watch and wait for something to happen.

So that's what I did, day after day, night after night, collecting the trash bags, sitting in the car, looking for signs, watching.

The driver's seat became a sanctuary. I never used the same car twice in succession. I hung a dark blue suit against the window and leaned against it, pretending to sleep, or I read a newspaper as though I were waiting for someone. I knew the form of many racehorses. The Lova, On the Rocks, Last Dust, Petits Pois, Sweet Naggy, Without a Paddle, Zog, Nite Dancer.

I had a lot of time to think. It upset me, the way my unit had been treated. We might on paper share responsibility with the army for Ezequiel's case, but in reality we were not governed by compatible regulations. We had ceased to be the people's guard-ians. To my counterpart in the military, a burly colonel who re-minded me of the cadet at the Police Academy who led the bullies, we were indistinguishable from the mob.

Calderón, by relying on the army, had marginalized us. Yet,

pushed out to the edge, I found Ezequiel coming into a perspective that disarmed me.

I remember, in one of the books I would find on his shelf, Ezequiel had underlined a saying of Mao: "People turn into their opposites." It is curious, but if you have been looking obsessively for someone—if, as I had, you had been stepped in Ezequiel day and night—after a while you do start to assume the characteristics of the person you are hunting.

Look at my hand. I can warn you I am about to touch this vase—and I do so. Or this book. But what if I told you of occasions when my hand didn't respond, when I mimed a bodily memory independent of my self—and instead of turning a page I watched with a grinding horror as this hand glided over my chest, to the base of my neck, searching for an itch which I couldn't feel but which my fingers desired, in spite of everything I might do to prevent them, to scratch?

I don't mean that I had moved any closer to finding Ezequiel. His character still seemed to me impenetrable—like the despair into which he cast us. But as I sat in that car, I had the sensation that I stalked nearer to the rim of some understanding.

Then, at the end of March, there was a swirl in the air—and I knew I'd disturbed him.


I had been watching the house of the American. He'd made his fortune in the States from pond-raised catfish. Ten months earlier he had come to this country to buy some Amazonian strains and to walk the Inca trail. At the travel agency in Cajamarca he met a very sexy, large-breasted girl, a model. They married, and in February flew down to the capital. A love story, he told his friends. He'd never left America before and within six weeks he was married! But it wasn't a love story. You see—and I'm not sure how well I have conveyed this to you—Ezequiel's assassins could be anyone. One day you might switch on the television and find the killer was your daughter. Another day, it might be your wife.

I spoke with him a few hours after he had found out, a fat man in a yellow golf shirt and tight-fitting Sansabelt slacks. He had a straw-colored beard and expensive glasses. Beneath his glasses his eyes were bloodshot.

He leaned over Sucre's desk, both hands flat on the desktop, talking uncontrollably. I was on my way to the basement when I heard him. Recognizing his clothes, I paused.

He had reached a point in his story which caused him to rub his eyes. He was telling Sucre how he'd been making dinner. He'd taken his carrot soup out of the microwave. In the act of settling down to watch the television news, he'd looked up and gone through hot flushes because there on screen, smiling, chic, looking out from the latest *Vogue,* was his wife. She was a model, see. That's how she paid her way. Then comes this news she's been captured. Oh no, he thought. They've got her, she's been caught in a car bomb, and they've got her. But it wasn't that. It was crazy, it was totally crazy. They were saying she was a terrorist. A killer.

He held Sucre by the shoulders, shaking him. "You've made a mistake, bud. She's not one of them. She's never voted in her goddamn life." He questioned whether she knew the President from her ass. "You've gotta let me see her, pal."

"Sucre," I intervened. "Let me."

Hearing my voice, he turned, his arms subsiding.

"You're American?"

"Yes."

"Where from?"

"We've got houses in Jupiter, Florida, and Lake Tahoe. I was born in Boston, Massachusetts."

"Didn't William James come from there?" My father had been an admirer.

"I have no fucking idea."

I took him to the video room. He sat meekly down while I poured him coffee, added lots of sugar and inserted a videotape.

He was close to tears. His wife was innocent, he kept repeating. He was one hundred percent certain. He believed all she told him. They had been married seven months, were so happy.

The screen brightened, filling with jerky images filmed by Sucre through the windshield of our car. A slim woman with long, stockinged legs was climbing into a black Suzuki Jeep. With both hands she hefted a Puma bag, sliding it onto the passenger seat.

"That's our car!" He was childish in his recognition. "She's going to her aerobics class."

I fast-forwarded the tape, chasing the Jeep through the afternoon traffic.

"She has this studio in San Isidro, Calle Castaños."

Out along the Malecón, past streets of substantial houses, their turrets rising over the walls, past Calle Castaños.

"She's picking up a friend. She does that sometimes. They take turns."

Out along the Pan-Americana, the dust bowl visible beneath the billboards advertising Hush Puppies and swimming pools.

"Some of them live as far out as La Molina."

Past rows of nondescript, squat brick houses with tin roofs.

"I don't know, maybe she's going to the Inca Market."

Past derelict, window-shattered warehouses from the days when we were a country.

"I guess she's meeting someone at the airport."

Past featureless districts, as yet unnamed, through untidy grids of adobe hovels, without electricity, without water.

Into more featureless districts, the hovels the same pigeon-gray as the dust, not adobe any longer but rush matting, a family to each roofless hovel, five hundred new families a day, jumping down off the trucks, dazed by the journey, run out of their valleys, no one to turn to, terrified.

By now we've slipped back so she doesn't see us. We've got her in the zoom. She bounces off the road, trailing a dust devil through a bank of rush-mat shacks, stopping outside a low white shed, one of the few concrete buildings in sight.

"Sometimes she does charity work." The words could hardly be heard. His face was shrinking. I could see the wide pores on his nose.

She looks around, hauls the bag off the seat and, without knocking, enters the building.

I fast-forwarded again. We'd waited a minute before going inside.

The tape wasn't well filmed, and once or twice crossing a slippery tiled floor, Sucre lost focus. But no one could mistake the look of the woman kneeling there as she jerked around to see us, nor the bag from which she had begun to unpack three submachine guns.

"Paulita," he said, a hand over his mouth, not believing it.

I had been on my way to the basement to interrogate her further. It was time I returned there. There was no point in telling the American, but this evening we would have to turn Paulita over to the military.

Already I'd spent six hours with his wife. So far she'd said only four words, repeated over and over again.

"*Viva El Presidente Ezequiel!*"

8

On the next day my bank refused me credit.
        Have you been in that situation? I notice you use a MasterCard to pay Emilio. But supposing tonight he came over and said, "Sorry, señor, can't take this"—think how you'd feel.

The cash dispenser was near my office. When it refused to return my card, I stood absorbing the flashing message, the cramps of impotence. Behind me concerned voices asked, "What's wrong? Is it out of cash?" Shamed, I walked down Calle Irigoyen. A couple, smartly dressed, entered a restaurant. What would the meal cost them? A hundred pesos? Across the road a man inserted his tip through a taxi's window. Inside a shop a woman decided on a dishwasher. Everywhere my eyes settled on people spending money. How could they afford it?

I counted my change. Three pesos. Enough for a pair of underpants.

Perhaps I could cash a check. Or request an advance on my salary. I saw myself reduced to telling Sucre I'd left my wallet behind, and might I borrow twenty pesos to tide me over?

At home I found Sylvina sitting on the end of our bed.

"What's wrong?" She had been weeping.

She looked away. "The shoemaker cut up my credit card."

On the bank's instructions, El Chino had before her eyes scissored in half the credit card with which she had tried to pay for Laura's birthday present, a pair of goatskin pointe shoes. "Thank God, I was able to put it on my Visa." But she had never been so humiliated. El Chino, an unpleasant man who kept a raucous crow in his shop, was a gossip. When he went around the dance academies with his box of sample shoes, he would relish peddling the story of Señora Rejas's MasterCard.

His shop became a place of horror. And not just his shop, but the department store where she had hoped to buy Laura a leotard. She had come home disgusted with herself.

"Why, why, why?" She wasn't extravagant. "Why, Agustín?" I couldn't answer. Her friends bought dance shoes, but they could afford them.

She held up a red-wrapped package. A present for Laura had got her into this mess. Now everything was called into question.

"Maybe I shouldn't have bought these." She turned the package over, squeezing its contents. "Maybe they were too expensive." She started to unwrap the paper, then passionately hurled the parcel away from her and collapsed back on the bed, her face white and glittering with unhappiness.

"Sylvina, why—" I began.

"Why do you say 'why'?" She spoke to the ceiling. She propped herself up on her elbows, her skirt drawn tight about her thighs. Her legs were askew on the bed, heels caught in the bedcover.

"We are—"

"Were. Were. Were," and she lay back again, a hand over her face, sobbing.

I sat down beside her, picking up the package from the floor where she had thrown it. I removed the red paper, laid the shoes on the bed, then, tenderly, pulled my wife's hand away from her eyes. One by one I separated the fingers, but they were not there for me as they once had been.

She talked mechanically, as if making a list. There was the telephone bill, her tennis club subscription, the groceries. How did I expect her to buy food?—talking of which, there were no pears today at the market.

"This is the time of year for pears. Why aren't there any, Agustín?" She snatched back her hand. "How can I make you a pudding without pears?"

"I don't know, darling." Whenever she wanted to forget something, she shopped.

"I still can't find a pepper grinder."

So it was on that bed that I confronted Sylvina with the true state of our finances. "I'm not accusing you of anything, but that's the way it is."

She sat up. Instead of reacting defensively, she said with great calmness, "What about Marco?"

"Marco?"

"I have discussed it."

"What do you mean?"

"He made the offer himself. He'd heard things were bad down here. We could rely on him, he said."

We had a terrible argument, after which she shut herself in the bedroom and telephoned Miami.

The following evening, without telling Sylvina, I drove to the ballet studio in Surcos. I made certain the mothers had driven away before ringing the doorbell. Yolanda had no telephone. If I wanted to catch her, it would have to be at the studio.

The street had fallen quiet. A bolt rattled and the door in the wall opened a few inches. I recognized her silhouette. Seeing who it was, she drew the chain.

"Señor Rejas?" Under dark eyebrows her look was intense. "But Laura's just left, with Samantha."

I knew this. I had watched them leave. Since I could no longer be certain of my movements, we had decided that Sylvina would alternate with Marina in collecting the two girls.

"It's about Laura I need to talk with you."

The door opened farther and a finger of light slanted down one side of her face. Her mouth was traced unevenly in dark lipstick, as though she expected someone. She wore a clean, faded pink shirt, which she must have changed into quickly, because it was misbuttoned.

"Do I disturb . . . ?"

"No, come in."

I don't know what questions passed through her head as she led the way through the sliding glass doors. Private teachers must expect the worst.

In the studio, as before, she put on a cassette.

"Dvořák, isn't it?" I asked.

"We were dancing to it just now."

She listened to the music, then turned down the volume. On her neck a tendon vibrated. "I can't offer you much. A coffee?"

Walking back from the kitchen into the studio, she dragged over two inflatable exercise mats. She blew them up until her face colored. When she inserted the stoppers, I saw that her fingernails were bitten to the quick.

"Sorry. These are all I've got to sit on. I don't encourage visitors. To begin with, I let the mothers watch, but I banned them after a week. They all sat in a row, which was rotten for the child who fell over. Mind you, some of their children I could push myself."

She laid out the mats. I sat cross-legged. She sat upright, her legs folded to one side, and drew a white handkerchief from her sleeve.

"I've got a bit of a cold."

I was about to tell her Laura had caught it, too, when she exclaimed, "I like your daughter so much! She's unsure of herself and anticipates the music and doesn't loosen her neck, but we were so right to try her on modern dance!"

Laura, with Sylvina's agreement, had exchanged a classical class for a modern one. Which was now immaterial, of course.

"I'm afraid I have to take her away."

A plaster had stuck to her mat. She peeled it off and looked at it intently. "What do you mean? Am I too strict?"

"No, she's very fond of you."

I explained my situation. I didn't want to withdraw Laura, but I could no longer afford the fees.

She kept staring down, and I thought she didn't believe me.

It wasn't merely a question of my salary being late. I'd been paying for Laura with my overtime earnings. Now all overtime had been canceled.

I was humiliated and she could hear it. She continued gazing at the plaster, then tossed it over her shoulder.

"That's all right. I'm happy to carry her until you can meet the fees."

Is this why I decided to talk to her before Sylvina? It must have been at the back of my mind, Yolanda's reluctance to disrupt her class.

Before I'd even thought about it, I said, "Next month. I might be able to pay then."

"Pay when you can. But don't tell anyone. Please. You can't imagine the misery my life would be if some parents found out."

I started to thank her, but she interrupted. "I've been teaching children in the mountains for free. Anyway, it's not kindness. I'm thinking of the others."

"Laura tells me you get your ideas from the sierra."

I knew that, before opening her school, she had studied traditional dance in the highlands. But I had mentioned the sierra only out of politeness.

"I've been studying the dance groups at Ausangate."

It is possible for a word to leap out and slap you after twenty years. "Ausangate," I repeated, and she must have thought I didn't understand, because she started to explain.

I wasn't listening. The word, last spoken by my mother, had exploded in my head. Now, on this dance floor, its mention extinguished the smells of rosin and sweat and cigarette ash and I was standing on a narrow path called the Knife Edge.

It was four in the morning. The moonlight blazed on the ice. We had been walking for three days and I was playing my flute to a sheer white cliff across a gully. We listened in awe as the glacier sent back my music, giving us the strength to climb to the summit.

I said, "I was once a pilgrim to the ice festival."

"You weren't!"

"Thirty years ago. I was Laura's age."

"You're the first person I've met in this city who's heard of it."

"I played the pipes in the *wayli* dance."

"No! Which pipes?"

A word formed on my lips—"*Pinkullo*"—and in uttering it I felt the sores in my mouth. The cold air cramped my chest. My neck ached and I heard the reedy notes of my flute and, from the pilgrims around me, voices imitating the animal whose costume we wore, whose bells tinkled round our necks, whose spirit we had been transformed into while the festival lasted.

"Then you know what I'm talking about!" Yolanda jumped up. She kicked off her slippers and raised one arm until I recognized the wrung neck of a dead bird. With her other hand she masked her face, kicking back a leg to mimic a creature scuffling out its urine. She danced a few steps, her body slim and decisive, then sat down again, eager to hear more.

"So you provided *kun*—what is it, the word for comfort and joy?"

I laughed. *"Kunswiku,"* and there was no way to halt the sequence of images: the short spears of frost on the stubble; the blast of orange heat from the candles in the sanctuary; Father Ramón, breathless, not used to this altitude, awaiting our return with Santiago beside him; while up ahead, leading us, scrambling onto the glacier with his axe, the distant figure of my friend Nemecio.

She touched my knee, forthright as a child. "Is it true every year someone dies? As a sacrifice?"

I was evasive. "There are accidents."

On the last night, we climbed to the summit and fought. There must have been a thousand people milling on the glacier, all from village groups like mine. At that height, in that strange light, something happened. Without anyone to guide us, we divided into two bee swarms. For an hour we ran at each other, throwing snowballs and yelling. The noise—rattled bells, shouts, drums—echoed off the ice as we rushed forward and retreated until someone slipped too near a crevasse. That year it was a pilgrim from Pachuca. We knew it as soon as he fell. We stood in the snow, not moving, and I'll never forget the relief—that it wasn't someone from our village whom the mountain had chosen.

She shook her head. "To think you played that flute. I can't believe this. So that explains what I've noticed in Laura. I wondered what it could be. She has her own way of moving, which you can't teach, just like the girls I've been living with in the sierra. She's also got that plumbline of balance these rootless Westerners don't have. She should be studying the *wayli*, like her father, not *The Nutcracker Suite!*"

Yolanda stared into space. I looked at her face. For whom had she inexpertly applied her lipstick? She lowered her gaze, unsettled again.

"You're sure I haven't disturbed you?" I said.

"No, it's nice talking. You don't meet many people outside the studio, and never anyone who's been to Ausangate. What were we talking about? I've forgotten."

*"The Nutcracker Suite."*

"Why does Madame Offenbach do it? Every year she still sends letters to Panama on Margot Fonteyn's birthday and every year she puts on *The Nutcracker.* Is that our response to the kidnapping of those drama students, to dress up in white tutus and behave like fairies or flowers?"

"And that is why you left the Metropolitan?"

She ran a hand down her leg at the memory, rubbing her ankle. She wore no stockings. On her ankle was a narrow scar, the same pale color as her skin, but shiny.

"No. I had a leg injury. Every time I tried to get my heel down to jump, it was agony. One day Señora Vallejo was watching to see if I'd recovered from my accident. There was an idea I might be the prima ballerina. Well, I put my leg in a developpé and I did this unheard of thing."

She stood up quickly, faced the mirror and unfolded one leg, the foot higher than her hip, then slowly lowered it.

"I thought: I'm giving up, I'm stopping. This is ridiculous. I put my leg down and I left the studio. Everybody knew what that meant. They knew it was final, as if I was in the army and had disobeyed an order. I ran into the dressing room, everyone's clothes hanging on pegs like ghosts. I heard the music outside, still carrying on. It was a Brahms adagio. At last, no more struggle, I thought. I want to go out into the world. So I went to the jungle for two years—I'd always longed to be a missionary. I dropped everyone in the ballet world and went to Iquitos, with the Teresiana nuns. For two years I couldn't bear to hear ballet music. I pretended I'd never been a dancer."

She had noticed in the mirror that her buttons were done up wrongly. She undid her shirt and rebuttoned it correctly.

"You gave up dancing, yet you started your own school."

"Because I can't help it," she said with feeling. She stood, arms crossed, chin up, on the tips of her toes.

"What do you mean?"

"I mean that everything that goes on inside me—joy, passion, rage, love—I want to show it with my body." She whirled around. "Don't tell me you didn't feel the same way at Ausangate."

"And this feeling, it came back gradually, or in a flash?"

"A flash." She pointed at a poster pinned to the kitchen door. "I was taken to see these Cuban dancers at the Teatro Americano—where soon I have to do my ballet. They reminded me of what I had forgotten."

"Which was?"

"Something Señora Vallejo always quoted. 'Movement never lies.' She never tired of reminding us that dance is a contemporary art form. It can incorporate our reactions to what's going on now, this minute. It can allow us to be ourselves, not parodies of some European ideal."

"Have you found an idea for your ballet?"

"It's unlucky to talk about work in progress."

That I could understand and respect. "Forgive me."

"Silence is part of the dance," she joked. Her face became serious again. "I'm going to dance a ballet in memory of the Arguedas Players."

"The drama group?"

She bit her lip and her nostrils flared a little. "Wasn't that terrible? Poor kids. I feel such hatred for anyone who could do that. What would you feel if one evening Laura was seized by a group of gangsters and that was the last you heard of her? No, that's a terrible thing to say." But she looked at me. "Do you think they're alive?"

"Who knows?" I'd wondered the same things myself.

"It's been three weeks. The parents have heard nothing. I've a pupil here—her cousin Vera was one of the students. Everyone knows it was the army behind it. They're dead, they must be."

"Probably."

"The other day I watched a program about their abduction. Then I had this idea."

"To dance the kidnap?"

"No, to dance *Antigone*."

"*Antigone*?" I was out of my depth. "Isn't that a play."

"But, you see, that's it! That's the reaction I want. If I had told you I was going to dance something called, I don't know, *Hexagramma,* then all I'd hear from the ballet mothers is 'Why do you have to do pieces like this? Why do you have to show us all these dead bodies?' That's why I'm going to go back to Sophocles! Something everyone will think is taking place a long, long time ago, but which we're living now."

"Can I see this ballet?"

"You wouldn't like it."

"You said it was at the Teatro Americano."

Upstairs someone moved. She raised her head. "What's happened to our coffee?"

Yolanda went into the kitchen, flicked the switch on the kettle and waited for it to boil again.

She was pouring the water when the lights blacked out.


People think they know how they'll react in extreme circumstances. I *think* I know how I would react if this ceiling fell down. But I can't be sure. Nothing so far had indicated to me that Yolanda would behave as she now did.

In that first shock of darkness I heard her cry out. Something crashed to the floor.

"Are you all right? Have you hurt yourself?" There was no sound.

"My arm," came a thin voice. "I've scalded it . . ."

I fumbled my way across the dance floor into the kitchen. My hand sent a tin object clattering into the sink, an ashtray by the smell of it. Dampening a cloth, I felt my way to the fridge, probed inside until I found the metal tray, then pummeled out the ice cubes, packing them into the cloth.

"Where are you?"

"Here. Over here." Her voice rattled with panic.

I knotted the cloth around her arm, but it was impossible to tell how bad the burn was. She clung to me and I heard her taking in gulps of air.

"A flashlight, have you got one?"

I had to repeat the question.

"I don't think so."

"Or candles?"

"No, no. I don't know where they are. Can we get out of here?"

In the studio the mirrors, reflecting the night sky, smoldered with a reddish glow.

I slid open the door and guided her outside, across the patio, then out through the door in the wall. There was chaos in the street. Cars hooting. Names shouted. "Inez? Margarita? Juan?" Crazed parabolas of light and voices calling, "Watch out! Where are you? Over here!"

The blackout had blindfolded the city, save for the starry firmament above, like recollected dazzle, and one ember-red patch above the roofs.

"Miraflores," I said. "They must have electricity."

I helped her into the car and drove at a crawl toward the red tint in the sky. Tall buildings blocked our view of the hills. So we couldn't see what they were staring at in Las Flores and Monterrico and La Molina, a pattern of blazing oil drums that spelled out in acrid, flaming letters, brighter than any star, the single word EZEQUIEL.

"I'm sorry." Her voice was calmer. "These things always take me by surprise."

"We should look for a chemist."

She seemed distracted. But she wasn't concerned about her burn. "I never know when to expect them. And I wanted to play you some flute music."

By the time we drove into the light, she had recovered.

"You don't want anything for your arm?"

"No. Thank you."

"Let me buy you a drink then," I said.

"I'd like that very much."

The Café Haiti was packed. I checked the tables for Sylvina, who had been playing doubles with Consuelo. Would she be here? I wondered how I would explain myself. You must surely know that if you go somewhere with an attractive young woman, even if the occasion is an innocent one, and you don't tell your wife, you can't help feeling guilty. But there was no one I knew in the café.

The waitress, shy, with expressive eyes in a highland face, waited for our order.

"Whatever you're having," said Yolanda.

"Two beers."

"Here, let me pay."

"No."

"An hour ago, you were telling me you had no money," she teased. She was flirtatious, though there was nothing more behind it. I felt a rush of affection toward her.

From our corner table I took in the room. There was a lot of shoulder tapping and chairs leaning back as news of the blackout was broadcast and digested. It was strange to consider Miraflores as a beacon in a blinded city. For the first time the café struck me as beautiful.

I felt a sudden sharp pain in my hand. Yolanda was examining the fingers.

"You've hurt yourself." When thumping out the ice, I must have stripped the skin.

"How's your arm?" I asked.

She drew up her left sleeve. "I look idiotic wearing this dish-cloth, but—truly—I hardly feel a thing."

Relief to be in the light again showed in her face. All her movements were revealed in the unreflected suddenness of her smile.

"I'm sorry about my panic attack. I don't like the dark."

"Is there a reason?"

"Do I need one?"

"I suppose not."

"I've never been able to sleep without a light on in the house. That's why I'm so relieved you were there tonight."

"I'm glad I could help," I said.

"Last time there was a blackout, I was rehearsing and I lost my balance. I couldn't see myself in the mirror and everything went to pieces and I fell flat on my ass."

"Is there no one you can call?"

"What can they hope to achieve, really?" clucked a voice from the table behind us. A woman in sunglasses, with flattened down, very golden hair, spoke to a woman with prominent, heavily mascaraed eyes.

"But haven't they got a point, these poor people?" said her companion.

Yolanda looked around as the blond lady removed her sunglasses. A reflection was admired in the lenses, some grease was polished off, and the glasses were restored to their perch on a large nose.

Through them, the blonde appraised Yolanda. There's nothing like the sight of an ugly woman taking in an attractive one. Wistfully, the blonde said, "Perhaps they'll kidnap Maimée."

Yolanda leaned forward toward me in a confiding way. She was about to speak when a woman's voice, obviously trying to be heard, announced, "You know, I've always been on the left, deep down."

Neither of us could help it. We burst into laughter.

Rejas glanced at Dyer. He seemed to have forgotten where he was. An all but empty restaurant. Not a ballerina sharing his table, but a man pretending to be a historian.

A foghorn prompted him to check his watch. Dyer saw the relief with which he said he must go. Somewhere in that night, in a house Dyer would never visit, Rejas had another woman to attend to.

"Emilio!"

Rejas, having called for his bill, began to stroke some bread crumbs into a line with the back of his hand. Unexpectedly, he reached across and removed the knife from Dyer's plate. He held it by the handle, over the table, between thumb and forefinger, blade pointing downward.

"How long do you think it takes a rat to drown?"

The question surprised Dyer. "Half an hour?" he guessed.

"It's a story I was told by Ezequiel," said Rejas. "He used it to explain to me the sheer will he managed to unleash in our people. But which could apply to any of us."

"How long?"

"He told me that if you drop a rat in a tank of water, the rat will swim about for fifteen minutes and after fifteen minutes he will drown." Rejas released the knife. It clattered on the table. His eyes blurred with despair.

"But if after fifteen minutes you pick the rat up by his tail and give him a good shake to start him breathing again and drop him back in the water . . ." He gazed at the dull blade. Once more he took the knife by the handle and dropped it. The noise bounced through the room. Dyer was aware of Emilio swiveling from the till.

"How long do you suppose he swims after that?"

"I don't know."

Rejas sat back, though his eyes never quitted the blade.

Dyer, too, stared at the knife. "Half an hour," he guessed.

"Two days."

"Two days?"

Rejas accepted his bill from Emilio and counted out the money. "I must go back to my sister."

The Colonel stood, but Dyer sat there, still imagining that creature swishing through the water.

"Her condition, is it serious?"

"She's in a coma. Well, in and out of it."

Dyer had failed to understand the seriousness of her illness. A case of food poisoning, he'd thought. Was that why Rejas had talked all this while, all these evenings—to take his mind off his sister?

"There's a good hope she'll recover, surely?"

"Hope? That's what it boils down to."

Rejas was not talking about his sister.

9

When Dyer entered the restaurant next evening, Rejas wasn't there.

Half an hour passed. Still no sign of his coming. At eight Dyer ordered Emilio's grilled fish, though reluctantly.

It had been very hot during the day. After writing down the policeman's story in a yellow spiral-bound notebook, he had slept late and again in the afternoon taken a long siesta. Now a little breeze came through the window.

He turned a page, listening for steps. Outside he heard the imperturbable throb from the fortress, and the peacocks in the bird market screaming from their cages. He tried to read, but could not concentrate. He looked at his watch. Eight-thirty. The policeman had never been this late. Had Rejas found out who he was, or had he, for whatever reason, suddenly thought better of telling his story to a stranger?

Dyer had not asked Rejas why he might want to talk in this way. It helped that he was Vivien's nephew, of course. Besides, people do tell their secrets to strangers, and it stood to reason they would feel for each other a certain sympathy. They were men of an age, both miles from home. And like Rejas, wasn't he about to be discarded, or used in the wrong way? But that he should have hit his target inadvertently . . .

And yet, Dyer thought, isn't it the desire of wanting to hit the target that makes you miss it? If you want things too badly, you end up with nothing at all. It's the act of not hankering after something that somehow, weirdly, brings it about. And wasn't he himself a kind of target? He was one of the few people in the world whose fascination Rejas could rely on. Many of his countrymen, perhaps even his own sister, might not have given a damn. But Dyer understood. Hadn't he been looking for Rejas in the first place and hadn't they both chosen this restaurant in which to read—both of them—the same book? Which was why, as Rejas had begun talking, Dyer had been able to quell any doubt about the policeman's motive. He had simply thought, This is the story I've been waiting for all my career.

It was past nine when he heard the *click, click, click* on the stone staircase and the strands of the bead curtain parted. Rejas sat down, apologizing. The specialist had been on the telephone to discuss his sister's tests. Over the plate which Emilio served him, he continued to brood on her illness, slowly enfolding Dyer in his misery.

Two months earlier a storm had kept her overnight on an island opposite Pará. At one of the stalls by the jetty she had eaten undercooked pork. Soon after, she became lethargic, complained of headaches, a pain behind the right eye. One day her husband found her speaking incoherently about snails. The symptoms— vomiting, nausea, disorientation—were consistent with cysticercosis. As the seizures became more frequent, he summoned Rejas. She was thirty-seven, and quite likely to die.

For the past three weeks the two men had taken turns by her bed. Rejas kept vigil during the day, his brother-in-law at night. Her level of consciousness fluctuated from hour to hour. One moment she was quiet, the next agitated and disoriented. After she swallowed her drugs, her limbs shook. Frequently she hallucinated.

Who was that making coffee?

Why did Agustín wear so much eau de cologne?

Didn't he like this beetle she'd found by the river?

"She thought I was our father. As a girl, she was always coming into his library with frogs and snails."

In the mornings Rejas sat in a wicker chair and read aloud

from their father's books. Propped on pillows, she listened, stuporous, sucking her thumb. In the afternoons as she slept, he brushed the flies from her mouth and the liquid trails from the corners of her eyes. At six, when her husband returned from work, Rejas could leave the room. He would be careful in his movements in case she heard the wicker creaking. In that confined space it had the effect of a shriek. Once, waking up, she insisted on coming with him. She knelt, rummaging through a drawer for a favorite dress of black velvet. "Wait, Agustín, wait till I find it. We'll have such a good time."

The doctor, observing the deterioration in his patient, advised a lumbar puncture. The hallucinations could indicate that the drugs were destroying the parasites. Or her condition was untreatable. The answer would show up in her spinal fluid. With the two men's approval, she was laid on her left side, curled up like a baby, while a long needle was inserted into her back. The sample had been sent for analysis to a lab in Rio. That was a week ago. They were still waiting for the results.

"You think you're grown up," said Rejas. "Then you see your sister ill—and she's a ten-year-old again. But there are some people—their youth never leaves them. It's the only time of life which interests them and they respond to everyone they meet as if they were still ten-year-olds. Yolanda was like that. In some ways she could be grown up beyond her years, in other ways oddly childish—as ballerinas can be who've not been around people much.

"Then there are those like me who don't think about their childhood. Which is a common experience in the sierra. When their parents die, people who've moved away don't come home anymore, not to small towns. I'd gone back to La Posta only once after I left—with Sylvina for a fortnight's holiday the summer I graduated. After the military had seized our farm, there was nothing to go back for. I didn't investigate Ezequiel's influence in the valley, because you never think things are going to be so bad in your own village. Then Yolanda mentioned Ausangate.

"That night I lay awake, remembering in detail the village, my friends, the skipping-rope rhymes, our coffee plantation. It was at this period I learned the fate of our priest."

He searched for something in his trouser pocket. "Tell me, did your aunt mention a Father Ramón, who might have worked with her on the children's project?"

"Ramón? I don't think so."

"I was one of his altar boys. There were three of us—me, Nemecio and Santiago, his favorite."

Dyer had been so relieved to see Rejas this evening that for a while he didn't mind what the policeman talked about. Now he was anxious for him to continue his story. "Last night you were talking about Yolanda."

Rejas, his hand now rummaging in another pocket, ignored him. "This old man. He wasn't just any priest, you understand. He was a priest I loved. It's a terrible story. But it was he who led me to Ezequiel."

He had found what he was looking for. "I want to show you this. It's important."

It was an airmail letter, the paper so thin that the blue writing pressed through like veins.

"My last contact was this letter from Portugal."

Rejas waited for Dyer to read it. The hand was large and neat. "You remember my hope of one day visiting Our Lady's shrine at Fátima? My prayers have been answered. I have been lucky enough to be appointed religious guide for a tour comprising eighteen pilgrims from our diocese." The priest, who Dyer gathered had never before left La Posta, was excited by the airport, by the food on the plane, by the way the time changed as he flew. "Five hours of Palm Sunday lost! Where did that day go? Was it a sin not to be in church, do you think?" In Portugal he had eaten well, if curiously—a dish with pork and clams . . . "On the way to the shrine we took a bus to Coimbra, where I saw the library. Gold everywhere. Your father would have loved it!" At Fátima the shrine to the Virgin surpassed his expectations. "I walked on my knees all the way with the same speed as if I had been on my feet. You have no idea how holy this place is. The Virgin's presence is palpable. I said a prayer for you and your sister. Also for the village. Things are not so good in the valleys at the moment, Agustín. I have had to send five children to an orphanage in the capital. You will understand why Our Lady's message of peace has never seemed more needed. I prayed through the night—and I did feel I was listened to."

I had not heard from Father Ramón since receiving that letter. Then, about a week after my meeting with Yolanda, Sucre handed me a newspaper cutting.

"La Posta? Isn't that your village, sir?"

"Why? What's wrong?"

"They've killed the priest."

The cutting, three weeks old, reported that Maoist forces had executed Father Ramón because he had been "participating in the counterinsurgency struggle designed by the government and armed forces."

I heard the details later. It was hideous.

They waited for him by the Weeping Terrace, which is now an airstrip. He walked there every Saturday, composing the sermon he would broadcast over our local radio station. They seized his hat, his stick and the small Bible he carried everywhere—a gift of my father's, with gilt-edged pages. He was forced to his knees on the grass, his hands tied behind his back. A woman knelt in front of him. She searched the Bible for the appropriate page.

"Read it out," she ordered.

The passage was from Job. He started reading. His voice was famous. He would have said the words as if he was touched with their emotional truth.

" 'His breath kindleth coals and flame goeth out of his mouth. In his neck remaineth strength and sorrow is turned to joy before us.' "

She tore the page out, screwed it into a ball, forced it between his lips. "Eat."

"What do you mean?"

"Eat!"

I picture his lips parting.

"Swallow."

I see him making the effort to swallow and the woman, a dreadful expression on her face, tearing the first page of Genesis, telling him, "In the beginning God created the heavens and the earth," making another ball, holding that to his mouth. I see him willing himself to transform this page into the Host. I remember there are six hundred and twenty-seven pages.

After he passed out, he was stabbed repeatedly. They scooped out the guts and filled his stomach with the rest of the Bible—which, according to a message left inside his hat, had been written as a propaganda tool.

Lastly, they attacked his face. Those who found his corpse couldn't tell if it belonged to a man. But when the face is mutilated like that, it means one thing: the killer is known to his victim.

Father Ramón had baptized her.


My father, a timid man with few close friends, believed that a part of the reason we love someone is because of the person we become when we're with them. When they're dead, we can never be that person again. It's that other person, my father would say, for whom we're grieving. When I read the bald fact of Father Ramón's death, I had no intention of journeying to La Posta. But I had to speak with others who had known him.

The three altar boys had drifted apart. The last I heard of Nemecio, he was teaching in Cajamarca. Santiago was in a seminary. I had no idea where they were at that time.

As you will see from that letter, Father Ramón mentions several of his fellow pilgrims. One of them was Santiago's mother.


Rejas waited for Dyer to find the reference. Although it puzzled the journalist—this concern for him to know every detail—he reread the passage.

> My feelings for Leticia Solano will always be informed by the utmost tenderness, but I will be relieved when we part. She would prefer it if her feelings toward me escalated to a level of greater intimacy, although this I attribute to her failing eyesight. We have known each other a long time—most of my life!—and she is so possessive of my company that once or twice it has led to friction with other members

of our group. Since leaving the valley—she lives somewhere in Belgrano: is that near you?—I hear she is more troubled than ever. I do not know if Santiago is at the root of her disquiet. I believe there has been a falling-out. Do you see your friend ever? We lost touch when he abandoned the ministry. It grieves me to think he didn't trust me enough to share his doubts. I would have told him what my Bishop told me when I contemplated the same action: maybe God doesn't exist, but people who believe in Him generally lead better lives.

I found two Solanos listed as living in the Belgrano district, one of them with the initial L. The telephone company said the line had been disconnected owing to nonpayment.

One evening I followed an orange cat between puddles up an alley, looking for Solano, L.'s house.

*Clap, clap,* went the echo of my knock on the shabby door. The cat darted under a gate. Beyond the wall a fig tree writhed unwatered. Presently a shutter rattled open. A bowl of white azaleas was shoved aside and, partly obscured by a line of drying clothes, an old woman's face appeared over the ledge.

"Yes?" She looked down between a pair of black stockings.

I stepped back. "It's Agustín. Agustín Rejas."

She weaved her head. "Who?"

"Santiago's friend. I've come about Father Ramón."

"What does he want?"

Her voice was bothered, her face lost in the flowers.

"Can I come in?"

She withdrew. On the sill the cat watched me. I thought, Why do people who go to pieces like cats so?

I heard a shuffle of feet and then metal squeaking. A gruff voice reminding itself, "Rejas, Rejas. The coffee farm."

We sat upstairs in a dingy kitchen, where she warned, "I've nothing to give you. No coffee." Her face and chest had flattened and she couldn't see very well. She relied on a neighbor's boy to bring provisions. He hadn't called today. She was thinking of Father Ramón, but too proud to ask.

"I wanted to get in touch with Santiago," I said.

Something fluttered across her face. "Santiago? Why Santiago?"

"We were at school together."

"In Pachuca?"

"No, before that. La Posta."

"Why didn't we meet?" She pretended she could see me. The eyes which had once caused havoc in the valley and beyond had a cloudy look. "Why didn't he bring you to the hotel ever?"

"He did. But you weren't there." She had abandoned hotel, husband and son for the alcoholic who pretended to be a wealthy cotton grower. Everyone but Santiago had known of the affair.

I said, "We both were servers at Mass."

I thought of walking with Santiago to the church. Horses grazing in the browned grass. A young goat shivering. Santiago wanting to be a priest. He looked very like his mother.

"I played the flute and he sang."

Santiago had the best voice in the village. I thought of Father Ramón, tone-deaf, encouraging Santiago to the eagle lectern; my friend's nervous face popping over those wings as though he were clinging to a condor.

"He gave up singing."

"Why?"

"Same reason he gave up the priesthood," she said bitterly. "He preferred to talk, didn't he?"

"What about?"

"Foreign names. All nonsense."

"What foreign names?"

"Why are you so interested? Why should I tell you?"

It's something I inherited from my father. If asked a direct question, I tell the truth. "I work for the ATP."

"The police?" She brushed the cat aside. Her cataractal eyes slunk back along the table toward me. "Paco told me they've found those actors you killed."

Bones had been discovered under the seats of a cinema which the university was restoring as a cultural center.

"That was nothing to do with us."

"The army, then. What difference does it make?"

"It hasn't been proved."

"Why are you all behaving like this?"

"I don't know."

"Why is it you want to see your schoolfriend?" The last word sarcastic.

"I want to talk to him about Father Ramón."

"That's what the others said."

"Who said?"

"Two men who came to see him."

"Who were they?"

"Friends from university. They needed Santiago, they said."

"When was this?"

"Two, three weeks." She lifted her head. "Why does everyone want to talk about Father Ramón?"

"What did they want to know?"

The cat had crept back. "His sermons—"

"They didn't like what he was saying?"

She folded her arms. "I told them to get out."

"Did you tell them where to find Santiago?"

"I have no idea where he is."

"Is that true?"

"Why should I tell you?"

"Then it's not true."

"He writes. He sends money."

"What do the letters say?"

"I don't know," she repeated, her eyes unable to make tears. "The boy who brings the food doesn't read."

"Don't you keep the letters?"

"Pass me that."

I unhooked the imitation leather bag from the back of a chair. She fumbled with the clasp and felt inside, bringing out an envelope.

The postmark was two months old, from La Posta.

She said, "Tell me, what does he write?"

I unfolded the letter. The page was blank, something to fold the money in so it couldn't be seen through the envelope.

"He says he loves you and everything is fine and he will write again soon."

The outline of a smile. "That's Santiago."
She moved her head to the wall. The thermometer was a Fátima Virgin. She bit her lip. "Tell me," she said more brightly. "How is Father Ramón?"

I requested a fortnight's absence. The General refused. The bowl on his desk was piled high with oranges, as if stocked against a great siege. "I tell you, tomcat, it's pandefuckingmonium out there." Calderón had given himself dictatorial powers. Everything went first to Lache. "If I know General Lache, the Arguedas Players, they're just the beginning. He's adopting the French solution—and the French haven't won a war since 1812. It's vital you stay here."

I held my ground. "And it's vital I go to La Posta, sir."
"Why?" He stood up and looked uncertainly at his map.
"Ezequiel has been trying to contact a friend of mine."
"So?"
"This friend may be involved."
It had burst upon me in Leticia's kitchen. All the time I had been searching for Ezequiel I had been looking in the wrong place.

10

On the morning I left for La Posta, Laura sidled into the bed-room. She was miserable. Children hold adults to their promises.

"Look." I watched her through the camera. "I'll take masses of photos for you."

Her face hardened.

"I'll bring you a flute—like the one I used to play. I promise."

She said nothing.

"The military have declared it an emergency zone, Laura."

To prove that she was the child I took her for, she locked herself in her room and sang aloud to the cat.

Sylvina drove me to the airport. An unusual peace had settled on her, and on the city we passed through. If you live with vio-lence, you become acclimatized to it. After a car bomb, people will jog around the dead bodies. They will go to their tennis courts. One of Sylvina's cousins, to circumvent the curfew, had bought a second-hand ambulance to transport his friends to parties. There is a routine even to menace.

As we drove past the Inca Market, Sylvina said, "Agustín, I have a way we can make money."

She had been discussing our problems with Marco. She knew I'd be cross, which is why she waited until this moment to talk about it. The fact was, Marco had come up with a fail-safe plan for us to become millionaires. In the vague terms in which I grasped it, Marco's solution—upon which, shortly, all her hopes would fix—required Sylvina to sell certain beauty products to her friends and induce them to do likewise while taking a percentage.

"If you persuade people to work for you, you get ten percent of everything they sell, so if they sell fifty dollars, I receive five dollars, and if they in turn find two people to work for them, eventually I'll be at the top of the pyramid and it can't fail." A lavender Cadillac seemed to be involved at some point, because she brought up that again after the engine stalled at the security checkpoint.

"Marco's obsessed with it. Just in his own street two women have made millions."

We kissed through the car window. "You know what communications are like in the sierra," I said. "But I'll try to ring."

"Anyway, Marco's sending me a sample kit."


I flew in a military transport to Cajamarca, from where I caught a lift with a truck heading north. The driver was a round, thick-set man with an overhanging forehead and huge, offended eyes. We left for the mountains that night, splashing out through the mud, our headlights shedding a watery dazzle in the pelting rain.

The truck had been climbing for three hours when Ezequiel struck. We were approaching a high pass and the driver was telling me about his family, killed by the police. I sat, appalled, watching a bank of mist nudge into the sweep of our lights.

He said he knew the policeman who had killed them, knew his name and nickname, knew where he lived. Every night since his wife and daughters had been found in a sheep field, strangled with khaki webbing, he had driven back and forth past the policeman's house, fifty yards one way, then reverse and fifty yards the other way. Up, down. Up, down. Up, down. Until daylight. He lifted a plump hand from the wheel and pointed a finger at my temple.

"Pow!" he whispered.

"Watch out!" The headlight picked out a barricade of rocks in the mud.

He braked hard and the truck slithered toward the hillside, shuddering to a stop against a bank of earth. Soon another vehicle pulled up behind us, and another, until the lights of six cars illuminated the bend.

He slapped the flat of his hands against the steering wheel. "What the fucking hell is this about?"

It was ten o'clock. The mist was rolling in.

And then four figures solidified in the haze, stepping between the rocks, waving powerful flashlights, advancing through the rain.

The driver leaned from his window and yelled, "Let us pass."

"Shut your face." It was a young boy, speaking through a woollen mask. His gloved hands gripped what in that light appeared to be a gun, but might have been a stick. He wasn't nervous.

"Turn out your lights and wait in the cab." There was the flop of feet and he continued down the line of cars, flanked by his three companions.

The driver turned the truck's lights off and slumped back in his seat.

I said quietly, "If they order us out, we'll be shot." I carried no weapon, but concealed in my right shoe was a military pass and my police identity card. Should they discover these, there would be no mercy. Not for me, not for the driver either.

A shadow, then a tap on the window. A light beamed in my face. The door opened and a moment later my first gasp of the chill mountain air froze my lungs.

"Your money. Quickly." The light remained in our eyes while we groped for our wallets. A hand seized them, then the flashlight was flashed at my feet.

"That bag. Pass it here."

The bag was unzipped, a hand in a long, damp orange glove thrust inside. It emerged with my old Leica, one of the few nice things my father left me. On the film were pictures of Laura and Sylvina at Paracas: standing in the waves, offering potato chips to a sea lion, pointing at a turtle on the sand. I would later regret the theft of those happy images even more than I did now.

I could easily afford to contribute to the revolution, snarled the voice. This instrument was worth more than he earned in a year.

He jumped to the ground and ran off, leaving me to shut the door. Beside me the driver expelled his breath. There's something frightening about a twelve-year-old with a gun. Then, suddenly agitated, he twisted in his seat. "Hey," he whispered, "what's that?" The truck squealed on its chassis and we could hear the heavy boxes sliding in the back.

They were unloading his vegetables. With the hand that had been a pistol he covered his eyes and sobbed.

Five minutes later the boys came by again, not looking at us. They reached the rocks and switched off their flashlights; shadow-thin, sheathed in denim, they slipped down the bank and vanished.

It was something tremendous, this silence. We waited, waited, as the quietness dripped around us. Eventually the car behind switched on its sidelights, and after an interval a strained voice was heard calling, "Shall we risk it?"

Two men stooped over the rocks and began lifting them. The driver and I got out to help. We didn't exchange words. Then we climbed back in and everyone started their engines and we drove from that place.

Two days later I reached the valley where I was born. The road signs had been stolen, but I knew where I was.

I banged on the cab roof. As the pickup slowed, I jumped from the back.

The air smelled sharply of wet earth and the barky scent of catuaba shrubs. Gnats, bloated by rain, danced over puddles reflecting terraces of corn and cactus.

I paused at the top of the track. La Posta lay below, a village on the edge of a drop into a valley at the headwaters of the Amazon. I could see the white domed church, the ironwork bridge and the thread of road winding through the valleys beyond the town. It led to our farm, though the house was hidden by an escarpment.

You know how you feel when you see your name in print? I experienced the same shock of recognition. Nostalgia engulfed me and the landscape trembled a little and I walked down that track as if the rest of my life hadn't happened. The landscape hadn't changed—therefore, nothing else had either.

Just outside the village I heard a cry. A boy came around the corner, whipping a donkey with a strip of rubber. When he caught sight of my bag, he leapt off down the slope, not looking back. The donkey, ignoring me, lowered its peeled-back lips to the verge.

I was too excited to be offended. I walked on down into the main street. It was eleven in the morning, but I was shocked by what I didn't see.

I expected the sidewalks to swarm with women from the lower farms. Every morning they would sit cross-legged behind pyramids of coca leaf and manioc flour. At the same age as the boy with the donkey, I had loved to watch their hands sneak from under impossibly colored shawls, to ladle a cup of reddish chicha; turn over a chunk of sweet-smelling alpaca; or offer a roasted guinea pig with a mouth of charred teeth.

Today the muddied sidewalk was deserted save for three small figures hurrying away. I breathed in deeply. Even the air seemed tainted.

In the Plaza de Armas, steam gargled from an open drain and drifted over a scraggy hedgerow, smudging the knees of a statue. I remembered how, on Sundays, dissatisfied young women would loiter before our band, making eyes at the musicians. Parents would push their prams across the cobbles to meet other parents, and the benches would creak with watchful old men, tapping their feet to badly played tunes. This morning two girls knelt by the fountain in the square. They crouched at the spout, spraying water at each other from the dribble. José's daughters? They had the butcher's curly black hair. When they saw me, they ran off through the threadbare topiary into a house beyond.

On his plinth Brigadier Pumacacchua averted his concrete gaze.

I paused on the corner at the butcher's shop. Twice a week my mother would send me to buy the lambs' tongues for which my father had a weakness. The idea had entered her head that this was every man's favorite dish—Father Ramón included. She adored the priest and was always fussing over him, inviting him to dinner, serving him these tongues which, uncomplainingly, he ate, telling her they were wonderful.

Twenty-five years ago I'd been waiting my turn in the queue, a lamb's head resting on a blue chair beside me, when the door burst open and the printer we knew as "the Turk" bustled in holding a thermos flask of calligraphy fluid, warmed up, and a stack of blank invitation cards under his arm. "They've expropriated the coffee farm!" He didn't know I was in the shop, and at José's dismayed expression he turned, dropping the flask when he saw me. I watched the steaming ink spread under the chair, mingling with the lamb's blood until the floor was a vivid pattern of reds and blacks streaking one into the other.

"Oh no, oh no, oh no. I don't believe it," said the Turk, on all fours among his silvery thermos fragments.

I tried the door. It was padlocked on the inside. I pressed my face to the filthy glass. No meat slapped across the stone slab. The blue chair stood in the corner, its seat missing.

In the glass I saw my face. I looked disordered and alarming. Horrified, I found a comb and ran it through my hair. I was still combing as I turned into Calle Jirón and walked headlong into an old lady.

She was stooped beside a mound of potatoes. I was so startled I dropped the comb. The old woman—amazingly quick—darted to pick it up, then held it away from my reach, refusing to return it until I rewarded her. She extended her other hand toward me, pleading for money. Her face was terraced with age and she had an almost peaceful look.

Then her glance slid down to my bag and she screamed.

"*Pishtaco!*" She threw down the comb, gathered up the potatoes in her black shawl and hobbled away as fast as she could.

At No. 119, a white house with a red door, I paused. This was where my parents had lived after the military expropriated our farm. When my father died, my mother continued to share the house with his books. In her curt old age she saw in them the enfeebled crops and the money he should have spent on fertilizer and parrot killer.

I didn't want to see inside and walked on. The next street, parallel to the church, was Calle Bolsas. Outside Nemecio's house I put down my bag and knocked. Nothing. I pushed the door, but it didn't give and, pressing my ear to a window, I could hear no sounds.

At the bottom of the same street I tried another house, a metal plaque bolted to its door: F. LAZO, ORTHODONTIST.

A little girl opened the door. She had an Elastoplast on her arm and held a rag doll by the leg.

"Who is it?" asked a worried-sounding man from inside.

"I'm looking for Fernando Lazo," I called.

"But I know that voice . . ."

He came up behind the girl, holding her shoulders as if to support himself. It was frightening how little he had changed.

"Joaquín?"

"It's his son," I said.

Later, after the embraces and the disbelief, he led me to his office.

One always expects people to react more emotionally than they do when you haven't seen them for a long time. It wasn't me the dentist wanted to remember. During our conversation he called me by my father's name. What had happened to our library? It was a sad day when we left the farm. He had kept our dental records. Just in case.

"And you? You became a lawyer, right?"

"That's it."

"Didn't you have a sister?"

"She's married, lives in Brazil."

He contrived a smile. "So. How are your teeth?"

"No serious problems."

"That's good. Tell everyone how well I looked after you."

I sat on a stool beside his desk while he fidgeted with the cast of a jaw. It was odd once more to be in this room, more museum than dentist's office. Above the desk, thirty or forty burial urns were arranged on shelves reaching to the ceiling. As a younger man, Lazo had been an ardent collector of Chimu and Chachapoyan pottery. Once, he was treating my mother when his daughter, dusting the pots, felt one of them stir and, peering over the rim, discovered a knot of gray snakes. My mother had come home full of the question, wanting to discuss the puzzle of how they had got there in the first place. No one had any idea. Nor did they know how to get rid of them. Hot oil—the snakes might thrash and break the pot. Water—wouldn't they swim loose?

Fire—the pot itself might crack. Lazo decided to smother them. He sealed the pot with tinfoil, lowered it into a plastic bag and turned it upside down. It had stayed like that for days, a source of macabre and ceaseless fascination for his open-mouthed patients until, with a great song and dance, it was judged safe to remove the covering, and the pot, cautiously examined, revealed a withered tangle of what looked like strips from an exploded tire.

That morning I had disturbed Lazo while he was making a plate for the Mayor, who'd lost a front tooth.

"He has to have it today. Talk to me while I work." He inclined the white jaw to the light with the care of someone inspecting the innards of an ancient clock. He had seen to the teeth of three generations of my family.

"Says he slipped in the shower." He pulled toward him a jar of brown teeth. To tease us, he used to tell me and my sister that the teeth were really peanuts. He poured a selection onto a shoebox lid; suddenly I wanted to eat one.

"You've brought the rain, Joaquín," he said, bending over his work. "We haven't had rain for two years. Not rainy rain. Have you seen your coffee fields? There are cracks so wide you can't see the bottom." His voice quavered. He hadn't expected me. I brought back too much.

In the courtyard emaciated chickens, plucked-looking, poked their heads between the fenceposts.

"What's happened to the market?" I asked.

"Our friends destroyed the lower road."

He tweezered an appropriate tooth, a molar, from the box lid and clamped it in a small vise. "Anyway, there's no one left to feed. Just babies. You remember my daughter? You were friends. That's her little girl."

"Where is she now?"

"Graciela? In the capital. The young ones have all fled there, those that didn't join our friends, those that weren't put dead into a hole. We're a village of old men and women. With grandchildren to look after."

"When did you see her last?"

"A month ago. Just before Father Ramón died. I want to follow her, but I can't. They've confiscated our identity cards."

He unhooked his drill, directed it at the molar. When we were children, he used to fasten a piece of cotton wool on the drive cord. He hoped the white flash, zipping up and down the drill's pulleys, would distract us from the pain.

"We're sick of the army, we're sick of Ezequiel, we're sick of anyone we don't know. You're lucky you weren't lynched today." His voice was husky. The drill jabbed at the tooth like a weapon.

"Tell me about Father Ramón," I said.

He appeared not to have heard. I repeated the question.

He switched off the drill, sat back, watching the pulleys slow, the needle lock to a sudden halt.

"I can't do this and tell you." The Mayor's tooth could wait. Not every day did Joaquín's son sit here.


Two months before, the villagers had voted in a left-wing councillor. This was their angry response to officials who had ordered parents to pay an education fee. In the local elections, encouraged by the councillor, the village abstained. One morning the military came driving down the hill.

The councillor was not seen again.

But it didn't end there. The soldiers went from house to house, demanding to know who had supported him. It was then that Father Ramón stepped in. He insisted on an inquiry into the councillor's disappearance and would neither give up nor moderate his demands. He contacted the Diocesan Commission for Social Action in Villoria. To the Synod he sent letters and rolls of film chronicling the army's excesses. He accused the commanding officer to his face.

And then Ezequiel's men retaliated. They executed the Turk as an informer.

"Remember the Turk? He'd taken over the hotel after Leticia Solano left town. I don't know if he was an army informer, or if he wasn't. I don't know, Joaquín, really I don't. Friendships only last as long as we don't talk about these things. The fact is, they killed the Turk and they shot his wife as she tried to pull the hood off one of them."

Father Ramón had been enraged. In his broadcasts to the valleys he attacked Ezequiel, whose behavior was no different from the military's. He showed no respect for those he claimed to liberate. This killing was something intolerable.

"I had not seen Father Ramón so wound up since his visit to Portugal," said Lazo sadly.

One Saturday afternoon a month ago the priest walked down to the river, presumably composing his next tirade, and never came back.

"Nemecio found him. Identifiable only by his hat and his stick."

"Who killed him?"

Lazo stared at the shelves of primitive pots. His voice was tight, his eyes pinched and sore as though he hadn't allowed himself to cry.

"Who can say?"

Outside, the chickens pecked the ground. In the next room his little granddaughter sang to a doll.

"I thought Nemecio lived in Cajamarca."

"He came back to assist Father Ramón."

"Where is he now?"

Lazo shifted his gaze to the brown tooth.

"He was one of those in church."

"What do you mean?"

The dentist's eyes rippled in astonishment. "The massacre. I thought that's why you'd come . . ."

"What massacre? What are you talking about?"

He searched my face. "The military's reprisal for Father Ramón. But you heard about that, didn't you? Didn't you?"

Afterward, after he had stuttered it out, I had to tell him no one in my office knew. As soon as I heard his story, I saw that everything the General feared had overtaken us.

Falteringly, in a voice from which all emotion had been exhausted, Lazo described the military's revenge.

Ten days after Nemecio discovered the priest's body, the villagers watched two loose columns of men in black uniforms jogging toward the church. It was a Wednesday, about four-thirty in the afternoon, a time when Father Ramón would have conducted his Bible class.

Nemecio had taken charge of the class. Suddenly, from behind the altar, he heard a banging.

The men kicked down a door at the back of the church. They squeezed through a storeroom, knocking over boxes and paintings. The congregation were petrified. The soldiers fanned out along both aisles, leveling their guns at the twenty men and women, ordering them to kneel.

"Palomino Cordero?" they shouted. "Which one of you is Cordero?"

The man they wanted was the producer at the radio station. One of the soldiers gathered the identity cards, flicked through them, then handed the bundle to someone else, who repeated the process.

They didn't believe it. They had been misled. They searched the sanctuary, the pulpit; they tore off the cloth over the Communion table. But Cordero wasn't there. Their leader retreated to the altar to radio for instructions.

There was the rasp of static. A remote voice said, "Proceed as planned."

The soldiers grabbed Nemecio first. Then Lazo's son-in-law, the postman. They yanked all the men outside, leaving others to deal with the women.

"Sing!" they yelled. "All of you, sing!"

The women were terrified. What should they sing? One of them suggested a hymn. She led the way nervously. Her words were hesitant, her throat dry. From somewhere she found a voice.

"Louder!"

Guns cracked outside. One of the women screamed.

"Louder, louder," lashed the soldiers, from behind them now.

The voices rose in fear. *"Oh buen Jesús, yo creo firmemente que en el altar Tu sangre está presente . . ."*

They had begun the second verse when something bounced onto a wooden pew.

Lazo felt the explosion in his office. It was five o'clock. From Clemencia's shattered mouth he would hear what had happened. Nemecio's sister was one of two survivors. The other, a farmer's wife who lost both legs, died later.

Since then they had threatened Clemencia. If she opened her

mouth, they'd dig up her dead husband and make her eat him. Neither she nor Lazo believed this to be an empty threat. She swore she would say nothing. But while she was sitting in the dentist's chair—Lazo doing what he could with his inadequate supplies—her remaining teeth started to chatter.

When Lazo had finished, I said, "Weren't there bodies to prove this?"

"They used horses to carry them away," he said.

Horses were the only way of transporting the bodies to the airstrip. Ezequiel's men, after killing Father Ramón, had blown up the bridge. Near the hangar the soldiers had dug a mass grave, but three days later they'd come back with their shovels and dug it up again and thrown the bodies—wrapped in plastic trash bags— across the backs of the screaming animals.

"The smell wasn't any more pleasant to them, poor things, than it was to us," said Lazo.

The military must have feared an investigation, because four soldiers barged into his office and demanded that he hand over his dental records.

"Which I did immediately. But I have copies. I've foreseen something like this for years."

Anxious to know the fate of his son-in-law, Lazo one evening made his way to the airstrip. He'd smelled the decay lingering above the disturbed earth. Dug for a while; found nothing except the end of a candle, a strip of white cloth and a bunch of keys.

Saliva shone on his yellowed false teeth. He looked up at the ceiling. "When they buried them, not all the victims were dead."

Words formed, but I couldn't speak.

"Ask me. Go ahead and ask me. How do I know? One night a soldier got drunk. He began shooting in the air, yelling that he missed his mother. Knocking on doors. He demanded to see my documents. I invited him in, calmed him down. Then he put aside his gun and began crying. He was from the coast, hundreds of miles away from home; he'd been made to do these terrible things—and he described what they had done.

"I haven't told my daughter. She thinks her husband's just missing. But they buried him alive. They dug that hole and threw him in it and shoveled earth over him. Alive, alive."

Lazo fiddled with a gas cylinder by his feet. He flicked a cigarette lighter, holding the flame to the tip of a blowtorch. The gas blew it out, but lit at the second attempt, burning with a blue-orange flame. I watched him melt the amalgam and fix the tooth in the plate.

"There. That'll have to do." He turned off the gas and the flame died. It wasn't perfect, but the cylinder was running low and months might pass before he could get another. The Mayor was a sonofabitch anyway.

He swiveled in his chair. "I tell you, Joaquín, we've been afraid so long, we're not afraid. We're mad. Our blood has boiled over. It's bubbled into our eyes, our brains, and we're crazy. We'll strike at anything. I tell you this for your own safety."

Next door the girl began another song, a skipping-rope rhyme I used to chant with Nemecio.

*"Este niño mío, no quiere dormir . . ."*

Embarrassed, I said, "Señor Lazo, can I ask a favor?"

"Be careful, Joaquín, what you ask."

I told Lazo about the theft of my wallet at the high pass. "Could you lend me some money?"

He reached stiffly above him and tugged a pot from one of the shelves. He rooted inside, plucking out a bundle of notes.

"Take this. No, take it all. There's nothing to spend money on here. But pay it back to Graciela, would you?" On the back of an invoice he wrote down her address in the capital.

"Shall I take a letter from you?"

"What would I say?"

"You must have something you want to tell her."

"What? That she has no husband? No friends? Is that what you want me to write?"

"Then I'll tell her you're well and so is her daughter."

He closed his eyes and opened them. "No. In return for this money, you please tell her the truth. What happened."

"Very well."

I stooped, folded the address and the money into an inside pocket of the sports bag. I was about to close it when he said, "This is for you."

Lazo, hands trembling, held the portrait vase above my head.

A beautiful one, reddish-colored, with the traces of black brush-marked crosses and a face. He could have sold it in the capital for the equivalent of his annual income.

I got to my feet. "But that's—"

"Please, Joaquín. I'm too old to be argued with. I want you to have it." He was breathing fast, as if he had run up the road to bring it to me.

I turned the jug under the light. Off the shelf this was not a dull ornament in need of a good dusting. It struck me then—there, in Lazo's office—that within its simple shape, its rough patina, the nameless red of its pigmentation, the strong face, the sensual quality of its jaw and lips, there existed the gamut of beauty and terror.

He had dated it to the Chimu dynasty, he said. He'd bought it off a grave robber from the coast, near Moche. Probably it was the portrait vase of a king or shaman and had been buried with his shrouds.

I stammered my thanks, knowing what this gift meant to him.

"Your father, Joaquín. I loved him."

"Then I accept it in my father's memory." I wrapped the pot in a shirt and zipped up the bag.

He opened the door for me. "I keep the records in the other pots. In case we find the teeth."

We shook hands. There was a furtive quality to his touch, and I knew there was something he held back. Despite everything he had told me, about Father Ramón, about the army's reprisal, there was more to tell.

"*Porque el cuco malo está por venir . . .*" The song's words drifted from the dark hallway.

"Santiago Solano—was he killed too?"

"Santiago?" His fingers fretted at his temple. For a moment he was trying to recall whether that ditch had taken Santiago too. Then his face cleared. "No. I don't think so. I think he was out of town that day."

"Where would I find him?"

"He teaches at San Marcos."

I had to walk past the church to reach the school.

At my approach the pigeons on the dome exploded into the air, leaving the brickwork bald and white. Sandbags packed the entrance to the height of my chest. A chalked sign declared that the building was undergoing essential redecoration.

I felt the urge to pray. Between the sandbags a passage led to the wooden door. I assumed it would be locked, but the hinges were wrecked and it opened.

From my childhood I remembered aisles watched over by gold-haired saints, and a caoba wood floor dappled with green and blue window light, as if seen through deep water. My father, who calculated the windows to be three hundred years old, had traced their origin to a glassmaker from Salamanca. The grenade had blown them out.

I walked into the nave, one step at a time, over creaking floorboards. I had been baptized in this church. My parents had married here. Beneath the pulpit I learned to play the flute. Yet I didn't recognize the place. No plank pews. No saints. No Communion table. The nave glowed with a hygienic, Protestant light from the empty casements.

A plywood board, an inch thick, rocked beneath my feet where the grenade had landed. A stain darkened the floor all the way back to the entrance.

Whose body had they dragged outside? Nervy Jesús, who smiled with relief at her friends every time she sat down after reading the Gospel? Or Aguilina, who wore a hairnet, which gave to her head the appearance of something imperfectly, patchily dyed? Or Prudencia—a gossip with balcony-hardened elbows—always patting her wet hair and saying "La Posta is such a dirty place"? Or María, who had never been the same since the Turk's tin sign for paraffin had fallen on her head in a gale?

Perhaps this bloodstain wasn't a woman's. Perhaps one of the men had crawled back into the church. Lazo's son-in-law, the postman, who often delivered letters to the wrong houses, a nice man with a pencil-sharp chin whose name I couldn't remember but didn't have the courage, just now, to ask for. Or Nemecio.

The afternoon sun simmered on the pillars. Blotches of cement spoke of an attempt to conceal the damage. Limbs, eyes, blood, glass, screams. Standing on this spot, I hated myself. I had left this valley to work for the law—and this was how the law had repaid my people.

The soldiers had thrown the headless saints into the storage room. Chips of gold plaster scattered all over the floor. There were ripped hassocks and cigarette ends and something metallic. When I held it to the window, I saw that it was a spent cartridge case, regular army issue.

The mahogany lectern toppled at an angle against a twisted metal chair. I pulled the eagle upright. The blast had removed one wing. I wanted to feel an emotion, be moved, but my only desire was to get outside. I had reached the storage room door when my eye was drawn to the wrecked diptych behind it. Through the mangled fronds of canvas I saw Father Ramón's cassette recorder. There was a tape still inside.

On this machine, every Saturday, the priest would record his twenty-minute talk. He would give the tape to one of the altar boys—Santiago usually—who would then run with it to the radio station. His sermons were immensely popular, their influence extending into the neighboring valleys. On a tape like this our priest would have recorded his attacks on Ezequiel.

I pressed the start key. The spools revolved. In a voice from which he couldn't keep his delight, I heard Father Ramón telling a story about Leonardo's *Last Supper*:

". . . try as he might—and how hard he tried!—he couldn't find the model for Judas! He had painted all the disciples. There was this one blank. Years passed while he searched for a model with the appropriate expression. But no. There the fresco stood. Incomplete. And I have to tell you that Leonardo had given up on it. Until—incredibly—one day in the market he found the face he had been seeking all this time. Judas to the life! He showered money on the man, flattered him, dragged him back to his studio and set to work. Can't you imagine the energy with which he picked up his brushes? Then he looks up and what do you think he sees? His model, head buried in his hands, is weeping uncontrollably. What's up, asks Leonardo? What's wrong, man?

"At first the other shakes his head, like we all do when we

don't want to confess something. Finally, he blurts out the reason for his distress. Many years ago he had sat in the same chair. He had sat like this, exactly as he was required to sit now. But then he had been posing as Christ . . ."

I stopped the tape. I didn't know the moral of the story, didn't care. I was conscious of my own tears tickling my cheeks. Blindly I tried to get out of that room. I knocked an object to the floor, and I might have left it there, whatever it was, under the lectern where it had fallen. But something made me retrieve it.

An ashtray from Fátima. In the center was a reproduction of the apparition of Our Lady. Three children, watching in rapt attention, prayed to the Virgin, who was balanced on a cloud above some sheep. She held, flaming in her hands, a human heart, in shape and color resembling a red pepper. Circles of dark brown tar obscured the Virgin's face and part of a message reading GOD'S FIERY SIGNATURE.

I packed the ashtray in my bag and went to look for Santiago.


He was teaching a class of bored children. He lifted his arm and scratched a sum on the board, savored its meaning and chalked another sum, not glancing around.

After the class he came up to me and we stood there and looked at each other. His face, always so much his own, seemed composed of other people's features. He hadn't shaved and his beard escaped from his chin in wisps, while his fairer hair sprang straight from the scalp as if something had shocked it. When young, his eyes had had the expression of a child in a playground. Now, thin as a lamppost, he had the stone-gray eyes of a plundered soul. Perhaps that's what he thought about me.

"Hello, Santiago."

"What brings you back?" He was not surprised to see me.

"It doesn't feel the same place."

"Blame your people for that."

"They're not my people."

"Military, police, what difference?"

"I've just seen the church. It's monstrous."

We walked out of the gates into the street.

"But any organization is like this," I said. "People can go mad within it."

He shot me a look. "Why have you come back? What do you want?"

"To see you," I said.

He strode a pace ahead, keen to get home.

I said, "I talked to your mother."

"We haven't been in touch."

"She hadn't heard about Father Ramón. I had to tell her."

He unlocked a door. The spirit of the sixties lingered like a joss stick in the room. A poster of a Brecht play. The sleeve of a Beatles record. Books stacked against the wall: Marx, Kant, Bakunin, Camus. I had parroted their ideas during Fuente's revolt. Once, in an "underground" café in Pachuca, I had listened to Santiago quote Lukács in defense of murder, a hint of madness in his eyes. My revolutionary ardor dimmed when the left-wing military took power. I ought to have approved of their seizure of the coffee farm. My correct reaction should have been: if our hacienda, seized in the people's name, would better serve the masses, so be it. But that's not what I felt.

"Weren't you going to be a priest?" I put down my bag and sat. The sofa, covered in pillows, lacked an arm.

"I changed my mind at university." Santiago, holding a tray, came out of the kitchen. He poured a mug of strong tea.

"You're not drinking?"

He patted himself. "Stomach upset."

He drew the curtain and sat down, crossing and recrossing his legs.

"What with the drought and the bridge being closed, we haven't eaten well."

Do you have friends you half apologize for, but whom you would hope to defend if they were criticized? At school Santiago had possessed a guileless quality which moved me to protect him. What had kept our relationship from developing into the sort of friendship I enjoyed with Nemecio was his stubbornness. No sooner did he find a phrase that pleased him than he would repeat it like a rosary. The same with his ideas. If anyone interrupted him, his lower lip would tremble. He had the inflexibility of an actor who has grown too much into his part. An unscripted line he saw as a terrible threat.

I think this explains what happened after his mother left the valley for a stranger, a man much younger than herself. I was already at the Police Academy when she discovered her lover's cotton fields were no more extensive than the bar in Cayara where he was employed to collect empties and wipe the tables. My sister wrote to say Santiago had been badly affected by his mother's defection. It must have been at about this time that he shifted the focus of his reverence.

"What did you study?" I asked.

"Religion, for a term. Then philosophy."

"The opium of the people, eh?"

"If you like."

"Because you were very religious, and all of a sudden you changed your mind."

"It seemed irrelevant to what was happening around us."

"Do you think Father Ramón was irrelevant? You used to admire him, all the good things he did. What seems irrelevant to you is the fact he's been killed."

"At least Ezequiel has drawn the attention of the government—who would rather forget us. We ask for clinics and what do they give us? Grenades. No, Agustín, the revolution must put up with its own violence or be fucked."

"Then you accept Father Ramón's death?"

His mouth folded up. "That—it's not something I can explain. It—"

"Don't you feel disgusted?"

His eyes blinked, gray, nervous, strained.

"Well, no. Not really. But yes."

"If there's a word to justify such an action, then tell it to me, Santiago."

He stared at the back of his hands, licking his lip.

I said, "Then you understand how I feel when I'm confronted by the sight of that church as evidence of what I'm doing, or what my side is doing. But I tell you this. I'm leaving here tomorrow and my first action will be to file a report. I want to see the people who did this in prison as much as you do. You, on the other hand, have to play your part. What happened to our priest is no less reprehensible. You didn't kill him any more than I threw that grenade, but if this sort of thing is to stop, we must help each other."

"There are bound to be accidents," said Santiago. " 'To act immorally is the highest sacrifice the revolution demands.' Remember? Besides, Ramón had been speaking out against Ezequiel. He was judged an enemy of the people." The rhythm of his speech was too fast, too stuttering.

"Rhetoric is rhetoric, Santiago. Could you have stood there and spouted that stuff as they forced him to eat his Bible? Any more than I could have stood and watched that soldier toss his grenade into the church? I would have done all in my power to stop him."

"Kant says—"

"What does Kant have to do with anybody in this valley? Didn't they teach you Plato, for God's sake? Philosophy is impossible among the common people."

"The communists ban Plato."

"So do the fascists," I said.

"Kant is relevant. If we live according to his precepts, we will achieve perpetual peace."

"And old priests will be found slaughtered on riverbanks till the end of time."

"Through Kant and Mao," he persisted, "Ezequiel has constructed a cosmology that can be understood by the masses."

"Reality is stronger than any cosmology. Ezequiel's ideology has no basis in fact. Look around you, man. Communism is dead, even in Albania. If Ezequiel is the rational person he claims to be, he would have come to accept the changes in the world. He's like a chicken tottering about after its head has been cut off."

"I promise you, his revolution—"

Santiago was scrambling now. He retreated into the bleak, unsubtle territory of revolutionary socialism, the Kantian dialectic as promoted through the books strewn on his floor. Capitalist society reduced our people to objects. Those old women outside were of no more importance to the state than their pathetic shawlfuls of potatoes. Clinging to the wreckage of familiar jargon, he addressed his words not to me but to the world. But it was the shadow of a speech composed by another.

I listened, and I understood what had happened. At university, while I studied law, Santiago had transferred into the political sphere this moral stubbornness of his, this obstinacy that brooked no opposition. He had wanted to be a priest, but he had come up against an absolutism more attractive than Father Ramón's bustling humanity.

*Such people are always hungry for imperatives when those imperatives coincide with their own.* And who was it who supplied what Santiago sought? Ezequiel, that poisonous red mushroom created by Kant. My fellow altar boy would, of course, have perceived in Ezequiel's Kant a disembodied Christianity. Treat all mankind as your equal, everybody as a person, nobody as a thing. Look to yourself as the source of order. How alluring it must have seemed. But it was not what Ezequiel had meant at all.

I had heard enough. I interrupted the speech. "It's cowardly to set philosophy above life when such atrocious things have happened, are still happening. Cowardly and evil. Tell me, why is it that people who espouse Kant's liberation doctrine always end up putting other people in chains? I could use Kant to justify bourgeois morality, yet you use his categorical imperative to justify Father Ramón's murder. Why, Santiago? Why?"

"So I'm nuts, completely nuts. What do you want me to say?"

"I want to know who killed him."

"Forget it."

"Under the Emergency Code, I could arrest you for everything you've said. These books alone—"

"Look, don't make threats about arresting me—I just need to yell 'police' and everyone in town will come running."

"Fine. I'll go away. I'll build the evidence against you. I'll watch you night and day. And then I'll come back. Do I have to spell it out?"

He looked down at my feet. "Why do all policemen wear white socks?"

"Who supplies the food? Who are Ezequiel's contacts in the village?"

He threw himself back. "I don't know. I don't know."

"But you know about Father Ramón. I'm certain you do."

His lower lip trembled and he clutched his knees. When he raised his head, his eyes were not looking at me but at the side of my face. "You don't understand. I've signed a blood pact with these people."

"You're a lot better off dealing with me, buddy. You know Ezequiel's ways. If he discovers we're friends, he is likely to make the same moral sacrifice of you that he made of Father Ramón. And you've seen how the military behave. It's a miracle they didn't get you last time. You're fucked, Santiago."

I gave it time to sink home. Then I said reasonably, "It could be lucrative, you know. How much do you earn teaching algebra? I can offer you more. A reward. Start-up capital. Settle you in a new country, new identity, leave all this despair behind. Miami. White beaches. The good life."

"Go on, Agustín, squeeze my balls some more."

"Don't you see? Ezequiel's made an idiot of you. Is that what you wanted when you were an altar boy? To see your priest, the person in the world you most wanted to emulate, choke on his Bible, see him gutted like a fish, see his face sliced off?"

No reply. He was not listening. In a faraway tone he addressed the sofa beside me, breathing uneasily. "They came here after they'd done it. They wanted bed and food."

"How many?"

"Three."

"Male, female?"

"Two men, and a woman who was in charge."

"How old? Where was she from? Was she educated?"

"It was Edith."

"Edith? From Pachuca?" A girl with cold, mint eyes and makeup who wouldn't dance with us.

"Ramón had to be punished by someone he knew," he said doggedly.

"Where is Edith now?"

"No idea. They operate away from home. Like your army friends."

"But she used to live in the next valley."

"Not for twenty years."

"How did she behave? What did she say?"

"She said be patient, the revolution was in our grasp."

"And the men with her?"

"Kept pretty quiet. Said almost nothing."

"You knew them?"

"No. They were from the capital."

Had Edith slept on this sofa afterward?

"Did they want you to lead them to Father Ramón? Is that what they wanted?"

"They were angry about his sermons. His attacks on Ezequiel."

"He had also spoken out against the army."

"Anyway, I wasn't here."

"But you were here when they came back."

"That's right."

"Where were you, Santiago?"

Dismally, he said, "A woman. She's married. I see her in the afternoons. You can have her name, if you like."

I didn't want to hear more. "How do you feel? You waited all these years for the call, and this is what the revolution demanded—and you weren't even here. Nor when they killed Nemecio and the others."

"No, I wasn't. And by God, Agustín . . ."

"How did you know who these people were? How did you know they weren't spies?"

Santiago got up and went into his bedroom. A cupboard creaked. He came out again, unfolding a piece of paper.

"Here. This is all I can offer you. This is all I know. This is all I have."

A photocopy of a computer printout. Four names, each listed for a village in the area. At the bottom, on its own, a telephone number prefixed by the code for the capital.

"You're 'Comrade Arturo'?"

"That's what they called me at university. I had no choice. Don't ask who the others are. I've no idea."

"What about this number with no name?"

"She said to use it in an emergency."

I copied down the information.

"Do you still play the flute?" he said in a not very interested way.

"No."

"I'll never forget the sound you made as we came down the glacier."

"And you, Santiago, do you still sing?"

Before he could answer, voices sounded in the street. He jumped up, parting the curtain. "I told them to play in the yard!" Someone pounded on the door. Santiago said, "Excuse me." He puckered his lips in a schoolmasterly way and charged out into the street.

I heard animated snatches of conversation. Then he came back in. He shut the door, leaning against it. "The class is waiting. I have to go back."

I picked up my bag. For the first time Santiago seemed to notice it. "Wait. Where are you staying?"

"Your old hotel, if it's still open."

"When did you arrive?"

"This morning."

"You had no problems?"

"What kind of problems?"

"I don't know. From the people."

"An old woman screamed at me. A donkey boy ran off when he saw me."

He blocked my way, staring at me hard. I had seen the same look in Lazo's eyes. He looked down at my bag again. "They've had enough, Agustín."

"What do you mean?"

"They're suspicious of everybody. A man carrying a bag like yours, he was killed last week."

"A man? From the village?"

"Nobody you'd know. A commercial traveler from Pachuca."

"What was he carrying?"

"Just samples."

"Samples of what?"

"Brushes, scissors, combs, the usual stuff. He was going from door to door trying to interest people. But the whisper went around. He was a *pishtaco*. He'd come to abduct our children, cut them up, boil their limbs for grease."

Do you know the *pishtaco* myth? My mother, who worshipped mountain spirits, tried to make us believe in this creature. She warned us not to go out at night or we would find, waiting for us, a stranger in a long white cloak. He had been sent by the authorities to rob us of our body grease. He would carry us to his lair, string us upside down and collect our dripping fat in a tub. She said the *pishtaco*'s favorite delicacy was the meat of young children, which he sold to restaurants in the city. My sister and I assumed she used this bogeyman to stop us roaming too far from the farm.

I said to Santiago, "They can't believe this. Not seriously?"

"They don't know what to believe. They say those who have disappeared are demanding some explanation. They say policemen in disguise have been sent to extract our grease. They say that with this grease the government can buy weapons to fight Ezequiel."

"Who believes this?"

"Who doesn't? I'm telling you, don't go out at night, Agustín. Because that's when they seized this man. He'd been trying to sell to the barber and they descended on him. A crowd, fifty at least, old men and women, terrified for their grandchildren. The noise, I can't describe it. They were beating pan lids, screaming and chanting. One of my pupils saw it from her bedroom. They knelt on him. They searched his pockets. Nothing. Then his bag. Inside they found scissors, nail clippers, penknives, needles. That proved it. So they lynched him. It was like a *ch'illa*."

You see, this was another thing about a *pishtaco*. You couldn't shoot him. My mother said the only way to kill a *pishtaco* was to gang up and use his own methods on him. A *ch'illa* was how the farmers sacrificed their llamas.

"They tore out his eyeballs, but they didn't stop there. They ripped off his balls and then they plucked out his heart. He was still alive. I heard the screams from this room."

The army buried him near the bridge. No one knew his name, nor what he had looked like. The people had dragged him through the streets until his bones showed through the scraped flesh.

"I hear the pan lids every night."

"Is that what you were discussing outside?"

"One of the kids spotted someone on the upper road. It's exciting for them. In daylight it's easy to dismiss as a joke. But it's not. If you go to the hotel, take my advice. Stay inside." He nodded at the sofa. "I'd offer you a bed here . . ." He couldn't hide his thoughts.

"It's all right, Santiago." I had exacted enough.

He jerked up his thumb, relieved. "So long, then, Agustín. If you catch Ezequiel, give me a call."

"Look, I'm serious, what I said about money. About a reward."

Emphatically, he shook his head. And that's how we left each other, making vague promises which neither of us thought we would keep.


I decided to sleep the night at our farm.

The bridge had reopened days before, repaired by army engineers from a base in Pachuca. Below me the gully squeezed out a torrent of icy water.

The rain had come too late to work its miracle on the valley. The drought had filched the colors from the mountains, and the familiar contours were streaked with the dark brown shades of a buzzard's wing. The sight of the pinched terraces, slipping away into ridges of cracked earth, ploughed up buried voices. I heard my mother saying, "If you don't play your flute, the rains won't come and the coffee won't grow."

I followed a line of hoofprints. They stamped ahead of me over the clay, disappearing off the road down a steep track. Down that track the frightened animals would have stumbled to the airstrip. I stepped onto the verge and looked from the river—glinting, a little swollen, through a bluish haze—to the flat field below. Unable to contemplate the passage of the horses and their load, I grasped at another image.

I thought of the day I left home.

My mother is driving our truck along this road so I can catch the bus. I'm eighteen, going to the capital to study law. I sit between my mother and my father, who has my sister on his lap.

Since it's my last day, everyone is making an effort. But it isn't a happy occasion. A week ago an army jeep delivered an envelope to my father. We haven't been told what it contained, but after overhearing the Turk in the butcher's shop, I know.

I am about to speak when my sister points. "Look!" Covering the field, a flock of green parrots.

You must have seen them. You can tell you're up north when you hear those birds. They're hard to make out on the ground. You see a green bush, and then the whole thing lifts and the way the light falls on their feathers as they tilt makes it seem the birds have changed color in midair. What has been green is violent red, and you are looking at another creature.

I expect my mother to stop the truck and shoo the parrots from the bushes. She detests these creatures. They eat the crops and she is forever asking my father to buy some poison. Whenever she hears a wingbeat, she dashes into the field and raps a kettle, shouting "hey-hey-HEY!" until they rise, shrieking, against the mountain.

But, as she sits beside me, her lips are closed.

We reach the road. My father slides out of the truck to open the wire gate. He waves my mother on, closes the gate and climbs back in. Normally this is my job. Today it's his treat to me.

I look back at our farm. It is an honest house and the view over the split-wood fence is identical in every direction. Bleached grass on the terraces. The shadows of large birds. Rain-streaked rocks. In winter, shoals of puffy clouds neatly arranged to the horizon. In summer, nothing but the sky. When it grew really hot, you'd get fireballs. On that sort of day the eucalyptus trees would explode.

Ezequiel grew up two hundred miles to the north, his house not unlike ours. He shared our river too. The Marañón springs from a limestone basin above the village. It becomes the Amazon a thousand miles away, but is already a substantial flow by the time it passes our fields. From the truck I can see the rapids.

"You'll miss the river," murmurs my father.

Last week when the moon was up, Santiago, Nemecio and I

tied hunks of meat to a string and threw the bait in the water. When the string went taut, we scooped the net under what clutched the meat and boiled up a paraffin can.

"You won't eat crayfish like this in law school," said Santiago.

My father, leaning against the window, observes his fields. The farm has been in his family since 12 August 1580, which he has read was a Wednesday. By the time he inherited from his uncle, it had dwindled to an estate of a hundred acres. But still large enough for the military to expropriate.

"Ouch," he says, adjusting his position. "You've become too heavy." This is an excuse. He wants to shift my sister off his lap so he can see the black roof now coming into view between the trees. His library.

I've never met a man so interested in books. Any hope of establishing a conversation with him is predicated on your being interested in what he is reading. Otherwise, as my mother says, it's a long cold night.

She jokes he is more concerned about his books than his family. The reason he pays attention to my sister is because, from when she was a small child, she liked to show him animals she'd captured by the river. She would ostentatiously play with them at his feet—toads, beetles, lizards, snails she'd scraped from the cactus. But he is not often seduced from his text, unless he treads on something on his way to the shelves. Scraping a snail from his shoe, he would exclaim, "The boys throw stones at the frogs in sport, but the frogs do not die in sport, they die in earnest."

At four o'clock every afternoon my mother joins him in his library, nudging open the door, with a glass of red syrup for his chest. Together they raise Pachuca, the nearest big town, on the transmitter and take orders for coffee beans—fewer and fewer orders since the creation of the government cooperative. Then, until it is time for dinner, she abandons my father to his books.

And last week a man he has never met, made important by a soldier's uniform, has written to say: all this, it's over; it's no longer yours, it's mine.

He jerks his head. "Martha . . ."

"Yes, dear?"

We wait for him to speak. But it's my last day. "Oh . . . nothing," and he investigates his foot.

My mother is an Ashaninka, pure. She has been his house-keeper since he was twenty and is sharp and sweet. She has high moral standards and shoulders lopsided from picking his coffee. If I look at my face, I see my father's Spanish nose. From my mother I inherited my coloring.

"I've packed your flute," she says.

"Oh, good. Thank you." I had wrapped the *pinkullo* in a sweater and hidden it in the back of my drawer so she wouldn't find it.

"They'll keep you busy at university, but try to practice."

"I will."

Her eyes, which nest in the fine lines of her round face, smile trustingly. She wipes the condensation from the windshield and drives off the road, down the track, toward the Weeping Terrace.

Before I catch the bus, family and friends are to assemble on this field where by tradition the villagers meet to say goodbye. It's a rare event for any of us to leave the valley and we will hug and cry and sing special, very sad songs. I've witnessed these farewells, and hated them. My mother has forced me to learn the flute so I can participate in ceremonies like this one, but I don't believe in her music any more than I believe in my father's books. They haven't saved the farm. These rituals embarrass me.

Political, ignorant, mad to get away, I am a young eighteen.

We are early. We wait on a bank of sharp sedge grass while my mother extracts the *pinkullo*. She plays some notes and hands me the flute.

"Dirty girl," says my father, picking grass from my sister's back. But the set of his shoulders says, What are we going to do, Martha?

"Papa . . ." I wish he'd speak to me. He wanted me to inherit the farm.

"Look, there's Father Ramón!" My mother points at the priest, who is stumbling toward us down the hill.

"You'll trip over your surplice," she calls.

"Agustín! Agustín! Thank heavens, I've caught you . . . ." He slows to a walk as he nears us, then stops and slaps his belly, catching his breath.

He has been at the radio station, he gasps. Delivering his sermon early so he could join us. He grips my shoulder while addressing my mother.

"Before I forget, thank you for the most delicious dinner last night. The tongues were excellent. Nemecio and I agreed . . ." and the rest of his sentence is consumed in a fit of coughing.

"Shouldn't smoke, Father," flirts my sister. She is the one who gets around everybody.

"Now, now," and he coughs louder.

I ask, "Where is Nemecio?" But I can see him with Santiago, waving from the road above. He spreads his arms into wings and zigzags down the bank. It's the last time I will see him.

"Agustín, I want to give you this." Father Ramón hitches up his surplice, revealing dirty tennis shoes. He plucks a hand from the folds. "No." I take a step back. "I can't. Not possibly."

Coiled in his palm, his silver chain with its pendant. Our Lady of Fátima.

"Trust her, and you'll get through your law exams." He advances, spreading the chain into a circle. "Always remember, God's mercy is more powerful than God's justice." He drops it over my head.

Look. I still wear it.


I got to our farm in the late afternoon.

It stood at the end of a subdued avenue of eucalyptus. The view of the house held no surprises, but I was not prepared for the emotion it aroused. I hastened toward the buildings as if the river would drag them away before I reached them.

The trees opened into the yard where we would heap the dispulped berries. I stood by the concrete water tank. Faintly on the air came something I hadn't smelled for twenty years: the scent of the rotting honey which coated the beans.

The buildings were deserted. All I heard was my breathing. Lack of sound in these valleys meant lack of life, another reason my mother made me learn the *pinkullo*. Music and dance for her were practical necessities, the melodies she urged me to collect as vital in their way as my father's crops. Silence spoke only of blight.

Now, up close, I saw the devastated fields around the house. The earth had separated into fissures wider than my outstretched arms. Shrubs poked into the air, unprotected against the sun, strangled by vines. My father had not been a successful farmer, yet those who replaced him had understood his crops less.

I walked through the rooms, not taking much in. Broken glass on the kitchen floor. In my bedroom, a cardboard box spilling over with magazines. A drawer chinking with dead light bulbs. The farm had been seized in the people's name, and the people had not known what to do with it.

I crossed the yard to the old depot. Beside the door, on its side, crouched the rusted carcass of the English-built generator. My father boasted that it had pumped in the same peevish rhythm since 1912. It had powered the dryer for the berries and the transmitter in his library and the lamp by which he read.

The door had been torn away. The floor was a mess of empty sacks and gasoline drums. Termites had crumbled the pillars, and the roof in listing had shed most of its panels to the floor. I approached a heap lying at the end of a beam of sunlight: the blackened remains of a gut-shot dog, the floor showing through its eye sockets. I heard my father's voice: "Wherever you see the military, you see stray dogs."

Something smelled; the dog, I thought—but it was me. I had worn the same clothes for three days.

I washed everything in the river, including myself. On the opposite bank a thin mare was eating a mouthful of yellow grass. Like a ballerina, she rubbed her head against an outstretched leg. When I fell backward, naked, into the water, she cantered off, kicking against the flies.

The sun was hidden by the mountains, but the air was warm and when I got out of the river my skin dried quickly.

I was hungry. Tucked under the bank, in a pool where we often trapped trout, I noticed two dark shadows and a lazy bubble trail. I went back to the house, mended a net I found hanging in the library, and in a short time landed two small fish.

I gathered firewood, built a fire in the yard and cooked the trout. But I could barely keep awake to eat. I had spent the previous night rolling and bumping in the back of the pickup from Pachuca. The night before, I had sat unsleeping in the truck. I changed into a fresh shirt, rested my head against my bag and fell asleep beside the fire.

A penetrating cry dissolved into stillness. The cry rose again. It became part of my dream, a dream in which I saw the eye whites of terrified animals, hooves kicking against a stenchy load, teeth tearing at their own necks. I heard the whinnies of those creatures as they picked their way, or were dragged or beaten, across the stream. And, again, the cry.

I scrambled to my feet. The road above jittered with orange lights. Tall shadows flared on the cliff. The sides of the gorge magnified the clamor. I heard animals howling, men shouting, a clashing of steel like the sound of my mother beating her kettle.

The flames jerked down the bank. A line of upright shapes stumbled into the avenue. Dogs barked. Back and forth, torchlight flashed on the eucalyptus, shooting up the trunks to a great height. Then the lights were snatched away to kindle another patch of darkness.

The shouts were distinct now, male and female, but mostly female, older rather than younger; after so many years of frugality and silence, a hysterical release of pent-up rage, despair and grief.

*"Pishtaco! Pishtaco!"*

I leapt back from the fire, ran across the yard, took refuge inside the library. The blood seethed through my head. Who were these people? Whom were they chasing? Did I know the person? Half-asleep, exhausted, I asked myself these questions. I believed they had pursued their quarry all this way from the village. They had frightened him into the fields and now were flushing him out with their pan lids and burning brands.

I peered down the avenue, expecting to see a figure flitting like an exhausted bat between the trees. Nobody. Nothing moved toward me, save for those flames.

Now I could make out the forerunners. As well as their torches, they held sticks. The dogs tossed their heads, teeth flashing in the lights.

Then from that swarm of shadows I heard a woman's scream.

It was a sound from which all the flesh had been removed and only the raw bone showed. A voice ecstatic with hatred.

"*Pishtaco!* There he is!"

I ran to the river, wading into the fast-running water, the bag with Lazo's jug in it poised over my head. In midstream I slipped on a stone, but the current buoyed me up and I allowed it to bob me along. A short distance away the river broke into rapids. I floated on—not far—to the next bend and found my feet, splashing to the bank. As soon as I reached the level of the field, I doubled back through the shrubs until I knelt about fifty yards from the crowd. Slowly I raised my head.

They hadn't followed me. They trained their attention on my fire. To a frightened people looking for what they needed to find, these flames in a deserted farm signaled one thing. *Pishtaco.*

An old woman—perhaps the one who had screamed—danced toward the fire. She stamped her feet, sending up scuffs of earth, twisting her body in an untidy sway. Once, livid with my father over something, my mother had shuffled the same steps.

Spread out around the flames were other shriveled figures. Chanting together, they urged her on. Light played over their quivering throats, their downturned mouths, their brainwashed faces. They looked like creatures made of earth. "*Pishtaco, pishtaco, pishtaco,*" they sang tonelessly.

The woman was dancing away the alien, the flesh-eater.

She finished. A man's voice said, "He's not here. Where is he?"

The faces disappeared. Dogs were called and the lights doddered through the house. Sparks drifted up through the library roof. A fierce beam of torchlight investigated the rafters.

"Over there! Something moved!" But it was another's shadow.

From the river, in a voice I thought I knew, an old man shouted, "He's in the water!" My shirt and trousers—which I had spread on the rocks to dry—were brought for inspection, then cast into the fire. The thrower knelt down, puffing at the embers. The flames illuminated a face that could have been Lazo's—but from that distance, in that glow, I was not certain of anything.

If it was Lazo and he caught me, would I be able to reassure him, make him call them off? Or would he tear out my eyes?

An old woman, her back framed by the fire, suddenly turned

and scrutinized the darkness that engulfed me. She held up a lantern, and its light slanted across a ravined cheek. I heard her say to two other women, "Come on, let's check this field." One of them whistled. A dog lifted its nose from the fish bones. Swiftly—very swiftly, given their age—the three of them struck out in my direction.

I scrambled through the undergrowth. Brambles tore at my face. I wasn't sobbing yet, but I felt a stab of terror. I crawled on hands and knees, feeling a way between the roots and over ditches. After twenty yards or so the ground suddenly gave way and I fell through black air. My arm flailed, striking a bush—which I grabbed. Rigid with dread, I hauled myself back to the surface and lay on the lip of the crevice, hugging the bag to my chest, panting and trembling. Branches snapped. A dog barked. Daggers of light converged toward me. I had no time left.

How wide the crevice was, I couldn't tell. I kicked out and touched earth a yard away. But how deep? *There are cracks so wide you can't see the bottom.* To measure the depth, I gripped the bush and lowered myself, feeling for the bottom with one foot. The sides started to narrow almost immediately. I let myself down a little farther. The crevice seemed to shrink to the width of a man's waist. But I could not feel the bottom. The ground reverberated with trampling feet. What if Lazo was right? What if this plunged into the heart of the earth? I twisted my head. The tips of branches glinted twenty yards away. I could hear a hungry snuffling. A bush shuddered.

I released my grip and slithered down until I was wedged. Above me was the vast indifference of the night. Then sparks drifted among the stars. They had set fire to the house.

At that moment I wanted to kill Ezequiel. Had he been sandwiched in the earth and I had appeared on the lip, I would have stamped him into that bitter-smelling oblivion.

# 11

Next evening, waiting for Rejas, Dyer had opened a second packet of breadsticks. Without a word, Emilio lifted the book and flicked the crumbs into his cupped hand. Then, in his grubby, overlarge jacket, his bow tie at an angle, he walked ponderously onto the balcony and flung out his hand, scattering the crumbs.

Nine o'clock. A samba racketed from the fortress. Through the window drifted dog barks, engines panting and the leathery smell of night.

"Where is he?"

Coming back inside, the waiter shrugged.

"Do you know where his sister lives?"

Emilio flicked a napkin over the seat of the empty chair, avoiding Dyer's eye.

"Do you know her name?"

No reaction. Across the river, darkly spread against the last traces of a dramatic sunset, the jungle lifted ragged wings. Dyer could see, between the acanthus scrolls of the balustrade, the water rolling by and foam curling from a prow. A garbage boat. Sluggish, unimpressible, varnished by a low moon, the river had Emilio's face.

Dyer ordered a beer. At nine-thirty he heard someone on the stairs. The curtain rustled and two faces poked, one above the other, through the beads. The taller, European-looking, wore a ponytail and chewed a mango noisily. At first Dyer thought they were musicians, wondering whether to play. Then he saw a pair of flippers dangling from the taller man's neck, and, attached to his belt, some goggles. Two divers, more likely, looking for a buddy or a good time. "Come on, Mr. Silkleigh, there's nothing for us here," decided the lower head, impatient. "Righto, old thing." The discussion over, they withdrew. Dyer heard their footsteps descending and a catcall from the square.

Ten o'clock.

Last night Rejas had left Dyer down a dark hole, expecting to have his eyes torn out. Surely he couldn't have intended to leave him hanging at such a point? Dyer had listened to people's stories all his life. Why was he so engrossed by this one? However dimly, he must have suspected where Rejas was leading. The policeman's narrative beckoned, and not just because he had fought against a darkness unlike any Dyer had known.

"Another beer."

That darkness, that darkness—suddenly it flickered through him like a nausea. Jaime, wasn't that his name, the journalist from Villoria who'd had his tongue cut out? No, Juan, that's who it was. Or maybe it was Julio. Dyer had met him only once, for a beer, at the Versailles Bar in Plaza San Martín. Gray jersey, shiny black bomber jacket, fattish. Dyer must have seen the tongue when Julio licked his fingers to turn the pages of the thesis he had brought with him. He'd written this about Ezequiel, his years at Santa Eufemia University. It was one of three copies; the military had one, Ezequiel the other. The two professors assigned to supervise had both resigned out of fear. Ezequiel's comrades had rung him. A strange voice said, "Burn your copy. Show it to no one." If you're afraid of dying, you'll die many times. But if you've spent four years writing six hundred pages, what you want most in the world is readers. That's when Julio licked his fingers. The world needed to know this, how it started. He had been vehement on this point, fervent, but Dyer couldn't tell him that the world didn't care a fig, could not say that to a colleague, so he asked him, "Jaime, listen, who've you shown this to?" And Jaime had listed them, this American journalist—who Dyer knew was CIA—also a French journalist and one from Reuters, and now he was showing it to Dyer.

Wasn't he in danger? Oh, no. No, no. No. Besides, who would find out? Jaime didn't believe in Ezequiel's thousand eyes, Ezequiel's thousand ears. Propaganda.

Journalists can get like that with a story, when it becomes more important than their lives.

But someone found out. Must have. Jaime had been so pleased too. Kept saying "scoop." Wanted to know if that's what they called it in English. "Scoop?" In fact, that was the last word Dyer heard him say as they were leaving the bar, Jaime hopping from one leg to another, terrifically pleased with himself. A group of Ezequiel's followers imprisoned in Lurigancho had agreed to speak to him. In jail. "A scoop."

It was too. None of the press corps had been able to interview Ezequiel's people. This was Ezequiel's policy. He didn't like journalists. Journalists took sides, he said. So far he had killed forty-two.

Well, the prisoners granted Jaime his interview. The guards unlocked the door into the compound, let him through, turned the lock after him. An hour later a hand scratched at the grille. They had cut out his tongue.

Perhaps it was Jorge. The name didn't matter. The point was the tongue, and once Dyer thought of that gargling hole, he couldn't stop himself. The awful daring of a moment's surrender, wasn't that what Eliot had said? Or Pound?

Unasked, Emilio brought him another beer.

He was drinking to forget what he couldn't remember. Now that he thought about it, had Jorge's tongue in fact been cut out? Dyer hadn't seen it. Had anyone seen the tongue or the absence of tongue? What was to say that it didn't happen? That the whole story had been made up, its horror improved with the telling? Hadn't Dyer been culpable of treating Ezequiel like this? Hadn't he boasted he knew all about Ezequiel—yet if he was honest, if the man were sitting right opposite him now, in the seat he'd reserved for Rejas, who wasn't coming by the look of things, did Dyer know anything about the man? Really know? Some people devoted whole lives to this subject. Forty-two of his peers had given their lives to it. Dyer had been lucky so far, but there was no reason why his luck should continue. If he hadn't had connections, and Vivien Vallejo for an aunt, nobody would have had anything to do with him.

And Brazil? What did he know about Brazil? Come to that, what did he know about South America? He knew Spanish and Portuguese and a smattering of Guarani, but not so well that anyone would take him for a native speaker. In his articles he was able to present the continent as a novelty in England, but what right did he have to act as an intermediary?

His heyday had been the war in the Falklands and its aftermath. His dispatches towered above the others, not just because he spoke Spanish but because, by virtue of his upbringing in Latin America and his marriage to a Brazilian girl, he already had unrivaled contacts in the region. He won two consecutive press awards—one, for his interview with Lieutenant Colonel Rose, minutes after Rose had brokered the peace in Port Stanley; the second, for his investigation into the treatment of Amazon Indians. Excited by Latin America for the first time since Perón nationalized the railways, his newspaper had opened a bureau in Rio.

But interest had quickly flagged. Either he could keep up a steady flow of revelations about the destruction of the rain forest or Nazi-hunting in Paraguay, or the public did not want to know. *Our C2 readers aren't switched on to your neck of the woods.*

And now his aunt had disappeared and it was eleven o'clock in Pará and Rejas hadn't turned up and he felt like a shit because he hadn't told him who he was. Rejas had thought he was talking to a receptive stranger, but had grown suspicious. He must have used his contacts in the police force and found out about him and that was why he wasn't coming tonight and why Dyer would never see him again and would spend the rest of his life thrashing through the water without having heard the end of the story.

When he got to his room in the Hotel Seteais, he threw up. It had been a mistake not to order dinner.


In the morning Pará celebrated Corpus Christi. The young priest stood beneath an awning in the bed of a lorry, which took him at walking pace across the square, stopping at the steps of a church with three clockfaces. Attached to the fringed awning, two coffin-sized loudspeakers distorted the Eucharist. The congregation, dressed up, fanned their throats with hymn sheets until invited to sing. Their words emphasized the connection between Pará and the Old World: "O Jesus, you were born in Bethlehem, our brother city." Firecrackers burst noisily between the hymns.

Shaken from his bed by the din, Dyer got up—still in his clothes from the night before—and walked to the square.

His mood was penitential, but he lacked the energy to insinuate himself into the crush. His mouth was dry and he had an undergraduate's hangover. What he wanted most was coffee and a large glass of orange juice. He looked toward the restaurant, peering over the hymn sheet someone had given him, to see if Emilio had opened his shutters, when he saw Rejas standing in the recess behind the balcony.

Dyer, climbing the steep stairs, was worried in case Rejas might want to avoid him, but the policeman regretted his absence the night before: he had not been able to leave his sister. She had been unwell all afternoon. When she opened her eyes, her left pupil was turned outward and didn't respond to light.

"No news yet from the lab?"

"No."

They watched Emilio put down the coffee and orange juice. Rejas waited until the waiter was gone, then said, "You've been suborning my friend."

"I did ask him where your sister lived," admitted Dyer, embarrassed. "But he wouldn't tell me."

"No, he wouldn't. He comes from my valley. His family used to work in the hotel when it was owned by Santiago's mother. His wife looks after my sister. They were driven out by Ezequiel's people. My sister was happy to take them in."

"He's very protective . . ."

Rejas, changing the subject again, said, "What did you do yesterday? Did you find some Indians?"

"There's something I need to tell you," said Dyer.

"What is that?"

"I told you I was a writer. That's not the whole story. I'm a journalist."

Rejas gave him a quick, hard look. "I know who you are. I know your name, and your date of birth, and the name of the paper you write for."

"How did you know all this?"

"I knew it as soon as you told me that Señora Vallejo was your aunt. I've read your work." Rejas mentioned an article which had been translated in *La República,* one of the first studies of Ezequiel's movement to have been published in the West.

"Well, yes—yes, actually, I did write that."

Rejas said, though not disagreeably, "It was rather shallow, I thought. There were some inaccuracies too. And another article which upset a great many people in my country."

"I hadn't known until quite recently that it caused this offense."

"It doesn't matter." His smile was more a shrug than a reprimand.

"They were rather shallow," agreed Dyer. "What I write is bound to appear shallow to a participant. Journalists can't tell the whole story." He stopped. "But if you knew I was a journalist all along, why tell me your story? You must be aware of the risks."

Rejas, face between his hands, evaluated Dyer. "Do you write everything you are told?"

"If I judge it has political interest for my readers, yes."

Rejas considered this. "When you came here, what actually were you researching?"

To be able to tell the truth was suddenly more welcome to Dyer than fresh air. He explained the background to his journey to find Vivien, his failure to get an interview with Calderón.

"It seems I may have blotted my copybook."

Rejas shook his head. "Frankly, you ought to have known he wouldn't speak to you. He's practically ungetatable. That is the source of his power, as it was for Ezequiel. Why should he see you? He won't even see me."

"Calderón has reason to be frightened of you. It's hardly any wonder."

"No, it's not that. He just doesn't see people. That's not the way he works."

"But why would you want to reach him, Colonel? Except to tell him of your intentions."

For three nights, Dyer had kept his ferreting brain in check, hoarded the questions he wanted to ask. Now they tumbled out. "Ledesma of the PLP is vying with Temuco of the CPV for your hand in political marriage. Yet here you are, miles from home. All right, your sister's ill. But surely you have a plan? You must know that if the elections were held tomorrow, you'd have a chance of winning. You're an ideal figurehead for the People's Party. You would have an immense following. A great many people outside your own country, too, are aware of you, what you've done. The Brazilian press, if they had any idea you were here, would be marching up those steps in battalion strength."

He watched Rejas, waiting for a reaction. But he was trapped by the other man's unblinking gaze into rushing on. "So what would stop you running? What is stopping you running? Is Calderón frightened of your popularity?"

Rejas, a little impatient, said, "Who can say what Calderón thinks? I've left the stage, haven't I? I've gone away—which is what he wanted. I can't help it if the stage keeps coming back to me."

"I don't want to appear impertinent, but I have to ask. Will you run?"

"Maybe not. Maybe I will. Today is too soon to say. Neither yes nor no is yet the right answer."

"What do you need, then, what are you waiting for, to make up your mind?"

Rejas threw back his head, exasperated. "Let's just say that I need, in some way I haven't been able to arrive at, to reach an understanding."

"Are you talking about a deal? I can perfectly see, Colonel, what you could offer Calderón. But what could he propose to you?"

Rejas looked at Dyer a very long time, as if weighing whether to continue with the discussion.

Finally he said, "Let's get to the end of the story."

## 12

I returned to the capital by bus. The journey took three days. What sustained me was the piece of paper with Edith's emergency number on it. I had no idea of her position in Ezequiel's hierarchy, but she was obviously high up. If I could locate the address, I believed it would connect me to Ezequiel. I knew that number by heart.

We reached the outskirts at dusk. There was a blackout. Blue fireworks spattered the sky, a signal of some kind. I was certain a message lay encoded in those bursts of color, but could not guess what it might be.

The bus inched through the crowd. Fanned out beside the window, panicked men and women, heads down, walked rapidly from something. Families fleeing with their children, heading they didn't know where. A face twisted up at me, mouth open.

I had been gone nine days. Terror had sunk its fangs into the city.

We drove through the blacked-out suburbs. Pyramids of truck tires blazed on a hillside. The night smelled of burned rubber. Inside the bus we started coughing.

At eight-fifteen we were spat out into the chaos of the terminal. I pushed my bag through the crowd. The streets dinned with people bashing their car doors, hooting. In the middle of the road, as if answering to some weird impulse, a barefoot figure in striped pajamas and brandishing a straw hat directed the traffic.

"That's it, straight on. You'll get there."

Figures weaved between the car bumpers selling objects they

had looted. Beneath a set of dead traffic lights, a boy held up a canvas, ornately framed, of a peaceful European river scene. An accomplice, in jeans and a woolen hat, lowered his head beside a driver's window, offering a silver goblet to an alarmed woman. I crossed the road, searching for a bus to take me to Miraflores. Another firework exploded. A few feet away an antlered head reared glassy-eyed over the car hoods. Its throat lifted skyward, and then with a desultory toss, the head tilted and disappeared. Gripping the horns, a disheveled man in flapped-open coveralls said, "Twenty pesos, señor?"

There was no blackout in Miraflores. The bus might have rattled out of the darkness into another planet. Couples sat on benches, holding hands. In a café, brilliantly lit, a girl raised a glass of iced coffee to her lips and, laughing, wiped a cream spot off her nose. By the flowerbeds a man slapped his green mackintosh and called to his dog.

I stepped off at Parque Colón and hurried toward our flat.

I had not spoken to Sylvina since she'd driven me to the airport nine days before. I hoped she had not started to worry. Whenever my work took me outside the capital, I made certain to telephone. I would write down a list of things I wanted to say and never get around to saying them. But always I called.

This evening I desperately wanted to talk to someone.

Laura, her face lifted to the ceiling, sat at the end of the table while Sylvina applied a gray paste to her cheeks. A pink vinyl case gaped open, and scattered about it were a number of small gold pots with their tops off.

Sylvina stood back. Her mouth shone unnaturally bright and her eyes had the undaunted stare of the convert.

I looked at Laura. "What is going on?"

"Laura's been filling in for one of my clients, haven't you, darling? No, give it time to set."

"Clients?"

She kissed me, but not so as to disturb whatever she had smeared on her lips. "I've got six, Agustín. Six in three days! Patricia, Marina—I won't go on. They're coming tomorrow. Consuelo said she'd pop in, but wouldn't buy anything. Otherwise they've sworn to place an order, even if it's only an eyebrow pencil. People are wonderful."

Sylvina's scheme. Our salvation. I'd forgotten. From a leaflet on the table, a frosted blonde, teeth framed between bright lips, smiled at me. STRATEGY. A REVOLUTIONARY SKIN CARE FOR THE MATURE WOMAN.

"I know you don't like him, but Marco's office expressed these samples last week." She'd spent the last two days with Laura, learning the spiel, how to apply the cosmetics. "It's so exciting, Agustín."

My tired eyes took in the gold pots. Lip gloss. Throat creams. Concealers. Moisturizers. Foundations.

"We're going to make money, darling. Thousands of dollars in weeks. It's the Sally Fay promise. They're keen to get into our market. There's no one doing this here."

Laura lifted her head, trying to say something.

"No, don't speak yet. She's been very good, listening to my pitch. There's this pack of promotional material I'm expected to memorize."

"Sylvina—"

"They want me to put over the idea that Sally Fay works best when the products are used together."

"Sweetheart—"

"I've asked everyone to come over tomorrow without their makeup—so I can confirm their skin types."

She had stopped paying any attention to me. Here on this shrinking island of Miraflores she had found in that vinyl briefcase her answer to the horror.

She inspected Laura's closed lids. "Yes, it's ready to come off. How was your trip?"

I pulled out a chair. I wanted to tell her, but my words dissolved in the air between us.

"I'll tell you later." I sat down. "What's been going on here? You know there's a blackout in the suburbs?"

"To tell the truth, Sally Fay's been devouring my time. But you remind me: I must get more candles."

I turned to Laura. She was rubbing off what looked like dirt. "How are your new classes?"

Sylvina said on her behalf, "Going well, aren't they? I do like her teacher. Deliciously pretty and so dedicated with it. Nothing too much trouble. But it's all dance, dance, dance. I told her—not too sternly, I hope—'I want to see you with a boyfriend. This city is no place for a single girl.' By the way, Agustín, remember that pepper grinder? I can't find a new one anywhere. There. Show your father."

"How do I look?" said Laura.

"All right." The paste had turned her skin blotchy, as if she had stood too long in the shower. It made her resemble Marina's daughter.

She spat something out. "It tastes like seaweed."

I made myself a sandwich in the kitchen. I hadn't eaten since breakfast. The radio, which Sylvina sometimes left on for the cat, was playing classical music above the fridge. I made an unconvincing animal noise and the cat bolted.

A moment later Laura entered, holding it in her arms.

I looked at her and my heart turned out. "You wouldn't have enjoyed it."

She stamped her foot. "How do you know?"

"You couldn't have seen the Weeping Terrace. It's become an airstrip."

"Did you bring me a flute?" She saw I'd forgotten. "Oh, Daddy . . ." The cat leapt from her arms as she ran out.

I finished eating the sandwich and made a pot of tea. Outside I heard Sylvina speaking.

"What?" I put my head around the door.

She had taken up position in front of the mirror and was speaking to herself.

"All those companies you can't pronounce. It's so easy to understand and say Sally Fay. We're not trying to hide behind some exotic French name. Sally Fay takes you into the next millennium of skin care without you having to leave the comfort of your own living room . . . Laura? What comes next?"

". . . and because we don't have overheads . . ."

I took a shower. She was still speaking to herself when I came out of the bathroom, smiling in a way I'd not seen before.

She offered the mirror a tube.

"Now this is a really good defense against skin fatigue."


As soon as I awoke, I telephoned Sucre.

"Any luck with the chiropodist?"

"Nothing."

"Dr. Ephraim?"

"Ditto. No one suspicious."

"And the trash?"

"Nothing out of the ordinary, sir."

I read him the number Santiago had given me. "I want to know the address. A month ago it was hot."

"It could take a day."

"Take a day."

"Where can I reach you?"

"I'll ring in. I've got to repay a loan."


Lazo's daughter worked in a cavernous, ill-lit bakery opposite a tin-roofed church.

The manager agreed to spare her for five minutes. I didn't tell him who I was. Family business, I said. I'd come directly from the bank.

"Agustín."

She met me at the door, sleepy-faced. She had her father's eyes and her daughter's tight mouth. We kissed. Her cheeks smelled of flour.

"How did you find me?"

"No other bakeries on the hill."

"Your voice, it's deeper . . . but the same."

"You haven't changed either."

We were being polite. If you know someone as a child, you'll recognize them as an adult. For a few seconds she was the Graciela who loved detective stories and pizza with grated cheese. And I was the Agustín who played in a band.

"You're crazy, Agustín. Look at me. I'm exactly the same as I was twenty something years ago? Is that what you're telling me?"

Coquettishly, she fanned out her dress, releasing a floury puff, and pushed out a cumbersome hip.

The day was hot, but I could feel the hotter blast of the ovens. From inside, a man shouted.

"I'm coming," she called—then with sudden anger over her shoulder, "Jerk." She rubbed an eye. "Tell me, how is Papi?"

"He sends you his love. And some money."

"Didn't he write?" She leafed through the notes. "Nothing for me, no word?"

"He couldn't talk for long. He was mending the Mayor's teeth."

"Agustín, they—the military, I mean—found a piece of red cloth in my bedroom. It meant nothing. Tomasio used to wave it at the bulls. They said he was one of Ezequiel's men. I had to leave . . ." She looked down the hill, over the ghetto of dust-colored houses. This was not what she'd anticipated when she stepped onto the bus in La Posta. The night before, the second in succession, the army had choked the streets of the capital, had beaten down doors, had thrust people into vans.

"But you say Papi's well, and Francesca, did you see her, how does she look, Agustín? Has she lost that sore on her arm? It wouldn't go away."

"Your daughter's well."

"I want her here with me, but I'm waiting to hear from Tomasio. Did you see Tomasio? He said he'd write—but I haven't heard."

"I didn't see him."

"It would be just like Tomasio to send his letter to the wrong address."

*In return for this money, you please tell her the truth. What happened.*

I could not look her in the face, embedded my stare instead in her dress. Then, gently, I asked if we could find somewhere quiet to sit down.

An hour later, exhausted and on the verge of retching, I drove over the Rímac bridge.

I could taste the Styrofoam cup which Graciela had filled with lukewarm coffee. Not thinking, I drove to Miraflores. Whenever Sylvina needed to forget an unpleasantness, she shopped.

I walked into an arcade, looking for presents for my wife, for Laura. But in each window the glass reflected back a dress scrunched at the knees, and two flour-covered hands clawing at printed yellow flowers, mashing them.

I turned away. What was I doing in a shopping arcade? I couldn't afford presents anyway. I moved toward the daylight— and it was at that moment I recognized the silhouette of Laura's ballet teacher.

She wore, despite the heat, a pale pink sweater—V-necked, far too large for her, made of some fluffy angora stuff like kitten fur— over a black leotard and leggings. She stared at an enameled urn in the window.

"Yolanda!"

She had a Walkman on. Her head swayed from side to side and her knees brushed against her shopping bag in abbreviated movements, shorthand for a dance.

"Yolanda!"

She had her hair pulled up with a dark green band and was wearing black Doc Martens—like combat boots, only with something very childish about them. Laura has a pair. They made her legs look thin.

Yolanda moved off, clasping a plastic bag to her chest. Not looking around, she walked out of the arcade, her stride long and loping.

Running into the street, I touched her shoulder.

She spun.

"Yolanda! It's me."

The muscles of her neck relaxed.

"I didn't see you," she called. She plucked off the headphones, slipping them over my ears. Her face, excited, awaited my reaction.

Have you had this feeling? You are sitting in a car, radio on, and across the street someone tunes in to the same frequency—but much louder. For a second you are physically somewhere else. That's how I felt. I was looking at Yolanda, but at the sound of those pipes a different air filled my chest and I knelt on the moon-blue rim of a glacier. I was planting candles in the ice while, beside me, Nemecio axed out a block to carry on his shoulders. The ice, melted into holy water, we would use as medicine.

"For my *Antigone.*"

"What do you mean?"

She stopped the tape. "That's the music I'm going to dance. I'd been stuck on something totally inappropriate—Penderecki. Then we—you and me, I mean—started talking about Ausangate and I had the idea."

I returned the headphones. "So your ballet, I haven't missed it?"

"It's this Sunday. Since I last saw you, I've been rehearsing, rehearsing, rehearsing. Suddenly I felt I had to get out or I'd go mad." She dropped the Walkman into her bag.

"It's wonderful to see you." My voice sounded far off to me, as if on the mountain.

"You're thinner," she said.

"I've been away." I hadn't combed my hair and my fingernails were filthy and she looked so alive with the sun on her face.

"I've missed our conversations. I've thought a lot about the other night. But what are you doing here?"

I shuffled my feet. I hadn't polished my shoes. My hands felt large, my palms sticky. "I was looking for a pepper grinder. And a flute."

"A flute? Don't you have one?"

"Let's see, what have you bought?"

She opened her bag. "A jersey for my brother."

"Let's see."

She held a yellow alpaca cardigan against my chest. I sucked in my stomach, conscious of the white-flour fingermarks on my shirt. Afterward, I'd held Graciela for ten minutes.

"He must be big, your brother."

"He is large."

I peered inside again. "And underpants!"

She folded the jersey back into the bag. I noticed how her nostrils flared a little whenever she wanted to change the subject. She said, "I've spent my money, but the real reason I came out was to buy a jug."

For a second time that day, I reached for my wallet. "I've just been to the bank. I owe you six weeks' tuition at least."

"Are you certain?"

Having paid Graciela what I had borrowed from her father, I had intended the rest of the money for Sylvina. Marco's dollar guarantee had not solved the problem of our finances, but because of it the bank had agreed to extend my overdraft.

"Take it while I have it." I waited while she tucked the money inside the jersey in her bag. "Where are you going now?"

"The theater where I'm dancing on Sunday. I must check the stage. Do you want to see?"

I needed to ring Sucre, but it could wait. "Is it far?"

"Five blocks. Come on." She touched my arm.


I must tell you about this in the right order. Before today I had met Yolanda twice. I had liked her, but it would be stupid to pretend that the thought of Laura's teacher sent me into a state of excitement. When, in the truck from Cajamarca, I had tried to recall her face, it had eluded me. She had contracted into a ballet dancer with a good figure and shoulder-length black hair.

As we walked up Calle Argentina, I found myself drawn to her again. You know how some people affect the air around them? You enter a room, a party, and immediately the crowd divides into those—the majority—who suck energy from you, and one or two who with their every look and gesture restore it. Yolanda was like that. She had—well, she had life.

She took my arm. "I thought you were afraid of me." Her cry was full of affection.

"Why?" I cut my eyes away to a stumpy man who was staring at Yolanda's chest: the low V of the fuzzy pink sweater, the scoop of leotard beneath it. He walked by, swinging his arms higher.

"You never come to the studio," she said.

"I've been away."

"You've been in the mountains. Laura was upset not to go with you. I want to hear everything."

I looked back at her face. The light falling through a tree played over her collarbones, her cheeks, the dark notes in her hair. Her eyes were big and slanted, but in a beautiful way. I felt an urge to tell her everything.

"The new classes—are they a success?"

She stopped. "That girl of yours, now there's someone who can really do it. She's talented and it sings out, and then doesn't she know it. She knows. I told you I was right. If you'd watched her last week . . ."

I couldn't listen very well. All I could see was the distinctive slant to her eyebrows and the lipstick which didn't suit her, and then suddenly I could think only about the woman I'd left in the bakery.

"I'd recorded this group of women from Chimbivilca. Their song—well, it describes how they ride like horses through the snow, celebrating the gold they have been given. A new age, if you like. Laura took to the floor and danced as if she had known the steps all her life! The other girls are starting to be jealous."

"Thank you for encouraging her."

"Hasn't she said anything?"

"I haven't caught up." I tried to describe what I'd found on my return home, but my head buzzed as I spoke.

"That is hysterical."

"That people should be worrying about oily skin . . ."

"Actually, your wife came to the studio a few days ago."

"Sylvina?"

Very funnily—as I said, she had a gift for mimicry—though not unkindly, she imitated Sylvina's voice. " 'I hope you're not teaching my daughter anything too absolutely contemporary.' "

She walked on in her loping gait, her feet in their heavy boots rising unconsciously on tiptoe at each step. Without warning, her face grew solemn.

"You know, the only moment I was possessed by dance, really possessed, was at Laura's age, before I knew too much. It's what most of us lose as adults. The older you get, the more you edit out the daydream. Discipline takes away that feeling. You become so controlled."

She withdrew her arm from mine and swapped her bag into that hand. She fell silent, thinking something over.

The Teatro Americano, a cream-painted colonial building, lay behind spiked railings in a rectangular garden planted with lavender and cassias. It was currently being used as the venue for an exhibition by a Chilean artist. A placard on the railings announced A HISTORY OF THE HUMAN FACE.

The attendant, slim with a scanty mop of gray hair, was about to tear us tickets when she saw Yolanda. She chucked back her head and called a name through an open door. A short young man with a close-cropped beard and cautious eyes strode out. "What is it?" At the sight of Yolanda he threw up his arms. He hugged her, speaking into her ear in a jaunty, whistling voice. "I have the lights, the loudspeakers, two hundred chairs. I've rung Miguel. He promises to write a review."

Over her shoulder, he peered at me from between heavy, red-veined lids.

"Lorenzo, this is my friend Agustín. I wanted to show him the stage."

He pulled back. "Sure, carry on. How's everything going?"

"I'm not there—yet."

"You need help?"

"That's sweet of you. I'll manage."

He looked at me, then in a low voice said to her, "I'd love to see a dress rehearsal. The others would too."

"There really isn't that much time."

He thought about this for a moment. "Listen, I've someone on the line. We'll be in touch." He squeezed my shoulder. "Good to meet you, Agustín."

We passed into a lofty room hung with silk sheets. She whispered, "Lorenzo, when he isn't running this theater, is a depressed

choreographer." She glanced back. "We used to work together.
You can't believe his jealousy. Worried continually I'd run off with
his steps."

The room, arranged with uncomfortable-looking cane chairs,
was lit naturally from a glass roof which revealed the gray-wool
sky and the top of a palm tree. Stage lights cast elaborate shadows
across a stained wooden floor.

Yolanda waited for two students to leave the room, then
slipped off her shoes, handing me the shopping bag.

"I need to measure this." She walked to one wall. Abruptly,
she pirouetted once, twice, three times, then leapt five paces across
the floor. "Zsa, zsa, zsa, zsa, chu!"

Burned in my mind is the flash of her feet, naked and white,
through the bright air.

A yard from the opposite wall she stopped. "That's fine. I was
worried about the width."

Another couple wandered into the room. She retrieved her
shoes. "Isn't this a nice place?" She spread her arms and her voice
rang beneath the glass. "In my first year at the Metropolitan I
danced Stravinsky's *Symphony of Psalms* here. Hey, look at these
faces."

My attention fixed on Yolanda, I had failed to notice the faces
staring at us from the silk sheets. Up close, they defined themselves. They had been lifted from newspapers in Chile dating back
thirty years, blown up to life size and printed on the silk.

The faces of pickpockets.

The faces of murderers.

The faces of terrorists and freedom fighters.

The faces of their victims.

The faces of their pursuers.

The faces of their judges.

The faces of patients from a schizophrenic ward.

The faces of extinct aborigines.

"Many of these people had one thing in common: they were
not included in the society that was photographing them—either
for the purpose of anthropological observation or as objects of
police control. Are you a good judge of character?" she asked.

"I think so."

"Everybody thinks they are. Let's see."

We played a game. She darted to a sheet, covering a caption with her bag. "Now, answer me. What kind of person is this?"

"Thief?"

She raised the bag. "Murder victim." She ran to another face. "What about . . . her?"

"Policewoman?"

"Policewoman it is. Him?"

"Judge?"

"No. Murderer. Her?"

"Freedom fighter?"

"Schizophrenic. Him?"

"Extinct Indian?"

"Right. Two out of five. Which means that half the people you meet, you get wrong."

Across the room the couple, who had been watching us, began to copy our game. They likewise had been confident of their ability to distinguish a murderer from a freedom fighter, a general who had been blown up in his bed from a Yaghan who had died of a common cold. But this was the artist's challenge. He was saying: put them side by side and the schizophrenic assumes the personality of the judge.

"In other words," said Yolanda, "we know nothing about anybody."

Not every face had been alive when photographed. I had been about to test Yolanda's skill when she halted before the mummified features of a body in a dress.

"Yaghan?" I asked.

"Look."

The caption read, "One of General Pinochet's disappeared. Eva Vásquez, student, for seventeen years buried in a mine shaft."

Yolanda said, "It's the same story, over and over again." She added, fiercely, "Bastards."

I looked at the torn drum of skin, the wretched angle of the head, and thought of Nemecio, his mouth filling, drowning in earth. Thought, too, of a widow five miles away, scrunching her dress at the knees. My years as a policeman, what had they achieved? What if I had followed Santiago's path? A sense of my emaciated duty all at once made ridiculous the distinction between Ezequiel and Calderón. You might have asked me to choose between Emilio's grilled fish and his grilled pork.

Yolanda said, "I don't know what you are like, Agustín, but I can't look at a face like this and say nothing. What happened to her is happening to us, now."

She told me that while I'd been away the university had held a service for the Arguedas Players. She had joined the parents lighting candles for their missing children. The remains found under the cinema floor included a scrap of green blouse and two keys on a keyring, one of which fitted Vera's locker. But no body, or at least not enough of one to be identifiable.

Yolanda, looking at the desiccated face on the silk, spoke as if to herself. "You have to have a body to be able to grieve. It's something you can't understand unless you've seen a loved one die. You have to see the corpse to be certain they're dead, so they can begin living in your memory. Without a body, you can't be rid of the horror." She broke off, covering her eyes. "Stop it, Yolanda, stop it, stop it." She composed herself, not without effort. Giving a quick look around, she said, "Come on, let's leave."

Outside, people pushed their baby carriages or stretched out on the grass, reading. Through the railings I saw a yellow handcart and bought two lemon water ices on sticks. We sat on the grass, but a darkness had brushed Yolanda and she had retreated into herself.

"What would you do," I asked, "if you were Eva Vásquez and your boyfriend asked you to fight that war?"

"I don't know." She nibbled at her ice. Her eyes were red. "I don't have a boyfriend."

"I'm thinking of Laura. If I were her age, I'd be tempted to fight."

"She's a dancer."

"Does it frighten you, that I talk like this?"

"No, I'm thinking. What I would do." But she had retreated from me as well. She finished her ice and buried the stick in the grass. "I give up. I need a cigarette."

Ten yards away a young man lay on his stomach, reading a newspaper. Yolanda went over and talked to him. She came back, drawing on a cigarette.

"I didn't know you smoked," I said.

"I don't. I feel like one."

Forcefully, she blew out the smoke. "What about you?"

"I don't smoke."

"I mean what would you do?"

Something about the jut of her chin, her glowing eyes, must have reached me, stung me even. I said, "There was a moment when I sacrificed everything."

"When was that?"

"I was younger than you."

"What happened?" She had been distracted. Now she was focused.

"I had a good job with a law firm. I was just married. I was going to be rich, maybe become a judge. One day my conscience spoke to me. When I heard it, the barriers went down. My wife, career, friends. Nothing mattered when I heard this voice. Next day I left my job."

Her hand slapped the ground. "That's what she felt!"

"Who?"

"Sorry, I see everything through Antigone. She didn't want the dogs to eat her brother's corpse. She was saying, life and death, those obligations are more important than a state's decree—and that's how I feel. I value Eva Vásquez's life—or Laura's, or yours—much more than the laws of this country."

"So our political situation can never change?"

"I'm not interested in politics. The only command you have to listen to is the one inside you—which you listened to."

She flattened a hand against her chest. "I'm interested in doing the things you know in your heart are right. Burying your brother is one of them." She spoke like a child, seeing what a child saw, then became serious again. "That's what stirred me up about the Arguedas Players. They were people's brothers and sisters." She was crying.

"Lovers and sons and daughters too."

She shook her head, coughing, stubbed out the cigarette. "Not so important. You can find another lover, give birth to another child."

"You mean, you'd sacrifice your child?"

She stroked the grass. She spoke as if she were onstage. "It doesn't take much to break a man-made law. A little dust, that's all. So what can we do, Agustín? We can follow orders and do nothing. But aren't there other demands? You've been back to your people. Don't they need our help?"

I didn't move. She stared at me, her face swollen. The path her tears had taken shone down her cheeks. In a hurt voice, she said, "Agustín, do you have a reason for not telling me about your journey?"

I had been concerned to protect Yolanda from knowing the things which churned me inside. My eyes fastened on her ankle and the scar an inch or so above her boot where the leggings had pushed up.

"I'm not who you think I am. I've deceived you." I nodded at the Teatro Americano. "I'm like one of the photographs in there. Laura may have told you I was a lawyer, but I'm not."

I couldn't reveal to her the work I did, but told her that it involved lies, violence, death. I had been engaged in it when I returned to La Posta. I kept back the details of Father Ramón's murder, but not the church massacre, nor the communal grave at the airstrip, nor the people beating their pan lids along the eucalyptus avenue.

"They never found me, nor did their dogs. I can only think it's because I had changed my clothes."

I told her how I had lain tucked under a lip in the crevice throughout that cold night, my clothes damp with urine, insects crawling over my face, under my shirt. At sunrise I climbed out of the hole, my arms and legs aching. I was filthy.

After washing in the river, I walked back to the village. During the night I had made a decision. Because of it I had to move with extreme care so that neither the Mayor nor the army would discover my presence.

I wasn't going to leave La Posta until I had gathered depositions.

"People were too scared to talk to begin with. But when word got out it was Agustín from the farm, they filled Lazo's office. I didn't like to think how many of those faces had chased me the night before."

I spoke still to her ankle. I was conscious of my hand jerking in the air and the lemon ice melting, running down between my fingers.

"For many, this was the first time anyone had paid attention to them since they'd been at school. They reverted to the elementary habit of raising their hands to speak. One old lady, no longer able to walk, told how three soldiers had escorted her to the far end of a field and raped her, beginning with the officer."

Yolanda took the stick from my hand and poked it into the earth.

"Another woman lost her son when soldiers found the toy gun he carried for the Independence Day Parade."

She rested her hand on my hand, the lemon ice sticking her skin to mine.

"There was a woman holding a baby, born as a result of a rape she'd suffered on a previous invasion by the military. She'd been asked for her identity card. The soldier had ripped it up, put the pieces in his mouth, eaten them. He had repeated his demand. 'Where's your identity card?' "

Yolanda raised my sticky hand to her lips. She spread out the fingers. One by one she inserted each finger into her mouth and licked it clean.

The air went still and in that instant something altered between us. It was as unsuspected as a conversion, and as explosive.

Absentmindedly I rubbed a damp finger over her eyebrows, down her cheeks. She pressed her head to my knee. Her face had a cracked look. Neither of us said another word, but when we got to our feet, she was no longer Laura's teacher.

———

Much later I contacted Sucre.

"Still no luck with that number," he said.

"It must be on the computer."

"The exchange is down, sir. Truck bomb."

"If you hear anything, call."

I had collected the car from where I'd parked it behind the shopping arcade and driven home. The lights blazed in our street. On the night of my wife's presentation, Ezequiel had decided to be charitable.

I could hear Sylvina talking. I closed the door softly behind me. Reflected in Laura's mirror, six ghostly visitants sat chin-up in a line, towels bibbed under their necks.

Sylvina was saying, "You risk tragedy if you mix different products from different cosmetic companies."

"I've just spent a lot on a new Estée Lauder." Marina's voice.

"Well, you could try Sally Fay's under-eye cream and see how you like that."

"We're not supposed to mix, you said."

"I was thinking of having a facelift," another said, doubtfully. "Like Marina's."

"Then I suggest before you undergo the knife, Consuelo, you try this alpha-hydroxide cream. It works something like an actual facelift—it's the most revolutionary product we've created."

"It does exactly what?"

"It will protect you against environmental damage. It will combat free radicals. It's even got Vitamin E. Here, put a little under your eyes. No, let me help you. Maybe on your chin, I see a little blemish there."

She took up position behind the next chair.

"María, you have reddish undertones to your skin, so we're going to use this color to even them out. Yes, it does seem a little green, but don't be scared . . . Oh, Agustín—"

"Don't get up, don't get up." Six hands gesticulated from beneath their towels. "How's it going?"

From the chairs an uncertain chorus. "How do we look? Horrible?"

Necks extended, they peered at Sylvina's husband. My unpredictable hours, my weekend shifts, my unexplained absences in the countryside, ensured that many of them could barely remember what I looked like.

I gave an enriching smile of encouragement. "You're going to be angels."

Patricia said tartly, "If there's a blackout, we'll need to be."

I mumbled my excuses and went into the kitchen. Since leaving Yolanda I'd felt hungry. I toyed with the sandwiches Sylvina had made for her guests.

My appearance, far from discomposing the women, had relaxed a tension. I heard them swapping blackout stories.

Patricia had come home ten days before to find her angelfish belly-up. The filter had gone off and it had died of heat and suffocation.

Margarita, a cheerless woman who complained about bleeding gums, had come home to find the freezer thawed and already squirming with maggots. "They'd hatched in the beef—so there was not only this bad smell, but the meat was alive!"

Tanya's husband had not come home at all, having started an affair with a total stranger with whom he had been stuck for three hours in an elevator.

Sylvina spread her lotions.

"Now this is a really good defense against skin fatigue."

Patricia said, "This old man, he was directing the traffic in his pajamas."

"It goes on like silk, see, and it doesn't have to be reapplied."

"There are characters who like to direct the traffic," said Marina. "In Miami the nuthouses were full of them."

"It'll give you a more youthful appearance."

"Daddy!" Laura's head appeared at the door. "Those aren't for you."

I sprang up. I wanted to make peace with her.

"Someone's on the phone," she said, writhing away from my kiss.

Sucre had an address.

———

"Eleven twenty-eight. That one!"

He'd collected me in the Renault. Behind us Sergeant Gómez and three others sat in a van we'd borrowed from Homicide.

"Tell them to overtake and park the other side."

Sucre spoke into his handset. The van crept past. Its headlights uprooted a tree outside the house, kaleidoscoping its shadow branches against the blue stucco.

Santiago's last resort in an emergency was a flat-roofed, single-story building five minutes' walk from the sea. Paint curled from the wall in page-sized sheets. The shutters, unvarnished and lop-sided, were closed. No one had cared for 1128 Calle Tucumán in a long time.

"Not much squeal on the place," said Sucre. "Lease ran out in February. Until then rented to a Miguel Angel Torre. Says he's a poet on his lease form."

"Where's Torre now?"

"We're looking for him. But someone's paying the bills. Electricity and telephone haven't been disconnected."

The van drew into the curb fifty yards beyond the house. Opposite, boys threw stones at a beer bottle on a low wall. One boy, spotting our car, detached himself and loafed toward us. He stopped some way away, trying to look uninterested. The radio in the car came alive.

"What's that up there?"

"A cage, it looks like."

I took the binoculars. A wire coop on the roof fluttered with birds.

"Stake it out for a day or two, sir?"

"No." Santiago might have alerted them. I lowered my gaze. Sprayed on the door in gray paint was the name of a novelist who had stood for President.

"Ask Gómez what he sees."

Sucre spoke into the radio. In the van someone, not Gómez, was saying, ". . . she promised she'd clean my straw if I let her go."

"Gómez, what do you reckon?"

Gómez came on. "Light in the yard at the back, sir. Otherwise no movement."

To me, Sucre said, "Go in now?"

"Tell Gómez to drive around the other side and keep watch. There might be a garden they can escape from."

I heard a snarl in the air. A helicopter tilted northward into a sky scratched with red fireworks.

"Red, what's that mean?"

"No one's worked out the colors, sir. Yesterday they were shooting blue. The day before, green."

All kinds of confusion had been going on when Sucre left the headquarters. Roads piled high with burning tires. Windows smashed. Stores looted.

"The General reckons some enormous piece of shit is floating down the pipeline." He took the binoculars and raised them to his eyes.

We watched the street, waiting for Gómez to radio back. The boy knelt in the road twenty yards away and retied the laces on his gym shoes.

"The General, you won't recognize him, sir. Calderón and Lache, they treat him like he's garbage. Cut him out of everything."

He unwrapped something from a sheet of newspaper. "Pear, sir?" They'd come from his farm.

A shutter opened in the house next to us. Through the window I saw a girl in a rugby shirt. One arm raised, she leapt to touch a slowly revolving fan. She reminded me of Yolanda. Everything did. A laugh floated out and a fat man in a vest appeared at the window. He leaned on the sill, glass in hand. Give his red nose a twist, I thought, and it would come off. After a while he stopped laughing and turned back to the room.

I ate my pear, concentrating on the girl, wondering why she wanted to touch the fan like that, when my vision was blocked by a hideous face. Sucked to the car window, the lips of its distorted mouth moved down the glass.

"Beat it!" Sucre, throwing the newspaper over his pistol, reached across me and slapped the glass.

"Can't I stand here?" The boy's voice, faint through the glass, sarcastic.

"No."

"Why not?"

"Just beat it."

His gaze roamed over our laps. Then he pushed himself upright. He sauntered back to the others, on the way stopping to pick up a stone. I heard the tinkle of shattered glass, followed by a shout. Then a quietness settled over the street. A quietness which terrified.

Gómez radioed that he was in position. A firework exploded, hidden by the roofs. Sucre, fidgeting with his pistol under the newspaper, said, "Ezequiel, if he's inside, I'm going to stop his clock for him."

If, behind those shutters, we did find Ezequiel, how tempting to believe it would cease overnight—the shooting, the murders, the knives at our throats—and the days would be unsoured and Sylvina could take Laura to the beach and buy her a balloon or polish her toenails in the sun. But Edith would not have handed out Ezequiel's number to a bit player like Santiago.

"What's that?" I said.

"Sounds like a dog at a trash can."

"Let's go."

Filling the house was the smell of a burned filter from a cigarette crushed into a mug. The television set was warm and the door to the yard was open. A lamp on the porch swayed in the breeze from the beach.

Sucre barged back in from the yard, followed by Gómez.

"They were tipped off, sir. We should have gone in immediately." He smashed his foot into the door.

I ordered Gómez to round up the boys in the street, then went through the house. Alerted by Ezequiel's thousand eyes, whoever had been here had left in a panic. Clothes jettisoned over a narrow iron bed; on the kitchen table a tin of peaches, half-empty beside an architecture magazine; in the front room, stacked on top of the television set—three videotapes.

A stepladder led through a hatch onto the flat roof, from where I watched Gómez running down the empty street. I waited, looking at the fences and rooftops. In the cool, dry night no shadows moved.

My presence had disturbed the birds in the cage. Agitated by the fireworks, they clawed against the wire, opening and closing their cramped feathers. I had assumed they were doves or pigeons, but now I saw that they were parrots. Raging, impervious to the screeching and scratching and clatter of wings, I heaved the cage to the edge of the roof and I pushed.

When I went downstairs, the ruined green wings flapped blood over the porch, and dying birds sang their pain through smashed beaks.

The Café Haiti, where I waited at twelve the following morning, was emptier than usual. I sat at a table in the corner and ordered coffee.

The waitress retrieved the menu. "I remember you."

The prospect of leaving Yolanda without having made a firm date for another meeting had been intolerable. I hadn't known how best to broach the subject. Then, talking about *Antigone,* she had said she was coming into town to collect her costume.

"Could we meet afterward—at the Haiti?"

I had had to extract myself from Calle Tucumán. We were going meticulously over the house. So far all we'd found were a black horsehair wig, a combat jacket on a door hook and a cardboard box containing more of the pamphlets Hilda Cortado had distributed. There remained the three videotapes in my briefcase. I'd watch them at the station, I told Sucre. Then, for the first time in my career, I played truant.

At twelve-fifteen Yolanda pushed open the glass door. She wore a sea-blue dress—sleeveless, loose, above the knee—and, over her shoulder, a bag of raw silk patterned with white llamas. She stood on tiptoe and looked about the café twice before she saw my upraised hand.

She walked over, head down, and we embraced clumsily. She had washed her hair and I could smell the new cloth of her dress and I knew she wore it for me.

"You look lovely."

"Don't let me forget this." She tucked her bag under the table. "May I see?"

"It's unlucky. Not until I come onstage." She didn't want to begin on a wrong note and wasn't ready to catch my eye.

She said to the waitress, "You know what I feel like more than anything in the world? A *suspiros de Lima*."

"We don't have them."

"Oh, dear. A *masita*, then?"

"Only *pan de árabe* or *pan de Viena*."

"*Pan de árabe* then." She looked around. "Isn't this where we sat before?" Her eyes rested on me. "See? Already we have a history."

I don't wish to say too much about that afternoon. What I mean is . . . is that I can't be precise. What happened between us is not a complete picture in my mind, any more than is she. How long had we known each other? If I count up the hours, I don't suppose much longer than the time I've spent talking to you.

Put it this way. For many years I had looked neither right nor left, but stared ahead, my thoughts settled on one object: the capture of Ezequiel. Now, out of the blue, this young woman had taken me by the arm and offered something which I ought to have resisted.

There was still light in the sky when we left the Haiti. We spent the end of the afternoon walking. Toward the sea and along the Malecón. I had no sense of being curbed, only of endless space. When I looked at her, the ghosts of my happiest childhood moments nudged me.

"That sea," I remember telling her. "It takes you nowhere, but I love it."

And later: "I've been walking down this street for twenty years and never noticed that funny gray turret."

In some square—I was never to find it again—we sat on a bench.

"What are you looking at?" I asked.

"Your wrist. I was looking at it yesterday, on the grass."

"My wrist?"

"I always look at a man's wrist. Or the side of his neck, or his ankle. The vulnerable parts."

I inspected my wrist. It had never struck me as vulnerable.

"What does it tell you?"

"All intelligent people can fake modesty, Agustín, but you *are* modest."

Her hand suddenly flew at my face and I ducked away.

"What are you doing?"

"I'm not going to hit you." From the corner of my mouth, she neatly flicked away a large crumb of *pan de árabe*.

Was it on this bench that she released the few details of her life, or do I introduce these from another conversation? It wasn't much. Conservative upbringing. Only daughter of a construction engineer, to whom she had been close. Her mother, a pious teacher, made her attend the Fátima church in Belgrano four times a week. From an early age she longed to escape. The opportunity presented itself when she was fifteen. The nuns from the Sophianum school took her on a trip to the shantytowns. The Mother Superior led her to understand that she would regard it as something dreadful, worse than a lie, if Yolanda ignored the conditions in which these people lived. She decided to become a missionary in the jungle. Her father put his foot down. He wouldn't allow it.

"So I became a dancer."

Whenever she talked about her calling, a splinter of ruthlessness would enter her voice. "You may think I'm a nice person. But ask Laura. In my studio I'm different. Once you come inside, you're there to be disciplined, to get rid of your ego."

Another time she said, "You don't know how dance is. You can't talk about it—but it is a calling. You feel different. You feel special. You have to be very much yourself, but that's so you can be someone else."

"How do you mean?"

"Look, I have chubby cheeks. Too much flab here—and here. Nevertheless, people always say, 'You're so beautiful, Yolanda. What a marvelous body.' But to me a marvelous body is not interesting unless it can represent something. Because what are you? You are many people. I can't become real to myself unless I can also become, say, Antigone."

I had not met anyone like Yolanda. Yet if I describe her qualities, they sound slight. As I say, she was astonishingly alive—she really did excite the air around her. She was attractive, but didn't assume she could do everything. She was an idealist; at the same time, she could behave like someone who had lost her beliefs. She was tender. She was interested. Above all, she had this alertness. In repose, she always seemed ready to whirl about. Sometimes you had the impression she waited for a signal which none but she might register—and that it had sounded as you spoke to her. Then she would break off and her face would set in an attitude of the most intense expectation. She would look into space and with a jerk of attention focus back on you. She might listen deferentially to what you were saying—but a few minutes later something would distract her and she'd cry, "Isn't that man ridiculous? No, come to think of it, I'd like hair like that."

Prompted by the bag at her feet, which contained the dress she wouldn't show me, I asked about her performance. Who had choreographed the ballet, who was to be Creon, what props would she use?

She rolled her eyes. "Oh, it's a mess. There were going to be four of us, including Lorenzo. Remember, you met him at the theater? We'd been looking to dance a drama. Then I saw this piece on television about the Arguedas Players, and that's when I had the idea. What about *Antigone*? So we read Sophocles. Then Anouilh. Then Brecht. Then fought a lot. When the group broke up, two of them wanting to direct, all of them wanting to dance *Antigone,* I said, 'Forget it. I'll dance on my own.' "

We walked around the square. Prim houses. A woman behind a grille who looked up from her book. "Did you see that lady smiling to herself?" A couple not talking in a car. "What is she doing with him?" "What is anyone doing with anyone?" Laughter.

On the edge of the square a large dog, black with a spine of orange fur, hurled himself from the leaves and nudged his head between us, panting.

I pushed him away, afraid he might attack Yolanda. He bounded to her side and licked her hand.

"Down, boy, down." She stroked his shining face, then took my arm.

"Tomorrow I will be twenty-nine."

"How will you celebrate?"

"Rehearse. Then classes. Then more rehearsing."

"On your birthday? What about your family?"

She looked abstracted. She might have been working out a complicated dance step.

I thought of the yellow cardigan she had spread against me. "Isn't your brother going to take you out?"

"But, Agustín!" she cried. "My dance is one week away. I haven't finished the choreography. I'm having nightmares."

"Nightmares? About what?"

She pressed the fingers of one hand to her chin, contemplating the dog, which had run on ahead. "Very well. I dream I am late for the performance. I hear a flute in the background—maybe it's your rain pipe!—and I can't get to the stage, I can't run. Something, someone holds me back. At the last moment I break loose and it's dark onstage and there isn't enough light to see."

"But you shouldn't spend your birthday alone . . ."

"It's not a problem."

"My wife is worried you have no friends."

She burst into laughter. "Your wife is right. Yesterday, before I bumped into you, I felt so useless. I wanted to pack it in. Then I said no, better not, too much work to do."

"That's why you have no boyfriends?"

"Oh, I've catted around," she said unexpectedly. "And I was engaged, to a poet, a frivolous poet who only liked cars and clothes."

"You didn't love him?" I said, without reflecting.

"I loved him. But work got in the way."

Childishly, she withdrew her arm and dashed up the path to kick a can. She kicked it again and the dog chased after, pushing the can away from her with his nose. Then he trotted off, the can in his mouth. Yolanda looked back at me, raising her arms in a shrug. I felt another stab of intimacy, and I knew a strength in me had lapsed.

I drove Yolanda home and around seven o'clock returned to police headquarters. In the viewing room on the fourth floor, I gave the videocassettes from the house in Calle Tucumán to Sergeant Clorindo and went to fetch a cup of water.

"Okay, Clorindo. I'm ready."

I settled down without much expectation. I held the cup to my lips, about to drink, when on screen there appeared the face of Quesada, our late Minister of the Interior, making a televised speech to the Assembly. I finished the cup and sat back. Already this promised to be a waste of time. Probably the other cassettes were movies. I was so used to disappointment.

It would last less than a second. It was no more, really, than a trivial act of clumsiness. But our smallest gesture is never so small as we think. You hand over a camcorder, you rub a crumb from someone's mouth. The consequences are incalculable.

The first tape was a compilation of news reports. Quesada's triumphant speech. Quesada, wife and bodyguard onstage at the Teatro de Paz. Prado's body on the roadside. All items recorded from Canal 7, fifteen of them.

The second tape featured exteriors filmed through the back of a fast-moving car. The Presidential Palace; a barracks in the south of the capital; two houses I didn't recognize. The sites, I presumed, of intended targets.

I did not immediately gauge the significance of the last tape. It consisted of a single grainy recording, rather blue in color, as though it had been copied from another copy. Filmed in a nondescript room, a group of darkly dressed men and women danced in a ritual celebration.

"Turn up the sound."

Clorindo adjusted the volume to a high-frequency, insect hum. "There isn't any," he said.

The floor was strewn with flowers. The celebrants surged back and forth, arm in arm, stamping on the blossoms. At the same time, their faces concentrated on the dancer who held the camcorder, about whose expertise, despite the uncomplicated eagerness of their smiles, several eyes implied reservation. From the angle of the pictures, it was obvious that the dancer/operator, who moved in a sort of inebriated sway, didn't know how to work the machine. A short-haired woman, rather flat-faced and with a mannish mouth, could be seen shouting directions. Then a hand must have found the volume control.

There came the sudden loud sound of stamping feet and reflected voices and Frank Sinatra singing "Summer Wind." I could hear the cameraman's heavy breathing, like the wow-wow resonance of a seashell removed from the ear.

The flat-faced woman pleaded, "Give it here, give it here."

As she took the camera, I glimpsed the person behind it—a large man in a pale jersey, filmed from the side. When he realized the tape was running, he flinched, held up a hand, spread the fingers over the lens. The tape ended there.

"Go back to the beginning," I told Clorindo.

Could that blank-looking face be Edith's? I remembered a woman with thick makeup and longer hair.

"Let's see the color of her eyes."

Clorindo froze the tape. He connected the image enhancer and blew up the pixels. An icon appeared in the corner, which, with the computer's mouse, he dragged down to her eyes. He clicked twice. The image needed sharper definition.

"Try a different algorithm."

He typed in the coordinates. Once again he grabbed a frame and digitized it. Her eyes became the screen. They were the same color blue as the print. But I knew them to be green. I was looking at Father Ramón's killer.

"Go forward." I wanted to see the dancer at the end, the operator.

Edith, animate again, took hold of the camera. It jerked to the floor, recording several pairs of trouser legs. Then it arced up, over the walls, filming the man's shoulders.

"Wait. Focus on that area."

The icon was clicked. The hand juddered frame by frame toward the lens. I could see between the fingers a fuzz of beard, the black frame of a pair of spectacles, two narrow eyes.

Ezequiel.

We reran the tape. It's amazing what you miss when you're looking for something else. I was concentrating so much on Edith and the bearded dancer that I did not notice the road sign until I'd played the tape a dozen times.

The three letters had been recorded during the fumble when Edith took the camera. At first I had assumed they belonged to a picture on the wall. It was Clorindo who said, "That's not a picture, sir. It's a window." The window overlooked a tree. Outside, it was night.

"Can't you make it clearer? Try a vector map."

The computer enhanced the definition. From the letters and the way they were formed, it was a street sign. The window frame cut off the left-hand end of the word, and branches hid the last letter, but clearly visible was ERO.

I ran downstairs. Ordered a computer search, a list of all streets containing this sequence of letters. Nothing said this was a street in the capital, but I wasn't going to widen the search. Not yet.

How long would it take? "An hour, two hours?"

My secretary said, "Maybe an hour."

I rang Sucre. He was still picking through the house in Calle Tucumán. The General, eager for such propaganda as he could make out of our raid, had been on his back.

"He's keen to speak with you, sir. He wants to inform the media."

I didn't want to talk to the General. I told my secretary I'd be back in an hour and returned to the viewing room. I had intended to spend this evening plotting my report on the army massacre in La Posta. But suddenly nothing was so important to me as this tape. I had Clorindo play it again and again, trying different filters. For the first time since I had questioned him in Sierra de Pruna, I had a tangible sense of Ezequiel's presence. Over successive generations the image had become degraded. His features were blurred and imprecise, as if seen in the light of an eclipse, but I had no doubt in my mind: those fingers clawing at the lens and the eyes they half concealed were his eyes. His fingers. Ezequiel the cameraman. Ezequiel the dancer.

At ten-thirty I received the printout. There were two addresses. I knew them both. Calle Perón I remembered from my days spent guarding diplomats. A smart cul-de-sac with several banks and embassies.

I was familiar, too, with the second address, a quiet, tree-lined street in the suburb of Surcos consisting of a hundred or so houses. And my daughter's ballet studio.

From the very first I deployed two teams to watch Calle Diderot and Calle Perón, five in each team, men and women, disguised as sanitation men, municipal gardeners, loving couples. They were to report on everyone's movements, what time they left home, returned; whom they let through their doors. In the evenings the refuse from both streets was to be collected in a special sanitation department truck and sifted.

"Get a list of chemists in both neighborhoods," I told Sucre. "Who's buying what ointments, how regularly. Anything to do with psoriasis, I need the details. Same with tobacconists. I want to know of anyone who always buys American cigarettes: Winston, Marlboro, Camel, L&M. And a list of householders. Occupations, how long they've been there, where they've come from. Everyone is suspect. Even the Argentine Ambassador."

Except Yolanda, of course. I had to warn her.

Yolanda, when she spoke of it, had tried to play down her birthday, but she couldn't hide from me the child in her who wanted to celebrate. The occasion became my pretext.

At nine o'clock, half an hour after the modern dance class ended, I walked down Calle Diderot and pressed her bell. I carried a package, not well wrapped, and a flat box containing a banana cake.

The cake wasn't the cake I had wanted to buy. I'd seen a

beautiful *suspiros de Lima,* positioned cleverly in the window so as to convince me that I could afford it. When the girl inspected the pedestal, she discovered it had a much higher price. What I could afford was something pitiful. Anxiety assailed me as soon as I had left the shop. The cake wasn't enough. What else could I give her?

The present I chose in the end was meant only as a friendly gesture. Now I wondered if the act of bringing both a cake and a present could be taken for a sign of something else—something more emotional. Was I fooling myself? What was she going to think?

The studio lay in darkness. Upstairs, screened by the yellow curtains, someone watched television. I rapped on the door. Part of me hoped she had slipped out. I was falling for her and not wanting to. Yet my job had taken me to where she was.

I knocked again, then gave up. I had walked two or three steps when I heard the door open.

"Agustín?"

She leaned in the doorway, one leg lifted so that the foot pressed against the frame, her hands on her cheeks.

"Happy birthday," I said.

She brought her brows together and looked at me for some time. She had hurriedly thrown on a thin black dress and her hair was sticking in wet strands to her cheeks.

"Why didn't you knock properly?" she said at last.

"I thought I did."

"I shouldn't let you in." She withdrew a hand and tugged at the straps of her dress. Her shoulders were red from the shower.

"But you can't dance all day. To be cooped up, these four walls—"

"What's that you've got?"

She looked at the parcel, her eyes curious. She wasn't sure what to do.

"And a banana cake." I held up the box. "We could eat a slice. Then I'll go."

She stood aside to let me come in, then shut the door and walked ahead, barefoot, through the sliding doors into the studio.

"I was washing my hair." She pushed a cassette into the

player—the Pretenders singing "Stop Your Sobbing"—and turned up the volume. She was pleased to see me, but she didn't want me there.

I gave her the parcel and we sat down cross-legged on the floor and I felt like a teenager again, sitting in a chairless room with music playing loudly and a pretty girl and from somewhere the smell of lilies.

"It was nice of you to remember." She pulled the string loose. Raising Lazo's red pot to the light, she gave a little gasp of pleasure. Turning it over in her hands, she let her fingers caress the rim.

"It's a portrait vase."

"You're giving me this?"

"Didn't you need a jug for *Antigone*?"

"Could I put in flowers?"

"It's very old. And porous, probably. The water might leak."

With a fluent motion she lifted her hands and waved the pot from side to side above her head. When she moved her arm, I could see soapsuds in her ear. She flung the jug into the air.

"Careful!"

She caught it, swung it gracefully to her breast.

"See, now it's a baby." She was overcome. "It's beautiful. Thank you." On all fours she crawled over to where I sat and kissed me on the cheek. A soapy smell mingled with the sharp scent of her skin.

"Now I have something for you." She scrambled to her feet and skipped from the room.

I was taking off my jacket when she ran back holding a long wooden flute.

"I bought it at Ausangate. It's a *pinkullo*. Play something." She turned off the music and lay down on her side, her legs tucked in, watching me.

I pressed the mouthpiece to my lips. Pushing out my chin to raise the pitch, I played the opening notes of a rain melody. Followed by Yolanda's eyes, my fingers opened and closed the six holes as I blew, producing a muffled, flattened sound. It wasn't a *pinkullo*, it was something else, and I had no idea how to play it.

"It's for you," she said, face shining.

"No, Yolanda. This is too special. Please. You keep it."

She rubbed a hand up and down one leg as if she were cold. The soles of her feet were black from the patio.

"But didn't you want a flute? Weren't you looking for one?"

I didn't want to distract her by bringing Laura into the conversation. "I suppose so." It sounded graceless.

She sat up, put her hands on her thighs and rose lithely to her feet. "I'm not accepting this jug until you accept my flute." But before I could reply, she added, "Now let's try your cake."

I followed her into the kitchen. A hotplate beside the sink was stacked with half a dozen unwashed mugs and an ashtray piled with cigarette ends. A green oilcloth covered the table on which was a fountain of lilies in a cream-cracker tin. There were two chairs and a fridge. A door in the far wall led—presumably—into her bedroom. The ceiling beams were decorated with photographs of dancers.

Impatiently, Yolanda pulled open the cake box. She cut two slices onto a plate.

"Here, have some," and she fed me one piece, putting it into my mouth, making a mess. She ate hers quickly, with a child's appetite.

"It's good."

"Isn't it." But I thought of the cake in the window.

Before I'd finished eating, she jumped up, mouth full, and ran to the kitchen cupboard, bringing out a bottle of red wine. I opened it and filled two glasses.

"To your birthday."

Suddenly she hesitated. "We shouldn't be doing this, Agustín. Our birthdays are not important." Her voice was chastened, different.

"Nonsense. How old did you say you were?"

Soon the bottle was empty, the last of the wine in our glasses. An impish smile spread over her face. "Shall I tell you something? Shall I tell you a big secret?"

She crossed her legs. I looked at the scar on her ankle, like an anchovy. My heart stopped and I thought, She's going to tell me she's fallen in love.

"Oh God, another plaster!" She peeled something from her heel and rubbed it between her fingers until it was tight enough a ball to be dropped into the ashtray.

"What's the secret?"

"No, no." She had changed her mind. "I won't. I can't."

"You're probably right." I put down my glass. My hand had begun to shake. "How is the ballet going?"

"I'll show you."

She got ready in the bathroom. To busy myself, I removed the plates to the sink. My eyes strayed to the door at the end of the kitchen. On it were pinned a list of pupils' names, with ticks against each one; a poster of the National Ballet of Cuba; and photographs of ballerinas: Patricia Cano, Carolina Vigil, Vivien Vallejo at the Colón in 1951. I was looking for Laura's name on the list when a hand covered my mouth and Yolanda said, "Come."

We took our glasses into the studio. She wore a loose Andean dress, sand-colored with braided edges, reaching nearly to her feet. She sat me down on the leather trunk and picked up the rosin box, tapping out a small heap of powder until its musty odor vied with the scent of lilies. From a hook on the wall, she lifted a pair of platform clogs and a white mask. She set them beside the rosin and put another cassette on the machine. As the tape hissed, she took up her position, her elbow rubbing a hole in the steamed-up mirror.

She rose on tiptoe, checking herself. One hand gripped the barre, the other performing small involuntary gliding movements as though a live creature lay beneath her skin. A foot caressed the air. Her doom-eager face was beautiful, as implacably set as Lazo's jug. She was ready.

The notes of a pipe—similar in tone to the one she had given me—zigzagged through the room. Her body stiffened. She picked the jug up and tracked in hesitant steps to the opposite mirror. Back she flitted to the rosin heap, her feet squealing on the parquet. With a bump she put down the jug, tied the mask over her face and bent double, gathering her dress up between her legs, like a pair of trousers. The music quickened. A charango strummed

and she became her helmeted brother, riding across the plain, fleeing the battle. She was breathless, but she had clearly been a marvelous dancer.

A brash clap of cymbals broke her advance. She halted. No
longer her brother, she slipped onto the high clogs and kicked
away the mask, which skimmed with a crack into the wall. Now
she danced her uncle, Creon, stamping about the floor, one hand
lanced toward the jug, forbidding Thebes to bury a disgraced
brother.

There was a final crash of the cymbals. Upstairs, a chair
shifted. Then, unaccompanied, a *pinkullo* began to play its pithy
notes. I recognized the instrument, and the music snatched at me.
Yolanda freed her dress and lay down on her stomach, her arms
stretched forward in the air, begging. She was Antigone, entreating
her uncle—but her fingers also reached out to me. I caught her eye.
Did it mean anything, the way she looked at me? I held her gaze
and felt a blast of desire.

Slowly, elegantly, she stood up, preparing herself for the movement she had practiced at the Teatro Americano. She pirouetted,
once, twice, three times. And leapt. Then the lights went out. The
music stopped, and a thump resonated in the darkness.

"Yolanda!"

She lay against the sliding doors. I tried to lift her, but she
pushed herself up and away from me. "This time I was prepared."

She stumbled to the leather-covered chest. Inside, there were
candles. She lit two, sticking them upright in their own melted
wax. We sat, close together, on the floor. In the candlelight her
skin had a lustrous shine. Sweat polished her shoulders and rolled
in bright beads down her throat, between her breasts. Her nipples
pressed dark and hard through the sandy-yellow dress. The last
blackout had panicked her. This time she was aroused.

I had to remember the reason why I had come to the studio—
to warn her. I put an arm on her damp shoulder. I forget what I
said, but I spoke vaguely, in hints. It was not possible for me to
confide to her the nature of my business in Calle Diderot, nor
could I reveal that I would not be far away in the days to come.
But I had to alert her to the danger.

I was telling her of the need for vigilance when she interrupted. "But I am careful," she said. "Everybody has to be careful these days. You too."

I took her hand, feeling the rough-bitten edges of her fingernails. How could I say what I had to say? That they wouldn't care if she was a dancer. That they wouldn't care about her girls. That, to them, we were expendable. All of us.

As if to tell me not to worry, she tapped my wrist, then lightly kissed my cheek. She wanted to get up. "We can look after ourselves."

"I know. But I was worried for—"

"Stop it. You're scaring me," she said, and the moment had passed. She stood straight. "Anyway, I haven't finished."

"You want to go on? In this light?"

Above me, her face had been sculpted by the candlelight into something older, stronger, fiercer. "I can see perfectly well."

"But what about music?"

She picked something up from the floor. "Here."

That night in Yolanda's studio I mustered the notes of a forgotten tune. I didn't really know how to play it, the flute she'd given me. It was hard to produce a good clear tone. But as my breath warmed the wood, the color of the sound changed. The flute vibrated to the same pitch as my body, as though it were another limb, another flow of blood. And Yolanda, dancing her forbidden steps, became the music of this flute made flesh.

She cradled the pot to her breast, then moved on scissor legs toward the rosin, scooping handfuls into the pot. Her body was something unimaginably alive. She wept with her limbs, yet at the same time they blazed. She truly was making something unseen visible, so that I never doubted her identity as the sister about to cover a mangled corpse with dust.

She pirouetted and jumped. In that leap her body was in complicity with the air. Her legs dismissed the ground, her shoulders expressed their wings, and the image of her flight was painted there.

"Play. Play." She spoke to my reflection. The steam had cleared from the mirrors and in them I could see her body from every angle. With trembling arms, she raised the jug above her head—and I am certain that, with this frozen gesture, as if offering a libation, she intended the ballet to end.

"Don't stop, Agustín." A whisper.

She was then to do something I will never forget. It was the last thing I expected, and I doubt whether the idea had entered her head until that moment. She stared up at the base of Lazo's jug, and I wondered if she had seen something there. With a tidy flick of her wrist, she overturned it. A torrent of white dust poured down her hair, over her dress, puffing out over the candles, where it burned, sparkling, in the flames.


Rejas fell silent.

"Go on," said Dyer.

"Half an hour later I left the studio, having promised not to see her until Sunday."

Dyer was not certain he had understood correctly. "You mean, you wouldn't meet again until after her performance?"

Rejas blushed. "That's right."

"Why?"

His fingers tugged at the chain around his neck. "She was an artist. She was consumed by discipline. She needed her privacy— her loneliness, even."

Dyer's eyes hadn't moved from his face. There was more to be said, but he saw that the other didn't want to say it. At that moment Emilio appeared with two dishes of pork and pineapple. Dyer supposed that Rejas would have no appetite, but he ate hungrily.


When Rejas resumed his story, Dyer hoped he would pick up the thread in the ballet school. But the meal had restored in him some sort of equilibrium. He wanted to talk about Ezequiel.


Ezequiel signed his name when he handed the video camera to Edith. I knew as soon as I discovered the street he had filmed that I would find him. You might have thought this would be easy: I just had to look for a house near or opposite a street sign. But on either side of each street, vertical posts stood every hundred yards beneath the jacaranda.

There are ninety-six houses in Calle Diderot. In Calle Perón, fifty-four. I took charge of the Diderot operation. I'll spare you the details. Watching a street, vital as it is, is tedious work. Compare it to the act of blowing up an air cushion: although nothing appears to be going on, no breath is wasted. It is only with the last few breaths that the cushion takes shape. Yet you have to keep blowing.

Some people get a headache just waiting for something to unfold. Hour upon profitless hour. Contemplation immobilizes them. They end up like my father, drugged by doing nothing. They become disciples of sitting down and facing a blank wall whenever they feel a storm of rage or passion. Because it is not enough to be patient. You have to know how to be impatient, when to act quickly. The trick is to recognize the moment.

The Calle Diderot team worked eight-hour shifts. It was a crude operation by Western standards. But anything more sophisticated at this stage might have aroused curiosity. Sucre was the sanitation man. Gómez, alternating with Clorindo, did wonders in the blue and yellow outfit of the municipal gardener. A couple transferred from Narcotics spent hours in the café and nestling in the front seat of their worn-out Volkswagen. The operation was kept secret even from the General, whom I had not told what we had found on the videocassette.

I used a different car for each shift. Sometimes I parked in a narrow cul-de-sac, sometimes on the corner of Calle Leme. People aren't that observant. They don't stare at particular cars in the street—and I wasn't driving a lavender Cadillac. I listened to the radio. I read the newspaper. I broke up the day by using the lavatory in a bar on Calle Pizarro where they sold sandwiches. I sat for eight-hour stretches, watching passersby.

At night, since it was too risky to rent a room from anyone in the street, I exchanged the car for a van. I used a blue engineer's van, no windows at the back and with a black stripe along both sides. From the outside it looked like a band of paint. In fact, it was darkened Perspex, and I could see through it.

I sat on a folding chair in the back. I had night glasses and a bottle to pee in. One of my men, usually Sucre, would park the van, get out, lock it and walk away. At the end of the shift he would come back, repeating the process in reverse.

I soon became familiar with the faces of the street, what preoccupied them, whom they liked or didn't like. No one seemed ill at ease or fearful. This was a prosperous neighborhood, far removed from the tension of the outskirts. A bird sang in the jacaranda. A dog lay asleep on a porch. The very tranquillity of the scene was reason enough to be on guard.

I compiled notes. On that first afternoon, for instance, at about two-fifteen an elderly man, tall with patched sleeves, entered No. 339. After forty-five minutes he drove quickly away in an orange Volkswagen Beetle.

An hour later the maid from No. 345 visited the Vargas Video Store. She came out holding two cassettes, talking to herself. The storekeeper charged extra if you didn't rewind the videos.

At four o'clock a female jogger, late forties, in a turquoise tracksuit, left No. 357. She returned after thirty-five minutes, walking.

Ten minutes later a young woman, tidily dressed, arrived at No. 365, the estate agency run from a garage. I could see the car behind her desk. She left at five-thirty carrying a handful of envelopes.

Which of these people was hiding Ezequiel? You see, I was certain he had settled here or in Calle Perón. He had remained as silent and derisive as a god right up until the moment I saw him on the videocassette. A few frames of film had made him fallible, human at last. The sound of him may have been no louder than the distant thrumming of an insect, but in those warm nights I felt his presence.


I am able to picture him in that room. He's lighting another cigarette. He is listening to the music we would find in the cassette player: Beethoven's Ninth. Perhaps it is the last movement playing as he leans in his customary position by the window, having watched the sixteen girls go into their class.

It strikes him as a warm evening, but he often misjudges the temperature, so that Edith, wearing a thick sweater, will come into the room and find him with nothing on but a vest.

I see Edith nudging open the door with a tray. She rests it on the trolley while he lingers at the window, watching two lovers go by. He hears a bird. He scratches his neck. For twelve years he has been cooped up in airless rooms like this one.

Edith confirms the meeting on Monday. At eight that morning the Central Committee will present details for his approval. Nothing can go wrong. In less than a week the final act of the Fifth Grand Plan will be played out.

He listens, eating. He planned it himself, twenty years ago. The strategy has remained unblemished in his head. He nods and forks toward his tongue another mouthful of ceviche.

The night crackles. Edith parts the curtain a fraction. Yellow fireworks confirm the operation tomorrow, against Cleopatra's Hotel. She comes back into the room and sits on the edge of the bed, plucking hairs from her black trousers.

At seven o'clock she turns on the television, keeping the volume low. The police announce an important breakthrough in the hunt for Ezequiel. A police general, interviewed outside a blue house, holds up a wig and says, "Have no doubt. We are closing in."

Ezequiel watches for a minute, then picks up his book. There are marks on the page where wax from a candle splashed during the last blackout. It upsets him because it is a good edition.

Edith says, "Is there anything else you want? Cigarettes? Water?"

"I need more Kenacort." He doesn't need to speak loudly to be heard. His voice is a solid thing, the words creating in the room another presence. This second figure stands at his shoulder, like a maquette of damp gray clay, arms crossed, featureless—but watchful.

"Is it bad?"

He nods. The rash has started to creep inside the membrane of his penis. When he pissed this morning, he wanted to scream.

He brushes her hand from his knee. Reluctant to pull herself away, she watches him drink his water. She decides to make the bed. The Dithranol has marked the sheets with purple-brown stains. She strips them off and is about to leave the room, pregnant with dirty bedclothes, when she hesitates, returns to his side.

His mouth is full of water, his tongue and lips dry from the Acitretin tablets. He swallows. "What is it?"

"It might be nothing."

He listens as she explains what is troubling her.

"Should I have him followed?"

"No. I've seen him. It's nothing. He's infatuated, that's all. Another Gabriel."

"Are you sure?"

Although the words are quietly spoken, his black eyes are charged. "You can't check everybody." He drains his glass and pushes away the tray.

"You're finished?"

"Yes."

"Do you want to watch some more?"

"No."

She switches off the television and leaves the room. She will not come back tonight.

From below he hears the squeak of shoes, a sound as of something sharply wrenched. He looks down to the rug. Downstairs they are beginning their exercises. For the next hour and a half the floor will become a sounding board for the thud, thud, thud of feet and the "one two three, one two three, one two three" of the teacher calling out the rhythm, and for the music, interrupted again and again, of his favorite composers.

These interruptions are a torture to him. At the same time, he demands in his followers the same obedience as the ballet teacher seeks from her pupils. He makes tolerable these evenings by recasting the girls beneath him into the image of his invisible army.

Tonight it is a classical class. The girls begin at the edge of the room and, in a quickening tempo, proceed to the middle. At the end of the lesson they will have exercised every part of their bodies—except the vocal cords. On the dance floor, only the teacher speaks. They listen to her, not talking, because she can make them perfect.

"Okay, we'll start with the same plié as yesterday. Let's remember what we discussed, about keeping the strength in the middle and freeing the arms."

He slips a finger under the page as he reaches the bottom. He is rereading Kant. He turns the page.

"Listen to what I'm going to play, and push from the front foot. Good, Christina. Practice that."

They're dancing "The Song of the Moon" from *Rusalka*. Hands wave in the mirror. Bodies sway like branches in a wind. The hands and bodies flow to the Dvořák composition he most loves. He stretches a leg.

"Down and up, down and up. Hips back. Listen to the music. You're not listening to the music, Gabriela." It stops in midbeat. "I'm sorry, girls."

Shoes brush across the parquet. The teacher, he imagines, will be adjusting a head, plucking up one shoulder, placing a finger in the small of the girl's back.

"Now, your arms are condor feathers."

The music strikes up, accompanied by a handclap in time to the beat.

From the trolley he picks up a fountain pen. He unscrews the cap and with an effort writes in the margin: "Can we then infer from the natural world that man ought to be free? Is that bird I hear free?"

He reads another paragraph, but the words are evasive. They, like the music, fail to move him. He coughs, catching a movement on the blank screen before him. From the television his reflection is beamed back at him. Sitting behind the trolley, he is made shockingly aware of the contrast between this body and the hands which tremble at full stretch below him, taking aim at the ceiling.

"The eyes must go up," says the voice downstairs. "Open them, open them, look at the ceiling."

Ezequiel turns a few pages and lays the book, pages down, on the arm of his chair. He pushes himself up and walks to the door. He unclenches his hand, lets it hover over the stainless-steel handle. But he does not make contact. In the end the hand drops back to his side.

"You must be careful of that foot, especially Adriana."

Grimacing, he unwraps his scarf, throws it onto the bed. The meal has made him sweat. He feels the jowls dragging on his face and the weight of his belly. What can he expect if he eats and doesn't exercise? Sliding a hand under his vest, he begins to scratch.

The move to the city has not arrested the spread of the disease. His hairless chest is patched with white fleck marks where the skin is peeling. These sores, the shape and size of tears, also speckle his arms and the insides of his legs, while a thick red rash torments the back of his neck. An unkempt graying beard conceals the eruptions on his plump face. His scalp shows pinkly through a thin scrub of curls. If he scratches it, the fingers come away stuck with the hairs.

To handle a book, even, is an agony. There are brown pustules on the palms of his hands, on the soles of his feet, on the skin of his armpits and inside his ears and belly button. Since he left the jungle six months ago, his nails have grown crumbly. On his right hand, three have lifted from the nailbed. He bathes them every morning in a bowl of warm oil, but the delicate flesh around and under them is weepy. Against the pain, a doctor has advised, "Find an image you like. Imagine yourself on a beach, or your skin being soothed by the sun."

The only thing that can help is to be in the sun.

He tries light therapy. In the evenings he sits under the sunlamp and reads, but it is never wise to read for long. He has articles brought to him on the current state of research into his condition. He experiments with the latest medicines. He prays for a miraculous breakthrough, but his head tells him there is no cure. A doctor has told him, "It's your Spanish blood coming through." But he still hopes.

Downstairs the tempo quickens. The girls have changed into pointe shoes and are leaping through the air. He hears the yelp of the shoes, the thump of feet as the dancers land, the occasional, less exact, sound of someone falling over, the teacher's handclaps passing like gunshots through the floor.

"Laura, do you want to have a go?"

Ezequiel closes his eyes.

He is awakened by the young dancers applauding their teacher.

A mosquito feeds on the back of his hand. He watches the blood fill its belly. He lifts his hand and the insect is gone.

A minute later he limps into the bathroom and claws a flattened tube from the basin. He squeezes a length of greenish jelly onto his fingers and rubs it into his neck and behind his ears and on his chin until the beard glistens. Lifting his vest, he smears the foul-smelling stuff over his stomach. Then he unbuckles his trousers and does the same on the inside of each leg. Having shielded the exposed skin, he spreads the Dithranol—very carefully, since it burns. Finally, he swallows the last two pills from a brown box. He has been taking these pills since June. They make him liverish, but on parts of his body he has noticed the rash has stopped spreading. He drops the empty carton into a bucket under the sink.

Beneath his feet, below him, he hears the girls turning on the showers. The sounds are distinct. He hears their giggles, the water hosing their bodies, their complaints about the lesson.

"I told her from the start my neck's out from last night."

"Doesn't she understand we're exhausted?"

"My physio told me I shouldn't be pushing it, and there she was—pushing it."

"Shit, my feet are bleeding again."

Sometimes the girls talk about sex while they soap themselves, or as they whip their long hair from side to side under the hot-air vent. But tonight in the shower they talk about Laura.

This dance they're talking about, she had performed it while he slept.

"You used to dance like a lollipop," says a grudging voice. "What happened to you?"

They ask questions, trying to sound nonchalant.

"Was it as amazing as it looked?"

"Go on, Laura. What was it like?"

The girl called Laura speaks. She sounds embarrassed. She dreamed she was standing in the air.


Twelve hours after I last saw Yolanda, in the early hours of Friday morning, a car bomb exploded on a traffic circle in the main street of Miraflores, killing twenty-seven people and gouging a truck-sized hole in the road outside the Café Haiti. The debris maimed scores of others, among them the cheerful waitress from Judío, whose nose was sliced off. There was no doubting the intended target: Cleopatra's Hotel, where the Foreign Minister was to have entertained ambassadors from countries of the European Community at breakfast. But an accident spared the hotel. At the traffic circle the getaway car crashed into one loaded with a mixture of fertilizer, diesel oil and dynamite. Their bumpers became entangled. When the café's security guard walked over to help, the drivers ran off across the park. The collision must have damaged the detonating mechanism, because ten seconds later the front car blew up, the force of the seventeen-hundred-pound bomb catapulting it into the Café Haiti, which caught fire.

I heard the thunderclap from ten miles away, having just arrived in Calle Diderot. It was seven in the morning and the street was rubbing its eyes. Opposite, a schoolgirl leaned against a wall talking to a friend, their legs the color of cooking oil in the sun. The bottle boy cried out and they glanced up, which encouraged him to bicycle past waving both hands in the air. Red-faced, talking both at once, they turned back to each other, ignoring him.

"Bottles! Bottles!"

The earth jolted between his cries, but the girls did not look up.

There were few details to be had over the radio link with headquarters. I tried to contact Sylvina on the mobile phone. As I left, she had murmured about some shopping she needed to do. I rang home, but the line was engaged. I waited five minutes and tried again. Still busy. An hour later she answered.

"Yes?"

"It's Agustín." I was so relieved to hear her voice.

"What's wrong? Are you all right?"

"What about you? What about the bomb?"

"Bomb? I thought it was the gas mains."

"You're not hurt, then?"

"No. I was washing my hair. I was going to complain. The oven's not working."

"You know I love you."

There was a pause. "Agustín, you can't just ring up and say

you love me as if that will make up for not saying it when we're together. It won't."

"Darling, I was worried."

"I was expecting another call."

My news had disturbed Sylvina. She wanted to know from me how I thought the bomb would affect her presentation on Sunday night. She'd had acceptances from ten prospective clients, including Leonora—which was a coup (although Leonora's dachshund had become pregnant by Patricia's Irish setter, and Leonora was worried the puppies, expected to be premature, might have to be born by cesarean). Sylvina didn't know how she was going to seat everyone. She needed extra chairs, but she refused point-blank to ask the people upstairs before I had even suggested it.

"Do you think the bomb will affect international flights?"

"Why should it?"

"That's another thing. I have to go to the airport."

"What on earth for?"

"I'm expecting more samples this afternoon."

"Can't they wait?"

"No. Patricia placed her order on the strictest condition she had the lipstick in time for the American Chargé's party tomorrow. I've been invited too, which is very sweet, since I've met Señora Tennyson only once. It's her fortieth birthday, which means a present, I suppose . . . Perhaps a nourishing night cream . . ."

Dr. Zampini drove by, raking a hand through his long gray hair. The bus drew up and the two girls climbed aboard.

Sylvina said, after another pause, "Agustín, would you do me a favor? I've spoken to Marina. She's free to collect the girls later tonight, but she doesn't think she can take them to their lesson. Would you do that? I don't often ask and it would help matters."

"Shouldn't we pull Laura out of the ballet—for the moment?"

"When everything's going so well for her? Agustín, I simply don't read you sometimes."


Gómez relieved me at three o'clock. I drove back to headquarters. In the corridor a long-faced Sergeant Ciras gave me an update.

When the car crashed through the Haiti's window, twenty people were in the café. The dead included a director of the Banco Wiese and a junior Foreign Office minister, blown up with his undelivered speech in his briefcase. And there were yet more injuries when tenants of the high-rise blocks recklessly tapped out the shards from their smashed windows onto the pavements below.

I walked upstairs, thinking of an obliterated corner table.

When the General heard I was in the building, he sent for me. "What's going on?" he said woozily, as if he had fainted. He grabbed my arm and shut the door. "Calderón has been shitting on my shadow all morning." He sat down heavily. The fruit bowl was all but empty. The crisis had stripped away his eccentricities, of which the final remnant was one shriveled orange. The General started to peel it.

"Latest orders: whoever captures Ezequiel, we turn him over to Calderón and keep it secret." He put the first segment of orange into his mouth.

"What does that mean for Ezequiel, sir?"

"It means they'll shoot him."

He pulled a face and spat out a pip. "The army's become the government—the government's so desperate they're trying to buy their way out. The reward for Ezequiel's capture is now ten million dollars. I've heard they are debating bringing in the Americans."

He leaned forward, rubbing his cheeks. "I tell you, tomcat, this is a cluster-fuck."

His face had a bedraggled, unimportant look. "Tell me, anything in Perón and Diderot?"

"So far nothing."

"Gut feeling?"

"Gut feeling is we're close, but we mustn't hurry—"

"Yes, yes, I know about your inflatable bed theory." He played with the orange peel, plucking out strands of pith, which he dropped into the bowl. In a voice so quiet that he might have been speaking to himself, but didn't mind if I overheard, he said, "Fact is, tomcat, in one sense Brother Ezequiel's won already. The Americans, who believe everything they read in *Der Spiegel,* reckon he's taken control of the country."

He lifted his head. "It was a pity he had to bring in all this Mao and Kant, you know. It was perfectly understandable without that claptrap."

I sought out Sucre in the basement. He stood behind a table, face mask pushed up over his hair, tagging a card to a trash bag. He had opened the door to allow in air from the courtyard, but the place stank. Bunches of flies rose from the concrete floor as I approached.

"What's exciting today?"

Behind Sucre, dressed in coveralls and wearing blue rubber gloves, other men raked through a little hill of filth.

"Nothing to give you gooseflesh."

He studied a chart, wrinkling his nose. "Best of the day? Calle Perón. Item One: three copies of *Marxism Today* from No. 29. Item Two: traces of cocaine in envelope addressed to cultural attaché in No. 34. Item Three: serrated bone-handled knife from No. 63, probably thrown away by accident, since the bag also contained duck à l'orange."

"Any medicines?"

"Aspirin, Nivea, French talcum powder, mouthwash, yards of dental floss, used Trojans. What you'd expect from diplomats."

"Calle Diderot?"

"We're collecting tonight. You told us not to be too clockwork. Make the customers uneasy."

"Clorindo report anything?"

"He frightened off a man climbing into 456. Probably just a thief. Otherwise he's whitewashed most of the trees."

"Gómez?"

"Problem with the maid at No. 345, who said her employer liked to plant the geraniums himself. Yesterday he put in all the annuals I gave him." He set down the paper and tried to wipe off a grease stain he'd made with his thumb. "Soon everyone will want to move in."


At six o'clock I drove one of our surveillance vehicles to Laura's ballet school. About the dangers posed to my daughter, I suffered a father's anguish. Should I tell Sylvina, who, in a sort of ecstasy, spent each day ordering lipsticks? Should Laura from now on ride to and from her class with Marina? I didn't want her associated with me. Ought I to remove her from the school? Would you have wanted *your* child to go to dance lessons in that street?

"Laura!"

She didn't recognize the car. I repeated her name, but she turned away.

I opened my door and shouted. "Laura! Samantha!" They turned, walked over.

"Where's Mummy?" said Laura, climbing into the backseat.

"She's gone to the airport."

"Is she leaving?"

"She's collecting something. It's for her presentation on Sunday. Marina will take you both home later."

In the mirror her face was serious. "Daddy, do you think we'll ever be rich?"

"No."

"Yes, we will be. Mummy says we're going to be rich and she's going to buy a house in Paracas and drive us there every weekend in a big purple car."

"Let's not argue in front of Samantha."

At this Marina's daughter, small-eyed, ruddy-faced, looked superior. The month before, she had stabbed Laura with a pencil.

Laura looked out of the window. "This isn't the way."

I was driving along the coast road. The streets around the Haiti would be blocked off. "There's been a bomb."

"Samantha knows one of the people who was hurt."

I looked up. "Is that so?" In the back Samantha tried to feign sadness but looked proud.

"It's not my friend, Laura, it's Mummy's."

"You said it was your friend."

"I did not."

"How's your flute?" I asked Laura.

The night before, I had come home from the ballet studio. After taking a shower, I found her in the kitchen. She threw her arms about me.

"Daddy, thank you! I was so horrid. I thought you'd forgotten. Mummy said you must have been keeping it as a surprise."

"What are you talking about?"

"I shouldn't have opened your briefcase, but I was looking for your newspaper . . ." She slipped her head from beneath my hand. Her fingers, their span not yet great enough to cover the holes, clutched Yolanda's gift to me.

Behind me in the car, Laura's voice: "The flute's all right."

"Is that all?"

"That's what you say whenever we ask you something. I can't wait to show it to Yolanda."

"I don't want you to take it to the studio," I said hastily. "It's too precious."

"But Daddy—"

"What have you both been dancing this week? Samantha?"

"Yesterday we danced *The Nutcracker*. The day before we tried a dance from the sierra."

"What dance?"

Laura, reminded of her aborted trip, said, "You won't have heard of it."

"Try me."

"I know what it's called," said Samantha, perking up.

"Don't tell him."

" 'Taqui Onqoy'," pronounced Samantha, accurately.

"The dance of illness?" It was a messianic dance.

"Samantha has an audition at the Metropolitan," said Laura.

Samantha, looking out of the window, said in a lethargic, grown-up voice, "But I don't really know if I want to go there. Daddy says I might be better off in Florida."

"What about Yolanda," I said, "are you pleased with her, both of you?"

Laura came forward, hugging the headrest on my seat, her breath on my neck.

"We think she's got a boyfriend," she said slyly.

Both girls giggled. I flushed. Were they talking about me?

I adopted Samantha's bored tone. "Who is he, do you know?"

"Christina saw a birthday cake in the fridge," said Laura. She had removed her hairclip and now shook loose her hair. "And the two wine glasses, Samantha—remember?"

"Someone's given her an old pot," Samantha added. "She was furious when I put out my cigarette in it."

"Samantha! Sssh!"

I was too interested in Yolanda to take up the matter of a forbidden cigarette.

"Must it be a boyfriend?"

"Oh yes," said Laura. "She's changed, don't you think, Samantha? She's started worrying what she looks like. She never did before."

I felt an unpleasant tingle at the back of my neck. Perhaps Yolanda did have a boyfriend.

"Daddy," whispered Laura, "you shouldn't scratch like that. Your neck's covered in spots."

"You've missed the studio," noted Samantha.

"I'll drop you both here."

I parked on the corner and they climbed out. I tilted my side mirror, watching them walk back a block until they stood outside the door in the green wall. Samantha pressed the bell. Laura fiddled with the zipper on her Adidas bag. Aware that I was watching, she refused to look back. She tugged up one leg, then the other, exercising. She was the only reason my marriage survived.

The door opened. I saw Laura's face light up.


I drove past Gómez, who followed me at a distance to a car park behind the Banco Wiese in Calle Salta. I then climbed into Gómez's van and he drove me to Calle Diderot, parking in the narrow cul-de-sac opposite the studio. After he got out, locked up and walked away, I took up position in the back. Through the Perspex I could see the studio's strip lights. Laura had left her hairclip in the car and I held onto it, thinking of her inside with Yolanda.

You have to realize, watching—it's also about desire. I was deeply shaken when I sat down in that van. *We think she's got a boyfriend.* Laura's words were a punch to my heart. She was Yolanda's pupil and I was her father and Yolanda had *Antigone* to think about. It was none of my business—but suppose there *was* someone else in Yolanda's life? She'd mentioned a fiancé, had said,

*Oh, I've catted around.* Then there was the matter of her visit to the sierra. Had she made the journey to the ice festival alone? Or had she been with a lover when she was researching the dance groups? People tend not to mention former companions when talking to a third person they are fond of—and I didn't doubt Yolanda liked me. But how much? And was her brother really her brother? Or was I being jealous of myself?

How many times did I tell myself none of this should concern me? But after what both Laura and Samantha had said, my hopes and suspicions ran wild. One minute I was elated. The next, I felt the cold feet of jealousy climbing into bed beside me. With everything else that was going on, it was hard to reconcile myself to the fact I was in love.

There's no point trying to understand why people fall in love. My contact with Yolanda had been so snatched, yet the impact had been intense. I was forty-three years old, but I had lived only for a few days. Once you wake up like that, you don't drop back into sleep. Not easily. Since Monday, when I had bumped into Yolanda in the Bullrich Arcade, I had hardly slept. My heart had become a vast and uncomfortable thing. It reared out of my chest, throwing back my head so I could breathe only with difficulty. As I pressed my forehead to the dark Perspex strip, I could no longer hide from myself the reason for these feelings, this behavior.

In the few hours that remained until I saw her again, this is what I argued: I was in the saddle of a passion which could lead nowhere. I sifted Yolanda's character for faults, fumbled with them to that narrow bar of light. She was immature, unpredictable. She had chubby cheeks, an unquenchable appetite for cakes, ugly feet. I pictured her in revolting positions. I summoned her feet and stamped their deformed features on her face, over her eyes. There! Could I find her attractive now? I did. I did! I was in pain. I was miserable. I was ashamed. I was thrilled. The smallest detail rang with her name, from the outline of the jacaranda to the pattern of specks on the Perspex.

———

You remember I told you how she flipped the jug in the air? Well, what happened . . . happened shortly afterward. She remained in that position, eyes closed, arms raised, holding her breath. I can only say that, to me, the air about her was charged with the naked thrill of what she had done. She looked as if some extraordinary truth had dawned on her. I mean, think of it. She had with that simple gesture buried her brother, the state, herself.

Then she lowered her arms and this expression vanished and her breath returned in chokes. Her throat and shoulders were sweating. Tiny crystals of rosin sparkled in her eyes, on her breasts. The dress had opened at the front. Her dark ruby nipples showed through the thin cloth, catching at the material. She was devastated, but also intoxicated.

We fell against each other. I felt her hair rubbing my cheek and her breath, flavored with wine and banana cake, scorching my neck. Her closeness was unbearable. I longed to move my hands down her sweating back, to take off her dress. Her breasts pressed hard against my chest and I smelled her coppery skin. In that moment I wanted her more than anything I had ever seen or known or done.

I touched her and became something else. All the vital experiences of my life had predicted this moment. Touching her, I repossessed them and relived them, felt their reverberations. I was a candle burning in the snow. I was my father carrying my mother in his arms. I was grief and joy.

Slowly, she tilted back her head. She held my face between her hands and she kissed me.

Then she pushed away. "Oh, my darling, what are we going to do?" She blinked, putting out a hand to the barre. Rosin had fallen into her eyes. She rubbed them with the back of her hand.

"It's not allowed, you know that. What are we going to do? I—"

She couldn't escape my face in the mirror. Nor the effect on me of her words. "And believe me, I want to, I want to . . ."

Now she folded her arms, bowed in pain. "Agustín, you must go. It's impossible. It's nearly the curfew."

My voice came out thick, desperate. Our kiss, which had made her all of a sudden vulnerable and tense—like someone without a skin, really—had brushed me with fire.

"Tomorrow, can I see you tomorrow?"

She unfolded her arms, clasped and unclasped her hands. "It disturbs me very much to have you here."

"Disturbs you?"

"This is a really important decision. For us both. It is not one I can make now. Not now. The dance is an impediment, Agustín. I've been working too hard. I'm not clearheaded."

She glanced crookedly up at me in the mirror. It was easier to fend me off there. In a ravaged voice, she said, "It's not something to be entered into lightly. After the dance—after that, let's talk about it. Let's be sure."

The ballet class ended at eight-thirty. Through the Perspex I watched the girls being collected. Marina drove off in her red BMW, Laura and Samantha squabbling in the back. I trained my binoculars on the door, but I did not see Yolanda.

A mosquito wailed in the air near my face, then fell silent. I slapped my cheek.

Some time later, there was the noise of a key in the lock. The door opened and Sucre climbed in. The chassis rocked as he clambered to the back. I unfolded a chair for him. He had inspected the garbage bags from Calle Perón. Nothing of substance. He took a paper bag from his jacket pocket. "Sandwich, sir?"

He reeked of the basement. I had to ask him what the sandwich filling was.

The streetlight threw a band of orange across our faces. Sucre touched his cheek to indicate the spot. "You've been bitten, sir."

I wiped my face and looked at my finger. There was blood on the tip.

"I've a can of spray in my truck."

"It doesn't matter. I'm leaving soon. Tell Gómez to be here at ten."

Sucre would start collecting the trash once the curfew started. Piled outside each house, the black sacks had materialized throughout the day. As ten o'clock approached, they stopped appearing. The curfew wasn't for another twenty minutes, but its shroud prepared to wrap the city. Everything fell still and you heard sounds you never normally heard. The fragile hum of a drunk. The receding gargle of a motorbike.

The clink of a garbage bag against a doorframe.

I heard the noise, glanced across the street. What I saw made me sit bolt upright in my chair. All day I had longed for this sight. It jarred me to see her.

Yolanda, in black leotard, black tights and bright red headband, squeezed sideways through the door in the wall and onto the sidewalk. She held one trash bag against her chest and dragged another behind her. She swung them onto the heap at the base of the lamppost and wiped her hands. I expected her to return inside, but she paused under the light.

I focused the binoculars. That I was snooping shamed me. What would she think if she knew that, fifty yards away, I sat spying on her?

With her feet turned out, she walked two or three paces toward me. Her shadow lengthened out and revolved against the wall. Rising on her toes, she gazed down the street.

My head swirled: She's expecting somebody.

"That's got a nice little walk on it," observed Sucre. "Your girl's teacher, isn't it?"

"Yes."

"Single, is she, sir?"

"That's right."

"You know, a single girl like that—it's kind of tragic."

Balanced on the tips of her ballet slippers, again she looked down the street.

"Although," said Sucre, "that's a lot of garbage for a girl on her own."

She turned and loped, head down, toward the studio. I adjusted the focus, following her inside. I expected her to shut the door and draw the chain. Instead, she stood on one leg, eased off a slipper and wedged it between the door and frame.

Sucre scratched at the plaque on his teeth, sucking. "Hello. She's waiting for someone."

*We think she's got a boyfriend.*

Before leaving the van, I put my pistol in the glove compartment. "Time to start collecting the trash."


She saw me the instant I entered. All those mirrors—you're aware of who's walked into the studio without having to look behind you.

"It's you." She stood with her back to me, not turning, one arm up, one leg raised in an arabesque.

"You're still rehearsing?" I looked at Lazo's jug and the tapes, which she hadn't moved—which she had played for me. I looked at the two glasses on the floor where we had left them, the wine evaporated to a powdery red blush.

"I didn't expect you."

I put into my voice all the passion I felt. "I wanted to see you."

She lowered her leg to the floor.

"I love you."

In an empty dance studio—or anywhere else, I suppose—a whispered love is a deafening thing. I had not known I was going to say the words. But in the van, when I visualized our scenes together, I had been drawn back to everything that was truest about myself.

She bowed her head as if someone were saying grace. "Please don't."

"But this last week—"

She whirled toward me. "And I meant everything I said."

Then she crumpled to the floor.

It's funny, the memories you keep of people. The moments which fix them in your mind aren't always the most obvious. My last image of Father Ramón is the vision of him in dirty tennis shoes spreading a silver chain above my head. I remember my mother shooing parrots and my father in too large a suit at my wedding and my wife leaning against the kitchen window, tapping at the glass. She was tapping like that to make a bird on the lawn fly away, to save it. But, startled by the noise of her fingers, the cat pounced. "And Agustín wanted to put you down," she said afterward, stroking it.

This is almost the last memory I retain of Yolanda. It's a sight that stops my heart. She is seated cross-legged on the parquet. Her long hands are thrust over her face, her hair falls through her fingers, and the red headband is about to slip off. Lazo's jug is beside her and she sobs into her lap.

Curiously, I don't hear the sound of a woman weeping, but of a river breaking over the rocks and the wind dragging its feet through the grass and the slap of a tattered wind sock. I have this sensation I have led Yolanda along the bank and up a steep narrow path to the airstrip. I see the ice sheeting the mountains and the ancient field beaten from the valley floor and the moist square of earth where the grass has not grown back.

I said something and left.

# 14

You don't wake up, look at a blue sky and think to yourself, What a perfect day to capture Ezequiel.

It was another morning which began uneventfully. By ten o'clock the sky was overcast. The branches shifted a little, and from the window of the car—a Ford Falcon, I think—I watched a duck fly east. The air smelled of fish.

Everyone in the street agreed. Today, or tomorrow, it would rain.

At ten-thirty my mobile bleeped. It was the General. Last night a woman had been arrested near the city's main water plant. She had been carrying a bottle of urine

"The lab says it's contaminated with the typhus bacillus."

He was calling because he had no one else to tell. He saw no end to the giddying violence. He didn't ask if I had anything to report.

At eleven I called Sucre. He'd managed three hours' sleep and sounded exhausted. I waited for him to find his notes. Somewhere he had a list of those who'd broken the curfew in Calle Diderot.

Dr. Zampini, presumably on a hospital call. "But we're checking."

The owner of the video store. He'd come back at midnight, drunk.

Two women and a man going into No. 459.

I was slow to register. "But that's the ballet studio . . ."

"They turned up about fifteen minutes after you left with Gómez."

"In a car?"

"On foot."

"Description?"

"The man had a beard."

Lorenzo. The depressed choreographer. Of course! Why hadn't I thought of him before? *I'd love to see a dress rehearsal. The others would too.* He'd be bringing the members of Yolanda's dance group, the ones who had first wanted to be in *Antigone.* They would have taken a bus from the center. Perhaps the bus had been late, or they'd missed an earlier one. That's why Yolanda had wedged open the door with her ballet slipper. She didn't want them stranded outside in the curfew.

My jealousy eased. I felt happy.

"When did they leave?"

"They were there when I took away the trash. That was about midnight."

"What about the trash?"

"Seventy-six bags we've done."

"That leaves how many?"

"About the same number."

"When do you reckon to finish?"

"Five, six o'clock."

At three o'clock, after Gómez relieved me, I drove to headquarters. I intended to return later to Calle Diderot, spending the night in the van. For the rest of the day I would busy myself with my report on the military's atrocities in La Posta. I wanted to block out Yolanda.

According to the deposition of María Valdes, 67, the officers who dragged her into the field were addressed by the nicknames Pulpo and Capitán . . .

But I didn't see an old woman in a dentist's office, raising her hand to speak. I saw an anchovy scar, an ocher dress snagged on a breast, a flash of calf through a torn leotard, a row of white teeth pressed into a bottom lip.

At five I telephoned Sylvina. She was excited. Fifteen people had subscribed for Sunday's presentation! Because of tonight's party given by the American Chargé d'Affaires, she wouldn't be back till late. Patricia promised that several ambassadors would be there and, with luck, some generals and their wives. I sensed her hands winnowing the air at the prospect of new clients. "I tell you, Agustín, we're going to be rich."

So, anticipating this, she planned to rearrange the apartment and change the color of her hair.

"And I've bought you a polo shirt." She described it, navy blue, sleeveless, from a store in the Bullrich Arcade. "Marina said it's time I spoiled you."

I drank a Coke. Midway through my report I broke off to write to Lazo, to say that I had repaid his daughter and discharged my promise. Then I asked him for copies of his dental records—in case, as was my hope, we found Tomasio's body.

At six fifty-five the telephone on my desk rang. It was Sucre, his voice hoarse. "Sir, I think you should come."

Sucre had isolated three tubes on the table. Also, two pillboxes and ten crushed cigarette packets. The stench in the basement dispersed the moment I saw them.

The tubes had been rolled up to the mouth. I flattened one out. Dithranol. The brown pillboxes had contained methotrexate and cyclosporin A. The cigarettes were Winston.

"Which house?" Even before Sucre answered, a numbness invaded me.

He smoothed out the neck of the trash bag, inspecting the label he had taped there.

It was seven-ten. I didn't have time to stop and think. My first impulse was to warn Yolanda, but the class had begun on time. Gómez, sitting in a green Renault, confirmed fourteen girls inside, plus Laura. If I warned their teacher, it would create panic among her pupils and alert Ezequiel in the flat above.

I told Sucre, "Find out how long the place has been rented, who the landlord is, whether there's a ground plan. Get everyone from Calle Perón to the Banco Wiese car park in Calle Salta."

I telephoned Marina. Today was Tuesday. Her turn to collect the girls. No one answered. I tried Sylvina. She had said she was going to the hairdresser. No answer.

Twenty minutes later I addressed the unit over the radio. There was no time to speak to each officer individually, so I told them to listen carefully. I had, I said, been inside No. 459.

The house was divided into two. Downstairs was the ballet school. Our suspect might be in the first-floor apartment. There was no access from the studio and the ballet mistress didn't know who lived upstairs. Probably our suspect relied on a staircase at the side or back of the building, but I hadn't seen it.

Once they were over the wall, they were not to open fire unless they were fired on first. Anyone found inside must be captured alive.

"There's a dance class in there. I want to wait until the class is out."

Before leaving, I again telephoned Marina and Sylvina, but there was still no answer.

At seven forty-five I drove to Calle Diderot. Apart from my team I had told no one.

Not a day goes by when I don't return to that scene.

Dusk is falling. I park in the cul-de-sac. There's a bright light shining in the upstairs apartment and I train my glasses on the yellow curtain. Behind the cartoon elephants a shadow blurs back and forth as if addressing an audience. The shape disappears and the only movement is the curtain being sucked in and out by the draft.

Gómez, in his gardener's overalls, halts his wheelbarrow beside the car. The directional mike is hidden in the rake. For thirty minutes he has pointed its laser at the first-floor window, picking up vibrations from the glass.

"Meeting broke up a few minutes ago. He's now watching television."

"Who else is up there?"

"Four others. They're resting in a room at the back."

"And the dance class?"

"Just now a lot of clapping, but no one's come out yet."

He trundles his wheelbarrow away. Sucre gets in beside me.

Neither of us says anything. Such a long time I've waited for this moment, but I don't feel tired. I'm concerned for Laura and Yolanda. I must get them out.

The clapping means the lesson has finished. I fiddle with Laura's hairclip, trying to imagine my daughter waiting her turn in the shower. The older girls will have lit cigarettes. They will be lying exhausted on the floor, their feet against the wall, higher than their heads. They will be looking at the ceiling. At Ezequiel.

Will he have guns, explosives? Will there be a secret escape route? Will he let himself be taken alive? Or will he want his world to die with him?

There's nothing to do but wait.

I feel the relieving breeze from the sea and hear the bottle boy yell out from the next street. The maid from the house opposite the studio is beating a carpet against the railings. Elsewhere, people are putting on their makeup, going to a birthday party, meeting for the first time, falling in love.

Against the fatigued sky the branches of the jacaranda are blots of ink. A bird flies down to a lawn which is being watered by a sprinkler. On the porch, darkened by the spray, a dog wakes up and shakes itself. The bird returns to the tree, a branch sinking slightly under its weight. The light is fading fast.

In the café beside the studio a tubby fellow with curly fair hair caresses a young woman's ear. They kiss. Their job has been to monitor my side of the street; also to protect me. They have been there since three this afternoon. Behind them, Clorindo, in a gray pigskin jacket, buys some cigarettes and gets into an argument about change.

At eight there's a honk. Dr. Zampini parks in front of his house. The door opens and a wedge of orange light reaches down the path, pulling him toward his wife. She stands on the threshold, her hair freshly sculptured, her arms raised in welcome.

"Here they come!" whispers Sucre.

The door in the green wall opens, and out of it troop the girls. I count them, holding my breath until I see, second to last, Laura. Yolanda follows, in a long T-shirt and the black gauze skirt she was wearing when I first met her. She stands on the pavement giving the ballet mothers her pleasant "hello" wave. When she lifts an arm, rubbing it against her headband, I can see that her neck is shiny. Sucre can't keep his eyes off her.

Laura leans against the whitewashed trunk of the jacaranda, watching the other girls leave. Marina is late. Suddenly I realize that no one's collecting my daughter. She is alone, without even Samantha to talk to. Later I learn that Marina, on Marco's say-so, has removed Samantha from the class in reaction to news of the Miraflores bomb.

One by one the ballet mothers leave. Eventually only Laura remains.

"Oh God," says Sucre, "she's going back inside!"

Yolanda is saying, "Why don't you wait in the studio?"

Laura gathers up her Adidas bag and heads for the door. I'm reaching for the handle when there's the sound of a car horn and Sylvina jerks our gray Peugeot to a halt outside the door in the wall.

My wife is dressed for her party. I can tell, thank God, she's in a hurry. She throws open the passenger door and shouts across the seat. Yolanda, hands pressed between her knees, stoops to the car window.

I hear Sylvina's words, "Good luck tomorrow."

"Come on, come on," I'm saying.

Sylvina checks herself in the driver's mirror. A quick hand through her hair, set in a new style. More lipstick, she decides. Leisurely, she applies it. Yolanda, embarrassed, seems to think she ought to wait. She sinks to her haunches and says something to Laura, touching her shoulder through the window.

"Get on with it."

At last the car starts. They wave goodbye. Sylvina drives past, running her tongue over teeth and lips.

A desire rises unsteadily within me, like a rage. I want to leap out, scream, run as fast as I can down the street to prevent Yolanda from stepping back inside that door. Unaware of my thoughts, unaware of the eyes upon her, she removes her headband. With it she dabs her temples, her cheeks, then stretches it back over her hair. With a toss of the head, she disappears through the door.

The street is empty, frozen.

"Look, sir. Upstairs!"

Upstairs the curtain parts; against the yellow folds the outline of fingertips, a cheek.

"That's him, isn't it?"

At first I move the focusing wheel the wrong way, so that he dissolves into the curtain. Then I have him.

The head swivels as if in pain. Through thick spectacles two black, bright eyes sweep the street. About the throat, loosely knotted, there's a scarf. A hand appears and begins absentmindedly to scratch at the back of the neck.

The car radio crackles. "Men in position." Sucre, his voice edged with terror, fears a blackout.

But I wish to prolong the moment. I know my life is about to change. In a room behind the green wall Yolanda will be undressing. She'll be turning on the shower. I can see her soaping her legs, her breasts. I see her squeezing the washcloth, wetting it, reaching over her shoulders to scrub her back. She screws shut her eyes and lifts her face to the jet. Cymbals and pipe music sound in her head. Everything is ready for her dance tomorrow. I hear her humming through the falling water.

The lights snap on in the street. I look down Calle Diderot one last time. The bottle boy bicycling round the corner. The maid whacking her cane against the carpet. Just now, after the spear shot of recognition when I saw the face at the window, a wave of calm rolled through my head. The hush ebbs and I hear the slow handclap of I don't know how many thousand dead.

Sucre again. "We're ready to go."

I put down the hairclip. I pick up the handset.

## 15

There really is very little more to say.

I gave the order, after which seven of my men climbed over the wall. Finding no outside steps, they smashed into the studio through the sliding panels, and in the kitchen knocked down a door leading up a short staircase to the first-floor apartment. Ezequiel was sitting under a sunlamp with the *Critique of Pure Reason* still in his hands. The television was on. He was watching the boxing.

Sucre radioed me. "It's him."

The rain had started. I came in from the car and ran across the patio. Yolanda was struggling on the parquet with two of my men. There was glass everywhere. Oblivious to her screams, a third man was pointing a pump-gun at the ceiling.

Yolanda, aware of another presence, looked up. Shock blackened her eyes and left her cheeks purple and gray, the shade of an artichoke leaf.

Her eyes grabbed me. "Agustín! Help me. These bastards—"

"Let her go."

Gómez tried to say something.

"Shut up," I said.

He released Yolanda and she ran to me, throwing her arms around my neck, sobbing with relief.

I stroked her head. "Thank God you're safe. You don't know who we've got upstairs."

Behind my head, her arms stiffened. Extremely slowly, she disengaged herself.

"What's going on?" she said in a confused voice, her jaw at an angle.

I held both her hands. The veins in them stood out as she strained to pull away. "Don't be frightened. These are my men."

She glared at me. Some savagery transformed her eyes and there shot into them an expression I had seen on Laura's face. She stared into a middle distance that didn't exist, in which I did not exist.

She tore free one hand, punched the air and screamed, "Don't you dare harm him! You'll pay with your life if you harm him!"

"Yolanda—" As she whirled away from me, I felt the bite of truth.

"*Viva El Presidente Ezequiel!*"

Gómez seized one of her arms, Ciras the other, as she tumbled toward the floor.


Somehow I stepped past her, through the kitchen, up the steep, uncarpeted staircase, toward the dull nickel of my triumph.

He sat in his velvet-covered chair, a sick man wearing the yellow alpaca jersey which she had bought him. Sucre and Clorindo kept their guns on him.

He looked from Sucre to me and back to Sucre, who said, "Stand up before the Colonel."

Obviously in agony, Ezequiel slowly rose to his feet, watching me intently. Neither of us knew what to do. He offered his hand, and when I shook it, conscious of a rough-textured, vegetable skin, he flinched.

Sucre, encouraged by this contact, searched for a weapon. With care, as if he might not be dealing with someone of flesh and blood, he patted his hands down our prisoner's legs.

Ezequiel, still holding my hand, was calm. With his free hand he tapped his forehead. "You'll never kill this." He spoke with an insane clarity. His eyes were dark and unblinking, the black dots in their centers like shirt buttons. He was, I think, fully expecting to be shot. I had not even drawn my gun.

From a room at the back I heard women screaming. Edith and someone else, shrieking for me not to touch him. Downstairs, Yolanda's screams renewed themselves. Gómez must then have gagged her.

Since I wasn't in uniform, I introduced myself, addressing Ezequiel as "Professor." For the second time in our lives I asked for his documents. Gingerly, he emptied his pockets. He produced a spotted handkerchief, crinkly with dried phlegm. "I have none."

He did not appear distressed. I reasoned that someone who has caused so much havoc, so many killings, is not going to be worried by final capture.

"How many others?" I asked Sucre.

"Three next door—two females, one male—plus Edith Pusanga. Sánchez and Cecilia are covering them."

"And downstairs?"

"Only the dance teacher."

I turned to Ezequiel. Haunted by a ballerina with unseeing eyes, I couldn't distinguish the details of his face. "Is Yolanda with you?"

The beard opened and the answer slid out through a smile, stabbing me with the cold blade of understanding.

"Everyone's with us, Colonel. It doesn't matter if you shoot us. We're in history."

I told him that he must accompany me below. He wanted to take with him a Mao Tse-tung badge from a drawer by his bed. The Chinese leader had presented it to him personally.

I glanced at Sucre, but he was broken with emotion. I found the badge. After Ezequiel had closed his fist around it, I nodded to Clorindo to put on handcuffs. He seized Ezequiel's wrists and I thought, This is my victory. A sick man with nothing to say who wants to keep his memento from Mao.

Out of the room, he changed. He had been waiting for the coup de grâce. Once it dawned on him that he was caught, his personality abruptly weakened. He had no plan beyond this—not a Sixth or Seventh or a Twenty-fifth Grand Plan. Upstairs he could be Kant's dove, soaring in his own vacuum. Downstairs, when I took him into the street and the rain fell on his skin, he felt the beak of fear.

We used the back elevator to reach my office. I locked the door. Four men stood guard in the corridor outside. No one else was to be allowed entry. In accordance with the orders issued to me, and with enormous reluctance, I telephoned the office of Captain Calderón.

A clipped female voice told me he was attending a cocktail party at the house of the American Chargé d'Affaires. If my business was urgent, she was empowered to provide a contact number.

"It's urgent."

I started to dial. I was aware of Ezequiel in the chair and Sucre behind him and Gómez holding a gun. But my thoughts were not coherent.

I heard the ringing tone. I looked at Ezequiel, bright diamonds of rain on his yellow cardigan and in his hair. He must have felt an itch because he raised his hands and with the back of his fingers tried to scratch his temple. The handcuffs restricted his movements and he knocked off his spectacles. The sight of his naked face, suddenly revealed, brought a flash of recognition. I remembered the packed earth yard in Sierra de Pruna, the upturned beer crate, the cramped front room in the police post.

"Sucre, see to his glasses."

Ezequiel fumbled blindly on his lap, but his ruined fingernails caught in a fold of his trousers.

In the receiver at my ear a voice boomed in English, "Denver Tennyson, can I help?"

"Captain Calderón, is he there, please?"

"Who wants him?"

On the other side of the desk, Ezequiel grimaced. Suddenly I saw what the matter was. Gómez, in applying the handcuffs, had prised loose one of the fingernails. Ezequiel, when he dislodged his spectacles, had not been trying to scratch, but to press the nail back over the exposed flesh.

"I've made a mistake. I'm sorry to have troubled you." I replaced the receiver.

By that grimace, Ezequiel placed himself with the living. If, as were my orders, I handed him over to Calderón, he would be tortured and killed. I would be delivering him to the fate he expected, and against which he had prepared himself. He knew that in death he would become something else, a memory to spur his people on. To save his life was my greatest revenge.

I dialed Canal 7. "Cecilia, I have something for you. Yes. It's important."

At nine in the morning, having interrogated Ezequiel through the night, I presented him to the press. I learned more from our conversation than I am able to tell you, but nothing to make me alter my plan. Once word was out that we had him—alive and unharmed—the government could not shoot him. Your profession saved Ezequiel.

There was another consideration. I wanted to demonstrate that the institution I had served for twenty years was strong enough to ensure a fair trial. It was naive of me and it didn't happen. Yet he wasn't executed. Calderón drew up a Decree Law—even selected members of a naval firing squad—but the President feared the outrage abroad.

Calderón, if he couldn't execute Ezequiel, decided to humiliate him. He hit on the idea of exhibiting the captive in a cage. He dressed him up in a black and white uniform, like a cartoon figure, and locked him inside a large metal coop, a kind of box with bars, covered with tarpaulins. At what was judged to be the most propitious moment, Calderón had the covers removed. But it belittled us rather than Ezequiel. Like staring at a monkey in a zoo. As if we were superior. But you were there, with all the rest of those journalists. You saw how they treated him. That was in the piece you wrote.

"And Yolanda?" Dyer asked after a long interval.

Nothing in all his years as a journalist had hardened him to the despair in Rejas's answer.

"I was still interrogating Ezequiel when the message came through. Yolanda, Edith, Lorenzo and the two women from the Central Committee had been transferred from Calle Diderot to cells downstairs. Yolanda, I ordered, was to be put in a cell by herself. She had been hysterical, but the nurse had given her a shot. She was now asleep.

"I rang downstairs. 'I'll look in on her later,' I told the nurse. 'Please give her an extra blanket.' There was an astonished silence, so I said, 'She's my daughter's ballet teacher. She doesn't understand what's going on.'

" 'She doesn't, does she?' I asked Ezequiel.

"His hand opened and closed over Mao's badge, as it had throughout our conversation. Behind his glasses his eyes were tired. 'Comrade Miriam is not only a fine dancer, Colonel.'

"Even at this stage I hoped there had been some mistake. It didn't seem possible. Yolanda was naive politically, but if I could talk to her for an hour, we would find some way out of this. I didn't want to believe there wasn't a way.

"Minutes before the press conference, I tried to see her. I needed a special pass to enter the basement. My own orders. Sucre fetched the permit.

"The nurse looked at me angrily. 'Over there.'

"On a bench in a small cell, her face to the wall, Yolanda lay sleeping.

" 'When will she come round?' A blanket covered all but the top of her head.

" 'An hour or so. I gave her another shot at six.'

" 'She didn't understand what was going on,' I repeated.

"Behind me a drained voice said, 'You're wrong, boss.'

"Sucre nodded through the bars. His face had the look of someone who has steeled himself to say the unsayable."

Calderón gave me no chance to interrogate Yolanda. Twenty minutes after the press conference a convoy of trucks blocked off the entrance to the headquarters. Soldiers leapt out, followed by my furious military counterpart.

In my office he threw an official order down on my desk. It removed from my charge Ezequiel, the four members of the Central Committee—and Comrade Miriam, as Yolanda would from now on refer to herself.

I last saw her stumbling between soldiers, her head covered in a black hood.

16

Next evening Dyer crossed the square for the last time and climbed the stairway to the Cantina da Lua. The following morning he would take a plane out.

Rejas had ordered the wine. He began to fill two glasses as Dyer sat down.

Good news. The specialist had telephoned about his sister's tests. The antibiotic was working. Her cysticercosis, which they feared might have been a fatal strain, was curable.

Alert, no longer disoriented, his sister had no memory of her recent confusion. For the first time in a fortnight, she had asked Rejas to read to her. She wanted her mind to be taken out of that stuffy bedroom.

Rejas smiled. "I read a few pages of *Rebellion in the Backlands.*"

He poured another glass of wine, but he drank without tasting it. He had ordered the bottle to celebrate his sister's recovery. He was not drinking to celebrate.

He was coming to the end and he wanted Dyer to listen.


I have blanked out a lot since the night of Ezequiel's capture. Calderón forbade me to say a word, with very clear threats of unpleasant consequences if I chose to disobey him a second time. In the months ahead he would have me watched. But my wound was private. I hardly remembered how to breathe, or walk, or perform the simplest gestures. The press would declare repeatedly how, by my action, I had cured the country of "Ezequiel's pestilence." I had achieved all I had set out to achieve, but in achieving it I had lost what I most wanted. The truth was that I had sundered myself from all that was precious to me.

There followed the darkest days of my life. Why had fate determined that Ezequiel and I should be linked in this way? Nor could I get used to the coincidence that Ezequiel's safe house was the school where Laura learned her ballet. Every time I dropped my daughter off, I had been, without knowing it, delivering her to his lair.

I wanted to hate the person who had taken her hand, led her inside, but I didn't. I kept seeing Yolanda on the parquet, two men pinning her to the ground, her eyes loaded with hatred and madness combing her hair. I was stormed by her image and my heart could not bear it.

We know so little about people. But about the people we love, we know even less. I was so blind with love for her I hadn't been able to see. I had been like that American watching the video who could not believe it was his wife. *There must be thousands of poor bastards who don't know what's going on in their women's minds.* I had just kept making excuses and making excuses.

Shall I tell you something? Shall I let you into a secret about Yolanda?—and this is such a sad thing. I believe that until the last moment, when it could not have been clearer who I was, Yolanda had found a way of convincing herself. If true, it's pitiable—but how else do I explain our intimacy? On that day when we sat on the grass and I told her about the army massacre, she must have told herself I was on her side. I was one of them. Of course, she had no means of proving it. She couldn't run upstairs to Ezequiel and say, "I've just met this man . . ." That would have been a breach of his discipline. So she demonstrated her loyalty by not informing him. When she said to me, "Silence is part of the dance," she was speaking the truth.

At her level you weren't permitted contact with more than two comrades. And you'd address each other as Comrade this or Comrade that, so that you'd never discover who they were. After your mission you'd go back to being the person you had been before. It ensured you revealed nothing if you were tortured. That's why Ezequiel was effective.

But, isn't it funny? Isn't it the most appalling thing? There I was, pouring out my heart to Yolanda, all the time exhibiting the same tensions and worries she was suffering. It's possible some of the cryptic phrases I used to protect my work chimed with phrases she had been taught—and it would have been in her nature to think if she didn't recognize the code, the fault lay with her, not me.

Then there was this other problem. You see, in Ezequiel's world, love was forbidden. Sex was okay, but he demanded that his followers live a loveless life, dedicated to him. But for whatever reason, whether it had to do with her father or the sad figure who'd been her fiancé, poor Yolanda, who in every other way proved so perfect a disciple, wasn't quite capable of filling that emotional hollow with Ezequiel's philosophy. There was a gap which the revolution couldn't satisfy.

All her training, the nuns, the months in the jungle camp, ought to have drummed into her the unsuitability of a man like me. But in my comforting her during the blackout, something happened which she couldn't have predicted.

A week, ten days maybe, passed before I decided to speak to the one person who might reduce my madness: her old fiancé, the poet.

He was a thin, angular-faced man with trout-colored eyes and Yolanda's habit of staring into space. We walked through Parque Colón and sat on a bench, while, opposite us, a blue-and-yellow-uniformed gardener patted geraniums into the black earth.

The poet was reluctant to talk. He was still in love with her and so was I. We were rivals and I felt shameful, but I needed to see what he and I had in common, and if he bore any stamp of her.

I gave him little choice. Either he talked to me informally, here in the open air, or I would detain him for questioning. It was imperative we speak. There were matters I needed to clear up regarding Yolanda's trial.

It was a mild day, too cold to sit out really, and he was nervous. He spoke himself.

"I couldn't believe it. When I saw her photograph, screaming, I said, 'No, it can't be Yolanda.' And then it was Yolanda." He picked up a book wrapped with a battered-looking dust jacket. I supposed he had brought it along to prove his innocence. "It was as if I'd opened this book and it had exploded."

I asked to see the book. It was *When the Dead Speak* by Miguel Angel Torre. "No one pays attention to poetry," said its epigraph.

"Not a good time time for lyrics," he said.

I noticed a poem dedicated to Yolanda.

> . . . *world invisible,*
> *the skillful poison of*
> *your changeless pose* . . .

Envy overwhelmed me. This young man with the red mole on his forehead had felt the same as I did, but his desire had lived to enjoy its full flesh.

His shadow fell on the page. "She danced that one."

He started talking about her. Their first meeting, a friend's birthday party at the Catholic University. Her taste in music (she liked The Doors, Pink Floyd, King Crimson). Her passion for cakes. (A day later I found myself queuing at her favorite bakery in San Isidro.) A born seductress. Never said a bad word about anyone. Didn't have enemies. If she wanted to go from A to B, she went. Whatever the cost.

A force to be reckoned with.

Soon they were living in the blue house in Calle Tucumán. He installed a caoba wood barre in their bedroom so she could dance. That was a good time. They went to the beach, cooked, made love. Then, while she was convalescing from a leg injury, she was invited to Cuba, to a conference on the arts.

She was to be away for a fortnight. When she stayed a month, he became worried. Maybe she had met someone else. He was always jealous if, onstage, she danced with another man. But, no—there was no man. She had found the society in which she could believe. Four months after returning from Cuba, she resigned from the Metropolitan.

Classical ballet was too rigid. It was ballet for the bourgeois. From now on she would devote her energies to modern dance. Modern dance represented a liberation of the spirit from its state of repression.

"Her talk, it was all about dance. That's what I believed. But she was acting the whole time. She was seeing with other eyes."

"Did you never suspect?"

A hand squeezed his face. He was afraid. He had believed in many of the things she did. He also believed that to admit this to me would be to condemn himself. He feared, perhaps, that I would discover his status as an underground poet. But from my university days I had been familiar with the bars he frequented. Like him, I knew how to weave tough dreams from cigarette smoke. The Kloaka, the Dalmacia, the Café Quilca—these were the haunts of people who talk revolution, talk and do nothing about it. We were more alike than he knew, he and I. Yolanda would have branded us cowards.

"I thought what she felt was religious, not political," he said carefully. "There was a group of nuns she liked. Twice a week she would borrow my car and drive them to the shantytowns. She'd bake the children cakes, teach them to dance. At least, that's what I supposed she was doing. But she was very reserved, never talked of anything that was purely personal to her.

"Our relationship began to come unstuck when she wanted me to join in. 'How can you represent the masses if you don't live with them?' I had said. Besides, I was a poet, not a revolutionary.

" 'Then let's live with them,' she said.

"Early on, I might have done. But our affair was not as passionate as it had been. There were frictions. A writer has to live in his own world at one moment and relate to his public at another. A dancer needs to be the center of attention at all times. For Yolanda I had become something day-to-day, while every day she burned with a desire to impress a new audience.

"She attended a studio of modern dance in Calle Mitre, mixing with people I didn't approve of. She started coming home late, talking about Truth and Justice. She spoke of the Greeks, of Plato and Sophocles. She had read nothing—then Sophocles!

"Of course, you don't know her, so you can't imagine this. But Yolanda, reading Sophocles . . .

"One day she received a call from the youngest of the nuns. The army had stormed the prison in Lurigancho and killed two hundred of Ezequiel's men. I overheard the nun asking Yolanda to distribute leaflets about those who'd been murdered.

"I protested: 'Yolanda, those are Ezequiel's people.' And I forbade her. That night she came home late, driving my car.

"She didn't deny what she had done. She had brought back a potted plant for me. I threw it at the kitchen window. She swept up the glass, the earth, the terra-cotta shards. Later, when I apologized for breaking the window, she said, 'It isn't a window you have broken.'

"We didn't speak for a week. Then I found a pamphlet advertising a discussion at the Catholic University about the prison massacre. 'I want to go,' I said.

"The evening was dominated by this bearded chap—Lorenzo. He kept waving his arms about, shouting for everyone to rise up, assassinate the President. Afterward he joined us and he was very friendly with her.

" 'Yolanda,' I said, 'I don't want that man in our house.'

"Three days later I came home and he was sitting in our kitchen. I threw him out. It was the second time I had lost my temper. You couldn't lose your temper with Yolanda. She went with Lorenzo to the door and watched him leave. She didn't scream or say anything. But that night in bed she said she had begun to question our relationship.

"She became cold and distant. I worried for her health; among other things, she hadn't menstruated for twelve months. And ate nothing, only cakes. She'd become so thin she would put stockings in her bra to make herself look bigger there. But her belief was rocklike. I think she had already made her decision.

"Two days go by. Then at breakfast she says she's going on a retreat in the jungle with some Canadian nuns.

"I sat down and said, 'Yolanda, you're not going to a retreat. Are you?'

"She didn't lie. She didn't know how to lie.

" 'You're going to your political friends.'

" 'Yes.'

" 'Then we can't live together in this house anymore.'

"She packed and left. A week after that, when she hadn't come home, I abandoned the house.

"I saw her again about six months later. She was sweet, and talked for two hours about the jungle, what she had seen and done there. At the end of the conversation she asked for money. She had moved back into Calle Tucumán. She needed to pay the bills. I refused, said I knew what she wanted the money for. Now, for the first time, she lost her temper. She shouted at me, and then she turned on her heel and was gone.

"I saw her again once, walking along Calle Sol. I didn't recognize her at first. She had put on weight. I thought she looked terribly attractive. As she came toward me, I called her name. She walked past."

A man plonked himself down on the bench next to us and opened a newspaper.

We got to our feet. Behind us another gardener had been lifting turf. He didn't have gardener's hands.

We walked under the African tulip trees to the gate at the edge of the park.

"Is it possible she will recant?" I asked.

He shook his head. "No, this will have made her even stronger, even more determined. She'll never relent. Ballet gave her this discipline."

"What about her brother, was he involved too?"

"Brother?" he said. "She had no brother."

We stopped at the gate. I shook his hand, thanked him for his time. I knew he would have been distressed by our conversation. A barman at the Café Quilca had told me that he thought the poet had attempted suicide after Yolanda left. Now he was reluctant to let me go. There was a question which plagued him.

"Tell me, what was her relationship with Ezequiel? They say in the papers he slept with all his followers. She didn't sleep with him, did she?"

The same thought tormented me. We stood there, two rivals seeking from each other assurance it was impossible to give.

"There's no way of knowing one way or the other."

He nodded seriously to himself, zipped up his jacket, and I watched him sidle off, his head on one side, book under his arm, the other hand trailing along the railings.

Still, there are answers I can't find. What position did Yolanda hold? How did she relate to the Central Committee? To Edith? I would have bet on Edith being jealous of her. Yolanda was privileged, middle-class, not a jungle-tested killer. Or was she? Had she planted car bombs and cut throats? When I asked the poet, he remembered a Sunday lunch they'd had once and her squeamishness over a chicken. She couldn't sever its head and the creature had scampered around making the most awful mess until he had to finish the job for her.

I ask all these questions, but always I go back to her relationship with Ezequiel. What went on between them?


Yolanda's trial was a charade. The few details I have were passed on to me by the governor of the prison at which she is held.

She was flown to Villoria, and from there transported in a truck to a military base on the lake. The trial was staged so quickly that it would have been impossible to prepare a proper defense. She never saw her judges. They sat behind reflecting glass, and she spoke to them as she might have spoken to the mirrored walls in her studio.

The voices accused her of fifty-four charges. Her lawyer's plea that she was solely the errand girl for No. 459 Calle Diderot was dismissed out of hand. She belonged to the Section of Operative Support. She found safe houses, made connections, linked one cell with another. Her calling, her privileged position allowed her to move freely in society without arousing suspicion. The most damning evidence was a mention in her notebook of the name of the café outside which the Miraflores bomb had exploded.

She was sentenced to imprisonment for the rest of her natural life at the women's penitentiary in Villoria. The senior judge acknowledged the severity of the sentence. It attested, he said, to the state's determination to prevent "the superficial attractions of the accused from serving as a beacon to others." In passing sentence, he had acceded to the prosecutor's demand for a symbolic punishment.

She would be condemned to a cell without light.

I've never been to the compound in Villoria. And I suspect it's worse than I've been told. But I do have this certainty: if her cell is anything like Ezequiel's, it's unendurable.

Picture a tiny, windowless room thirty feet underground. If you open your arms, your fingers scrape unpainted concrete. If you raise your hands, you touch the ceiling. If you walk three paces, you smash your face.

Along one wall is a narrow bed with a mattress and a blanket. The air battles its way into the room through a vent in the ceiling. Apart from the bed, there is nothing other than a towel, a plastic water jug and a plastic basin which can be used as a toilet. At least that is what you see with the lights on. What it's like without light, I cannot even begin to imagine.

Do you realize the horror of this? A woman used to movement, who is afraid of the dark, who is used to a lighted stage, now living in absolute darkness, no one to acknowledge her except the guard who collects the tray. There are no mirrors. She can't know what she looks like. Perhaps her eyes will milk up, like one of those deepwater, dark-dwelling fishes they net from the lake at that altitude.

She can't see what she's eating, what she's drinking, where she's defecating. She can have no idea whether it's night or day. How does she know when to sleep, when to wake? Dreams must be her only light, but what can she dream of, and how does she feel when she wakes from a dream and there's darkness and she knows she'll be waking to this room for the rest of her life, that until the grave this is what will greet her?

Of course, one hopes that it won't be for the rest of her life, that there'll be a remission, an act of clemency. I think of Father Ramón's last message to me: "God's mercy is greater than God's justice." But in a way it's worse, not knowing. If she knew she was going to live like this for the rest of her life, she could simply give up. Or else she could take heart if she knew she would have to endure it only for a certain number of years. But to face so uncertain . . .

Rejas stopped. He started again, pausing between each sentence, measuring each word as if he had few left.

During the whole first year she was permitted one visit from a Red Cross official. Now her family are allowed a visit every fortnight. But she refuses to see them. She hasn't seen anyone for fifteen months.

It would be inconceivable, even in that lightless space, if she didn't attempt some form of movement. But if you're not born at that altitude, you risk *soroche*. You've been to Villoria—you can't jog fifty yards without feeling mountain sickness. So I expect she stretches to keep warm, gripping the bed for support. The nights are often well below freezing.

She still has touch, I suppose. But that's all she has. Her last anchor to this world is the feel of her bare feet on the concrete floor, her nose against the wall, the tips of her fingers on the ceiling.

I did manage to deliver some blankets to the prison governor, asking him to pass them on. The blankets were returned with a personal message: "Tell him I'm dead and I live only for the Revolution."

I know what people say. They say that what she fought for has enveloped her, that where she lies now is an appropriate punishment. Didn't Ezequiel for so long make this country a place of comparable darkness? Shouldn't she be held up as an example so no one will be tempted to follow this path?

But it is not what I feel. I think of her in prison like a candle burning down, her muscles degenerating. Soon she's going to be too old to dance. Such a waste. As if someone said you could never read again.

You will say that I feel this because I'm in love with her. But if you were to meet her, you would see the ballerina before you saw the terrorist. We're none of us, are we, just one thing? I am a policeman, but also a father, a husband for the time being, a nurse-maid to a sister who I pray will survive her illness. You are a journalist, a writer and I don't know what else besides. To look at a person from a single angle is to deform them. Even if Yolanda is guilty of protecting Ezequiel, she is also afraid of the dark. And I cannot forget that I put her there. In prison. To be in the dark forever.

Rejas had finished.

On the jetty the night-cart people loaded trash onto container boats. Black and yellow birds darted into the searchlights, and out in the river something splashed.

Astrud was buried in a cemetery overlooking Botafogo Bay. Hugo had picked out the black wood coffin, lined with bright blue satin. She was buried in her nightgown, the wrinkled neck of the dead baby girl in her shawl visible between her folded arms.

Dyer looked back into the room. "Why did you tell me all this?"

# 17

Her luggage had been left at the foot of the staircase. Dyer walked past it, chasing her laughter down a paneled corridor until he reached the conservatory.

Vivien sat holding Hugo's hand at the breakfast table, her other hand carving gestures in the morning light. She wore black velvet trousers, green ballet slippers, a white organdy shirt with an open collar and a sailor's bow loose at the neck. Ruby links—not Hugo's, he surmised—in her French cuffs.

"They should have been far, far quicker in the first act and they rushed the music in the second." Then: "Johnny!"

She jumped to her feet and stood on tiptoe to kiss him. "I'm telling Hugo about our performance in Pará. Although you, my dear, won't be interested in the least."

Hugo smiled his diplomat's smile at Dyer.

"There's coffee on the sideboard," she said. "You'll have to be nice and wait patiently until I finish my story."

Hugo, having heard about the ballet—a modern piece, specially commissioned—was fascinated to know what the Amazon looked like. "Can you see the other side?"

She touched him tenderly where his paunch pushed at his silk shirt. "It's too ridiculous. Two weeks I was stuck inside that opera house—and I only saw it for the first time last night. My dear, it's like any other river."

Dyer said nothing. He poured himself coffee and listened while Vivien described a party thrown by the Governor—"the girls nicknamed him Porpoise Eyes"—and the varieties of fish she had eaten.

At last Vivien clapped her hands. "Enough about me." She looked at Dyer, hard. "Johnny, darling, I want to hear what you've been up to."

Not until lunchtime was Dyer able to tell her.

She had booked a restaurant on the Malecón. "Just the two of us. Hugo, miserably, has another engagement. He says you were awfully sweet with him."

"I only took him to the Costa Verde."

"He couldn't stop talking about it. How did you find him?"

"In good form, I thought."

"He minded losing his eyebrows. Otherwise he is quite chirpy."

They ordered lunch. Vivien talked in her enthusiastic fashion about the orphanage, the children and a separate dormitory she had built for the girls. "Before my eyes they'd grown into adolescents. I'd find the boys the whole time under their blankets."

The details—cupboards, washbasins, new cooking pots— seemed fresh on her mind.

"Is that where you spent last week, Vivien?"

"My dear, why do you ask?"

"I went to Pará."

She held him with her pale blue gaze. "It's funny, I didn't somehow picture you with the Ashaninkas."

"I couldn't find you."

"Pará is a big place."

"Not as big as you would think."

She laughed, fiddling with a cufflink.

"When I found out there wasn't a ballet," he said, "I thought you might have gone there for other reasons."

"Darling, would I have done that if I suspected you were going to follow me?"

"Did you know I would?"

"Let's say I had an inkling. But how else was I to lose you? I had one or two things to do which I can do better on my own. I'm sorry I couldn't help with Tristan. But please understand why not. Your instinct always to find people in power morally dubious is perfectly commendable, but it doesn't go down so smoothly with those of my friends who happen to be political—not every time."

"You can help me now," said Dyer.

"Johnny, I can see it in your eyes. You're teeming with wicked ideas about what your aunt is up to. But it's not what you think. Without Tristan's patronage the orphanage would collapse. And I'm not going to jeopardize those children's future for the sake of getting you a newspaper interview. *Punto final.*"

"I've got something important to tell Calderón," said Dyer.

"Sweetheart, you're being childish. He's not going to see you. Not only is he not going to see you, he's not even going to let you past the gate."

"I don't want to see him."

"Good."

Dyer smiled. "You used a phrase once. 'My life has been a series of meetings and failings to meet.' "

"How very poetic."

"You were talking of your elopement with Hugo."

"That was forty years ago, my dear."

"I didn't manage to meet Calderón. But because of you, I bumped into someone more interesting."

Her eyes challenged him. "More interesting than Tristan?"

"Agustín Rejas."

Vivien put down her menu. "It's not true! You saw Rejas? Where?"

"In Pará. While waiting for you."

"My dear, no one's met Rejas. Do you realize how incredible that is? The press here are shrieking about how he's been out of the country, talking to the Americans. Now you tell me that he's been talking to you. What sort of creature is he? I've met his wife. She tried to sell me lip gloss. I want to hear everything."


Dyer's summary lasted through most of lunch. Vivien listened without interrupting. At the end she ordered another bottle of wine.

"Yes, yes, pour it out," she told the waitress in atrocious Spanish. "Why do you wait for me to taste it? If it was disgusting, I'd send it back. You didn't wait to see how we liked our fish, did you?"

She toyed with the glass. After a while she said in a sober voice, "So Rejas did fall for Yolanda. I'd heard as much. It's not surprising. She was lovely."

"Why did you never mention her?"

"I expect I forgot. So much was going on. I had rehearsals. Hugo had his stroke. All of us—the whole country—were picking up our lives after Ezequiel. You forget, the vast majority of people, like me, aren't interested in politics. I'm for a well-organized life. I don't like people dashing about with guns. I was simply relieved the lights worked again. It's only you, my dear, who goes on being fascinated by the bad news."

"That's not true."

"I never could share your obsession with Ezequiel. It is the one thing I won't forgive, the way he used that girl. A dance studio was the most brilliant cover. Who would have imagined that above those proper young ladies there would be this choreographer of violence?"

"Then—she was lovely? Yolanda, I mean."

"You're upset. I can tell."

"Everything Rejas said . . ."

"My dear, you're as bad as he is. This intense attraction, hardly consummated by a touch . . . He sounds as if he didn't know her—which is always for the best. Never get too close to the dance stage, Johnny."

"It isn't exactly my line, as you know, but she sounded so attractive, so—beguiling."

"She was, and she wasn't. I liked her, but then I didn't, or at least not so much."

"Tell me about her."

"Yolanda? I met her through Dmitri. Remember Dmitri?"

"The White Russian? Tall, bald?"

"That's him. He was a bit démodé, but great fun. Anyway, he was running the Ballet Miraflores then and he insisted I see this girl. She was fourteen, which is getting on a bit, but since it was Dmitri, of course I saw her. She came for an audition. Everyone performed a little dance and she did jazz, with a bit of mime and a

Paganini piece thrown in. She was glorious to look at and I was in tears at the end—Dmitri knew how to get to me, all right. She wasn't wishy-washy and she moved very well. Her mother, a small gray-haired Miraflorina, sat in the front and watched. Well, I accepted her and she was with us—let's see—nine or ten years. At one point I thought she might be prima ballerina material. But I must have decided she was too easily influenced. Then she had this problem with her leg."

Vivien took up her glass and sipped at it, then set it down on the table.

"She told everyone it was a dance injury. I wasn't so gullible. You don't get scars like that, my dear, not from dancing. Very suspicious, it was.

"One day she was helping at the orphanage and out it came. She'd been on a protest march at the Catholic University and had been tear-gassed. In the panic, the crowd trampled on her."

"Wasn't it a bit dangerous, to confess that to you?"

"Not at all. She knew I'd be sympathetic. She'd spent a good many Saturdays at the orphanage, cooking, washing clothes, teaching the children to do pliés. Initially, I'd been reluctant to involve her. Most do-gooders are a menace. Yolanda, I have to say, was different. A tremendous way with the children, she had. But after a few months she stopped coming.

"I have to say it was the same with her dancing. She started to find classical ballet too constricting. I thought she might like something more modern, more aggressive, even—Martha Graham, say—but no, she preferred folklore. Then she went to Cuba and that impressed her terribly. Came back with all sorts of ideas. Instead of getting down to rehearsing, we had to have these moral discussions, my dear. Fond as I was of her, I did start to find her a teeny bit wearisome. It was like talking to a glove puppet.

"But far worse than her debates, she used to skip rehearsals. That is no good, not if you're serious. She would disappear for a month at a time, and no one ever knew where.

"Then, one day, in the middle of a class, she gave it all up—poosh!—just like that. I understood, my dear. Or thought I did. I didn't know with her if it was love, or what. But politics—no, I never imagined politics. She was too naive.

"Who knows what was going on in her mind? She'd done nothing for other people, or so she felt. And then she must have met someone who talked about the creativity of the Indians, and how the only way to help them recapture their identity was to offer them salvation through revolution. A very romantic view of Indian society, my dear. It could have happened to a lot of women like that—educated, pretty, good family, religious. You start with a humanitarian idea, and before you know it, you're cutting throats.

"She soon dropped out of sight. Then two years ago I heard she had started her own school. I went to see her once or twice, for encouragement's sake; also to let her know I'd leave the door open if things didn't work out. I recommended her to a few parents. As far as I could make out, she seemed content. But I had other things to worry about. To me, she was a very good dancer who had stopped coming to rehearsals."

"Rejas is convinced she must have been exceptional."

"Some of my teachers have gone round making extravagant boasts on her behalf. But when someone becomes notorious, people do tend to say, 'Oh, my brilliant pupil.' Do you still paint your watercolors? If you had gone berserk with a machine gun, no doubt one or two people would have said, 'What a tragedy—he was such a good artist.' "

Dyer couldn't help smiling. "So atrocity is the province of the bad watercolorist?"

"My dear, I adore your paintings. We still have one in the spare room. No. What I'm wondering is, if she had been that good a dancer, would she have given it up?"

"You did."

"I had no illusions. The world was going to go on without me. I didn't think I would be able to go on without Hugo. That's all."

Vivien looked at him, a suspicion of sharpness in her eyes. "This doesn't make her fate any less unspeakable, but hasn't she become what she struggled to be on the dance floor? Isn't she entombed in her cave, like Antigone? All I'm begging you is, don't fold her into your life, please. I'm serious, Johnny. She is lovely, Yolanda, and it's easy to see what Rejas, poor man, must have felt. Imagine this attractive young woman walking toward him through the rubble of his life. Who could resist? That body! Those looks!

That sweetness! My dear, it must have been as though she had sat on his lap stark naked.

"But if I was stern, I could paint a different picture. I could say Yolanda had only her looks. I could pretend she wasn't blessed with the meat and gristle of character, and that when she grows old, this will reveal itself in her face. We old people aren't unfaithful to our characters. Your aunt here—what you see is the real thing. You can keep something suppressed a long while; then, at a certain age, your true self bounces out. Maybe in twenty years those big brown eyes will narrow, showing how thin the broth has been. Maybe her skin will grow dullish, her black hair lose its luster, her slender fingers flatten into hands like those of our dear waitress. Maybe the dungeon will snuff out her essential sweetness and she won't be lovely anymore."

"And I wouldn't believe you."

"The thing is, you'd be right," she said crossly. "But it's my duty to stop you forming sentimental attachments to people you haven't met—if only for your poor mother's sake."

She called the waitress for a plate to cover the fish against the flies. "No, don't take it away. I know we've had our pudding—but we might want to go back."

"What about her relationship with Ezequiel?"

"What does Rejas think?"

"He doesn't believe there was anything between them. Doesn't want to, perhaps."

"Men are so silly. Listen, have you any idea what Yolanda was like at the Metropolitan? She was wild, my dear. Wild. Blasts of vitality. No one was immune to her attraction—why should Ezequiel have been different? All those months in that compression chamber . . . Maybe they did, maybe they didn't. Does it matter anyway? No, don't give me that flinty look—Ezequiel I regard in the same light as the Devil, but he might have been amusing company with it. Perhaps he was considerate and careful with her. Women, who will tell themselves any number of consoling lies, forgive almost anything of a man who goes out of his way to be tender and make them laugh. A little bit of trouble goes a long way, my dear. I'm not saying that's what happened. But who knows what goes on between two human beings? And what did

Rejas himself say? That we know next to nothing about the people we love."

She sighed. "That goes for you too, Johnny. Sometimes I think of you as just another one of my orphans. I'm always saying to them when they leave, 'Get on with it, for Christ's sake. Up, up, up, on your own two feet.' And I wish you would do the same. When Hugo told me he'd been trying to fix you up with Mona, I said, 'That willowy girl is no good for Johnny. He needs someone much rounder.' "

Vivien drank her wine and looked serious again. "A ballet dancer would never do for you, my dear. Now. This message you have for Calderón—is it about the election?"

"It is and it isn't."

"Is Rejas going to stand?"

"What does Tristan think?"

"Don't play with me, Johnny."

"I think it's more a question of 'I won't stand if . . .' "

"What's the if?" Her eyes narrowed. Dyer had her complete attention. But he knew she was addressing someone else.

He saw this person clearly now, from their first meeting in the Cantina da Lua. Rejas, recognizing him from the start, had taken a gamble on the kind of person Dyer was—had gambled his all. By speaking freely, the policeman had broken the habit of a career. His anguish was unreachable, but Dyer, without being aware of it, had offered, through his kinship with Vivien, one feeble ray of hope. In order to win the journalist's trust, Rejas had told him everything, in the most careful detail, omitting nothing. At the same time, he must have hoped that when Dyer understood the reason, he would decide not to publish it.

Once he had relayed the message to Vivien, Dyer knew that he would put this story away. He would not forget it, but it was too personal, too unhistorical, too unpolitical to use as journalism. The only thing he could make of it would mean his having to leave the real elements out.

But it would not be wasted. Rejas had confessed to him for a reason—because Dyer was still capable of doing things that he could no longer do himself.

With Rejas's story, Dyer had the power to give Yolanda back the light.

"I'm bringing you a message for you to give to Calderón. Rejas wants to be certain that Yolanda—as quite distinct from Ezequiel—will be decently treated in prison, and that Calderón will use his influence with the President to release her in two or three years' time. If Rejas has this assurance, he will not contest the elections."

"You believe him?"

"Yes, I do. One, he is a just man. Two, Yolanda has no blood on her hands. That's why Ezequiel chose her. Three—he loves her, damn it."

"Didn't you see her on television? She was screaming blue murder for the revolution."

"Yes, but she's young. Rejas is convinced that she has never handled a weapon in her life. You knew her, Vivien. Was she a revolutionary? He's appealing to you."

"Did he mention that he'd given the orphanage the money from his reward?"

"No, he didn't. But I knew anyway."

"So his gift really was an *acte gratuit*," she said reflectively.

"You can't think he gave you that money to get at Calderón. He announced his decision on the steps of the police building—the day after he caught Ezequiel."

Vivien nodded. "You should tell your friend he's done a wonderful job, but he's not presidential material."

Dyer looked down at the table, pushing a fork so that its tines left faint parallel tracks in the cloth. He looked up at his aunt again. It was vital he persuade her.

"He's a good man, Vivien. I trust him."

She sat back, returning his gaze. "If, as you seem so certain, Rejas doesn't go into politics—well, anything might happen. Then there is hope. That hair-raising story Rejas told you about the rat . . . He's right, you know. But if he decides to stand against the government, or even to speak out in any way, the risk is obvious: she'll continue to rot in jail."

"So that's the message back?"

Her eyes twinkled at Dyer's concern. "He knew what he was doing, didn't he? Quite apart from the fact that you are my nephew. It's a terrible burden, a story you're not allowed to tell which the world has got wrong. And what better way of keeping it quiet than to give it to a journalist who understands more or less what you're talking about, but whose readers at home will never be interested in South America? You know what they would have said, don't you? At the paper, I mean—'Nice story, my dear, but can't you set it in Provence?' Telling it to you, he was telling it to the ground. So don't worry about Rejas, Johnny. He chose you."

They walked home along the Malecón. The trees were in their last days of flower, and in a small open park on the clifftop, the blossoms were strewn across the dry grass.

"I have another favor to ask," said Dyer. "I promised Rejas I would speak to you about his daughter. Laura. Who was Yolanda's pupil."

"How old is she now?"

"Fourteen."

"Too old."

"Her dream is to join the Metropolitan."

"I'm sure. Or is it her father's dream? It doesn't matter, in any case. This is not a sentimental profession."

"You accepted Yolanda at that age."

"Yolanda had talent."

"I believe Laura's good. Really."

"Or Rejas does?" Vivien, who had been about to shake her head, looked amused. "And if Laura does succeed in becoming a dancer—a good one—then a part of Yolanda will live on? Is that what you're both thinking? All these people you haven't met, Johnny . . . All right, I'll give her an audition. Now, watch out for that step. You're walking too fast. I want to catch my breath."

They looked down at a gray sea dissolving into a grayer horizon. A freighter moved out of the docks. Through the cranes, as though hanging from them, Dyer could make out the shape of an island. Under its cliffs, white-stuccoed with guano, spread the squat roof of Ezequiel's prison.

He thought of Ezequiel's captor, still in another country. He could not forget the policeman's grief-colored face as they had shaken hands twenty-four hours before. Here was a man who had fought against not one system but two. What he represented was better than either. Yet his cure had been his destruction; and what he had called his "madness," his salvation.

Halfway across the square, Dyer had heard the clatter of the shutter against the wall and stopped to look back at the Cantina da Lua. Rejas was on the balcony, gripping the iron balustrade, and for a moment the other had thought he might have left his chair to wave. He raised his hand in salute, but Rejas was staring into the river. At first Dyer couldn't work it out. Then he realized. A strong breeze played over the current, blowing upstream, so that the river seemed to be flowing the other way, inland to its source. His eyes adrift on that water, Rejas had looked so lonely and little, a man with part of his soul broken.

"Thinking of Rejas?" said Vivien.

"Yes."

"It's like the end of a book. He'll live on. We're very resilient, human beings. Maybe he'll find someone else. I've survived ten revolutions and as many heartbreaks. What they say here is true. Love is eternal for as long as it lasts."

"Vivien—"

"I'm sure Tristan will find out what you've told me," she said abruptly. "But I do need you to get that slipper copied—I am serious."

They turned into Vivien's street, purple with jacaranda and lined, between the trees, with old-fashioned lamps from the time of the rubber boom. It was early afternoon, but jets of gas flickered behind the glass shades.

In Pará, Rejas would be sitting down to dinner.

———

Dyer sent his fax from Vivien's office.

> It wasn't the story I thought it was. This gives me all the
> more occasion for writing to say that I can't accept your
> offer to send me to the Middle East. This is where my life
> is, with or without the paper. I don't suppose Jeremy is still
> in Personnel, but could you put me in touch with someone
> to arrange severance terms?

Meanwhile he had a book to finish. He threw himself into the
project as soon as he had finished closing down the office in Joaquim Nabuco. He would rise at six and write until lunchtime. In
the afternoons he took to walking the length of Ipanema beach, to
the point where the Dois Irmãos slipped into the sea. As he walked
toward those mountains, he would often think of better ways to
express what he had written; on the way back he planned the
chapters ahead.

He began to enjoy the work. The book would have a limited
market, but it was a subject he felt uniquely qualified to write
about. As the weeks passed, he forgot about Vivien's promise to
audition Laura. It was the sort of thing his aunt would not think to
mention, and besides, she was hopeless at keeping in touch. He
had rather expected it to turn out badly; such vague attempts to
help usually do.

He had reached chapter seventeen when the letter came
through the box. The envelope had been sent to Dyer, care of
Señora Vallejo. Vivien had forwarded it and on the back she had
written, "Shoes perfect. Color, too. Thanks. V"

Inside, there was a postcard.

The legend was "Pilgrims ascend Mount Ausangate on the final night of the Corpus Christi ice festival." The color photograph
showed a zigzag of lights against a dark blue slope and, dotted on
the snowy summit, a line of curiously robed figures.

It was from Rejas.

His sister had died. Emilio would be staying on and doubtless
would be pleased to see Dyer if he chanced to visit Pará.

His wife had gone to live in Miami.

Ezequiel had signed a declaration stating that he agreed with the policies of the government.

Dyer would shortly read that Rejas had been made Minister of Native Affairs.

Whenever Dyer came to the capital, Rejas hoped he would make the time to dine with him again.

And, "Laura has been accepted by the Metropolitan. Thank you." And his initials.

That was all.

# ALSO BY NICHOLAS SHAKESPEARE

### BRUCE CHATWIN

*A Biography*

Bruce Chatwin burst onto the literary landscape in 1977 with *In Patagonia*, which quickly became one of the most influential travel books of the twentieth century. Beautiful, charming, and intelligent, Chatwin was welcome in every society—from the most glamorous patrons of Sotheby's, where he held his first job, to the remote tribes of Africa. And yet for all the adoration he received, when Chatwin died of AIDS in 1989, he died an enigma, a panoply of apparently conflicting identities. Married for twenty-three years to his wife, Elizabeth, he was also an active homosexual. A socialite who loved to regale his rich and famous friends with stories about his travels and the people he met on them, he was at heart a single-minded loner.

Nicholas Shakespeare spent eight years traveling across five continents in Chatwin's footsteps. He was given unrestricted access to Chatwin's private notebooks, diaries, and letters, and has gathered evidence from Chatwin's peers, family members, enemies, and lovers. The result is a masterful biography that brilliantly leads us into Chatwin's world—and into his psyche.

"Does exactly what Chatwin's fans have longed to do: get beneath the alluring but elusive quality of his persona and prose."                    —*Entertainment Weekly*

Biography/0-385-49830-6